IN BETWEEN DAYS

IN BETWEEN DAYS

Anne Jamison

IN BETWEEN DAYS

The clock by her bed was flashing 10:15 when the tapping on her window got louder, became knocking, rattled the glass in its frame until it finally woke her all the way. She'd been sick, she told everyone, and she'd gone to bed early, too early for a Saturday night. Still, it wasn't as early as what the clock said. Something must have happened with the power.

The face floated pale in the darkened glass and made her jump. She felt terror before realizing the face was familiar and looked plenty scared itself. The moon lit the room enough for her to go to the window, unlock and open it, then the screen. She cringed at the metallic scraping sound it made beneath her fingers.

"What? Isn't it, like, the middle of the night? My clock is off, what are you doing here? What's going on?" Her voice sounded sleepy and panicked at the same time and seemed to echo loudly in the moonlight.

The whisper was tense and barely audible. "Sssh. Keep it down. What's going on is that our friend is bleeding all over the leather seats of my dad's Mercedes and can't seem to say anything but your name. I'm all alone except for a weepy stoner in the front seat who faints at the sight of blood. And we're running out of time."

"Look, then don't you need a hospital instead of—me?" As she looked closer, she could see the face outside the window was tearstained and streaked with blood.

"Yes. But." The face looked up and met her eyes, the distance greater than the space of night between them. Then it went on speaking. "Listen, I know it seems strange, my coming to you now, and I know things got a little messed up between us. But I know who you really are. You're the only person here I can trust. There's a bleeding person in that car who apparently feels the same way. Add it up."

So she did. "Wait one second."

She came back with a clean towel. "For the blood. You know, pressure. I'll be down in a minute with everything else."

"Hurry. Car's across the street, lights off. If you're not out in ten minutes, I'll assume you got caught and I'll have to leave without you."

And the face was gone. In its place, she could see that the lights were off all over town, so for that night, at least, the world she knew really was a darker place.

During those next moments, time seemed mechanized. The corners of objects grew sharper and thinner, digitized, like an arcade game. She watched a video game version of herself calmly slip on black clothes, cover her hair with a black hat, rifle through drawers and purses. Grabbing a dark-colored backpack from the closet, this calm girl shoved the few things she'd gathered into it, rolled up a blanket from the bed and stood a moment. In that moment, she was that video game girl, and what they saw was the same: one window, one face, one car hurtling through darkness.

Later, in the back seat, she'd direct the driver to the freeway as the lights began to flicker back on throughout town. She'd press a towel tight to where a head was bleeding or hold the bloodstained blanket in place to ward off shock. A voice would mumble, "You don't belong here, sorry," and her own voice would whisper, "How do you know where I belong?" And then a third voice would say, "Careful, there's a gun back there somewhere," and then no one would say anything for a while.

Looking back, it all happened so fast, it was as if she'd barely blinked an eye—except for the days that stretched so long, they seemed like half her life at least, she got so old in the course of them. And in between, those moments she wanted to stop, hold on to, wear like a charm around her neck. Or a scar.

Then, that moment, she turned toward the window and threw a blanket to the ground. A white Mercedes, lights off, edged through the branches of trees in the moonlight. She stepped onto the ladder with one last look to her room, its pale blue walls, rose carpet and white furniture luminous in the dark like ghosts. It was the room she'd grown up in except for the part of growing up that started now. It was the room she would never return to, because when she did come back to it, it would be the same, but she would be different.

Because no one knew who she really was, because who she really was, was in motion. Who she really was, was young, and alone, and scared, without a plan, or a rulebook, or any idea what game she was playing. And she knew she was playing for keeps.

1. VICIOUS

1:05 pm, October 7, 1985

It was completely amazing how long Mr. Richards could talk without taking a breath. Samantha Ward was trying to match him, and failing badly. She let the air out slowly so Richards didn't notice.

Jessica Levin was in the next row trying to look like she was adding and subtracting linear equations instead of cracking up. Her face was immobile, but her back was shaking. Every time Mr. Richards took one of his huge breaths, Samantha did too. On the fourth try, Jessica collapsed into a coughing fit.

Not for the first time, Samantha wondered if Jessica Levin was entirely good for her academics. She had no idea what Mr. Richards was talking about because she had to concentrate so hard on his not-breathing and Jessica's not-laughing.

Of course, Samantha also had no idea how a simple conversation about Richards' long talking had led to the biggest burnout in school calling her frigid in front of the entire lunchroom. After that, she wasn't sure how much concentrating on equations she'd be doing in any case.

It was the stupidest thing. At lunch, Jessica told anyone who would listen that she'd tried to hold her breath for as long Mr. Richards could talk. It was impossible. Three kids from the next period had tried, and none of them could do it either. Which clearly proved Richards was an alien or a robot.

Everyone laughed. Everyone laughed at whatever Jessica said, it was a given. And if Samantha said something remotely funny, like, "Duh, he's a math teacher," people laughed at that, too. It was just the way of things.

Then Dave Watson from the jock table said that if Jessica and Samantha wanted men who could go a long time without breathing, they should really check out the swim team.

Samantha rolled her eyes with the other girls, but she didn't get why Jessica would be blushing, which did not happen easily. Dave Watson had very nice back muscles that you could totally see through his shirt. But who cared how long he could hold his breath?

Then Bethany Moran called Dave Watson a perv and flung a grape at him. Samantha still had no idea what was going on, but if Bethany was calling someone a perv and Jessica was blushing, it was bad. She tossed her head and turned away.

She turned right into the stare of Jason Devlin, a.k.a. the Devil himself. He was standing by the end of Samantha's table with a couple of burnout loser friends on their way to throw out their trash or deal drugs or something. Samantha didn't know him, she just knew who he was because everyone did. He was always getting paged to the principal's office or thrown out of class. And now he was at her table, staring openly, like he had no idea how the school even worked.

Samantha realized he'd been listening, and he *knew* Samantha was totally confused. Jason and his slimebag friend Skinny knew what everyone was blushing and leering and laughing about. They knew, she didn't know, and they knew that, too.

It got worse. Jason Devlin's gaze, it had some kind of weight to it. Samantha felt her breath quicken, hated herself for it. It only lasted a split second.

She wouldn't look at those boys again.

But they were looking at her, and they could tell *some*thing. "Looks like Teen Barbie is already checking out the swim team, dude." Skinny nudged Jason in her direction.

Samantha could feel her cheeks getting pinker. Now, not looking at those boys made it seem like they were getting to her, like she cared even one bit about Skinny Nowlin and anything he said. If Jason Devlin was famous for being *bad*, Skinny was famous for being *nasty*.

She whipped around to face him. "Drop dead, loser. Was anyone talking to you?" It wasn't the best line, but wasting good lines on burnouts just looked desperate. People like Skinny were best crushed like bugs.

Dave Watson turned back toward Samantha—angry, but not at her. "Are these losers bothering you?"

Samantha barely knew Dave but that was how it worked. She and her friends were more swim team territory than burnout territory. They'd get protection just on principle. Something about this bothered Samantha more than even Skinny Nowlin did, but she couldn't put her finger on what. It hovered there for a minute, something not quite seen from the corner of an eye, and then was gone. And she had more than enough to worry about that she *could* see.

Skinny slouched further into Jason with a smirk that seemed like it might crawl right off his face and slither toward her. Jason drawled, "We just felt these young ladies should know that the swim boys aren't necessarily the best divers in the school."

Samantha could feel Jason Devlin's eyes were on her like she was on display. Which, in a way, she was. It was what lunch was about. But for most of the school, Samantha and her friends were strictly look but don't touch.

Jason Devlin's gaze made her feel more than touched. Undressed, maybe. And Skinny Nowlin made her feel even worse. Like fingered. In public. Without her consent. She hated it.

Samantha was staring at her chicken breast with teriyaki sauce as if it were the last thing in the universe left to see except Jason Devlin's eyes. Dark eyes. Darker under a long, low, slanty fringe of dark hair that slouched over his eyes like he slouched over her, over Skinny, over the entire lunchroom. Like his hair had been studying carelessness to cover for his eyes, which had a sharper edge to them.

"Looks like Teen Barbie would like to see how Devlin dives," sneered Skinny. "She can't even look him in the eyes. She's all trembling."

Never had a chicken breast been so entirely engrossing.

The rest of the swim team had taken notice, and Dave got up. "You know, scum like you don't get to talk to girls like these. Scum like you don't even get to look at them. So, beat it."

Skinny shrugged into his torn-off jeans vest, pretending to shiver. "Ooh, Jason. Swimmers have threatened us."

"Run for your lives, boys, while there's still time." Falsetto sneers from the background. More boys in army pants or beat-up jeans and plaids moved in to where Skinny Nowlin and Jason Devlin were squaring off against the Barbies and the swimmers.

Jason just laughed. "Swim boy, unwind your Speedo from your dick and chill. Dudes. No lunch rumble today. See," and he looked at Samantha again, "Barbie here is safe from me. I don't really dive in shallow water. I don't find it's worth the time and..." He took a deep breath, then blew the air slowly into his slouchy hair, showing his tongue between his teeth before finally saying, "...effort."

Samantha hoped only that an enormous hole would open where she was sitting and swallow her. Into hell. Which would be better than the cafeteria.

But then Jessica nudged her foot. Message taken. Some burnout had gotten the better of her, in front of a big audience. It couldn't stand. Because girls could smell blood in the water like sharks. They were always circling. If they smelled blood they went for it. Even if they were your friends, instinct would take over. And if they weren't your friends, they were waiting for it, any opening to the kill.

Guys were no different. They were just looking for an opening of a different kind. Samantha repressed a shudder. She could shudder later. Response required. Now.

Turning to the swim team, who looked like coiled springs ready to shoot out at any moment, Samantha smiled sweetly. "Thanks, guys, but you should save it and bring it to your next meet. You know, somewhere it'll count for something real."

"Because you?" She looked Jason Devlin up and down and her upper lip curled as if a cockroach had crawled across her chicken, "You?" She sounded incredulous. "I mean, it's true I don't speak totally disgusting well enough to understand anything that's coming out of your mouth, but it doesn't matter. Because you know and I know no one cares what you say or do. Really." She looked right into Jason Devlin's eyes and she did not flinch. "You know. No one cares."

She turned to her lunch, took a beat, then turned back, eyes wide. "Oh, are you still here? Look. Run along. Stop trying to make yourselves look better by talking to people who do matter. Go do some drugs or burn something down, or whatever it is that you do...do." She shrugged her pretty shoulders and began delicately slicing into her chicken.

Murmur of approval from the jock and Barbie tables. A few calls of "Face!" and burning sounds.

It was almost too easy. It wasn't a game she'd signed up for, but that was no reason to lose.

Jason Devlin raised his eyebrows. "Check it out, man, shallow and cold. You know, usually it isn't the shallow water that's so—" His tone grew sharper, which told Samantha she'd struck a nerve. "What's the word? Oh, that's right, frigid."

High fives and snickers. Jason looked at Samantha once more in that same appraising way, and then at Dave Watson. "Dude, good luck diving there," and he slouched off, fist bumping with some outstretched hands from the outlying tables.

These congratulations didn't escape Samantha's notice. They didn't surprise her, either. It was part of being popular that a lot of people hated you. Without ever saying a word to you. It was just part of the deal,

Samantha sighed. It wasn't like she loved every part of her life or every one of her friends. It was more that, as she scanned the lunch room—and she did this on a daily basis, the way a general keeps an eye on the territory he needs to hold—she didn't see a lot of better alternatives. Samantha was at the top, because she could be. And falling from that height, especially if pushed, would be painful.

She turned to her table. "Oh my God. Whatever."

Everyone started talking at once. "That was so bogus. That Skinny guy is like, super skeeve. I feel gross he even looked at someone I was sitting next to."

"Please." Jessica started gathering her stuff. "Like he even matters."

The rest of the girls made their way to the trash and out the door, the freshmen hanging back in respect, which was normal. Samantha smiled to include them, then spoke to one in particular.

"Is that a new purse, Michelle?" It was Kelly green and puffy with buckles and the butt ugliest thing Samantha had seen all week.

Michelle smiled, obviously pleased Samantha noticed. "You like?"

Samantha smiled back. "It is so perfect with that argyle." Which had to be, like, the second ugliest thing. But maybe she and Jessica could work with her. They'd done wonders with Kim.

"Hey, where the eff is Kim? Did she totally bag on us or what?"

Jessica rolled her eyes. "Richards. Algebra."

"During lunch? That is like, child abuse!"

"Right?" And Jessica was off again. "Wait! Kim can observe and document! Then we'll kidnap Richards for our alien robot science fair project and we will all be going to Harvard."

Now everyone was laughing. Again. "But that means every one of us needs to try to match his breathing. In class."

Samantha cracked up even harder. "Why exactly?"

"Omigod, do you have *major* tutoring needs? *Scientific method,* doofus. Multiple trials."

"And when I collapse of not breathing and they carry me out on a stretcher and Jason Bleeping Devlin joins cheer squad because he's so massively happy about my untimely death, what will *that* be?"

"That," proclaimed Jessica, "will be poetry. Which will mean my term project for English is also finished and my life will be one long par-*tay!*" Jessica swung into her locker and started singing "Holiday, Celebrate!"

Of course Samantha joined in. You had to sing and dance to Madonna. It was probably in the school rules. It was also apparently in the rules that if you were singing obligatory Madonna in the halls before algebra, the dickwad who dissed you at lunch would walk by and sneer, "Oh, look, now it's rocker Barbie," to another one of his burnout friends.

Samantha took a deep breath to practice for class.

But when no one was looking and she was sure no one could hear, she whispered to Jessica, "Did I do something to him? Because last time I checked, I had no idea who Jason Devlin even is besides, like, not someone I would ever know."

"Well, he sure as hell knows who *you* are. And you definitely 'do something' to him. I saw him looking at you this morning. He totally wants to bump uglies."

"Jessica. Gross. I'll barf right here and ruin your loafers."

"Ralph on my Guccis and die. Still. You have to admit, he's pretty hot in a burnout way."

"Jessica. Please. Gag me." Samantha lowered her whisper even further. "But what was up with the whole diving thing? Was it about making out or something? I so did not get that."

Jessica patted her hand. "I'll sully your lily-white mind with *that* and other news updates after class. But for now, just breathe, baby."

2. DAY AFTER DAY

7:35 am October 8, 1985

When Jason Devlin made his way to school early, he stopped behind the trees that separated Highland Central from Highland Cemetery. Just the sight of the long, low brick building stretched behind the bleachers made dead people seem like awesome company. He hopped the fence in a place it was weakened, sandwiched between two pine trees.

It wasn't like he wore all black or anything, but Jason liked the cemetery. The peace of the graves helped him breathe easier as he packed his cigarette against marble and struck a match on the rough stone edge. He put the filter to his lips and breathed the flame into the tip, then let the smoke slip from his mouth in a wispy stream with a slowness that helped soothe him.

Jason leaned against Mr. Studebaker's name and dates, rolling his head back on the flat stone of the beloved husband and father and smoking seat. He played with the bit of a watch he carried in his pocket, poking its sharp edge into his thumb, then releasing the pressure and rubbing the indentation it left in his skin.

He had fifteen minutes until first bell, having seen no reason to hang around the house with his mother and the spoiled solid fucking milk. He hated the house and its mess and its ghosts. Anywhere was better than there.

The cold gray markers stretched in their ordered lines across the grass like each one had a place, a reason for being there. It was like nothing else in his life.

Maybe that's what he could say the next time Stagnita had him up against a locker with an arm at his throat as he asked, each word a finger stab in the chest, what Jason wanted to be other than locked up or dead. "I aspire to be a tombstone, sir, they are so straight and orderly." Jason stubbed out his cigarette next to Mr. Studebaker and flicked it over to the trees. The thought of Stagnita's pug-ugly face did away with his calm, and it was time to take off anyway.

Jason strode back to the fence and grabbed onto it with both hands, glaring at Highland Central Penitentiary for Young Offenders in all its squat, gray glory. What genius designed high schools to look like prisons, anyway? He pulled the wire down, swung his legs over, then strode down the little hill. He tugged the collar of his army jacket up and stuck his hands in the pockets. There was more of a wind, out there in the open.

Further on toward the school, Skinny and Bogart and Dylan Dougherty were slouching around with a couple of girls, so Jason headed that way. As he'd hoped, Jason recognized one of the girls as Shelly—C-cup, rum and Cokes, last name unclear at this point. Wiseass girl usually up for some fun.

"Check it out, it's the Devil himself... in the flesh." Shelly did check him out, slowly, as if she knew a thing or two about the flesh of Jason Devlin. Jason nodded to her, a little private. She did know a thing or two. He could stand her getting to know a couple more, maybe later that day.

"Man, he is the Devil." Skinny gestured toward the graveyard. "You communing with your minions and shit?"

"Nah." Jason looked at Skinny. "That's what I'm doing right now." Everyone else laughed.

"Fuck you, man," Skinny said, but without any real bite to it.

"Chill, dude. You know how much," Jason paused and grasped Skinny's hand, "I really, really love you." Skinny was an ugly dude with skin that always looked like it needed washing, a kind of sour smell, and a really nasty sense of humor. No one, Jason thought, probably loved Skinny Nowlin. But he was loyal as hell and usually good for a laugh.

"Nah, you're just into me for the sex, fag, but I told you, it's over." Skinny shoved him.

"Whoa. Cool it. Watch the visual, man, I'll be soft for days now."

"Dudes, I'll lose my lunch!" Bogart looked up sleepily from where he was fiddling with some rolling papers and a film canister for no apparent reason. Bogart rarely had an apparent reason for anything he did. Skinny shoved him, too. He fell.

A voice Jason didn't recognize cut through the laughter. "So what *were* you doing over with the dead people, *devil man*?" The girl who spoke tilted her head to one side and smiled slowly around her words, making "devil man" sound both mocking and like some secret shared joke.

Jason shrugged. He grabbed on to Shelly's ponytail and gave it a yank so she didn't think he was going for that other chick. Not like he and Shel were a thing, because Jason didn't get into *things* with girls, but Shelly knew his deal and seemed cool with it, and after a morning like this one, a little human touch would definitely be in order.

But he was interested in this other girl in a different way. Like she might be interesting. She had blue spiky hair and a lot of eyeliner, and he was pretty sure he hadn't seen her around because that would be memorable in a cookie-cutter school like Highland. Thing was, she looked familiar, too.

"So who the hell *are* you, anyway?"

Everyone laughed. Dylan Dougherty totally lost it, stoned off his ass as usual. Bogart just looked confused. Jason hoped he didn't look as confused as Bogart. Ever.

"I'll give you a clue. Seventh grade homeroom. Two seats over. One seat back." Blue-haired girl made each word a revelation.

Jason stared, blank to incredulous. "Prissy all-my-clothes-are-pink-and-monogrammed-and-no-way-in-hell-are-you-her *Hines?*"

"The same. And that is the last time you ever call me Prissy if you want to keep your balls somewhere in the vicinity of your body, *Jason Devlin.*"

Jason put his hands up in surrender. "Dude."

"Wrong again. Just Pris."

Dylan's eyes widened. "Like from fuckin' *Bladerunner?* That is so awesome. Like, *dude.* Not like I'm calling you that, but with the neon, and those robots and time to die with the dove? Like, 'Hi Roy,' and Daryl Hannah goes all apeshit on Han Solo's ass?"

"I couldn't have said it better myself." Pris's eyes narrowed at the end of sentences like punctuation.

Dylan looked at Pris like she was an angel come to speak only to him.

Jason shook his head. Prissy in Pink to blue-haired freak. His mom used to work in the same office with her dad. Yeah, well. Things change a lot in a few years.

First bell rang and the group started moving towards the entrance. Jason whispered in Shelly's ear. "Behind the bleachers. After school. Bring a Coke."

She'd understand he'd have something to go in it. She nodded and took off with Dylan to their lockers. Skinny and Not-Prissy turned with Jason.

They passed a knot of jocks and Barbies, no doubt planning some after-school pep enhancement. Typically Jason ignored these kids, but he caught a look off one of them, some muscly dude in a pink polo shirt, that made his blood boil. The kid actually put his arm around one of the girls and steered her protectively out of Jason's path. Which she wasn't in.

The vibe the dude was putting out wasn't even like they were a couple. He was just taking care of a pure young girl whose shadow needed to be kept free of burnout footprints.

Turned out it was very thing Jason needed to focus his free-floating morning rage outwards on a worthy target. *I don't wanna hang with you either, dude, but I don't feel the need to let you know you're scum first thing on a Monday morning.* Maybe that was part of the problem. Maybe he should feel that need.

Jason grabbed a book from his locker and slammed the metal door shut with a bang of his fist. He let his face harden into the kind of loud stare you could hear and feel before you even turned around to see it, and he aimed it down the hall at Pinkshirt and his blue-shirted buddy. They wore the kind of shirts that had little lizards sewn on them. Jason *hated* those shirts and he hated them even more when they had the collars turned up. Bugged the shit out of him.

The *dudes* looked up. Jason made a show of blowing spit towards their feet. It was fake spit, just the sound of his tongue against the "O" of his lips, but it got the message across.

Pinkshirt nudged Blueshirt, gesturing in Jason's direction. Jason's stare followed the girl whose shadow had been steered. He made a point of looking at her and each of her friends. He also made a point of not looking too impressed.

The girls didn't look up or notice him at all, but their *dudes* sure as hell did. Good. Game *the fuck* on.

He looked at the girls again, then shrugged, then let his tongue show.

He didn't even like that kind of a girl, was the funny thing. They were so sure he and his friends were waiting like groupies at a stage door, hoping for their chance at the big time. But those girls—there was nothing special about them, just money and clothes and the fact that everyone treated them like gold and in return they treated everyone else like dirt.

Basically, they looked like what you'd get if you took a cookie cutter and set out to make girls. One with dark hair stood out some, everything about her flashing and alive, like she could be fun if she ditched the stupid clothes and stupider attitude, but she also looked like that wasn't about to happen. As for the one those jocks had been so concerned about, she wasn't even pretty, although there was a suggestion of pretty about her, like she might have been pretty if she hadn't spent all her time looking entirely average. But even *that* she ruined by this hideous green thing that looked like an aborted caterpillar she was carrying over her shoulder and clutching like some precious prize.

Caterpillar-Lover was talking to some Oriental chick who was cute enough but she had on a cheer uniform which was like wearing a big sign that said "Check me out, I'm brain dead." All in all, nothing to make Jason ache for the lost opportunities of teendom.

But then Peppy the Asian and Caterpillar-Lover moved out of the way.

Now. That was not the kind of girl he liked. She was the opposite. He liked girls with an edge and really, he liked girls who liked him. Because otherwise why bother?

But. He'd probably seen her before, but now—he really saw her. And he had to admit she was totally beautiful. In a blonde, pinky-perfect kind of way—but with these eyes like from some old painting, and —well. Jason shifted. He saw gold at her throat and pearls on her ears and when she turned, he swore to God she looked right through him. Like he might have stayed in the fucking graveyard. Like she would have had a better chance of seeing him if he'd been a ghost.

Skinny came up to him—literally, only part way, his head only reached Jason's shoulder. "See something you like, man? You've got those jocks down there beyond pissed off, I love it."

Jason shook his head. "Nah, nothing there I'd wanna shake a stick at, know what I mean?" That wasn't, strictly, how Jason thought about girls. In fact, he thought it was shitty to talk about them that way. But the same rage that had started boiling with the jocks now started freezing at that girl with her pearls and her gold and her unseeing goddamn eyes.

Not-Prissy-in-any-way-shape-or-form-Hines nudged him on the other side, back from her locker. Second bell rang and the hall was in motion. Pris and Skinny and Jason stayed in place, leaning against the lockers and watching the teens stream by. Pris said in a low voice, "That blonde girl? The really pretty one?"

Skinny snorted, "That hot as hell piece of ass with the stick rammed up it? Yeah."

Pris addressed herself more exclusively to Jason. "Whatever. Well, do you know who that is?"

Jason thought a minute. "Maybe her name is Samantha or Stephanie. She's one of those. You know. *Popular* girls. Barbies. I don't really give a shit about them."

Pris rolled her eyes. "Right. Like you were ignoring her just then in the worst way."

"Fine. She does—stand out a bit. But you know?" He turned to Skinny. "Those dudes *and* those chicks are really starting to bug the shit out of me."

The three of them started walking to class, late enough to be noticed but probably not late enough for the teacher to go through the hassle of a tardy slip. Pris was first to peel off. Calculus. Not typical burnout territory.

Pris turned to Jason one more time, eyes narrowed. "Her name is Samantha Ward. And check it out. We were *best friends* back when I was Prissy. And since I've been back? She doesn't even *know* me. Like she looks right through me. Like I don't even exist for her. We lived at each other's houses and now, not a glance."

Jason snorted in disdain but then thought a minute. "Well. Your own mother wouldn't recognize you. I'm not saying she's not a bitch. I'm just sayin'. Long way from Prissy, punk."

"Right. You sat behind me in homeroom. We lived at each other's houses for *four years*." Jason noted how the hurt in Pris's voice was emphasized by her sneer and her shrug. He got that. That was a dance he knew.

"So maybe she's got something coming. That's shitty. You jes' leave that to me, little lady."

Pris gave him the finger but laughed, "OK, but watch your mouth with that lady shit, Devlin."

"*You* watch it for me, 'kay?" And he made big kissing sounds.

Skinny tugged at Jason's sleeve. "C'mon, man, we're gonna get busted and I don't want detention, I've got a date."

Jason doubted that, unless it was with some especially willing inanimate object, but he followed his friend anyway, still chuckling. "Okay, that Pris girl is a *piss*. How'd she get so tough, where's she been at, San Quentin?" He stopped a minute and looked at Skinny. "Fuck it. Someone has *got* to bring some of those preppy assholes down a peg or two, you know?"

Skinny Nowlin smiled. "Those stuck-up Barbies too. Man. I am so there. I am in the goddamn *corner pocket.*"

Mr. Garcia glared at Jason through the door to his homeroom. "Mr. Devlin. You are minus thirty seconds from your third tardy slip, which is an automatic visit with Mr. Stagnita. Do you really miss him so much?"

"He's like a father to me, sir." Jason sauntered in and threw himself into a chair, shoving his combat boots on the desk in front of him. "An evil, sadistic father. Do you really want to get involved in that ugliness?"

Mr. Garcia looked unimpressed. "It might be preferable to the ugliness I have right here before me. Feet off the desk and open *Taming of the Shrew* to Act II Scene I. And Mr. Devlin. Read Petruchio."

"Mr. Garcia. Ugly? Me?" Jason batted his lashes. "That hurts, sir. But just to show there's no hard feelings, I'll read your Pinocchio." He looked down the page. "For I am rough ..." Here he ran his hand over his jaw as if to feel for stubble, and then ran it down his chest, getting a few snickers in the process. "... and woo not like a *babe.*" His hand traveled suggestively lower.

"Um, Mr. Garcia? I think Jennifer here can confirm that," came a voice from the back of the class, "from personal experience."

A metal chick Jason vaguely knew shrugged her shoulders, blew a small purple bubble, and sucked it back into her mouth. "I can't lie. The Devil don't kiss like any girl *I* know."

The class erupted in catcalls and whistles.

Mr. Garcia fought to be heard. "I'm sure Mr. Devlin is relieved to hear it, but it's actually irrelevant here. And Jennifer, gum in the trash. What Shakespeare means is that he doesn't woo like a *child.*"

Another girl chimed in. "He woos like woo-hoo!"

Two boys in the back started drumming while another sang, "Are you with me, Dr. Wu, Or are you just a shadow? Of the man that I once knew ..."

"That's enough!" Garcia sounded serious. But after a moment, the singing continued, "Are you crazy, are you high?" And there was another round of laughter. "Or just an ordinary guy?"

"None of the above, actually," commented Jason, studying the first principles of looking bored.

"Mr. Devlin. *That's enough.*"

"*Me?* It's *Shakespeare.* Can I help it if its greatness sparks lively conversation among schoolchildren? Can I help it if my classmates relate it to exciting experiences in their own lives? Or if some of them are stuck in the Seventies with their taste in music? Oh, I'm sorry, you might be a Steely Dan fan, too." Jason lowered his voice. "That was probably an insensitive comment, given your hairstyle and—"

"*One more word . . .*"

Jason considered. He had no reason to be riding Garcia today. Garcia was even a decent guy, in his own way. He was just trying to get kids to read books. It wasn't *his* fault that most of the books sucked ass.

He raised his hand. Garcia looked a warning shot. "Mr. Garcia, seriously this time, I'll read the speech for real."

"After Ronnie."

Ronnie sounded like he was reading a map. Written in Swedish. "Ay when the special thing is well. Ob—tined? Obtined. That is. Her love. For that is. All in. Oh. All."

Jason, though, could read with feeling when he tried. "Why, that is nothing; for I tell you, *father,/* I am as per-emptory as she proud-minded; /and where two raging fires meet together/ They do consume the thing that feeds their fury—"

"That's excellent, Mr. Devlin. Really. Can you take a shot at what it means?"

Jason scratched his chest again, laughing inside that Mr. Garcia had stopped him before he got to the yielding and wooing parts, which he'd had some more extravagant plans for. "Yeah, I think it means that this prize a-hole, Pinocchio or whatever, says the stuck-up bit—excuse me, *lady's* love— doesn't mean shi-, um, very much even though sparks do fly between them, because her attitude grates on him and he's gonna take her down a peg or two, which he knows how to do 'cause he's all bad-ass. And then those sparks are gonna, like, catch fire and burn up anything that was between them to begin with." He smiled. "But it sounds like it might be a hell of a ride on the way to ashes. Sir."

Mr. Garcia hid a laugh. "Mr. Devlin. And what do you think of Petruchio's attitude here?"

"Did you not understand what I meant by a-hole? Because I kind of thought being an English teacher and all, you could fill in the blanks. But I can translate."

Garcia declined the offer.

And, having paid his dues to his one semi-decent teacher, Jason Devlin set his mind to other things. Dudes who wore lizards on their collared shirts, mostly, and their stupid sense that girls were somehow property. That pissed him off. Even Shakespeare was actually kind of fucked when it came to girls. He liked the thought of Pris moving in to Shakespeare's stupid play and giving those dudes a run for their money.

Jason liked girls and basically, he figured, he was on their side. Though he was itching to let that blonde princess know that she didn't get to look *through* him like that.

3. MIRROR IN THE BATHROOM

After algebra, Samantha and Jessica grabbed Kim. They were speeding toward the girls' room when Samantha ran smack into *diving* Dave Watson, the swim jock from lunch. He caught her arms. "Slow down. I'll let you catch me, Princess."

"Um, in your dreams, maybe. Now excuse me?" Samantha let a little flirt creep into her voice on general principle. He was a senior swim star, and his interest couldn't really hurt—not her standing or her ego. Her friends' reaction at lunch, though, was enough to convince her that she wouldn't have liked his comment, if she'd known what it meant. So it was only a very little bit of flirt she allowed.

Dave made a big deal of hanging his head. "Listen. I'm sorry about lunch. Guy thing. But I didn't know *Devlin* would be there. I should get points for protecting you from *that* pond scum."

Jessica and Kim were tugging on her arm, mouthing her name broadly with lots of eye urgency. But Samantha couldn't leave that one lying there.

"I think you lose those points for assuming I *need* protection."

Dave laughed like that was an enormous joke. "You are so feisty. How about this? Joe Danuzio's party Friday night. I behave, you forgive and forget."

Samantha raised her eyebrows. "We'll see. I might show. Friday's a long way off. If I do, and if you're *very* good, I might forgive you. But I *never* forget."

At that, Jessica and Kim grabbed both her arms and pulled her roughly toward the bathroom, calling out, "Sorry. Eyeliner emergency!'" Jessica shooed out a couple of girls by the sinks checking their makeup. "Excuse us. Eyeliner emergency. It gets ugly. No one may see." She hustled them out the door with hardly a protest. Mostly, people obeyed Jessica. Kim checked for feet in the stalls. "Coast clear."

Samantha looked at them in shock. "Okay. What gives? What's worth an eyeliner emergency? Spill."

Kim and Jessica exchanged glances. "Well, for starters, Dave Watson was declared Vanessa Segal's personal property as of, like, last week."

"Vanessa Segal's boyfriend? Okay. So I'm dead." Samantha leaned over the sink. There had to be some kind of return receipt on her day. "Be sure to invite that Jason guy to my funeral. Wait—are you in league with him? Does he have you on burnout mob contract or something?"

"Honey. I'm just the messenger. There's the real culprit." Jessica pointed at Samantha in the mirror. "You broke commandment number one of high school survival. Thou shalt not flirt with the queen bitch's dude."

Samantha looked closely at her reflection. "Do you think I'll look okay as a corpse? But guys, that can't be Vanessa's boyfriend. That makes, like, no sense. She's a *football* cheerleader! Isn't she dating the quarterback because it's her God-given right as captain of the squad?"

Kim shook her head. "She caught Dougie Douglas with a junior from the West High squad. And that junior was missing, like, key parts of her uniform. So Vanessa's sworn off football 'playboys' and she's dating swimmers because they don't *have* cheerleaders. Get it?"

"Fuck." Samantha didn't swear often, but this was a situation that merited it. "But I didn't know he was her boyfriend, and I only said I might see him at a party." She tossed her hair and adjusted a few strands. Salvageable. Hair and situation both.

Jessica patted Samantha on the head. "Um. Samantha? Lunch."

"Oh. Shit. I mean, I think I was right the first time. I think I mean fuck."

Kim looked confused. "Wait a minute, what happened at lunch?"

"Oh, right. Sully my lily-white mind, Jess. This should be good, since it also involves Vanessa Segal's boyfriend and *diving*."

Kim was clearly no more enlightened about "diving" than she was. Both girls turned to Jessica.

"Muff diving. Duh."

Blank faces. Jessica rolled her eyes. "Okay. Going down. Eating out."

"*What?*" Kim curled her lip. "Eew. Right."

Samantha still didn't get it.

"Poor, sweet, excessively virginal friend. When a boy. Licks a girl. Down there. Get it?"

"Gag me," said Samantha weakly. It was too much.

"Ralph on my Guccis and die." Jessica moved her loafers to a safe distance. "But FYI and not from personal experience? I hear it's nice if the guy knows what he's doing. Now stop looking at me like I popped your cherry."

Samantha felt sick to her stomach. "Let me get this straight. Those boys, that is, Dave Watson, also known as Vanessa Segal's boyfriend, and Jason Devlin, my new worst enemy, and Skinny Nowlin, the grossest, most perverted person on the *planet*—they were all talking publicly, about *that?* About *me?*" She hugged herself smaller. "In front of the entire cafeteria?"

Kim made a whistling sound. "Wow. I am really mad I missed lunch. Or maybe glad?"

"Probably both. But Sam. You were awesome. And if you had known what they were talking about, you would have looked like you do now, like a beat-up eight-year-old, instead of an ice-cool *bitch* if crossed."

"Awesome. Right." Samantha put her face in her hands. She felt vomit in the back of her throat and tears in her eyes and hated all of her bodily functions at once. "I was just sitting there. I barely even like making out. Why would everyone get so hung up on *that* with me?"

Kim and Jessica both rolled their eyes at that one.

"Can't imagine," Jessica started in, talking all singsong. "I'm a natural blonde with perfect skin and a perfect body, what *do* they see in me?" She went on in her 'blonde' voice, which sounded nothing like Samantha. "What can I do? I just wake up beautiful. Every. Day."

"Right." Samantha hated when her friends talked like that. She didn't even *get* why it stung, but it did. "You're forgetting the perfect zit that has been a part of my excellent day since 5 am." Samantha very obviously examined her chin.

But Jessica wasn't having it. "Ooh, and I have this terrible, microscopic pimple in a totally unnoticeable place. And boys want to have *sex* with me because I'm *beautiful*. My life is *so* awful."

"Wait a minute." Kim crossed her arms and tapped her foot and glared in a way that would have been much more effective if she hadn't been obviously about to crack up. "Jessica. *Whose* chest has its own wall in the boy's locker room?"

"Oh, please. My highest honor. High school boys are such cretins."

"Duh," Sam whispered, burying her head in her hands.

Jessica patted her head again. "But Sam, trust me, when the right boy makes out with you, by which I mean one who *knows how*, you'll like it.

There's more to it than drunk jocks sticking their tongues down your throat at parties."

Samantha looked up. "Well, I assume so. Otherwise the species would be, like, dead. But maybe Jason Devlin is right about me and I'm just ... frigid. For extra fun, I could wonder who he heard *that* from."

She didn't feel frigid. Jason and Skinny and Dave and now even Jessica had made her feel *fragile*. Which was much worse.

Sam rubbed her eyes. "Ow. Damn. My contact." Her eye looked red and angry. Cover-up only made it worse. "That's it. I'm not even supposed to be wearing contacts. Glasses only. Right. That'd fix my unwanted boy attention problems. Anyway, I feel totally sick now. I'm going to the nurse's office to rest my eyes. And think about how to fix the Vanessa problem."

Kim nodded. "That'd be great. Because she *is* my captain, she does know we're friends, and she *could* make my life a living hell for the rest of the season."

Samantha sighed. There was no getting out of it. It was her mess-up with Dave, and that meant it was her responsibility to fix it, because everyone knew Kimmie was with Samantha. It was just the way it was. "Don't worry. I'll figure something out after I succeed in not losing the lunch I ate in blissful ignorance of the grossness going on around me."

On the way out, she said softly to Jessica, "Just FYI? No right boy ever *is* going to kiss me the right way because I'm not going near any of them. Ever. Again."

As soon as the bathroom door closed behind them, two black steel-toed boots appeared at the bottom of one of the stalls. One of them kicked open the door. Pris turned and spat a large brown wad from her mouth into the toilet. "About time," she said out loud, to no one. "Don't they care about anyone but themselves? Chew gets old, you know?" But she looked thoughtful.

She took out a toothbrush and tiny tube of toothpaste from the hip pocket of her Dickies. "Samantha Ward. How did you manage to grow up younger while I was away?"

Pris spat again, this time toothpaste, and wiped her mouth on the back of her hand. She stuck her fingers through her blue hair. They got caught on some clumps of dried gel which she flicked one by one off her skin. She whipped out an eyeliner and relined her eyes. The bell rang. "Oops." She slapped her hand into the mirror over the image of her face. "Late for physics."

4. THE HEADMASTER RITUAL

The hall outside the nurse's office was deserted, its gray-flecked floors stretching smooth and unbroken on either side. A girl was inside pitching some entire psycho hissy fit and the nurse had asked Samantha to wait outside for privacy, or the health of her ears, or something.

Samantha slumped down against the wall, letting the cold yellow tiles slide against her long sweater and clump it up around her back. Samantha's mother never looked at one of those sweaters without a tightlipped "tsk." She hated that loose-weave, machine-loomed cotton just like she hated the mall store it came from and the tangle of stainless-steel and rosary beads Samantha liked to wear in the wide V-neck. Her mother thought those sweaters looked *common.* So Samantha had bought seven of them. And counting. And as for the chains, her mother not only thought they looked cheap but knew they *were* cheap, which bothered her even more. Samantha bought another every chance she got.

But today, her mother had drawn the line. "I understand that cheap looking tent of a style is what the girls are wearing, although since you don't have to set yourself at that level, I don't see why you don't *want* to stay a little above the fray, sweetheart. But I will not have you wearing that ridiculous tangle of stainless steel, with *crosses,* of all things, like some cheap Italian call girl who never owned a decent piece of jewelry."

So fine. Samantha could live without the chains. It wasn't like she was some Madonna wannabe anyway. It was just fashion. And fashion, though she took it seriously, was not always worth fighting for.

Partly because there were other battles. But if anyone besides Jessica and Kim knew how hard she sometimes had to fight to stay in her stupid school, she would be a laughingstock.

Samantha's brother Stephen was in prep school. Had been *sent* to prep school. Where one went. Her parents had the same plan for Samantha and nothing short of the promise to get kicked out of any boarding school for pregnancy and drug addiction as opposed to maintaining perfect grades at Highland had been enough to change their minds.

For now, as they would remind her at any sign of rebellion. Such as chains.

Today her fight to stay at this stupid school looked like a pretty stupid battle to choose. But if boarding school was where her mother had acquired *her* ideas of what one wore and what one did, Samantha wanted no part of it.

As far as she could see, her mother believed that only about one hundred very boring people were really worth talking to or going to school with or marrying. Like one big, exclusive neighborhood of dull. The women dressed to show they'd had money for so long, they didn't even need to look good, which would be vulgar, just rich—but not *too* rich, which would look cheap.

So that was part of it. Samantha wanted different people in her neighborhood. Then there was her terror of living with *girls* 24/7. Samantha loved her friends—the ones she loved, at least. And then, she tolerated the ones she didn't love, and the ones she hated, she pretended to love because that was *so* much easier, at least until it became impossible to pretend, at which point, girl war broke out.

But even then, she could go home to her bedroom, open her closet door— the only place she was allowed to put vulgar posters—stare at David Bowie's face plastered all over it, and imagine a different, more interesting world. Alone.

But today, if it hadn't meant so much to her mother, Samantha might have reconsidered.

Samantha wasn't a saint, true, but other girls were so much meaner. So why was *she* the one in a crumpled heap outside the nurse's office? And all because a bunch of boys decided it would be funny to talk about putting their tongues in her vagina, or if it was worth their time, or how long they could do it for, or whatever.

Jessica was wrong. It was worse not knowing. It was like she'd had nothing to say about it at all. She was just *there*, like being pretty and popular made her Mount Everest of vagina jokes.

She felt *so* sick, sicker every time her mind made another lap around it.

Partly because it dredged up another memory, one that mostly stayed foggy. A party freshman year. The punch had been spiked with Everclear, she'd learned later, because the vodka had run out.

Samantha had spent the rest of the night dimly struggling to remove boys' hands and tongues from her body. "Can't believe I'm getting a chance with you," they'd slur as she tried to twist away. She'd pass out a minute and there they'd be again, tongues worming their way into her mouth, hands creeping up her shirt, fumbling with her underwires and fighting the tight waistband of her jeans.

Hands everywhere, all for the first time.

Spinning. Unable to leave because her ride was making out with Christian Shields in the pool house and Samantha was afraid to call her parents. Afraid to call for help. Afraid of being branded—can't hold her liquor, no sense of humor, frigid. And all the while, trying to avoid the shame of getting sick all over *them*.

Ever since Jessica's bathroom lesson, Samantha had tasted Hawaiian punch in the back of her throat.

That time, there were real hands and tongues, but it had mostly gone on in dark corners. No one had been looking. This time, the tongues were only talked of, but everyone was listening.

Suddenly, the idea of an all-girls boarding school seemed like the best idea ever.

Samantha hit her head back against the brick wall. She was now completely slumped down to the ground. She drew up her knees and pulled them up to her chin and pulled her baggy sweater down over them.

Just then, the yelling and sobbing going on inside the nurse's office was joined by some yelling and swearing from outside the nurse's office. Right around the corner, and coming closer.

Slam thud. The familiar sound of boy against locker. But who'd be fighting right around the corner from the principal's office? Guys. Were so stupid.

But as Samantha started paying attention to the yelling, she wasn't so sure she had it right.

"I'm telling you, I didn't do anything. I didn't do anything in that class except the fucking homework!"

"You watch that mouth, punk, or I'll give you a reason to watch it. Now for the last time, what was that knife in class for?"

"I didn't have a knife in class. Talk to anyone. It's not my knife."

"Right, I should talk to anyone because they'll know what knife you *do* carry?"

"*FUCK NO!* Because everyone knows I don't carry a *fucking knife.* I don't *need to,* I know how to fight, all right?"

"You'd like to show me that, wouldn't you, punk? Tell me. Tell me what you wanna do to me. Go ahead."

"Make your fuckin' day, *Clint?*"

Slam thud. The voice was much lower now, but the way the empty hall carried sound, Samantha could hear it. She definitely wasn't supposed to. "You listen to me. You mean nothing here, okay? No one cares. You don't matter to a single person who matters. Your teachers can't stand you, and most of the kids can't either. Some of them are just too scared of you to let you know, and that's who you call your friends. Your own mother can barely give you the time of day from what I hear. If you get roughed up a little, no one's gonna weep about it. So *watch yourself.*"

"You leave my mother out of this. This has *nothing to do with her!*"

"Who said it did? Get off your high horse." The voice was louder again. Much louder. "No one's saying anything about anyone's *momma,* okay? Your problem is you're getting booted from sixth-period history. And you can't graduate without another two years of Social Studies because you were booted last year, too. And now, we have a frightened teacher, a knife, and you, punk, in between them."

"I wasn't anywhere near that desk when that knife showed up, people *saw* it! I mean, not just my friends. People you count as people."

Silence.

Then, with less toughness, the teen voice continued. "Just get me into a different class. I don't wanna flunk out, I'm *doing* the work. But I'm not eating some bullshit *knife* charge."

Samantha flinched. No one's voice should sound like that. No one would want her to hear it.

With the heavy footfalls of someone being pushed, Jason Devlin rounded the corner, shoved down the hall by their Sherman tank of a Vice Principal in Charge of Discipline, Anthony Stagnita. Mr. Stagnita had Jason by the coat collar, which was a little funny-looking because Jason was about six inches taller. The looks on both their faces made it less funny.

If Samantha hadn't already folded her knees to her chest, Jason Devlin would have tripped on her. For the second time that day, she found herself wishing for the improved circumstances of total hell, but as before, hell totally failed her.

Stagnita grunted. "Miss Ward. No sitting in the hallways." He shoved Jason a little further. Jason turned to look at her. He *looked* at her, so hard.

She looked back.

She felt so tired, and so angry, and so punched in the gut by this boy, and there he was, getting punched in the gut back. And it didn't even feel good. It made her feel sicker.

Because maybe it was one thing for her to tell Jason Devlin he didn't matter. She was a girl and he was picking on her in disgusting ways. But it was another thing entirely for the vice principal to tell him that. It felt like walking in on her father with his secretary or something, like she'd stumbled in on some corner of her world she might have known was there all along, but *seeing* it made her feel gross and dirty and not saying anything about it made her feel like she'd had a hand in it herself.

It took away Samantha's pure feelings of righteous indignation and muddied them. Like maybe it wasn't even one thing for her to tell someone they didn't matter at all. Like maybe it just wasn't a thing to be said. To anyone. Period.

And then there was something in his face, as hard as it was, that hadn't been there before. Jason was tall, and although lean, he was pretty broad. He was a good fighter, and a lot of people were afraid of him. Now, though, Jason Devlin looked angry, but he also looked frightened. And sad. And for a moment, you could remember he was only sixteen or seventeen, and he was looking at Samantha with something like a question and something like recognition, and something else she couldn't even name.

Then just as fast as it had appeared, that look was gone, replaced by the bored sneer she knew from lunch. "Yeah, Miss Ward. Straighten those legs to standing position. Time for a new pose."

She turned away. It was nothing, after all. Maybe even just her contacts acting up.

"Devlin, you leave Miss Ward alone. She has better things to fill her time with."

"Clearly. Lots of hallway squatting. Sorry to keep you from it, *Miss Ward.*"

"Sorry, Mr. Stagnita. I forgot the rule—the nurse had me wait outside—some girl was really sick."

The yelling had subsided.

"Did it sound like anything I need look into?"

Samantha shook her head no. Two things seemed very clear to Samantha at that moment. One, whatever the poor girl's problem had been, involving Mr. Stagnita would only make it worse. And two, the difference between the way Mr. Stagnita talked to Samantha and the way he'd been talking to Jason Devlin was so large it felt longer than the hallway they were in. It was like they were different species.

As if on cue, Stagnita told her to wait in the hall as long as she needed to and smiled at her, a kind of reptilian, ingratiating smile.

Samantha didn't like being smiled at by the man she'd just heard slamming another kid against a locker while telling him that his mother couldn't be bothered with him. But social instincts run deep.

She smiled back.

Jason sneered and turned from her like *she* was garbage.

"And another thing, punk. I don't want to hear you mouthing off to Samantha Ward. She's not your kind of girl. Is that clear?"

Jason's eyes bored into Samantha. "Nothing could be clearer. I think she's more *your* kind of girl, *sir.*"

"I didn't say anything that you didn't deserve." Samantha spat out. Then she colored. She shouldn't have said that. Shouldn't.

"Oh, this punk's been bothering you before now? I'm this close to suspending him anyway. Make it easy for me."

Samantha stilled. She liked the idea of Jason Devlin getting suspended for how he'd made her feel. Unprovoked. Undeserved. But. Jason Devlin might be a battle she needed to fight, but Mr. Stagnita would not be one of her foot soldiers. They were *not* on the same side.

She thought fast. It was one of her strong points. "Oh, Mr. Stagnita." As if to say, "go on with you." "Like Jason could bother me even if he tried. We just got into it at lunch. My friends and I were practicing for this debate in Topics in American Culture and Jason and some of *his* friends kind of joined in. We totally didn't agree on *anything.* We were debating, you know, which is worse, institutional violence against minors, or sexual harassment of minors, and like, which is a bigger problem in our public schools, and stuff like that. The one thing that we could agree on, is that it is *totally wrong to participate* and that we should really speak out if we see it." Samantha smiled again. "Don't you agree?"

She watched with satisfaction as Mr. Stagnita dropped his hand from Jason's collar. Jason stopped still and turned to her with open and undisguised shock. Samantha continued, addressing Mr. Stagnita and completely ignoring Jason. "I love that class. It is so important. It's next period. I hate missing it, but something I had for lunch made me feel totally, totally sick."

Jason was still staring at her with a little more intensity and, from what she could tell of his eyes beneath his heavy fringe of hair, anything but boredom. Samantha could feel that stare under her skin. Then he spoke, cold and mocking. "Well, gee, maybe Stephanie here has a solution for me. It seems that...Sarabeth attends a class that fulfills a Social Studies requirement. Maybe—Sabrina would put in a good word for me, so we could continue our important debate about teen sex. We could continue it *all year long.*"

Stagnita turned towards Jason thoughtfully. "You know, Janine Kanter is no pushover. She could handle a punk like you." As soon as Stagnita's back was turned, Samantha shot Jason a death glare and showed him her middle finger. He raised his eyebrows and made a little "tsk" at her gesture. Then he opened his mouth enough to show her his tongue curled up by his teeth. She turned away in disgust. She could not *believe* she just helped him, and he had used the story to get in to her favorite class, where he would now be, being disgusting to her. Every. Day.

To Samantha, Mr. Stagnita said only, "Looks like you just bought yourself a new classmate, Miss Ward." But his gaze was sharper than anything Jason Devlin could muster.

5. DON'T SWITCH THE BLADE ON THE GUY IN THE SHADES

As Jason Devlin sat bent into one of the torture devices the dickwads who thought up high school used for chairs, he watched the second hand on the clock above the door and tried to tap his pencil eraser in the same rhythm.

Jason had his algebra book open to appease the detention supervisor, but his mind wasn't on algebra. It wasn't even on lunch—which had been all kinds of entertaining—or the hallway, which had been something, he wasn't sure what. Jason's mind was on history class. More specifically, on what bug specifically had crawled up Mr. Diangelo's ass.

No one thought it was Jason's knife. Even JAP Barbie, the friend of that Samantha girl who'd been turning up like a bad penny all day, even *she* swore Jason hadn't been anywhere near the desk when the knife had shown up.

Stagnita, of course, had been pleased as hell to think it was Jason's knife from the second he got Diangelo's panicked call. It had been so good for him, he'd probably be having wet dreams on it for weeks. But even Stagnita knew it was bullshit now, or Jason would have been suspended or expelled instead of just in detention which was already like his second home.

Of course, the one person who knew for sure it wasn't Jason's knife was Diangelo, who "found" it and threatened to call the teachers' union if Jason was not removed from his class.

Diangelo had a high, nasally voice when he got nervous and a thin mustache that made him look like some kind of old movie villain. The rest of him, though, looked more like the hero. Smooth. Dark eyes. A haircut that said how much it cared. Girls begged to be in his classes and hung on his every word like they would like to be hanging on his lips and he looked them in the eyes like he would like that too.

Jason despised John Diangelo.

Jason himself had certain standards. No middle-schoolers. No freshmen for anything but kissing. No one desperate for him—because Jason wasn't desperate for any of them and desperation seemed like it really needed to go both ways to be any fun at all.

Jason believed Diangelo did not share this code. He was pretty sure Mr. Diangelo thought a dose of desperation wrapped up in the body of a fifteen- or sixteen-year-old girl was just what the doctor ordered. Jason had no evidence, only warning flags that went off in his brain that said "bad news."

That sign had been flashing even before two weeks earlier, when Jason walked in on the teacher in the bowling alley bathroom nervously shaking hands with Artie Fisher. Jason didn't hear much, but it clearly wasn't just a friendly urinal-side chat.

Artie Fisher was not a nice guy. He was not a chatty guy. Artie was known as someone who could get his hands on and in all kinds of things and people for different effects and for the right price. He wasn't big time. He was just... flexible. So while hanging out in the bowling alley bathroom with Artie Fisher did not only mean one thing, the whole range of things it could mean were not things a high school teacher wanted made public.

The teacher had been wearing sunglasses at night and a leather jacket with a high collar pulled up around his face. Jason hadn't made eye contact. If Jason made a habit of noticing everyone he saw in Del Lanes Bowl and Pool who wasn't bowling or playing pool, his life would definitely be more painful and probably a lot shorter.

Sure, any idiot who thought he'd never run into high school kids in a pool hall deserved to be busted in the most painful and public way, but Jason was no nark, and even a stupid-ass sleazebag of a history teacher should know that.

What could Jason say, anyway? My teacher pisses at Del Lanes, arrest him? There was something missing, some piece Jason didn't have. And Jason hated, *hated* to be missing anything.

So Jason had plenty on his mind other than algebra when Pris the Unprissy marched in ten minutes late, threw herself into the chair next to Jason, blew an enormous pink Bazooka bubble and popped it all over her face.

Jason leaned over, whispering, "Can I help you lick that off, miss?"

Pris shot him a glare that was somehow also a smile and said at normal volume, "You can zip that thought and them parts as inspired it right back in your pants, devil man." She was rewarded with some titters from neighboring seats and a glare from the Ed Tech at the front of the room. Leaning back in her chair and stretching her legs out in front of her, she carefully began peeling back the layer of pink from her face, stretching the threads, wrapping them around her finger, and biting them back into her mouth.

Jason shook his head, letting his hair fall around his face. Those parts weren't actually much interested in Pris, but a girl could get insulted if you didn't at least pretend to try.

He held up his hands. "Hey, you don't know what you're missing."

Pris cracked her gum and answered in a much lower voice, "Yeah, right. Well-kept secret. If you never have to piss. Unfortunately, the *blow* by *blow* is on any girls' bathroom wall in the school. What I'm wondering is how you ever find time for all the other trouble you get into?"

Jason flicked some imaginary dust off the tattered collar of his army jacket, then nodded in great earnestness. "Good time management skills are indeed crucial to high school achievement, Priscilla."

Her eyes narrowed into slits at "Priscilla."

"Watch that if you want to have anything left to manage those skills with, Mr. Devlin."

"Ooh. It's 'Mr. Devlin,' now." Jason was surprised at how touchy she was about her name. She seemed so tough otherwise. He thought it was kind of endearing, but it meant he'd never let it go. He shivered and rubbed his hands on his arms. "So cold."

"Like ice, *baby*. Your balls should shrink just thinking about it."

The large and largely oblivious Ed Tech looked their way. "Anyone talking can look forward to the double session instead of just the one period. Principal's orders." She sounded as bored as the kids.

Jason turned to Pris in outrage. "*Ssshhhhh!* You'll get us in *trouble!!*"

"Would you stop distracting me? I'm trying to work here." She whipped out a physics book and started blowing another enormous bubble.

Jason and Pris sat straight up and focused exaggeratedly on their books. The whole room was stifling giggles. Jason got out a spiral notebook and started writing. Checking to see the Ed Tech had her head down, he passed the book to Pris.

"So what did you do?" it said.

The note came back. "Flipped off the gym teacher."

"Okay. Points. What for?" Jason wrote back.

"To get detention."

"Crafty. Why?"

"Jealous. You can't get in *all* the trouble."

Jason laughed out loud. The Ed Tech looked up over her glasses. "Are you *sure* you wanna stay here late? 'Cause I get paid. But not really enough, you know? So would you mind?"

Under the last line of the note, Jason wrote, "Wanna bet?" and passed it as soon as the Ed Tech put her head back in her magazine.

The book came back. "Duh. You'd lose. Here I am."

"Child's play," he wrote back. He was loving this.

Pris passed back a much fuller page and gestured toward her physics.

"No, child's play = sex joke to mess with a 15 yr-old virgin. She didn't even know what hit her—which let her hit U back. My heart whispers U did it 4 me, but go 4 the glory. Hit her where she's strong. Glory 4 U. Now physics 4 me. U work too or I'll feel guilty & not sleep nights."

Jason frowned. He hated when people used numbers for words. And when they saw shit about him he didn't mean to show. Because Pris was right, the girl had hit back, and hard. Jason Devlin wanted to *matter*. And not just in the school. Like in the world, somewhere. Maybe even in his own goddamn house. Somewhere where someone would think, hey, maybe Jason would like some breakfast.

Pris pointed at his algebra book, glaring.

It was the first time in years anyone reminded him to do his homework. He might as well. Not-Prissy had an edge to her Jason hadn't seen in a girl. Well—not in a fun way, anyway. Samantha had surprised him in the hall, but real edge didn't wear pink and pearls and little gold chains.

Fuck it. He had other fish to fry. Knives. Principals. And funny-as-hell punk rock chicks who showed up out of nowhere and wanted to be friends.

6. KARMA KARMA KARMA KARMA

Get it together, Samantha.

The sound of Jason Devlin's body hitting the locker, the look on his face when he'd seen her—these moments were spreading over her thoughts like scars, tugging at parts of her they shouldn't even have been touching. Jason Devlin had hurt her and hated her suddenly and for no reason, and now on top of it he was making her feel sad.

That was really where she had to draw the line.

If Samantha was going to get bent out of shape about stupid guys being gross, high school was going to be a long, horrible nightmare. And if she got even more bent out of shape when one of them got in trouble, then high school wasn't going to be long at all because she'd be in the psycho ward in no time.

Samantha was *not* some puddle of girl lying in a hallway to be stepped on and taunted by passing burnouts.

Samantha Ward was good at games, and she knew how to win at high school, Mario Brothers style. You sent out versions of yourself to fight your battles for you. Believable versions of someone you might be, but someone cooler, tougher, maybe dumber—maybe even less tough, if that's what was needed. As long as any softness you displayed didn't coincide with something actually soft inside you. And if it did, and someone scored a hit—shut it down, cauterize the wound, and never, never let them see you flinch.

Samantha had flinched big time, and Jason Devlin had seen it. She was paying for it now. But no one else should have to.

Kim Sato was as close to a genuine soft spot as Samantha had at Highland, and Samantha had set her up for hell. Anyone who thought that was a joke had never met Vanessa Segal and had no idea how much cheer squad meant to Kim. Which meant Samantha now had work to do.

So she cleaned up her face, took a pain pill for her headache, and left the nurse's office. Fresh makeup. Heavier eyes. Ditched the pearl earrings in her purse for cheap mall hoops.

Mission: damage control. Logistics. Samantha's specialty. She passed Kim a note in class: "V. S. after school, her locker, follow my lead. Rip this up." Notes got ripped up unless you *wanted* them found. Risk management. Kimmie tore the paper into tiny strips and twisted those into pills. Samantha reconsidered, changed back into her pearls while the teacher was writing on the board. Smooth and soft *in appearance* was better for this plan.

So by three minutes past the bell, Samantha Ward and Kim Sato could be seen hovering at the perimeter of Vanessa Segal's locker court. Dave Watson was there, perfectly mirroring a picture of himself Vanessa had taped on the locker door. He whispered into one of Vanessa's perfectly shaped ears while she smiled with her perfectly shaped mouth and pulled the collar of his polo shirt up to attention.

Samantha noted the other girls with Vanessa. Jewel-toned blazers, skirts, flesh-toned nylons, pumps. They matched. Too much. One girl wore too much black eyeliner for any blonde, ever. The other was trying to reshape her face with strips of foundation along her nose and jawline as per instructions in this month's *Seventeen*. She did it well, but not *that* well, if you knew how to look. Even without her contacts, Samantha knew how to look plenty well if she put her mind to it. Fashion failure was good information.

She waited, all faux-fidgety, until she was sure Vanessa had made eye contact.

"Hey, Vanessa, can I, um, talk to you for a second?"

Vanessa took every inch of her in. "Hey, Kim. Samantha, what's your damage?"

Samantha looked down and bit her lip. "It's a little personal—"

At a nod from Vanessa, her locker court clicked off in their heels. Kim backed up against the opposite wall of lockers and busied herself with a nail file.

Dave started to go too, but Vanessa grabbed his arm. "You can stay, of course."

Clearly Vanessa had heard all about lunch.

Samantha began gushing. "Actually, that's perfect, 'cause it's kind of about Dave. I mean, there were these burnouts? And they were totally saying the skeeviest things to us at lunch? I mean, I didn't even get what they were saying, honestly, but I'm sure it was gross. We—well, Kimmie wasn't there," and here Samantha nodded in the direction of her friend, exonerating her, "but Jason Devlin and these total losers were, like, staring at us and saying gross things? it was *so bogus*. But Dave and the other older boys—they stuck up for us? in, like, such a big way."

Vanessa regarded her evenly. "I was off campus at lunch, but the story I heard went a little differently. And Samantha, I had the impression of you as a girl who could look after herself."

For a split second, Samantha met Vanessa's eye, clear, hard, cold. "Oh, you're not wrong," she agreed.

Then the moment was gone. "But sometimes, you know, it's important that people stick up for you? So that you, and other people, know where you stand, and where *they* stand, you know? That was what Jason Devlin and Skinny Nowlin forgot, they forgot where they stand. But me, *I don't forget that*. So I wanted you to know how much we appreciated Dave—reminding them. It was like having a big brother, you know? Which was so cool because mine's away."

Dave Watson had been smirking but did a double take at the end. "Brother? Oh, wow. Steve Ward is your brother? Genius shortstop back in Little League?"

Fixing him with a look, Samantha said smoothly, "Oh, you know him? It's like you're doubly my big brother, then."

Without missing a beat, Dave ruffled Samantha's hair. "Any time, kiddo."

Vanessa nodded, her manner smooth as silk, or satin, maybe, something that resisted wrinkling. "I'm sure Dave was glad to help. And how is Stephen? I haven't seen him since New Year's."

"He's good. You know. Prep school thing, he's gone all Ralph Lauren."

"I bet it looks great on him. Everything always did. You tell him I said hi, okay? And Samantha, I'll see you around. Maybe that party on Friday—" and here she turned to Dave, "my friend Jeanne heard you tell Dave you might show?" Vanessa turned her gaze to Samantha, waiting. It made Samantha feel uncomfortably like prey.

Samantha shook her head and lied through her teeth. "Oh, *damn,* I forgot, I have this date with my dad's client's son or something. Major drag."

"Too bad." Putting her arm through Dave's, Vanessa smiled, "Samantha, it was good you stopped by. Kim? Game today, so warm-ups at four."

Kim looked up from her nails and nodded vigorously, "I am so pumped!" It looked true.

As Samantha and Kim walked off down the hall, a blue-haired girl emerged from behind an open locker and headed in the opposite direction. She walked past Vanessa and Dave, who glanced at her and muttered, "Who's that freakazoid?"

Vanessa sneered, "Please, as if I have time to know."

As soon as Samantha and Kim had turned the corner, they ran for the girls' bathroom and burst out laughing. The stall doors were wide open, coast clear. Kim leaned against the sink, gasping. "Oh. My God. Who *was* that girl you just were? and how did you get Vanessa to buy it?"

"That's easy. She didn't buy it." Samantha whipped out a lipliner. She wanted darker.

"Omigod, she *didn't?* She's going to *kill* me at warm-ups!" Kim looked genuinely afraid.

Samantha leaned into the mirror. Eyes still a little red, but she needed to see to play field hockey. She whipped out her contact case.

"Relax. Basically, I did what a dog does when it goes up to another dog and rolls over on its back. I told her, this is your tree to pee on, I know it's your tree to pee on, you peed on it first."

"Great mental image there, thank you, Samantha. But that is *not* what you said."

"Well, I can't just go up to Vanessa Segal and say, I submit to you, I know how this school works, because saying that would show I *didn't* know how the school works. So I gave them a cover story. No one's boyfriend started anything or was interested in *going down* on me."

"Wow. Okay. Missed that. But didn't that bother you?"

Samantha shrugged and shook her head. It did bother her, but it was only a little bit of a lie. A friend like Kimmie was worth much bigger lies than that. Samantha held her finger steady and popped the lens in her eye. "Anyway, she knows who I am. She doesn't want any trouble with me, either. I mean, she'd win. But I'd give her a run. She knows that. We had that moment, too."

"You did?" Kim looked dubious.

Samantha hesitated, concerned about the Dave Watson factor, but when she looked at Kim, she smiled. "Yup." Samantha looked toward the ceiling and put the other lens in.

"Wow. Glad you're on my side, Sam."

"Ditto, but Kimmie, you're a great cheerleader, mostly people don't hate you—"

"You mean I'm non-threatening."

"Maybe. But in any case, you don't really need me."

"Yes, I do, you buy most of my clothes and you saved me from AV club."

"The clothes are just fun for me and Jess and I'd say we *stole* you from AV club. I bet they're still pissed." She carefully, wiped the spilled tears from the contact lenses and reapplied eyeliner. "Okay, I seriously am going flatten anyone that gets in my way at field hockey. I am *so* excited to hit things with sticks."

"Well, count me stoked I'm not a ball, then. Oh, and Jessica said she'd see us at the game. She had Mr. 'Diangelove' after school."

Samantha rolled her eyes. "Could she be *any* more obvious about that crush?"

"I know, right? But she was also mondo excited about some big—oh, wait, it was new Jason Devlin gossip. Like, fresh gossip. Post-lunch."

"Well, I hope it's gossip about his impending painful death. Like I said. *So* excited to hit things with sticks."

7. LET'S GO WHERE WE'RE HAPPY

"Hey, go buy a Coke and come commune with the dead with me."

Jason still had the rum he'd bought for Shelly, who would be long gone by now. Pris ran off to the pop machines as soon as detention got out and the two of them walked across the field to the line of trees by the graveyard. Jason gestured to the place where the fence could be pulled down.

"I can give you a boost up." Pris gave him a look and was over the fence in a single fluid motion.

Jason nodded and got himself over. He looked at Pris. "So, I'm going to stop thinking of you as a girl at all and that'll make everything much simpler for me, okay?"

Pris vaulted over a gravestone, did a hopscotch turn, and vaulted back, landing just in front of Jason. She put her hands on her hips and leaned into his space. "How about this?" She narrowed her eyes and shifted her head from side to side as she spoke. "You use me to blow apart your dated, patriarchal notion of what 'girl' means and start treating everyone like people." She hitched herself onto a monument and sat looking at him, smiling and swinging her legs.

Jason put his thumbs in his pockets and shook his hair out of his eyes. "What's pa-parochial? Anyway, I like girls, and I do treat them as people."

"Girls aren't a subset. I mean, they-we-aren't a category of people. Am I more like you? Or like Samantha Ward?"

"I dunno. I've never seen either of you with your clothes off. But I'm willing to try. So, let's get naked and see what that's like . . . and then you can get Samantha over here, and get *her* naked, and *then* we'll be able to say . . ."

"Okay. I've got a better idea. Why don't you stop thinking of me as a girl at all?"

Jason chuckled as he slid down Mr. Studebaker's stone and sat. He pulled out a pack of Marlboros and slid one slightly out, offering. Pris shook her head, reaching instead into her pants pocket. Skoal. She stretched it out toward Jason.

Shuddering a clear no, Jason packed his cigarette on Mr. Studebaker. He lit up and watched in fascination as Pris took a pinch of chew and put it in her mouth between her cheek and teeth. "You know, that stuff is seriously nasty. And for the record, I have never seen a girl do that."

"I thought I wasn't one."

"I said, I've never seen a *girl* do it. So obviously, I wasn't talking about you, who just did it in front of me. Hand me that Coke?"

Pris made as if to throw it, but Jason grabbed her hand. "Very funny. I didn't want to wear it." He tapped on the top, opened it, and slurped off the brown fizz that oozed out onto the rim. "Rum?"

"I guess. I was straight-edge in London, but the suburbs are making me all kinds of sloppy."

Jason almost choked in the middle of a swig. "London, like, England?"

Pris nodded, as if to a three-year-old.

"You were in London? When?"

"Last three years. Give or take." Pris sounded casual and off-hand, but it also sounded studied. Like she knew it was impressive but even more impressive was to make it sound like she thought it wasn't.

Jason registered the pose, but he *was* impressed. "You *lived* in London?" Jason wasn't sure he'd ever even met someone who'd been to Europe. Well— probably the rich kids who had him to parties hoping he'd bring "favors" went there plenty, but it wasn't like they talked to him about their travels. It wasn't like he'd ever heard anyone he *knew* say, "when I was in London." Of course, dudes like Skinny's dad and uncle had been in 'Nam but that seemed so different it didn't really count.

He didn't even know what to say. "Was it cool?"

Pris shrugged. "Sometimes, pretty much a nightmare. Other times, coolest thing ever. It's a place." She leaned heavily against a grave opposite to Mr. Studebaker. Emily Goodchild, or maybe Goodman. Pris was blocking most of the lettering.

Jason couldn't believe he knew the name, but he also couldn't believe he wasn't sure of it. He didn't know which was more pathetic.

London turned Pris from interesting into a kind of royalty. Jason sometimes went in to Chicago. That was it. He looked up at the trees that ringed the graveyard and realized their every point and leaf was known to him.

Then Pris turned and spat into the grass, as far as she could from Jason. It didn't stop him from being able to see the brown, slimy stream slip from between her teeth. That helped rub off some of that royalty shine, helped him shrug back into his own cool and drawl, "It's a good thing I'm not thinking of you as a girl, by the way, because that right there might be enough to put me off girls forever."

Pris didn't miss a beat. "From what I hear, you might be over your lifetime quota anyway. Give the other guys a chance, you know?"

"Um, fuck you?" He gulped Coke to make room for some rum. He wasn't even a big fan of rum. Or drinking at all. It just—made a reason for hanging out in a graveyard, which otherwise—well, it was creepy to say to some girl, "Hey, wanna hang out in a graveyard" if you weren't going to make out or get high or something. But a little something illicit justified all kinds of weird stuff.

Jason blew a few smoke rings, watching them float and settle in the gray air above the stones. "So anyway, London—which parts were 'the coolest thing ever?"

Pris started ticking off London on one hand. "Once I found a scene, ditched 'Prissy,' ran away, got into politics and lived in a punk collective—that was cool." She moved on to the other hand. "Before that, public school—by which they mean private school, because they speak a stupid kind of English—plus my grandmother sick and dying, tons of family spam—less cool." She looked at her hands with the counting fingers sticking out, then clapped them together and made like she was dusting them off.

Jason took another deep drag and poured rum into the Coke. "Why the hell'd you come back?"

Pris took a drink and made a terrible face. "That stuff is nasty. How lame is it to be a white suburban punk, anyway?" She wiped her face on her sleeve. "Anyway. Long story. Short version: I missed Bazooka."

"Oh, I *get* Bazooka. Better than that other stuff you chew, anyway. But gimme the long version. I'm not in a hurry. I'm not in love with my home life."

She put her hand to her mouth. "Shocking." She took another sip, gagged a little, and passed the can back. "Okay, some stuff I don't talk about. But. I started listening to punk and running around, cutting school. Rentals found out. Huge explosion. Plus there was all this—" She paused.

"Stuff you don't talk about?" Likely she wanted to be asked, but not to answer.

"Yep. So I ran away to this squat and lived with my lover and a punk band."

"Lov-er." Jason made a face. "And what's a squat? I'm getting, not just a girl pissing position." Jason trailed his finger around the edge of the can where the tab had been, letting it dig in a little.

"You live somewhere without paying. It's easy in London. It's not even really that illegal."

"Yeah. Right. People just let other people live in their houses and stuff. Because London is apparently in Commie Russia now. And what's a flat? Squats are flat?" It seemed like Pris was speaking English and a foreign language at the same time.

"A flat is an apartment." A little smile hovered at the edges of her mouth.

"So why don't they say that?"

"I don't know. Stupid English. Like I said." Pris kicked at the grass clump growing over a small grave.

Jason wondered what else someone from his world would say to this alien creature.

The creature turned and spat again, then used her tongue to push the chew back between her teeth and gum. "So, when the Rentals finally found me, they let it slip that we were moving back here. We'll just say I freaked out." She crossed one leg over the other and stared fiercely at her boots. "So I ran away again, to this other part of London where almost no white people live, and there's riots. Hard core. And I don't just mean the music."

Jason hadn't really spent a lot of time thinking about what London was like, but he had a vague idea of tea parties and stiff upper lips. Or The Beatles. Even The Clash. Certainly nothing in his imagination corresponded to "no white people."

Pris spat again, this time spitting the rest of her chew. "Then they tried to arrest the people I was living with, and blah blah blah. They said they'd get the embassy involved, and it was this whole big thing."

Embassy? This girl was really intense. But he just said, "And? You're doing a good impression of not being there." Jason passed her the Coke. She shook her head.

"They gave me a choice. If I stayed, I was cut off. If I came back, they'd pay for university in London, and let me do pretty much whatever while I lived here, dress how I want, chew what I want, come and go when I want."

Jason snorted. "Sounds like a good deal. I have that same deal, by the way, without the London and college part. I think my mother calls it, what was it? Oh yeah, not giving a flying fuck." Jason took a big swig of rum and Coke. It tasted like crap and the bubbles burned on the way down. "So. Here you are. It might take you a while to adjust to the excitement. I mean, we have graveyards here."

"It's definitely different."

"While you were gone, a lot happened. Like, my bowling game—so much better now. Upper 200s, regularly. I don't wanna freak you out with the pace of change, but—"

"Devil man, you could leave too, you know? Go to college?"

Jason picked at his boot, twisting tiny fronds of leather that peeked out from a deep scuff in the toe. "Yeah. Well. That's not what it's like for everyone. If my mom decided to cut me off, I'd pretty much have more money than I do now."

Pris nudged Jason's leg with her thick black boot. "Jason Devlin, there were two people I was actually looking forward to seeing, when I finally figured out I was coming back."

Jason looked at her. He thought she was beautiful, in a strange new way that did not affect his groin. "Yeah, and?"

Her eyes narrowed, edged her words with black.

"You were one of them."

A little buzzing sense of pleasure spread through Jason's chest, a counterpoint to the cold stone at his back. "Get outta town. You barely *talked* to me in seventh grade. I mean, even when our parents worked in the same office or something."

"Yeah, My dad's company, he's back there now. But your mom isn't there, I checked."

"No, she's not." The way he said it closed that conversation pretty emphatically.

And Pris got that. Apparently, she, too, knew when not to press. "Anyway, you know why I didn't talk to you back then?"

"Um, because you were Prissy in Pink and I was what Stagnita calls a worthless punk?" Jason's smile was half proud, half bitter.

"Guess again."

Pris was staring. Jason found he had to deflect the intensity. He turned his own gaze back to his boot. "Because you remembered how much I love punk rock. Wait. No, I don't."

"Again."

"You heard about my bowling game." He leaned further into Mr. Studebaker's stone.

"Close. But, the reason is," and Pris regarded him coolly, gauging his reaction like he was some kind of experiment, "I had a toe-numbing, tongue-tying, breath-stealing secret crush on you from the second I laid eyes on you until well after I was in blue blazers in my posh London school. And you, right now, are the first person I ever told."

Jason was glad Mr. Studebaker's stone was so solid, because otherwise he probably would have fallen over.

"No way. I woulda known." Looking at Pris, it for sure seemed unlikely. But remembering Prissy, it seemed impossible. He passed her the Coke, this time without asking.

She drank, the smallest sip. "No one. Knew. Samantha Ward didn't know and she knew every one of my secrets since I was in third grade. She just knew you as Him."

Something inside Jason fluttered at the thought of Samantha Ward privy to all the secret details of little Prissy's seventh-grade fascination. With him. He shook his head. "Y'know, Pris, maybe it's the total volume of times you've already threatened to remove my man parts, but I'm not really getting that crush vibe from you. And believe me. I'm familiar with that crush vibe."

Pris nudged [him?] with her boot again, but this time it was a lot less gentle. "Devlin. I get it. You're God's gift. And you're right. I go' bet'er."

"That how they talk in London?" Jason looked down at her boot on his leg and his boot near it and noticed with some satisfaction that the boots were almost exactly the same.

She narrowed her eyes, withering. "No, shit for brains, that's how they talk on *Monty Python*."

"You know a snake that talks like that?"

Another kick. "You are so full of shit. Every boy in school and their cousins had that movie memorized by the end of seventh grade."

"OK, maybe. But I still don't know what paroch-patriar-what you first said when we got over here, meant."

"Patriarchal." Pris clasped her hands in front of her and raised her eyes as if reciting. "Of or relating to a system of society or government dominated by men."

"Okay. So, like, the right way of doing things?" Jason shot her a look.

"I can kick *very* hard."

"And I can take out any kid in school." She should know he'd earned his nickname.

"But you don't hit girls."

"But you're not a girl, remember?" In a flash he had her legs between his shins in a vise grip and watched her surprise as she could not move them.

She raised her eyebrows, shaking her head. "Okay, okay. Truce. So anyway, no more crush, but I still thought you'd be interesting."

"And?"

"Jury's still out."

"Gimme back my Coke." He threw her legs back down.

Pris swatted his hand. "My Coke." Then she leaned into his space, intense as a judge delivering a verdict. "I loved how you got into trouble, even if I would rather die than do it then. I thought you were just visiting from this whole world of cool, this world I could never touch it or be a part of, but it was exciting just sitting near you, looking on"

Jason couldn't really say anything at all, given how she had just said word for word what he'd been feeling.

She sat back down, or rather leaned, on her haunches. Squatting, as Jason noticed. "And so that's why I found you. To see if, now that I know a little more about trouble, we couldn't you know, make some."

Jason let himself smile a little.

"But, like I said. Jury's still out. The whole boy-slut thing, less than fascinating."

Jason allowed himself a full-on smirk. "I never take any money. Be fair."

"So, explain it to me."

Jason sighed and kicked out his feet, ticking off his explanation on his fingers like Pris had done, "One, girls like me. Two, I like girls. Three, I dig making chicks feel good, and it's something at which I excel. "He leaned back, rubbing his chest. "Demonstration?"

Much to Jason's relief, Pris ignored his last comment, absorbed in trying to etch tombstone letters more deeply with the point of a pen.

Clouds breaking allowed the sun to filter through the trees that edged the cemetery. Jason added, more quietly, "Course if someone is too into me, I don't have—I don't even start."

"And you never get it wrong?" The pen was still scratching into marble.

"Of course I fucking get it wrong." Times ten. Jason kicked the tombstone. "But I try not to."

A huge smile broke over Pris's face and it looked like what the sun had just done. "Jason, you're pretty much describing this *servicing* you do for girls, how it's not about you *at all,* like you're running some charity ..."

Jason had to laugh. "All right, all right. I said I like girls. I just like it when they like it, too. So what are you, some straight-laced, missionary position, no-sex-before-marriage punk rocker?"

The sun was out full force now, pulling out shadows from the tombstones but also making them gleam.

Pris was laughing too. "Trust me, seriously not."

"Good, 'cause I was really wondering how your London squat *lover* was feeling about—"

"I'm not even sold on monogamy. It's mostly about controlling women. Like, my lover—we don't have to be pure in our bodies. It's not about control. But our love is pure."

"Jesus. Gimme a drink. Can you not *say* stuff like that? And speaking of pure, how else can we fuck with your ex-best friend who doesn't even know who you are?" His voice sounded sharp.

Pris's eyes went all narrow again. "Ooh. So *harsh.* I guess they don't call you the Devil just because you're so nice to girls."

Jason ground his cigarette into Mr. Studebaker. "News flash."

"Not news. I heard about lunch, remember?"

"Yeah, well, isn't that what you wanted? She looked *through* you, or whatever? Ring any bells?"

Pris looked down. "The public sexual humiliation of a virgin wouldn't have been the way I'd go with that."

"How the fuck am *I* supposed to know she's a virgin?" Scruples were easy, after the fact.

Now it was Pris's turn to sound sharp. "Um, I don't know, maybe by looking at her or listening to her talk for a minute?"

Jason raised an eyebrow. "Um, you should know, you can't always tell by looking."

"And then, sometimes you can." Pris raised a brow right back.

"Whatever. I don't look at her." Jason began to consider his boot with renewed interest.

"Oh, bull*shit*. Remember? I saw you not-looking at her this morning. In the worst way."

"*OKAY.*" Jason stood up and kicked Mr. Studebaker. Hard. "*And* as for listening to her talk, that would imply she would ever talk to me, which she wouldn't, or to anyone I hang out with, which she also wouldn't."

"I thought you didn't know her?"

"You don't have to. That crowd. Just by hanging with them—you're, whatever, you're..."

"Acquiescing to what they do."

"Huh?" Jason was starting to get his fill of the big words.

"Saying that it's okay, or at least, not saying it's *not* okay."

"Yeah. So why don't you say that?"

"Because you want a better vocabulary."

"Like fuck I do." Jason blew another stream of bitter smoke.

"You don't?" And Jason stole a look at her. Pris was staring, head cocked to one side, as if he were a puzzle piece she couldn't quite make fit. But also like she wanted to keep trying.

As it turned out, he couldn't stay pissy around this girl for long. "Well, okay. I kind of do. But don't tell anyone." Jason shoved her with his foot again. He'd been right, anyway, Pris *was* interesting. Difficult as hell, but interesting. "So that Samantha girl is the other person you were looking forward to seeing?"

Jason watched fascinated as Pris pulled her knees into her body and hugged them. For a second, the hair and the eyeliner and the tough fell away.

She nodded, then rested her chin on her knees and looked off into the distance, past the trees, past the fields, past the school.

And then her tough was back. "Yeah, well. She didn't see me back."

"But again, you do look different." Jason wished he could show her, but at the moment, all he could see was how she looked the same—although the same as what, he couldn't quite place.

Pris kept talking, oblivious. "But if she hadn't turned into one of those *bullshit* people who dismiss, like, ninety percent of the human race because they don't have money or the right clothes or they listen to the wrong music, she would have *seen* me. Instead, I get to school, start walking up to her, smiling like a dork, you know? And nothing. We were blood sisters—in a treehouse, with a pin, you know?"

Pris picked up a stick and started digging a little hole in the grass with the tip of it, twirling the strands of green around it so they pulled out of the ground. "I didn't think we'd turn out to be, like, the same person. I mean, I had some serious experiences, you know? But I never thought, I mean, *never,* that anyone I loved so much would turn into the epitome of everything I despise."

As it happened, Jason knew what she meant so much that it was beyond speaking. So he didn't, and they sat a minute in silence.

"I saw her in the hall today." It seemed more natural to drop the subject, but Jason didn't want to let it go. "Stagnita practically shoved me into her lap." He looked at Pris, hard, an idea about someone else struggling to break through his resentment. "Except she didn't have a lap. Because she was sitting like you are. Like, exactly that way."

"Huh." Pris was quiet another minute. "She say anything?"

"Yeah, after smiling big and wide at the prick she just heard slamming me against the lockers."

"He *hits* you?"

"Nah. That'd leave marks."

"What a bitch." Pris's hard edge was back full force.

Jason stopped. Something didn't sit right.

"Well, she made like I'd done something to her, which, okay, maybe I did, but—" Jason took out another cigarette and held it between his fingers, turning it, adjusting the tobacco in its paper sleeve. "So maybe at lunch she didn't know what I meant at first, okay? I mean, she was clearly confused, but no one's *that* innocent."

He closed his eyes to the lost look of her in the hall. And then, without really knowing why, Jason explained how Samantha had covered for him, not making her look any better or worse than she'd been.

Pris was leaning forward with that intense look. "So she did a decent thing after all."

"I guess."

"Well, that's cooler than what I heard her say today."

"Yeah? What'd you hear?" But on sudden thought, Jason dug into his pocket for his watch. "Wait, let's motivate. I wanna catch some football."

"You have got to be kidding me." Pris sounded like he'd just suggested they go play hide-and-seek in a slaughterhouse or something.

"Nah. I love football."

Pris looked seven different kinds of skeptical. "Um, that is not what it looks like in the halls, I gotta say."

"I don't like football players. But football? C'mon, it's an American thing, like Bazooka."

Pris pulled the punk rock version of the popular girl lip curl. Not much different, really. "Um, that's only cool when you're *not in America*. It's not like I'm some kind of Springsteen Born in the USA fascist."

Jason threw up his hands at that one. "Whoa, whoa, whoa. Let's keep Springsteen out of this, 'cause I don't hit girls. And anyway, that's the stupidest thing I've ever heard. If something's cool, it's cool. And Bazooka Joe? Cool. Football-fuckin' cool, okay? And the Boss? *More* than fuckin' cool. You can't just deny your roots."

"Fuck that. I was joking when I said that. Your roots don't determine who you are, *you* do." Pris's voice was like a whip and Jason jumped back, startled.

She could be so prickly. Probably something sore, under the surface there. Jason could relate. He laid a hand on her arm, soothing. "Pris, come watch football, you American high school kid, you. Embrace your fuckin' fate, okay? You're not in England anymore."

"Fine," she grumbled, rising to her feet. "Just for a minute."

Jason and Pris got themselves over the fence and started down the hill together. To Jason's total shock, Pris crouched down, an imaginary football clearly in her hands. "C'mon, Devlin, out for the pass, Hup one, Hup two, Hike, Hike, Hike!"

And as Jason ran out, glancing behind him, Pris fake-snapped her imaginary ball to herself, dropped back into her pocket, made one fake-out, and spiraled like a pro. Jason adjusted his speed and leapt into the air, catching the non-existent ball and falling to the ground, right on his feet for the completion. He tucked and ran, dodging some imaginary tacklers and blocking others. One of them, he decided, would get him, but he would hold on to the ball, giving his team first and goal. As he hit the ground, he started laughing, and only laughed louder as about 130 pounds of punk rocker piled on top of him. "No shit, Prissy Hines. Where'd you learn that?"

"You should seriously watch the Prissy when these boots are so close to your balls, Devlin. But I learned from Steve Ward, actually, Sammie's brother, and his friends. Of course we thought they were the coolest. And they let us play. But where'd *you* learn? You looked like you would have scored."

Jason lay flat on his back, winded from so much laughing and running on top of so many Marlboros. "Nah. Getting hit—that's half the fun, you know? Whatever. Pop Warner. Ancient history. I hate the whole sports thing at school. It's about that popular stuff. I hate the—"

"Culture."

"I really wouldn't call it that. It's not like they're discussing books or art. They're fucking *stupid*. Or pretend to be. Like they might make good grades, but you should hear them at parties, it's all, where the next kegger is, and what they ran, and what ass they'll have next, and whose girlfriend found them with who, and—"

"That's kind of what I meant. Skip it."

"Fine, vocab girl. C'mon. I wanna go see those football dudes I hate kick some serious ass."

8. NEVER SAY NEVER

Samantha was happy. She'd always liked bleachers, a little hard, maybe, on the sitting bones but good for sprawling, leaning, dancing if you needed. Good for feeling high above the world and close to the ground at the same time. They reminded her of her brother's baseball games, before she'd realized what terrible people her parents were, when she was just happy to be there like a family, watching her brother be so good at something. And now, she realized, bleachers would remind her of moments like this one, and she would like them even more.

It was sunny. Highland was winning. Whenever Kim would cheer, Samantha and Jessica would jump up to cheer too, and whenever Samantha and Jessica would jump and cheer, Chip Davis and Johnny Rosauer would watch them. The boys were trying to sell the Danuzio party Friday night, but Samantha had to stick to her story that she couldn't go, and Jessica was making like she wouldn't go without her. The boys kept trying. It was one of those aimless, harmless, flirting conversations that was working for everyone involved and had no real point beyond that.

These were the moments you looked forward to when you were a kid, Samantha thought, the moments you'd look back on when you were a grown-up, the way grown-ups did when they told you high school had been the best years of their lives. Normally, that was like a bad joke, or you looked at them, open-mouthed, trying to get a handle on how bad the rest of their lives must have *sucked*. But some moments you could see spreading out into your future like sunshine, driving back the shadows that seemed so long while you were in them.

Sometimes you were there, just *there*, living the life you'd imagined when you were a little girl playing teenager, when you'd be the popular one, and you'd be at the football game with your best friend, and you'd be sitting with cute boys who liked you. Maybe one of them would push you playfully and you'd push back, and the air would be a little sharp on your cheeks but still warm, and your team would score a touchdown and you'd all stand up and cheer.

It was a golden moment. Football. Sunshine. Your team gets the extra point. Burnouts horsing around on the grass off from the sidelines, half paying attention in a mocking way, half playing their own weird game. She guessed, grudgingly, they were part of it too.

Of course it didn't last. "Check out that Devlin maneuver, see?" Sure enough, Jason Devlin, Samantha saw when she bothered to focus, was one of the burnouts she'd allowed in her perfect moment. The bunch of them were playing a kind of phantom football, going through the moves but without a ball. As the action on the real field heated up, they'd watch right along with everyone in the bleachers, but during the down times, they'd make a fake kick-off, throw a fake pass with a fake fake-out. The tackles looked real enough, she noticed.

"Kinda puts a different spin on fantasy football, right?" They all laughed. Even Samantha managed.

"That Devlin still has some moves, you know? I mean for real."

Jessica rolled her eyes. "Yeah, then why doesn't he do something real with them?" She made urgent gestures, trying to warn the boys off a tender subject. They didn't get it.

Samantha was glad they didn't. This way she got to gaze a little longer at the way Jason Devlin's body darted over the grass and leapt and fell to earth. He was much more agile than she would have thought. So while the boys she was with were talking, she could watch Jason Devlin move through the same sunshine that she was in. And no one would have to know.

The boys kept talking.

"What happened to him? He played Pop Warner every year."

"His dad died. Remember? He used to coach and stuff."

"I remember his dad. I never heard he died, though. That's tough."

"Car accident somewhere out of town, our eighth-grade year. Messy. You wouldn't have noticed his dad was gone, though, because that was the end of Pop Warner. Most of those kids didn't make the team here. I didn't. Devlin would've made the team, though, if he'd ever tried. For sure last year, after he grew that ten feet or whatever he grew—I mean, look at him, he's still so fast, and that's on top of however many dime bags and Marlboros he smokes in a day."

"You on the burnout cheer squad, now, Johnny?"

"Nah." Johnny looked down. "But my dad, he was in one of those Lions things with his dad. I always felt bad, despite what an asshole he can be—I always felt bad about the way things went down with Devlin."

Chip rubbed his face. "Huh. I swear to God, I never knew. I mean, I talked to him before—before he went all burnout, and he never said a word. *I* thought he went to hell when everyone started saying all that shit about his sister."

The stories went on. Samantha couldn't not listen. "See, freshman year, Jason was still a small guy. You know, how freshmen are."

"Yeah, and he's going after seniors, football players, whoever said a word about her. Got the shit kicked out of him. Every day. But then he got his growth spurt and he learned to fight so mean, people mostly shut up. But you were here last year, you must've seen."

Samantha shook her head. She had not seen.

Jessica shrugged. "Wastoids fighting jocks? Not high on the freshman girl radar when you're trying to not get eaten alive by Vanessa Segal. Before today, I don't think I ever spent two minutes thinking about Jason Devlin."

Samantha remembered another thing she loved about bleachers—the green paint, how in the sun it was almost like glue. It went on thick and left little bubbled craters and valleys, and if you found a good one, you could mold it with your nail, make it squish and slant and wrinkle. In a really good place, more like a blister, you could start peeling. You could peel off a whole strip of paint and it would be flat in your hand, you could let it flutter, or smooth it to your skin, or squish it up like gum.

She'd remembered the green paint because she couldn't look at Jason Devlin any more. She couldn't look at the boy she'd told that day that no one cared about him, that he knew it, too. Her heart felt shaky in her body. It made her feel like maybe she should never say anything again, if she could make such a big mistake. But the conversation slowed, and she had to say something or the something she didn't say would choke her.

"That's way harsh. His father died, and then people decided to pick on his sister? I didn't even know he had a sister." She spoke too fast.

"For sure, he has some sister. See, what made it worse, probably, there was hardly a word anyone could say about his sister that wasn't true."

"Did you say stuff about his sister?" Samantha was still fixated on the strips of green paint stretching between her fingers.

"Everyone did. Pardon my French, but she's a fuckin' coke whore, you know?" Chip shrugged. "People talk."

Samantha nodded. They did talk.

"Oh. My God!" Jessica exploded, "Could today possibly be even any more about Jason Devlin? First Samantha, and then that knife thing with Diangelo, who was so freaked out he needed, like, comforting. Now there's Jason Devlin, after-school special. I'm sorry. People's dads die. That sucks. But Kyle Schmidt's dad died and he's like, Mr. Student Council. And Kwame's a friggin' orphan from Africa and he's our star running back and a really nice guy. Anyway. Jason Devlin was gross to Samantha and thereby is dead to me. Now. Can we please watch the real football?"

Samantha tried to turn her attention back to the game, but the boys on the field now looked incomprehensible to her, their strange triangular costumes alien as they trotted back and forth on small legs that seemed in danger of failing to support the heavy helmets the violence of the sport required. It seemed, now, as if nothing made sense the way it had. The cheers seemed pointless, the flapping skirts and high-pitched voices out of place next to the cracking of boy against boy. Samantha, too, felt out of place in the sunshine.

She whispered to Jessica that she needed to call home and excused herself down the bleachers. The phantom footballers, she noticed, were mostly scattered, a small knot of them suspiciously gathered by the far corner of the grey squat building. None of them looked tall enough to be Jason. And what would she even say if she found him?

She took herself out of sight of the bleachers, near a side entrance to the school where there was a foyer with a phone she didn't need, where to one side some green and brown dumpsters loomed and blocked a small corner of asphalt. There, she could pace and worry and kick chunks of blacktop into the gray brick and wait for some solution to overtake her.

What came to her, of course—because things *would* work that way, just as Samantha had been deciding that talking to him was the last thing she wanted—what came to her was Jason Devlin, walking very fast, packing a pack of Marlboros hard against the palm of his hand. He almost walked right past her, then stopped in his tracks. "Well, look who it is. It's been too long."

"Are you following me?" asked Samantha, suddenly nervous.

Jason leaned into a dumpster and continued packing his cigarettes. "Yes. Yes, I am. It was easy, because everyone knows how you Barbies love hanging out here by the dumpsters for an out-of-the-way smoke. Oh. Wait. It's me who does that." Jason carefully peeled the cellophane string from the pack and crinkled the wrapper in his hand. "Who woulda thought I'd hit pay dirt with such a lousy stalker strategy?" He pulled the foil out, edged up a couple of cigarettes and gestured forward with the pack. "Marlboro, Barbie?"

Samantha shook her head and folded her arms over her body. She couldn't find words.

"Cat got your tongue?" Jason asked, lighting up. He shook his hair back and stared.

"Don't talk to me about tongues," blurted Samantha, which she considered later was the very last thing in the world she would have wanted to say. It felt raw. Then she said quietly, "I had enough at lunch."

Jason raised his eyebrows at her response, then nodded. "I could see that." He took another drag of his cigarette as Samantha went back to pacing. "So, did you come here to do some laps? Get a little exercise? Or just, you know, passing through to correct my idioms?"

Somewhere at the back of Samantha's mind, Jason's casual use of the word "idiom" registered a little surprise. She frowned. In a different part of her mind, a decision was made, although she couldn't have said later she'd made it. "I was looking for you."

These words seemed to knock Jason's head back and to one side. It was just a tiny movement, but it resulted in Jason Devlin's looking down at Samantha through his ridiculously dark eyelashes, his head slightly cocked. He was still leaning back, and he was still taller.

Samantha realized suddenly and to her total horror that she now understood exactly what dead sexy meant.

She watched, a little shocked, as Jason's tongue moved over his lips before he said, after a moment's hesitation, "Huh. I guess that explains the success of my less than stellar stalking technique." His hair felt back over his eyes. "Good to know."

And then Samantha thought, maybe it was now, maybe *that's* what dead sexy meant.

These thoughts flashed in her mind like light, but unlike light with some kind of weight and force. She was horrified. But she *had* to speak or risk being choked by the unspoken words welling inside her.

Arms still folded, Samantha studied asphalt. "So I—I don't know how to say this, without saying that you are anything other than a total pig for the way you—whatever. That's *not* what I came to say. What I wanted to say was, regardless, I don't like it that I said ... what I said. I don't want to have said it, I wish I hadn't said it, and it was wrong."

On the word "wrong" she looked up and she could see, for one moment, the total surprise on Jason's face.

"Okay," he said, forgetting for a minute to smoke, "I gotta say, I didn't see that coming." He looked like he wanted to say something else, but nothing came. No "I'm sorry too, I don't know why I did that," or, "I didn't mean to hurt you either." Nothing. Inside, Samantha felt something fragile being crushed.

And then she got mad. Which was, at last, familiar territory and allowed even the strange space behind the dumpsters to return to something like her world. "Yeah. I get that. Sometimes things just come out of the blue, and you think, wow. I wonder what I ever did to deserve *that.* For you, maybe, it's someone saying something decent to you. For me, maybe, it's someone coming up to you in the cafeteria and—" but she couldn't go on.

"Gee, Princess, it was just a joke. Maybe you should learn not to be so sensitive." He sounded bored.

"Right. Because you know me so well. Except I bet if you took a poll asking about, like, my big flaws, 'too sensitive' would not be topping the list. But actually, you don't know me at all. You just decided to—to *mess* with me. I was just there. Like Mount Everest or something."

Jason made a considering face. "You mean, like, you're so high above me—or, you just like to be *on top.*"

Samantha shuddered. "See. You want to prove you can *slime* anyone. But I'm going to tell you why I *am* high above you."

"This should be *good.*" Jason sounded genuinely pissed. He sounded raw, too, as if she'd finally pushed through a little. Samantha liked that.

"I'm high above you because when I overheard a—a difficult conversation *you* were having? I didn't use that situation to *totally devalue you.* Everyone was talking about it, about that knife and all, and I didn't say a single word. Not to *anyone.*"

"Yeah, did you figure maybe totally devaluing me once a day is enough? You're right. You're so high above me, you're a moral fucking goddess. Are we done here?" Now he wasn't looking at her. He was looking at his cigarette, turning it in his hand.

"Score," thought Samantha.

She narrowed her eyes and walked right into his space. "Not. Even. Close." She saw it in his face: total shock.

Maybe this was what getting high felt like.

She kept going. "I told you I was sorry. Because what I said was beneath me. Do you hear me? I'm sorry because it was beneath *me.* And the next time I had a chance? I didn't take it. And you know what? I *never* will. Because I have standards, and whatever I came by *unfairly*—I'm not going to use against you. Not because of *you,* but because of me. I'm not going to sink that low."

"Not as low as me, you mean." Each word sounded like a bite.

"That's right, you were pretty low today. And then, I'd say, maybe I stepped even lower. But I stepped up again. And in spite of what you said about me to *Skinny Nowlin*—I even did something decent for you. You *know* I did."

Jason met her eyes, nodded, then remembered what to do with his cigarette but blew the smoke out like it was bitter to him. "Medal forth *fucking* coming, no doubt."

"Maybe so. But don't *you* get in line for one. You even took advantage of my decent thing. And nowhere in any of this, do you ever consider that I might not be your Mount Everest, but like, a person with feelings that want to be doing something besides being stepped on with your big, ugly, black boots."

"Have you been watching lots of nighttime soaps?" Jason cocked his head again but looked a little less controlled.

"What?"

"Just that, you know, the melodrama is fine, but I think your scripts run a little long. Anyway, Princess, I know you think you own the school, but it's not your class, and I need it to graduate."

"Wow. I heard you were tough. But you're a big chicken. You just blow off every—every difficult thing I say, and you go for the easiest shot."

Jason did a double take. "*What* did you just say?"

"Skip it."

Shaking his head, Jason held up his hands. "Are we done *now?* Because as touching as this apology has been—and I am deeply moved—I hate too much of a good thing."

"Well, tough. Because we are *not* through. You started a war with me for no reason, and then you shoved yourself into my afternoon for the *rest of the year.* So what I have to say to you is, fine. I am *not* chicken. I do *not* back down. I never knew you from Adam, and I would have been happy to let it stay that way. But now? I am totally prepared to hate your guts and let you know it every day in the most painful way I can. Fairly. Just me. And just you." And Samantha started to turn, started to walk away.

"I have to warn you, I don't get exclusive with girls."

Samantha whipped around, completely floored. "Are you out of your effin' *mind?*"

Jason smirked. "Please. Your language. My virgin ears. But no, I really don't."

"Do you think that I would *ever,* after today, let alone, like, all the rules of nature, that I would ever think about you *like that?*"

"I would lay," he considered, "fifty-to-one odds that you already have." His gaze was steady, cool. "I get a lot of practice reading the signs. And you? Here? By the dumpsters with me, chest heaving, fine, delicate nostrils flaring, eyes—" and he made a big show of peering into her face, "eyes slightly dilated? Yep. Several tell-tale signs right there."

"Okay. So you *are* out of your mind. Interesting."

Jason shrugged his shoulders. "I just don't want you to get all hurt, you know, when you find out I've been hating other girls."

In spite of herself, Samantha could feel her mouth twitching. She bowed her head but could not help a chuckle. She crossed her arms again and looked up at him. "I'll get over it."

Grinding his cigarette butt under his foot, he looked down, and actually mumbled, "What, you can get over a pain like that but you can't get over a little joke at lunch?"

Like it might bother him, a little, if she couldn't.

So she spoke softly. "Okay. Since you ask. No, I don't think I can. And this is why. Sure, at lunch, I didn't know what you guys were talking about. That was part of the fun, right? Everyone laughing, everyone knows but me, right?"

Jason nodded, looking down, studying the pattern his ashes had made on the ground and scuffing them with the toe of his boot. This looking down, it was *so different* from when he looked down in disdain or stared in that steady, arrogant way.

She continued, quietly. "So of course, later, I find out. I find out what you were talking about. I didn't know—I didn't know people even did that. And actually, it makes me want to throw up. And maybe it always will. Maybe it would have anyway. But maybe, maybe that's something *you* did. It's supposed to feel good, right? Someone would want to do that to make me feel good?"

Jason looked up, and the look was unlike anything she'd ever seen. She didn't know how to read it. It was, she guessed, in that language that she clearly didn't know and he was somehow fluent in. "Right," he said, "it would be like that."

"Right." Samantha took a deep breath, fighting the sick she still felt so strongly. "But instead, maybe I don't get that. Maybe—instead, when I think of *that*—I have to hear your voice. Or see your face."

"*What?*" Jason started, stood up suddenly from the wall, sounded so shocked, so intense, so—she didn't know. "When you—*what* did you just say to me?" His eyes were wide and he looked like he might—explode, or something.

She could have enjoyed it, maybe, if she'd known what it was about. But it seemed like somehow she herself was speaking a language she didn't fully understand.

She backed off, a little panicked. "What? What do you mean?"

He stared, then looked down, shaking his head, muttering. "Jesus Christ. You really *are* that innocent."

"No—I'm—"

"No, not innocent, *clueless*. You have no fucking idea, no clue, just look at you—you just *say* something like that, and you don't even know—"

Samantha felt like she was swimming. Or needing to swim, and failing. "I don't know what you're talking about. I just meant—maybe you helped yourself be right about me, what you said. You know, frigid." She hugged her arms tight around herself.

Jason shook his head again. His lips made a circle, whistling without sound. "Jury might still be out on that one." There was something different about his eyes, just the brief glance he leveled at her before looking down again. Intense.

Samantha needed distance from that look. Whatever she'd been planning to even the score, it wasn't *that*. "Well, I give it to you in writing that *you'll* never have a seat on that jury. That's not what this about."

Jason followed suit. Back to square one. "I'm pretty sure I was clear about not looking for a seat on that jury."

"No, actually. How I remember it was, you had *already judged* on whatever evidence you thought you had."

"So, you're saying you could give me more evidence?" And then his voice was hard. "OKAY, Barbie, let's give you a different reason to *see my face* when you think about that *thing* you can't bring yourself to say. You know. Maybe I could kiss it and make it better." He showed his tongue curled around his teeth but it just looked gross.

That was getting old. Maybe he wasn't, after all, as impressive as she'd been beginning to think. "There you go again. How original. Who would expect the big burnout playboy to get over on the virgin *that* way. Except wait. It's your one note. Did you never think someone would learn to block the one punch you know how to throw?"

To her surprise, Jason was smiling. Not smirking. Actually smiling. She blew it off. "Anyway. I don't think you even get what this was about. Maybe you *are* as stupid as you look."

Then he was coming toward her, and then he was right there, in her face, one hand gesturing before him, owning the space between them, and after all, impressive maybe was the word. His voice had more bite and as he spoke his body had a jagged rhythm that offset the controlled movements of his hand.

"Oh, sweetheart, I get it. You came to show me yours because you saw some of mine you didn't want to see in that hallway. You want an even field, because you don't want to kick a dog when he's down, and you want to kick me again *really bad*. I get it *fine*. I got your back up, and to your shame and horror you actually give a fuck, and you're pissed as hell about it. So you wanted to tell me game on. And I want to tell you, *fine*. Game *the fuck* on, Barbie."

Samantha registered Jason's surprise as she did not back down. Instead, she reached out and slowly moved his hand from in between them. Her hand was on his sleeve, but the cuff shifted and her finger grazed his wrist, then hand. They both stared at the contact.

Samantha drew back, tilted her head and smiled sweetly. "That about sums it up, doesn't it?" she said, as if he'd just summarized an algebra equation and she agreed with his results. She began to walk away, then paused, looked halfway around. "But your math is off. It's really only half a fuck. Still, points, you know, for showing your work." And she kept walking.

Then he called out to her. "I should get points for more than that."

She turned. "I have *no* idea what for."

"Yeah—well what about this—if you know you can block a blow, it can't really hurt you again, can it?"

Samantha just looked at him.

"Cat got your tongue?" he asked, a small smile back on his face.

She rolled her eyes. But she could feel herself blushing and starting to laugh. It was true, she had no reaction at all. "Okay, so maybe you're a little bit right."

"And the earth opens and yes! Ladies and gentlemen, hell has frozen over..."

"Not really. You haven't said you were sorry yet."

Now it was Jason's turn for the eye roll, "Listen. Don't—"

But Samantha cut him off. "No, don't worry, I won't hold my breath."

9. THE FRICTION OF THE DAY

Jason watched the back of that girl for a while and then looked around at his surroundings, trying to clear his head of her just a little bit. He'd have to say, his surroundings weren't doing that much for him. Gray brick walls. Dumpsters. Broken asphalt strewn with cigarette butts, most of them his. They could only tell him what he already knew: He'd had one long-ass day, and it was time to get out of there, *fast*.

Plus he was *hungry,* and he needed time racking pins or washing pots if he wanted anything besides chips to eat that night. Chances his mother had made it to the grocery store were slim to none.

In the end, it would be Jason who would bring *her* food to pick at and leave for dead the way she did. But she still asked for it, BLT or burger and fries in their white Styrofoam packages, sealed up extra good, Harry always said, to keep it warm on the walk home. It was decent of Harry to send her food—mostly he didn't even dock Jason's pay. Holdover good will from when his dad bowled on the team at Del Lanes, and his mom with her Malibu-blonde feathered hair was the life of the after-party.

So Jason headed to the bowling alley like he did most nights. After a day like he'd had, the crash of the pins, the scalding water and the clang of the pans, even the grease to his elbows would be a pretty welcome change.

Walking fast through the front parking lot, Jason made a running cata-log of his day. He cut it into short phrases and set them to the rhythm of boot soles on pavement. Spoiled milk. Graveyard smoke. Prissy turned Pris. Jocks in the hall. Knife on a chair. The rhythm calmed and cooled him, he kept his eyes fixed forward. There was nothing to see, a few cars on the road and the scrubby fall grass creeping onto the pavement. Nothing but sound, words in his mind, movement. Back to the wall. Shove in a chest. Rum in a Coke.

Then it broke down. Barbie girl looking *through* him, eyes and hurt and blonde and mad and want. Pace broken, swirling. He stopped to light another cigarette, willing the smoke to billow through him, to smooth, deaden, calm.

He smoked too much, he knew it. But it was reliable like clockwork. Like tombstones. It got him through.

In the hall, she'd hugged her legs to her chest like a little girl. Like Pris had hugged hers, sad at losing the person the girl in the hall had been. Then stalker Barbie, calling him to battle in some honor duel to the death. Sneering that he went for the easy shots.

Something to think about: the tiny ghosts of each other he'd seen in both girls, lost phantoms appearing only to him.

He blew smoke from his nose and watched it fade in the autumn air.

Smoke was working. Black boots, pavement, gray smoke, bright air. Scope out the underpass, the one you had to walk under to get to school from Highwood. Everyone knew that. There was no other way. Great place for an ambush, used often. Coast clear, for now.

Jason could see the Del Lanes sign, enormous red and white bowling pin flashing neon against the graying sky, the orange block letters flickering raggedly as if showing two Ls at once was too much to ask. Play pool! it said in script, but one of the o's was dark.

One time Skinny had scaled the sign and added a big white poster saying "pot," so it read "Play Pol Pot!" Jason had cut class to take it down so the Vietnam vets who bowled there wouldn't go ballistic on them. Skinny's dad had helped bomb the shit out of Cambodia before he lost his mind, but not everyone was ready to laugh at the idea of bowling with the Khmer Rouge.

Jason thought it was funny as hell, but at the bowling alley he had better luck keeping his mouth shut than he did at school.

Fuck school. The way that prick Stagnita had it in for him, as if Jason Devlin, really, when you thought about it, needed to be taken down any further.

Something wrong there. People noticed, he could tell. But no one did anything about it. Maybe there was nothing *to* do, which should put it firmly in the *not* to think about column, but Jason had a hard time keeping it there.

Smoke. Cherry hit filter. Flick to bushes. Hope nothing ignites.

On the main road in Highwood, the buildings were low and dingy, a collection of gray and orange and brown and drink. Gas station signs added splashes of color. Even the bank looked poor. It was hard to see how *anyone* from across the underpass would think the people here needed taking down.

Fuck Diangelo. Just a tweaky prick doing bowling alley business, maybe nothing to worry about. Unless someone Diangelo was doing business thought *Jason* was something to worry about.

Which was something to worry about.

That world could get dangerous, not like, let's rumble with the jocks olde tyme teen movie dangerous, but guns and pimps and kilos dangerous. Small time stuff, maybe, but big enough to hurt bad if they thought you had it coming or just didn't like you.

The thing was—mostly they did like him.

To *normal* grown-up men, Jason was just some kid who needed a place to hang out and chill from his mom and school, like maybe the grown-up men themselves had, back in the day. Which was why Del Lanes was a good arrangement. It came with a little food and a little money and if anyone was messing with him there, he needed to find a way to take care of it.

He knew what happened when you got in too deep there. Lessons learned from a sister. Dark alley. Muffled cries. Too many men.

Jason shook his head. Heather was gone, living in the city with a dealer who moved serious size. He knew she made it pay. Didn't bear thinking about.

Jason didn't get in too deep. Not there, not anywhere. Lesson goddamn learned.

Matters at hand. The pack of jocks who had it in for him—but that could get fun. Throwing, taking a few good punches—blow off a little steam. But he couldn't take more than three of those guys—less if the football team got in on it.

So. The day had given him a lot of important life stuff to think about.

So what Jason was thinking about, of course, was girls.

Jason Devlin could admit he spent his fair share of time thinking about girls. Possibly more than his fair share. But he'd never spent more time thinking about girls with less actual action to show for it than he had that day.

Girls, furthermore, he didn't want action with, or at least he hadn't until one of them showed up in his smoking corner and turned his world upside down for a minute. For sure he didn't *want* to want action with her. And for sure, he was never going to get any action with her, so by his own totally reasonable rules, it wasn't worth thinking about.

But none of the good reasons he had for not thinking about Samantha Ward in what she'd call *that way* seemed to stop him. Reasons like the fact that she'd made him feel fucking bad. Showed up in his life in ways and places he didn't want anyone showing up, making him sick with her gold and her pearls, her looking through people, her rubbing his face in the fact that she mattered in a way he didn't.

Of course, she now hated him, and he pretty much had been prepared to hate her back and maybe enjoy it just a little.

But then she goes and says something so painfully sexy that he was pretty sure he was going have to get alone with it sooner rather than later and maybe more than once. You couldn't say to a person like Jason, who prided himself on certain talents, 'whenever I think of *that* I'll see your face and hear your voice.' He should be able to prosecute.

The thing was, saying it at all proved she had no idea what it meant, and probably proved that Jason was a little bit more of an asshole than he'd set out to be that morning. But her having no idea didn't change the fact that Jason had plenty, now complete with a video track *of her* saying *that* stuck in a loop in his head. Which guaranteed Jason would be up at night thinking about doing the very things he'd announced to the world in general that he was completely uninterested in doing to her.

So fuck.

Too bad he didn't really drink.

Pris was the girl he *wanted* to be thinking about, the one he liked so much it was almost strange. But there was just no sex vibe at all. And whatever story she might have about crushes, he was pretty sure Pris felt the same way. And that sex vibe was, unfortunately, pretty high on Jason's list of what you could possibly want a girlfriend for.

"So fuckin' sue me," muttered Jason out loud to a passing car.

And what made Jason Devlin think that really, guys *were* the jerks girls made them out to be, was this: the one he kept thinking about was the one he didn't like but *wanted*, not the one he could maybe even love, but didn't want at all.

And for that reason, thought Jason as he strolled into Del Lanes, God invented bowling.

Del Lanes had no bright lights or angles, nothing to catch sharply on your mind. If there was anything in the entire place that wasn't brown or black, it was green or orange. The beer mirrors on the walls reflected the pale brown of the lanes and the dark brown of the tables, the bar at the back was fake wood paneled, too. Even the gold of the trophies on the back wall looked brown in the dim light.

But when you put quarters in the pool tables and the balls came rumbling down, when you racked and broke, you got a starburst of color that you really noticed. And anyone's custom ball in swirly blue or green made them stand out like a rock star.

Jason called into the back room where the owner sat pouring over some of his chins and a sheaf of papers. Harry didn't look up. Miss October on the wall behind his desk didn't even clash with the color scheme. She was a brunette and her skin was tan. She was even spread out in a pile of yellow and orange and—yes—brown leaves. Harry had a red face and a gray-red crew cut that bristled around his head like a cut-rate halo, although at this point, Jason was hungry enough to swear it could be the real thing. Jason asked if he could bowl a few games before he washed the pots and pans. Harry nodded, still not looking up.

"Thanks, Har. I'm so goddamn hungry I could eat the menu."

"Have a burger instead, menu paper's like Chink food, leaves you hungry in half an hour."

Jason chuckled. Harry sometimes tried to make jokes and these jokes were never funny. It was part of Jason's job to laugh at them.

Jason popped his head through the swinging kitchen doors. "Yo, Eddie, Harry says make me a burger. Gimme some lettuce and tomato with it, extra. And pickles. And coleslaw. Anything you got that comes out of the ground."

"You got it," called out Eddie, the ash dangling from his ever-present cigarette miraculously failing to fall in the plate of food he was putting on the kitchen window. "Ham and cheese on whiskey down, fries is UP!" he shouted, and tipped the ash to the kitchen floor.

Food ordered, Jason looked around for anything that needed keeping an eye on. A dad with a couple of tiny kids trying to get them to bowl something besides gutter balls toward the front. Some ladies' after-work team squealing and drinking at number five. The serious players were at the back—bowlers at the lanes, dealers at the bar. Kids at the pool tables—no one he couldn't smoke with his eyes closed, but no one who had any money.

"*Devlin!*" Harry's voice boomed from the back. "Shoes!"

Jason waved his bowling shoes up in the air and started changing. He had to say, even being nagged like that, it was kind of nice someone was paying attention.

Eight and a spare, seven and a spare, three strikes. Not bad, Jason thought later as he hunched over the sink. He was up to his elbows in greasy water as he had foretold, Rush was blaring on the kitchen speakers, and Eddie was somehow managing air drums between flipping burgers and Steak-umms on the grill, all while not dropping the ash from his cigarette into anyone's food.

It was a beautiful talent Eddie had, Jason thought, and it was a beautiful thing he'd found a place in the world to make use of it.

Like the goddamn drummer for Rush. That shit was *amazing.*

Jason was feeling a lot better.

It was good listening to guys talk about normal problems—billing errors, late payroll check, a new carpenter's assistant not working out, good painting work to be had because of high turnover at the Mayweather apartments. Wife pregnant, wife nagging, wife has a new haircut, looks like a man.

Jason figured this was where he was headed, if he was lucky. Maybe not the wife part, but otherwise, it didn't look so bad.

Most of these guys had graduated high school, and one guy, Duane, had a year or two of college. But no one here had polo shirts, or alligators, or Mercedes or any other car that would count in the Barbie world.

None of that world counted here, either. Sure, kids from school would come and go—bowling for a goof, trying to play pool, scoring "party favors." But they were just customers, like the families who played early evenings and weekends. Jason *counted*—maybe in the same way that the beat-up brown furniture counted, but it still felt good.

Jason turned off the taps and wiped his hands on a greasy towel and hung up his food-stained apron. He checked on the food for his mother but Eddie gestured to a garland of white strips on the stainless wheel before his eyes. It would be a minute.

Skinny and Bogart and a couple of other kids were playing pool. Skinny was on a roll. "*There* the fuck you are, man," Skinny greeted him, "you're missing all my art. Check it out. Bank shot, nine ball, corner pocket off the seven."

Jason looked at the shot. "Pack of smokes if you make that, man."

"One lousy pack?"

"One lousy pack and, like, my eternal admiration and shit."

"Right. Well, once you add the *shit*, it becomes irre-fuckin-sistable."

"That's what I like about you, Skinny, you got that gift with words."

"Shaddup. I gotta concentrate."

Skinny did, and to Jason's surprise, sank the ball. "Dude. I got the smokes in my backpack."

"And the eternal admiration, and the shit?"

"Admiration is yours, but aren't you already pretty much full of shit?"

"*Fuck* you, man. Who made that fuckin' shot?"

"You did, Skinny. And I promise you," Jason deadpanned, "I'll give you all the shit you want."

Skinny went for the face and then, with a fake-out, punched Jason in the gut—not too hard, but hard enough to hurt a little. "Jeez," Skinny said, rubbing his fist, "got one in. You high, man?" He peered in Jason's face.

Jason shrugged. "Hang on. I gotta check something, and I'll grab your smokes. You hangin' out?"

"No doubt. I'm cleaning Bogart's clock."

"Right. Your kid sister could clean Bogart's clock."

"I don't have a sister."

"My point exactly."

Jason had seen Artie Fisher heading back to the bathroom and Jason wanted a word. He wasn't really clear on how deals went down at Del Lanes— but knew that Harry knew, turned a blind eye for a cut, and could probably put his foot down when he had to. Not that Harry's foot was any too heavy. Of all the people doing business, though, Artie was the only one Jason knew well enough to say hey to. He knew some of the other guys by sight or name but it wasn't established that *they* knew that he knew. Or if it was, it was officially forgotten, dragged out back beneath a dumpster, out of sight, out of mind. Better to leave it like that.

Better to leave the whole thing, usually. But Diangelo had left Jason nervous.

Artie was by the phones outside the bathroom, phone to his ear but clearly just waiting. The words and numbers etched into the fake wood paneling radiated out from his head, gold but faded against the brown. Jason eyed him a question, Artie showed him two fingers and a watch, and gestured with his head toward the bathroom. Jason nodded and went in. Some guy was using the urinal, Jason made as if to do the same until the dude took off, at which point Artie made his entrance, calm but purposeful.

Jason said hey, Artie said the same. Jason looked under the stall doors to make it clear he needed privacy. Artie rolled his eyes, kicked in the doors of the two open stalls, and stuck his head all the way under the closed one. "Out of order," he said, making a face. "Trust me, you owe me for the dirty work on that one. That little glance thing is gonna get you busted someday. Get real. All the way or no deal."

"Thanks, man. I appreciate it." Jason ran a hand through his hair—forcing Artie to check a broken toilet was maybe not the most favorable start. He kept his tone even, though. Cool was strength. "But I'm not, you know, up for any deal—not tonight, anyway. I had more of a question."

Artie looked at Jason with amusement and a twist in his lips that mimicked affection. "Listen to you, with your 'not tonight.' You think I don't know what the score is with you? You think I don't know what deals come through here, and exactly how many have gone to you, kid?"

Jason looked down and kicked at some tiles, unclear how to respond to someone outing him for *not* doing drugs. Luckily, Artie didn't seem to really need a response. He had his own piece to speak.

"But you know, it doesn't have to be like that. And I don't mean personal consumption either." Artie didn't move much, and after the strange lip twist, there wasn't much emotion. He simply made his case. "There's all kinds of money to be made, kid, I'd like to get in at that school of yours. Can't have too much traffic to kids here, Harry gets nervous. And the fact that your nose isn't three feet deep in ice, that's a selling point for us. You just say the word. We can do all kinds of business and it beats the hell out of scrubbing pots."

This conversation was so far out of Jason's game plan. Back-up rules: be polite, and make no commitments. The first was for sure not his strong suit but the amount of muscle backing Artie inspired a certain finesse. In general, Jason did well with the second rule.

Deep breath. "Thanks," he said, "but like I said, not tonight. But I—appreciate the thought. Definitely." He paused, nodding. "We cool?"

Jason tried not to think about what his life would be like if the answer to that question was "no." He realized that if the answer was no, Artie wouldn't tell him.

He also tried not to think about how psyched his sister would've been if he'd had a connection like Artie. Nothing he could do would please her more.

An image of bright blonde hair and sunburned shoulders flitted across his mind, a ruined sandcastle, tears and lake water, the impression so fleeting he did not remember who had done the building and who had knocked it down.

Jason stared at the bathroom floor. The tiles were beige with darker brown squares, some broken or missing.

There were things he tried so hard not to think about, he succeeded completely. They filled a black box in his mind that functioned like calm and blankness and a cool he was not feeling.

The tiles were dirty and made no pattern he could discern.

Artie regarded Jason for a moment in silence, then shrugged. "Have it your way. Offer's made, offer stands 'til you hear different. No hard feelings either way." He shifted, grimacing slightly to show teeth, one of them gold. He rubbed ringed fingers against stubble, then ran them through his longish hair. "So, what's up, kid, if it isn't that?"

Jason shifted on his feet, attention now completely on the present moment. "Well, speaking of school. I had kind of—I had a situation there today. Kinda messed up."

"My heart weeps, dude, but how is that my business?" Artie looked bored, gazing at his dirty nails and leaning against the closed door. His cheeks were hollow, the bones above them prominent. A gold marijuana leaf hung at his neck on a wide, flat gold chain. A sense of sex and menace and dirt came off of him in waves, thickening the air. Jason found himself wondering if girls like Samantha saw him like that, if they looked at Jason and saw an Artie.

But Jason's tone as he spoke betrayed none of this. Cool was the coin in trade for Artie, although too much was also a problem. Jason needed a cool that said not that he didn't give a fuck, but rather that he knew he had to give a fuck and he was okay with that. The right cool was a series of careful calibrations.

"Well, hopefully, it has fuck all to do with your business, because that's not *my* business, I don't see a goddamn thing, whatever shit might happen to pass accidentally, like, before my eyes. You know that, right?"

"Chill, kid. I got no reason to think different. Do I?" Artie looked at him and Jason thought the look might be a little off.

"*No*," Jason took a deep breath. This was harder than he thought. He figured the truth was going be the best, because dudes like Artie could *smell* lies no matter what else was going up their noses. "Just listen a minute. There's this teacher, he totally wigged out on me today. No reason. Didn't open my mouth, didn't look at him funny. Actually, I was pretty careful not to—normally at school, you could say I have a mouth on me—"

Artie's mouth moved up a fraction of an inch. "At school, right?"

"Yeah, well. Worse at school. Anyway. But not around this teacher, because maybe he was someone who had passed before my eyes here, you know? And I didn't want to make him nervous. But that was weeks ago. And today—" Jason brushed his hair back from his eyes but kept them steady on Artie, willing Artie to see his complete lack of bullshit on this topic. "Listen, it was totally obvious, he freaked out the kids, and it was a big, public, uncool scene." Jason could hear his voice shaking and he plunged his hands in his pockets so Artie couldn't see his hands were shaking too.

Artie was impassive, but clearly listening, completely still except for one muscle in his neck that was twitching, midway between his chains and jawline.

This stillness made Jason start pacing in the small room. "So, I got thinking—whether something could have gone down to make the twit *more* nervous, or if his nervous was coming—from someone here, who thought maybe *I* was something to worry about." There. It was said, but Jason was terrified to hear the answer. This was a set of problems he did *not* need.

At last, Artie shook his head no. "No guarantees, kid, but nothing that I've heard, anyway."

Jason could feel his eyes rolling to the back of his head in relief. "Okay. That's—that's how it should be. But this teacher dude? I don't think he's—if there was nothing, then he's too twitchy. I don't know if he was into anyone here for blow, or girls or—or rent boys—I don't fuckin' know, and I don't wanna know. But for my money, he's not someone I'd—I'd wanna rely on keeping cool. Not after what I saw today, okay? And I—" Jason shrugged, "I just figured I'd pass that information on."

Artie nodded, thoughtful. "Point taken. Now—I think I know who you mean, but it's possible I need to narrow it down a little, you know?"

Jason swallowed hard. One teacher from his school in for coke or under-age girls or boys didn't narrow it down enough. Assholes. "Right. So, this dude, he's like—girls would think he's good looking. Like in a—I don't know, like someone my grandma might've seen in a matinee, you know? Dark hair, little mustache. And maybe—if I had to guess, if it was girls he was into, I'd say he'd like them young."

But Artie was holding up his hand. "Whoa, enough said, okay, kid? I know the prick you mean. Let's just say, we reached the same conclusion as you independently."

Jason puffed out his cheeks with a huge breath of air he hadn't realized he'd been holding and sagged, relieved, against a sink. He looked around at the yellow stained walls, the phone numbers, the obscene drawings and explicit exploits penned on them, and for a moment, they looked beautiful. "So. Maybe that was it, then. Maybe he thought I ratted him out or some shit."

Hand on the door, Artie shook his head. "Could be, man. Like I said, not my business. Thanks for the heads up, though."

"So we're cool."

"As ever. And just say the word if you change your mind about that other thing." Artie paused again, apparently considering an idea. "Unless, kid, you want us to take care of him for you? Send a message? 'Cause we could work something out."

The image of Anthony Stagnita quickly replaced that of John Diangelo as Jason imagined the back alley beating that could right some deeply, deeply felt wrongs. Jason savored that image a moment before letting it go. "Now, that's tempting, but I gotta say no. Thanks anyway, man."

"'Nuff said. Later," nodded Artie, and he was out the door.

In another minute, so was Jason, back to the pool table and his friends.

Skinny looked curious and motioned him aside from the table. He said in a low voice, "You got something going on with Artie Fisher, dude? Can I get in?"

Jason shook his head and stuffed a pack of Marlboros in his friend's shirt pocket. He patted the pocket where he'd put them. "Nah. We were just chatting."

"He's not a chatty guy, dude."

"Yeah, but. You know. No one can resist me." He addressed this to the group at large, not wanting to even look like he was conspiring with Skinny or some shit. He shook his hair back and fluttered his eyes to a rumble of laughter.

"See, now, look at that." Skinny shook his head. "You are so full of shit, you can spare some for me."

"Okay, okay. If you love to take shit from me so much—"

Then Bogart spoke, "Devlin, man, that isn't news." Everyone laughed again and Bogart looked sleepily pleased.

Jason shook his head. "Shut up, Bogart, you'll hurt yourself." It's not like Skinny seemed to mind playing Devil's sidekick, but everyone didn't need to harp on it so much. Last thing he needed Skinny Nowlin with some kind of chip on his shoulder about it. He nudged Skinny and said under his breath, "How'd you wake him up, you doing lines or something?"

"Just a couple. You want one?" Skinny mostly knew the answer to that question was no, but it didn't stop him from asking. Jason was never sure if it was generosity, or showing off, or even just good manners, Skinny style. Probably a combination.

"Nah, I gotta take off. I had a long-ass fucking day, you know?"

"Yeah, you sure as *hell* did." Skinny looked like he did know, and it bothered him. "You find out what prick pulled that knife shit so I can fuck them up, man?"

Jason smiled. Skinny was a scary, nasty dude, but Jason was the one thing in the world he cared about. And that counted. "You would, wouldn't you, Nowlin?" And he gave his friend a little shove.

"*Fuck* yeah. Principle of the thing, you know? Like you need a fuckin' knife for the pussies in *that* school."

It wasn't even that Skinny didn't mind being Devil's sidekick, Jason thought. It was more like his chosen role. Whatever. It would come in handy for what he was pretty sure would be coming his way in the AM. He turned to the rest of the guys still gathered around the pool table. "Listen up. Tomorrow morning, we gotta get there a little early, okay?" He gestured around. "Who's up for meeting me and Skinny tomorrow morning before school?"

"Sure, we going at it with those preppy assholes?" General enthusiasm. "Was it one of them who pulled that bogus knife shit?"

"Coulda been." Any rumor but Diangelo was fine with Jason. "I stepped on a few toes today, know what I mean?"

"It wasn't *toes* you were stepping on, dude, it was *pussy*—"

The enjoyment in Skinny's voice was too much for Jason. "Yeah, yeah. But I gotta look sharp the next couple of days. I'm not up for getting jumped solo by a gang of pinkshirts."

Skinny rubbed his hands together. "But if we're all together, it'll just be a party."

"Exactly. So party on, man." Jason held up his fist, Skinny bumped it with his and everyone else followed suit. Eddie called his mother's food but Skinny tugged at Jason's sleeve on his way to pick it up. "Hey, check it out, it's a couple of those Barbies from lunch."

Jason whipped around, his pulse quickening. But it wasn't, of course, the one he'd imagined. It was that skinny girl and then JAP Barbie, maybe her name was Jessica.

"Huh," he said. "Figure they're just up for some late-night bowling?"

Skinny laughed. "C'mon, man, let's see what they do—who they're copping from."

Jason shook his head vigorously. "I don't really wanna know shit like that. Plus, I gotta bring some food home."

Skinny grabbed his shoulder a minute, then gave it a little shove. "I know you do, man."

Jason stopped by the kitchen and then mother's food in one hand, cigarette in the other, Jason was out the door. He gave the least perceptible nod possible to JAP Barbie, who returned the gesture, seeing his nod and raising by the tiniest imaginable smile. Interesting.

10. THIS IS NOT MY BEAUTIFUL HOUSE

Samantha felt a sinking feeling as she walked up the stone path to her door—which was only par for the course, especially since her brother had gone. The feeling, though, was sinking a deeper than usual, as if the dark world she'd glimpsed lurking at the corners of her brighter one was pressing in on her sides and chest. Samantha wished more than anything that Stephen was home.

She'd been standing for she didn't know how long, surrounded by ivy and gray stone, the cold metal key in her hand biting softly into her fingers. With a sigh, she unlocked the door and as it opened, her face adjusted into a smile. "Mommy? Daddy? I'm home," she called through the brightly lit rooms.

Samantha made her way past the early American front room, its simple antiques never used by the people who lived with them except for receiving people who didn't, past the library with its roll-top desk and leather-bound books, the paperback reading copies tucked away on the shelves that faced away from the hall.

Some of the household antiques had never been out of the family. Her parents, for example.

Samantha found them at table in the dining room. They were on to the after-dinner drinks. "Highland win?" asked her father, downing a mouthful of scotch. She told him Kwame had a great game, Dougie Douglas, the quarterback, ran 47 yards for a touchdown, and Kimmie was on top the pyramid again. Samantha herself was impressed by her level of perk.

"Is pyramid offense or defense?" Her father looked like he was trying to remember something. The performance was perfect, suave, teasing. Everything about Lincoln Ward was usually just that perfect.

"Very funny, Daddy. Kimmie, one of my best *girlfriends,* is a cheerleader."

"Oh, of course. Kwame—Kimmie. Hard to keep straight. Chink girl, very nice."

It wasn't all perfect.

"*Lincoln.* That's vulgar." Her mother's voice was rich with disapproval, which was its element.

Not 'Lincoln, that's wrong," or 'Lincoln, that's unkind,' or, 'Lincoln, are you out of your mind, it's 1985, what planet do you even live on, you racist pig?'

In a small voice, Samantha offered, "Actually, Kimmie's not even a little Chinese but—we say Asian, now, Daddy. It's like how we shouldn't call Ernestine a Negro anymore, remember?"

Her mother turned to Samantha in horror. "Sa*mantha.*" Nancy Ward inclined her head toward the kitchen. Nancy always used the word "black" and said it in a whisper, as if Ernestine might overhear and learn some shameful secret about herself.

Her father just chuckled. "That's right, sweetheart. You keep at it. Daddy's got no mind for details. So how's your little Jew friend?" Still just that suave.

Samantha thought idly of asking for some scotch. Maybe it would take the edge off *this.* And it would please her father if she drank scotch instead of wine coolers like her friends.

Her mother invited her to join them at the table but Samantha pleaded homework. Nancy Ward made her beleaguered "eating in the kitchen" grimace and nodded in tired acceptance, Ernestine was there, she'd work late the next night too as "your father and I have a function to attend."

"Dysfunction, more like it," Lincoln Ward sighed, "rich Democrats whining about how tough it is for other people to be poor."

Nancy Ward responded with a tight smile and relaxed voice, "Yes, dear, you prefer the Republican charity events that help well-off people get started in business. You and your Reagans." She took a sip of wine, her slightly graying hair motionless beneath a headband, her face a still, oval mask.

"At least Reagan had the good sense to get Poppy Bush behind him. You just don't like that we have a president who couldn't get on the social register."

"The President *and* his wife are *always* included in the Social Register, dear."

Her husband laughed out loud. "Nancy Reagan's in the book, then? Oh, that must *burn,* Nan."

Samantha wondered how one went about becoming an anarchist and excused herself to the kitchen.

After picking at her food for a while over her chemistry homework, Samantha pushed the plate back in frustration. "Ernestine? Did you ever get the feeling like—I don't know, your life just suddenly didn't fit? Like you grew or it shrunk, but all of a sudden?"

Ernestine wrung a cloth out in the sink and laid it over the porcelain divider. She gazed at the spotless kitchen, surveying her territory, looking for stragglers—dishes, crumbs, any matter out of place. Tiles, cabinets counters, everything was white, easily revealing offending evidence of human life. "When I was your age, sure. Reason is—it *doesn't* fit. Try and enjoy it. Some find that fit gets kind of dull, later on." Her mouth formed a line that with a little imagination might resemble a smile. "You want to hear about my life or tell me about yours?"

"Maybe a little of both—but do you mind? I know it's—you need to get home."

The older woman sighed, wiping her hands slowly back and forth on her white apron. "I'm paid till nine and I'm to help raise you." Ernestine sounded tired, but her tone was even, neither kind nor unkind. "You raised yet?"

Samantha shook her head, blushing. "Maybe a little ways to go."

"So shoot."

"You won't tell my mom?"

"That depends. Could it get me fired or you pregnant?"

"*Ernestine!*"

Spotting a smudge, Ernestine pounced with her rag.

"I'm sure my mother would say 'bringing me up' not 'raising me,' which is what she says one does to cattle." Samantha could *feel* her face darken.

"Maybe so, but that doesn't make her evil, Samantha. Just careful about her words."

"Whatever, maybe *that's* not what makes her evil." Samantha hated it when Ernestine took her mother's side.

"Samantha." Ernestine's eyes narrowed. "Your mother signs my checks. She and your father are putting Michael through Catholic school. When he graduates, they're going to help out with college. Samantha, I have *retirement.* Don't you put me in the position of listening to you talk down your parents." Ernestine pursed her lips and shook her head, disappointed. "Don't act spoiled, it doesn't suit you."

Samantha felt her cheeks burn. "Ernestine, I'm sorry. I just—I—" She tried to look up, but couldn't. "I don't have any excuse."

Unexpectedly, Ernestine put her hand on Samantha's shoulder. Samantha leaned into it, so lonely, suddenly, it didn't matter if the hand was paid to be there. Then it swatted her in the back of the head, not as gently as it might have, either.

"Samantha, listen up. We all go through it. I had days I thought my parents were from another planet. They yelled at me for my music and my dress, which they said looked cheap, like I was living up to the world's worst expectations of me instead of setting myself above. Any of that sound familiar, little miss closet full of weird punk rocker?"

"Glam. Glam rocker. Or art rock. Mostly. Some soul. And his new stuff is more pop." Discussing David Bowie with Ernestine. That was new. That was *awesome*. "What music did your parents hate?"

"All of it."

"C'mon, Ernestine. One name."

"Aretha," clipped Ernestine, as if saying the name cost her more than her paycheck was worth.

The thought of a younger, wilder Ernestine jamming out to Aretha Franklin delighted Samantha. "So, your mom thought you looked cheap and wanted you to set yourself above?" Maybe there had been miniskirts. Maybe go-go boots.

"She wasn't wrong." Ernestine shook her head. "Point is, she turned back into a human once I was done growing. Yours will too. Now, eat some more or they're liable to dock my pay."

Samantha took a grudging mouthful of potato. She still felt sick from lunch and tried to explain why.

Ernestine shook her head at the story. "Boys fighting over who got to pee on what tree—and you were the tree, and both sides were peeing on it."

Samantha smiled weakly.

"Well—you know, Sam, some girls love to be that tree. Some girls love it more than anything."

Samantha stabbed at a piece of potato on the plate in front of her until it was full of holes. "But Ernestine, I *really* didn't like being that tree."

"Now, Sam, not that anyone should be talking that way about you or anyone else. Period. But if you don't like being that tree, maybe it's time you stop being that tree."

"I didn't—"

But Ernestine wasn't finished. She raised an eyebrow. "Tree just stands there, looks pretty, lets it happen?"

"Well, I—I told them to stop."

Ernestine just kept looking at her. The pressure of Ernestine's eyebrow was so intense that Samantha found herself forced to examine the entire scene from the perspective of the steady gaze beneath it. "Maybe—I'm not sure I really told them I wasn't a tree. I just told them to stop peeing on me."

"Well, that's a start." Ernestine looked away, and Samantha couldn't tell what she was thinking.

Shaking her head, Samantha went back to punishing her potatoes. "But the thing is, I'm already covered with pee!"

"Well, don't take it out on your poor dinner any more, it wasn't even made yet."

Samantha went on stabbing and talking at the same time. "And everyone has all this stuff about me, because of how I look and what I have and—"

But Ernestine wouldn't let her go on. "Well, of course they do. You're pretty and you have a great deal at a time when the whole country's obsessed with having." Ernestine ran a hand over her hair in a gesture Samantha ached to believe was affectionate, but could just as easily have been absent-minded. Ernestine gave very little of herself away. "Time comes, though, when people are going to judge you based on what you do with what you have, less on what you have."

Then Samantha said the wrong thing. "I know—that's why my mom makes me do soup kitchen."

The hand stopped stroking Samantha's head and instead gave it another little slap. "Why on earth shouldn't she do that? And why on earth don't you want to? Everything you have. Shameful if a girl like you didn't give a little to those with less." Now Ernestine was regarding Samantha as if perhaps she was the smudge of dirt that needed polishing. "I serve at soup kitchen every week."

Samantha grew small in her skin and felt her eyes fill with tears. "I know—I mean, it's not like I think I shouldn't do stuff and help out. But, at our church, most of the servers—they're like us, look like my mom or are my age, and—" Samantha hesitated, unsure suddenly if this was the kind of thing she should be saying. "The people who are there to eat—look different and—-they're supposed to feel grateful to us, and then, we get to feel good about it. It makes me feel—weird."

Ernestine looked at Samantha steadily for a moment, her face unreadable. Then she half nodded, "When a person is hungry, that food makes them full. To that hungry person, that's what matters."

"I wouldn't know. I couldn't know." There was silence in the kitchen a moment as both women looked at Samantha's massacred potatoes. "I always have too much food," she murmured.

She thought of Bethany Moran getting up from lunch early every day. People were hungry across town and some of Samantha's friends were out to prove even food was optional for them. Or maybe Bethany had a different hunger, that food didn't help.

Samantha looked up at Ernestine. "Could I maybe try coming to your soup kitchen, at your church? Maybe just—mix it up a little?"

Ernestine said she didn't see a reason why not, though she'd need to run it by Samantha's mother first. Clucking disapproval, she cleared Samantha's plate, scraped the unwanted food into the disposal and turned the water on in preparation for grinding the waste down the drain.

But Samantha wasn't done yet. "Ernestine, I said something so awful to the Highwood guys." She couldn't stop the words from coming.

The sound of the water disappeared and the gaze of Ernestine was back upon her. Samantha felt it, but could not meet it. "I basically told them—not that I wasn't a tree, but that they weren't the right breed of dogs to be peeing on me."

The gaze let Samantha cringe for a while in the silence of knowing she was wrong, and spoiled, and mean.

"You say you're sorry?"

Samantha nodded.

"Good for you."

Samantha wanted to bask in that little scrap of praise but couldn't. He didn't say it back.

"Ernestine, do you think anyone will—ever like me?"

Ernestine's mouth curved up in another fraction of smile. "Aren't you one of those popular girls at school?"

"Being popular isn't the same as having people like you."

"Well, it sure isn't the same as having no one like you, either."

"I guess." And then the words just started tumbling out. "I just feel like— I missed out on the whole liking thing. Because everyone has something to prove, maybe, and I'm a good one to prove it on. So I missed out on handhold- ing, or eye staring or something. Whatever comes before a mouth full of tongue or—an arranged courtship with a boy from Daddy's yacht club or whatever."

Ernestine bent over the sink, her shoulders shaking. She was laughing. "Samantha, you'd best remember it's not over with you yet. You're in the driver's seat. If you want to hold hands, put your hand out there instead of something else."

Samantha let that sink in a little.

"Any of those peeing boys good-looking, Samantha?"

"Only the worst one."

"Is that what got your hockey skirt in this big old twist? You maybe liked that he was looking, just a little bit?"

Samantha found herself unable to lie to herself in front of Ernestine. "A little."

"Listen. I'm not excusing anyone. Just remember, boys that age, they're not all the way human yet. I should know, I have one myself. I'm sure if I had to know all the things Michael said and did to girls, I'd never sleep again."

"Michael's a sweetheart. I'm sure he's always a gentleman."

"You wouldn't say that if you could see his bedroom," muttered Ernestine, "let alone what he keeps under the bed."

Samantha almost choked on the image of Ernestine finding Michael's porn stash while dusting. Ernestine glared as she produced a small package from her pocket. "From your brother. Like *he's* any better."

Samantha took the stairs two at a time. The tasteful French prints in their gilt frames made Samantha want to scrawl vulgarities, but this desire was nothing new.

Instead of her own room, she headed for her brother's, climbed onto his forest green bed and hugged his pillow, the immaculate sham of it one with her childhood.

Stephen's room was like a shrine—one wall covered in pictures of Samantha and her brother, blonde hair against his black, one shot of long-gone Prissy Hines grinning from in between them. Formal portraits with her parents, stiff and smiling, hands clasping their children's shoulders. Sports memorabilia, meticulously framed, displayed, transformed from memories to decor.

Another wall had pictures of mallards—swimming on a pond, flying in the sky, taking flight from a steely ocean. Samantha remembered hours spent making forbidden forts in the bed, mocking the ducks and their green wings that picked up the green of the bed, of the drapes.

Samantha put the tape from the package into the tape deck. Cello background and a woman's moaning hum. Strange. But if Stephen sent it, Samantha would listen.

She dialed Stephen's number and waited for the other boy to bring him to the hall phone, and as she waited she felt tears prick her eyes. At the sound of his voice, they started spilling. "Wish you were here," she whispered.

His voice sounded far. "*That* wasn't on the tape."

But it was still him. "Fix my life?"

"Step one. Less obvious Floyd. Next?"

11. TONIGHT I'M ALL ALONE IN MY ROOM, I'LL GO INSANE

Jason lay on his bed propped up on his elbow, trying to write about why he did not think a play about spousal abuse should be taught as a comedy to high school students. Mostly, he figured, because it wasn't funny, but he had a feeling that wasn't what Garcia was after. "Helps institutionalize a patriarchal culture where violence against women is acceptable," he wrote. Thank you, vocab girls.

He might as well get something out of those girls, because they wouldn't leave him alone—in his head, anyway. At least they kept his mind off his mother for a minute, how she'd bought him a Snickers bar and a little bottle of orange juice, the thin, bitter kind they sell as mixers at the liquor store. Bought him that for breakfast, setting it on the grubby beige Formica counter like he'd won a big award. Thanked him for the bowling alley food and her hands grasped at it nervously to cover their shaking. Said she knew things were hard, but she had a temp job starting the next day.

She'd bought new stockings, too, she showed him the plastic egg they came in like a proof of better things to come. "Suntan" color, she'd got it to be hopeful, she explained, 'you know, babe, here comes the sun—it's alright?'

Jason had sighed and half-hugged her, which made his chest tight. "Yeah, ma, I know the song," he said. It was worse, he thought, when she was trying to be like a mom. Because when she wasn't trying he could just hate her, but when she tried he still had to feel sad. He took the Snickers to his room and ate it because eating the candy bar his mother had bought him for breakfast—actually eating it for breakfast—would give him that sad ache, but it was kind of good as a late-night snack for getting through some homework. Helped him, actually, get it done. Thought about that way, it was kind of nice.

Homework done before midnight—another day of insane academic success for Jason Devlin. He shoved his books back into his bag and went in to brush his teeth. The bathroom sink was crusted with some kind of yellowed scum and trails of his own hair. Time to buy some more of that stuff with the little chick on it and clean up.

Only going to a school where half the population had fucking maids could make cleaning up after yourself feel tragic. There was enough tragedy to go around, really, without finding it where it wasn't there.

He could swear he could hear Pris's slow, ironic clap at his genius in reaching this amazing conclusion. Probably not a bad thing to have a friend who could see through his bullshit. Not that he'd be telling her that any time soon, or ever.

Jason spat, turned off the tap, and shuffled back into his room, snorting at the Judas Priest poster still above his dresser. He hadn't listened to that stuff in years, but he couldn't get rid of it, he'd had it since seventh grade, just like he couldn't get rid of the little old-fashioned airplane border along the ceiling, or the faded airplane quilt on his bed. Postcards from another time—and what came later didn't make that early time any less good.

The dresser was almost empty of clothes. The floor had two piles—clean, dirty. They looked the same. In the top drawer, he had some old photos, rocks, baseball cards—things he'd treasured when he was a kid. He kept his money in a place he'd cut in the baseboard behind his bed. Caution, the legacy of a sister.

Jason threw something mellow on the turntable and started trying to groove into a sleeping place to some funk.

One sure-fire sign of this tiredness had been his first musical impulse, "Wish You Were Here." On repeat. And think about a girl who was seeking him behind dumpsters, with her eyes that got to him like a kick in the stomach or chest if something beautiful could kick that hard. A girl who looked at him with those eyes as they circled each other not so much like lost souls but like sharks—

"Okay. Kill me right now," Jason had thought.

Jason felt there should be a limit to the total number of pathetic teen guy clichés you could live out in a day, and he was probably one toke over the line already.

"Lost souls. Fuck me. Fuck me hard and up the ass if I ever have another thought like that," pleaded Jason.

So he threw on Brides of Funk, which he guessed that roughly zero of the other dudes in his class were listening to at that moment, as opposed to Pink Floyd, which had a 70 percent hit rate at any given time—just for that one stupid song alone. But the Brides were too sexy and he *couldn't* get into any of that right now. He was *so* tired, and he had some other kinds of thoughts he had to spend some time with.

There was a truth he'd been keeping at bay all day, or at least since he'd seen that girl crumpled in the hall, looking so young and lost. It had been laying for him all along, waiting to take its shot. But if Jason took hard truth out and looked at it late at night, he could put it deep in some pocket where it would rest dark and quiet through the day. Otherwise it would get restless, jump out at him some time when someone could see him flinch.

He liked Lou Reed for these times, his dark solo riffing reminding you that there were worse people in the world. Babies crying, couples fighting, cops coming for the kids, hookers dead in alleyways. All of them worse and worse off than you.

Gravel voice, dark tones, cool.

A comfort needed because—here it came—

He had in fact been the worst kind of asshole to that girl.

Fuck if he'd known she was a virgin and fuck if he'd imagined anyone could be that clueless. It had to be through some kind of supreme act of will or something. Still. Truth was, if Jason hadn't gone and said shit like that, then he wouldn't have traumatized her and he wouldn't have to be lying here, feeling like shit past eleven on a school night.

He would never have let anyone talk about his sister that way.

Something was fucked there. Something was *fucked*. Not just with him or her, but with the whole of everything. Now, though, he just didn't see any way out. Once you started something, it was started.

But hell if something didn't spark between them.

Her eyes kept staring at him, even when he closed his own.

And she said she'd see his face.

Enough. That was going nowhere but some sticky fucking bed in the morning.

He'd looked at his truth, now he could wrap it up and put it in his pocket, never need to look at it again. And the little burning want he had going was a poetic fucking penance for being just that kind of asshole he should know better than to be.

IN BETWEEN DAYS

It was hard for the world to filter through. Grainy waves passed over his mind and eyes, thoughts thick with static, or the sudden focus of a still weak image, broken with dots of light.

Memories bled into a shifting now he could not grasp hold of, where he was, why. Why his head was wet, and cold, and hot, and hurt, and hurt.

Waiting. At the place they'd set. No one came. Searing. Tearing at his chest.

The look on his friend's face before the fist connected. Maybe he saw stars. Ringing through time, the high maniac laugh of an eight-year-old boy, jumping from the jungle gym, ready to fly. He'd always won at chicken down by the train tracks. Flattened pennies jangling in his empty pockets. Some little boys, though, they grow up wrong.

They'd left him on the ground, coughing on the blood streaming from his nose. Wave. The pain could shift time.

It was true he'd sometimes take the simple blood, better than thinking. Something flickered through darkness as power returned along the lake. He could see that much, even with one eye swollen shut.

But you could see, reach out, and sometimes it wouldn't be enough. Even with a hand grasping back through the darkness.

They'd come at him, kicking him when he was down. Ghosts from the future, ghosts from the past. The pain of it was the same.

It was the way of things. Sometimes, you'd be on the ground, sometimes, you'd be the one kicking. Either way, you couldn't stop what you'd started. You just had to wait for the blows to stop. That, or wait for the gray to overtake you.

12. TALK OF THE TOWN

As soon as Samantha set foot on school grounds Tuesday morning, she could hear the buzzing. There'd been an ambush, a double ambush, a fight. Jason Devlin had gotten jumped under the underpass, but a whole crew of burn-outs had been hiding behind the bushes and broken-down barriers that littered the strips of grass by highway.

Dave Watson had a split lip, Skinny Nowlin had a black eye, and it seemed like half the school got bruises before the cops had broken it up. Jason Devlin, though, walked through the halls with his usual swagger. Andy Bishop swore he'd started the whole thing off with a killer kidney punch, but Jason was leaning against his locker with the same smirk he always wore, the one that flickered angry, or amused, or bored and made the boys with the turned-up collars see in blood.

The talk would stop the second Samantha walked past, but the silence buzzed just as loud. The fight had been about her, her name had been spoken between punches. Vanessa Segal was livid that her boyfriend had been bruised over another girl, but Dave Watson was claiming the big brother role Samantha had spoon-fed him and weathering lewd comments from his swim buddies about how that would mean incest.

Samantha squared her shoulders. Another banner day.

Jessica was practically bursting. "So how goes it with rehearsals for *The Outsiders*, baby?"

Samantha wondered if she should start going to a different bathroom. "Just more of my perfect life, Jess. I was cast without even trying out for a part." She rubbed gently underneath her eye. Not wearing the contacts just spared her a lot she didn't particularly care to see but today that wasn't an option. Focus.

"Samantha! Can you please get into this just a little bit? Half the guys in the school are getting into it, and it's all about *you!*"

Whipping out an eyeliner, Samantha flipped her hair back. "Maybe if I'd seen it I could get a little high on the testosterone or something. But if they think they're fighting over me, they're deluded. I'm not *property*."

"Well," Jessica sniffed—and then she sniffed a little more, wiping her nose delicately with the side of her finger—"where'd *you* get all feminist? Stop shaving your pits or something?"

"Nothing so drastic. I just talked to Stephen."

"Which somehow translates to Women's Power 101 now? I thought he was going to an all boys' school!"

Samantha laughed. "They could probably do with some woman power. But it wasn't anything like that. He just ... reminded me I know how to throw a punch or two myself."

"Oh—" Jessica looked Samantha up and down, frowning. "So you're pissed off *you* weren't under the underpass? Like, maybe *you're* the kid who can take Jason Devlin down?"

"Exactly." Samantha had her chains back and a carefully torn sweatshirt *just* slipping off the shoulder. Heavier eyes, darker lips. No more pearls. Not even for fake.

"Well—you've got the look down, anyway." Jessica paused, and for a second sounded one hair less sure of herself than usual. Maybe. "And without even a phone call to me."

Samantha shrugged, calculating the effect on her bare shoulder. "I tried last night but you were out. And I needed to get here early—this outfit wouldn't get past the Stylebuster so I changed in the locker room." She picked up her bag and turned to leave.

"Oh, and here I was thinking you might not have called because I was a total bitch to you yesterday."

Stopping in her tracks, Samantha turned back to her friend. Jessica was magazine-cover perfect, as usual, but her nose looked a little red. Crying? *Jess?*

"Well, maybe a partial bitch, but we hung out all afternoon, right?" Samantha shrugged again. The sweatshirt shifted further down. She hiked it up and let it fall just slightly less. "All cool here."

But apparently it wasn't all cool with Jessica. "Sam—I just—she started in on me again? And I don't know why it *bothers* me so much. But you've got your own mom."

Samantha felt herself soften a little more. Usually these moments only happened with Jessica at two in the morning after massive amounts of sweet and salty fats. "Yeah. But what'd *yours* do?"

Jessica took a deep breath and looked down. "So she stopped by my room yesterday morning and she was all like," Jessica sniffed again, "she *totally understood* why I might want one, it was nothing to worry about, just a simple procedure, and she would support my decision. I have *never* said I wanted one."

Mothers.

"Jess—it's *your nose*. It looks *good* on you."

Jessica peered at her reflection. "Hell—I'll probably *get* the damn thing, I mean, if my mom wasn't always telling me how much she'd understand, I'd probably be begging her for one."

"Jess, you look *great*." But both girls knew that Samantha would say it whether it was true or not.

So Jessica shrugged the compliment off. "It's just like, couldn't my mom be the one telling me I'm beautiful just the way I am and I shouldn't change a thing? Like, isn't that *her* job, while I'm worrying about how ugly I am?"

Samantha studied her own reflection and didn't know why anyone who could look like Jessica Levin would want to look like what she saw. She knew she was pretty, but Jessica was *striking*. "And *my* mom should not be asking me how my Jewish friend is. But the world's an imperfect place."

The two girls looked at each other's reflections. "Definitely got a few screws loose."

Samantha put her hand on her friend's arm, a little tentatively. "Jess, every time my parents say something like that, I just—"

"Oh, please, Sam, my mom doesn't like your people, either."

"I swear, *I* want to get a—an ethnic change operation."

"That? Would be the *ultimate* revenge. Mom? Dad? I've gone Jew." Jessica turned, eyes wide. "Wait—wait. It's perfect. A blonde walks into a plastic surgeon's office and asks for a bigger nose. Dr. Shapiro says, 'Oh, baby, I got what you need, and he pulls out his—"

Samantha swatted the arm her hand rested on. "My virgin ears, Jess. My lily-white mind!"

In the hall, Samantha put her arm through Jessica's. "We *have* to go shopping, like yesterday. And I think we should do the imperfect world a favor."

Here she lowered her voice. "And bring Michelle Fremd for a little treatment. Tonight?"

"The word is awesome. And Samantha? The data on Mr. Richards is rolling in. Just a matter of time for our careers in science."

"The world will bow to our awesomeness *again.* It will eventually get boring for the world. But I still better get to homeroom."

All day, Samantha kept the surface smooth, but a strange current was running through the halls around her, through her, flickering. She smiled and waved and giggled and underneath it all tried focusing her eyes, which meant that after third period she saw Jason Devlin at his locker, languidly cuddling a girl with big teased-up blonde hair and a tight t-shirt that said "Dirty Deeds Done Dirt Cheap." Jason let his fingers trail down into her back pockets, all the while joking with some other kid who was slouching against the next locker.

But from under his dark fringe of hair and lashes, Jason stared at the sight of Samantha.

She caught his gaze, focusing her eyes fully on him. She felt this gaze and his eyes behind it and his tongue as it wet his lips, and she felt these things in her gut and in her legs. It tingled.

She wanted to stop Jason Devlin's lazy petting of that other blonde and she realized she could. That it would be easy. Because he was touching that other girl but all his interest was on her.

Samantha stopped across the hall from them and leaned into the lockers. Jason's hand stilled on the girl's back. Instead of fighting what she felt looking at Jason Devlin, Samantha let it show on her face, affect her breath and her mouth and the way she held her jaw.

It was like a duel. He'd chosen the weapon. She tossed her hair over her bare shoulder and just stared. She got it now. Sex was a weapon. Samantha Ward had just been slow on the uptake.

Clumps of kids were walking by, going to and from class, but nothing broke the stare between them. At last, he whispered to the girl and she moved away, not before glancing resentfully at Samantha.

Easing into his walking slouch, Jason crossed the hall and Samantha noticed how kids moved out of his way like they were the Red Sea he was parting.

He stood before her and put his hands in his pockets. "Jealous, Barbie?"

Nodding, Samantha licked her lips before speaking and watched how Jason's eyes followed the movement of her tongue. "Yeah, I can't believe you were fighting with other people this morning. Don't have the guts to take it up with me direct?"

A slow half smile crept up Jason's face. "Yeah, you are so intimidating compared to the ten guys who jumped me. So, is that what got you so worked up?"

"Oh, my *God*, yes. I just wish I had been there. There's nothing like a bunch of dumb jocks and wastoids rolling around together in the dirt to get me going. Can you, like, call me next time?"

"Aw, shucks. You just want me to ask for your number. But then I might drunk dial and lead you on. And hate to pop your ch—I mean, burst your bubble, sweetheart, but this morning wasn't about you."

"*You* know that and *I* know that, but the halls say differently, *sweetheart*." Samantha moved a little closer and watched as his eyes focused on her lips, which she moved slowly around her next words, "I mean, *I* know it's Dave Watson you want to get it on with, *I* can see what really gets you hot, but how are you going to convince everyone else of that?"

Jason's face twisted in what looked like real disgust. "Uh, do you want a résumé or something? It's all about girls with me. Not plastic princesses, mind you. *Real* girls."

His reaction—better than she had imagined. Her brother was a *genius*. Hit him where he thinks he's strong, he'd said. She was going to bake Stephen cookies that night.

"Oh—don't worry. That girl you were with thinks it's all about me right now—shows how much *she* knows, right?" Samantha looked sympathetic. "I hope I didn't mess that up for you. But I guess there's always more where *that* came from. I mean, *we* know why no girl really holds your interest. From what I hear, you go through us pretty fast."

With satisfaction, Samantha watched as Jason's eyes widened slightly. But her body tensed as he leaned over to say closer to her ear, "And you wanna be next, or what? What the fuck are you playing at, Samantha Ward?"

"I just wanted to see if it was true, what it says on the bathroom walls— you know, that you..." She looked at him steadily and then tilted up to whisper near his ear, "... come really fast." She leaned back. "I guess that one's true. I mean—I just had to look at you and—" She shrugged.

"Ooh. Look at you all sex joking. Jeez, they grow up so fast."

"Sex? Who's talking about sex? You and your one note. I just meant—one look and you came right over to me. Blink of an eye, like they say. See you in hell, *Devil Man*."

The buzzing in the hallways had intensified around them, so thick Samantha could almost see it. Whatever. What more could people say? A public conversation about who got to lick her had erupted into a full-on fight. Definitely not the time to play shrinking violet.

Thank *God* she'd talked to Stephen. He *always* won at games. *"Throw your own punches. Jab, Jab, left hook. Like I taught you."* Or, *"You'll never be no one. So be the someone you want. Play dress-up, Sam."*

Samantha had laughed. "Like I need encouragement for *that*. It's my effin' life. But Stephen, what if you—don't you ever want to be just—who you are?"

Silence. Samantha could *see* her brother like he'd been in front of her, his striped cotton shirt unbuttoned three buttons down, tails hanging out of slouchy khakis *just* so, penny loafers, no socks, leaning into the wall of his dorm. He cradled the payphone on his shoulder, casual. Whatever look he needed, he had it down.

But his voice changed slightly. "You know that's kind of a brutal question to ask me, right?"

"Jab, jab, *left* hook. Like you taught me, right?"

"Yeah," he'd said, "like that." He sighed. "You'll be just fine, Sam."

She didn't feel just fine. Lunch was about Mr. Richards breathing again. Jessica was like a dog with a bone and the longer she obsessed about something, the more people listened and the funnier it got—not because it *was* funny, but it was funny that she got obsessed with it and could make everyone else obsessed with it, too, just because she was Jessica.

Today Samantha couldn't quite bring herself to care. At every other table, people were still talking. About her, him, them, *that*. She felt sick again.

She wanted to be no one.

But Stephen was right. When you were already this much of a someone, there was no going back. But maybe you could be someone else.

Way outside her usual role and script.

If everyone was going to be talking about her and those boys—so was she.

Samantha Ward stood on the table with a yogurt container in one hand and a fork in the other. She tapped on the yogurt container. "Excuse me, everyone—could I have your attention? I mean—come on, you know I have it anyway."

Murmur. Laughter. The smell of sickly-sweet sloppy joes, the stale banana from Jessica's fruit salad, the all but odorless vodka someone was slipping into a Diet Coke. She gave her head a little shake and bowed. And then she started in.

"Now, I know you're hoping for a repeat of yesterday's show, but, sorry, no diving lessons today. I just want to—to take this opportunity to let you know that—" and here she widened her eyes, counselor style. "I am saddened, *deeply* saddened by the violence that has broken out in our school community." The counselors always said the word community like each syllable was an integral part of the species' survival. People snickered, recognizing the tone.

Change-up. Civil rights leader. "We all embrace the dream of a school in which we are equally free to publicly insult a young girl's private parts. We share that dream of equality, and yes, some brave souls try to live it. We were witness yesterday to that great effort."

Samantha made eye contact with as many people as possible. Skinny Nowlin was glaring at her from a back corner looking apoplectic. Worm. She wouldn't make eye contact with *him*. All in all, standing there, the whole cafeteria staring at her, riveted—it was kind of a high. She was only sorry Jason Devlin wasn't there to see it. But it wasn't really about him. This one was on *principle*.

Samantha Ward was no one's tree to pee on.

Her words came faster, her own inflections creeping in.

"The sad truth is, in our school community, some people claim a greater right to publicly insult my private parts than others. And *I* do not seem to have thing one to say about it. Now, if it *were* up to me? Then frankly it doesn't matter to me if you're a jock or a burnout, you're not *ever* getting near the real thing, so—take a number! It could be like democracy—or at least a line at the butcher's, right?"

A girl's voice shouted, "That's right. A piece of meat. That's what they take us for!" Samantha paused. She was shocking people. Even the politicals looked impressed. From the corner of the room, though, the lunch ladies were looking at her like she was crazy, and she noticed one of the school counselors being hurried in by a concerned teacher.

Hands up for silence. She wasn't done. "But in truth, the right to insult my private parts, however important this struggle may be—is only a cover for the real problem confronting our school community." She paused for effect.

"*Ready about,*" her dad's voice suddenly echoed in her mind, "*hard-alee.*"

If Lincoln Ward knew how his sailing lessons were paying off, he'd eat his boat.

School counselor mode. "It is a tragedy, a terrible tragedy that in our community, there are boys—young men—who are obviously drawn to each other by strong physical passion but who, because of prejudice, can only find release in violence."

A murmur of laughter—shot through, here and there, with anger. Resentments brewing.

Steady as she goes, Sam . . .

"Yet so strong is this passion, that even a pathetically obvious excuse—like, for example, the right to be gross to a girl who you've never even spoken to in your entire life—is enough to get these guys rolling around in the dirt with each other using *my* name as some kind of perverse sex prop."

Catcalls. Gasps. Samantha struggled not to visualize what she was saying.

Her *name*, which they made stand for the right to talk about licking her. Lincoln Ward wouldn't like that much, either.

"So I am here to tell you today—no longer. I am here to tell you—I officially remove my private parts from this conflict! I mean—" she took a deep breath. "If bad boys wanna get spanked, I say live and let live, you know? I embrace my—my closeted brethren, I accept you, I really do." She really did.

Then she put her hand on her hip. "Just leave me and my parts and my girlfriends the *fuck* out of it." She held up two fingers and said, lightly, "Peace!" and sat down.

Change-up. K.O. Down for the count.

In her seat, a spiked Diet Coke appeared in her hand and she took a swig. She held the can back out, the hand it belonged to took it, and Samantha gave a thumbs up. She looked around at the open-jawed faces of her lunch table. Jessica's mouth was the widest. "You did not *even* just do that, Samantha Ward."

"Oh, yes I did. *Huh.*"

13. TEN IS FOR EVERYTHING

A massive fight with the biggest jocks in school, a run-in with little miss wind-you-up Barbie, and a half-hour of dishing from Pris had pretty much taken care of last night's problem. Whatever softening in Jason Devlin's attitude toward his new Barbie enemy had resulted from his late-night brooding was now hardened right back up. And not in his pants this time, either. Bitch.

He'd gotten Pris to ditch lunch with him—he was plenty sore from the morning and he felt like not hiding it for a minute. He could let loose with Pris—he pretty much had to, she'd see through him anyway.

But then Pris, pissed off to no end to see him hurt, told him about a scene between that prick Dave Watson and his bitchy girlfriend Vanessa. A scene also starring Samantha Ward. The story Pris told made him see blood.

In fact, Jason was so angry—at himself as much as at that *poser* whose act he'd bought—he didn't know if he'd ever feel anything else.

Oh, Vanessa, Dave was so brave to protect me from that scum Devlin. It's like having my big brother back.

That morning, Dave spat her name through clenched teeth as he and his friends pummeled into Jason.

You say another word about Samantha Ward's pussy and I will end you. Get your own goddamn pussy, scum. That one's ours.

He could hear Pris's voice mimicking Little Miss I Don't Back Down.

Jason Devlin forgot where he stands. I don't forget that.

Jason was so disgusted, so completely disgusted with himself for wasting time feeling bad about that horror show of a person, that if he'd eaten any lunch, he'd have lost it. After all that "let's fight as equals" crap.

And this morning. That look. Burning hot. Arrogant, sure, but he knew that look, and that look said want. And he wanted right back and he knew he was getting played, but it felt so amazing that she was playing at all. She'd barely brushed against him and he could still feel it. He didn't know when he'd been so worked up about a girl and all she'd done was talk to him for thirty seconds in the hallway, insult him, and get out of his way.

All after she'd thanked that asshole for keeping scum like Jason in his place, basically telling the guy to jump him.

She was a bitch and he was a loser for thinking about her. He didn't tell Pris about his run-ins with Samantha. He didn't want to risk Pris falling for any of that act the way he had.

So Jason was in a plenty foul mood even before they ran into Skinny on their way back from behind the bleachers.

"You would not believe what that Ward chick just pulled at lunch, the cun—"

"Shut your mouth!" The words slashed out of Pris like a blade. And then she was in Nowlin's face and her voice was dead quiet. "Devil's sidekick or no, if I ever hear you say that word to refer to a girl I will cut you one of your own. And I am *not* too tough to use a knife and just tough enough to know how to use one, so watch yourself."

At first, Skinny looked like he might hit her, but then he turned to Jason and just waited. And it was clear. Jason had to have his back. Because if there was one person in the whole goddamn world who had Jason's back, it was Skinny Nowlin.

Jason took a deep breath. "Chill, Pris, Jeez. It's just a word, no big deal. We're all pissed off at the same person. Back off, you know?" He put a calming hand on her arm and Pris whipped around, knocking it off and turning her glare full on him.

"It *is* a big deal." Her eyes narrowed around every word like it might hurt. "And I'm not backing off. I don't back off."

"Unbelievable," muttered Jason, shaking his head. Goddamn girl echoes.

But Skinny just shrugged it off. He'd gotten what he wanted. "Yeah, whatever, man. Tough punk rock chick, I get it. But your fine lady friend just called Jason and Dave Watson and me faggot fuck buddies in front of the whole school."

"What?" Pris and Jason spoke at the same time. Jason was outraged. Pris looked impressed. Jason wished he hadn't seen that.

"Yeah, she made this big speech, like she was at some rally or something, and she ended by saying that we used her name as a sex toy and—get this—if 'bad boys wanna get spanked' we should leave her and her 'private parts' out of it. And we were her 'closeted brethren.' Quote unfucking quote. The whole place cheered."

Looking down in disgust, Jason toed the ground. "Yeah, she was saying some shit like that to me today, probably just another thing she figures makes her so smart, you know?"

But Skinny wasn't listening. "What the fuck is wrong with you?" Jason looked up sharply—that wasn't a way Skinny talked to him, if he wanted to keep his head on—but he saw that it was directed at Pris. And no wonder. Pris's entire body was shaking with laughter.

"What, you think that's funny now?" Jason was a little pissed off. He'd thought Pris was on his side.

"Yeah, I think it's funny. Why don't you? She called the bunch of you out on your whole act, how you use a girl to justify the hard-on you have for fighting each other, that's funny—and—she's fighting on your goddamn turf with the weapons you chose." Pris was impressed and Jason felt intensely jealous. "She hit your strength. And she did it quoting The Pretenders. Yeah. That's a little more like my old best girl. A goddamn force to be reckoned with. Gives you something to live up to, Devil man."

Jason could hardly speak. "She called me a fuckin' faggot in front of the whole school, behind my back, and you wanna give her some kind of award? Like that's so original and real? I might be a lot of things but I'm not any fucking faggot!"

Pris narrowed her eyes and now her knife of a voice was directed at him. "So, you think that's like, the worst thing you could call anyone, right?"

Jason nodded. "For a guy, it's right up there."

Skinny had plenty to add. "Yeah, it's the worst, and if you're some kind of fag hag, you should know, they're gonna be dropping like flies, now, from that Rock Hudson thing—it was all over the news, my Gran's like, it's God's punishment on that gross shit they do. She's never gonna watch another one of his movies and he was her favorite, back in the day. I'm telling you, they're all gonna fuckin' die of AIDS and make the world a better place."

It was no news to Jason that Skinny didn't like fags, but Skinny didn't really like anyone much and as far as Jason could see it was pretty mutual. Jason guessed he was kind of used to Skinny, but he could definitely see how he could take some getting used to. Jason had been watching Pris's face. She was for sure not used to him.

Her face got white, then blotchy, like she might cry. It seemed kind of intense for the situation. Skinny was just being Skinny, talking shit, but Pris was all social justice and anarchy and he could see how Skinny's general political platform wouldn't necessarily go down well.

She didn't cry. She held up her hands all cool. "Yeah, I just don't know if I can do this. Later, maybe." And she was gone.

Skinny shoved Jason in the arm. "Little touchy, isn't she? Was it something I said?" And he laughed.

"Nah, man, I think it's just how you smell," said Jason, and he laughed, too. The laugh was a lie. Pris had ditched him, his entire body hurt from being hit, his hands hurt from hitting back harder, and he hadn't eaten since Skinny had brought him a package of Ding Dongs and a coffee in the morning.

Jason Devlin was just sick of it. "Fuck this. What you got on you? Got any smoke?"

Skinny raised his eyebrows. "Sure thing, man, smoke and a goddamn pharmacy. You wanna get toasted?"

Jason turned toward the graveyard. "Not toasted. Wasted off my ass. Just get me back by sixth. I got my new Social Studies class with that little blonde wench, can't get booted before I even show up. But some days are too long to get through straight, you know?"

"I hear that fuckin' loud and clear. You know me, all you ever gotta do is ask."

"I know, man." It was true. Whatever and whenever Jason wanted, good or bad, no questions. It *counted*. It *had* to count. Jason stared at his friend. Whether he *liked* him or not, that wasn't really the issue. Skinny and Jason just *were*. He punched Skinny in the arm, not too hard. They were all a little sore. "And thanks for this morning. Your eye kinda looks like hell."

"Ah, it just looks tough." Skinny started off toward the line of trees by the graveyard. He turned and did a little shadowboxing up in Jason's face, an old game. Skinny loved to make Jason flinch. "And hey, no thanks needed for this morning, dude. That was a *party*."

14. SEVERAL WALLS OF POSSIBILITIES

The counseling session was endless. The counselor's big, earnest eyes were made bigger and more earnest by earth-toned makeup that screamed 1970s louder than disco. She rocked slowly back and forth, from time to time cooing, "It's hard, isn't it?" as Samantha continued to say nothing at all.

Finally, Samantha spoke. "Look. Not like I don't appreciate this. But I'm not traumatized. I just don't want guys I don't know using me to fight over. So I said something, because, like, no one ever does—at least, no one anyone will listen to. I think they got the message. I think we're all cool here."

The counselor nodded earnestly. "You're a powerful woman, aren't you, Samantha?" Then her voice softened. "And yet, you're also a frightened little girl."

"Wow. That's amazing. You can tell that?" Samantha made her eyes go wide.

Samantha wondered how the counselor would react if the frightened little girl woman she saw got powerfully sick all over the office wall macramé. Which was sure to happen, soon, if she didn't stop talking like that.

Earth-tones nodded again, caringly. Samantha found herself really wanting to hit the woman sitting across the desk—a little blood spatter would alleviate the beige tedium of her face, her clothes, her walls. *Huh.*

"So," said Samantha, "growing up is hard. Can I go back to class?"

"If you feel stable enough to go—"

"Do I look wobbly?"

The counselor ignored her. "Then returning to class could be an appropriate course of action."

Why use one word when you could use seven? Samantha's eyes widened on their own this time. "So—I'm not in trouble? No detention? No Stagnita?"

"Samantha," soothed the counselor, "we understand that there are pressures on young girls—especially on someone like you, who is so attractive. It can be hard to process the—signals. We want to be there for you, not to punish you."

Right. "That's, um. Great. Not everyone understands how hard it is to be us." Samantha successfully reined in an eye roll. Not that it couldn't, sometimes, be hard. But she was aware that other people had worse problems than prettiness. "What about the guys?"

The counselor took a deep breath and rubbed her desk blotter a little nervously. "We are aware, of the—the regrettable violence this morning, and we have been in communication with the police. But since it happened off school grounds, our ability to, ah, assign appropriate consequences to those students is—is limited. But in the case of a few repeat offenders, I can assure you that some kind of action will be taken."

As clear as if it had been happening next to her again, Samantha heard the echo of Jason Devlin's body slamming against the locker.

"Repeat offenders."

The counselor nodded in her vacant, caring, reassuring way.

No.

Samantha watched as the world around her seemed to take on sharper edges, its forms and their functions suddenly unfamiliar, out of place. The twists and beads of the macramé, for instance, now seemed etched on her consciousness like hieroglyphics on stone, the knobby patterns full of portent. The beige walls, the ceramic earthenware cup for pens, the full and brown-tinted lips of the woman charged with consoling her—they all seemed edged with some darker purpose, some meaning that Samantha should have been able to read.

Samantha shook her head, trying to clear it. It seemed crazy, she knew that, but the conversation propelled her toward some thought, some action, a clarity that had no content, a mission without a plan.

"No, what I meant was, the guys—do they get—counseling? The guys I insulted in front of everyone?"

Chuckling, the counselor shook her head. "Dear. I know this, this was important to you. But boys—they are more likely to just—appreciate any attention they receive from a girl—especially one like you, Samantha. I don't think we need to worry about your victims."

As if that's what Samantha was worried about. Samantha took a breath. The fact that people underestimated her could always work to her advantage.

At the very least, it bought her time to think. "But what about how they're beating each other up?"

"Of course, that is a concern, especially when one—one of the repeat offenders—was brought up on a knife charge. Those who consistently violate the letter and the spirit of our school community charter may face some specific ... targeted consequences. That, of course, is Mr. Stagnita's department. But I don't think you need to worry about your friends who may have been involved. And Samantha—boys—boys fight. It's natural."

Boys will be boys, and girls will be—patients? Samantha shook her head again. "'My friends'—you mean, like, Dave Watson and the rest of the sports guys?"

"Of course. And Samantha, however misguided it may seem to you, to them, they were—protecting you, protecting your honor. Of course it sounds terribly outdated, but boys—they feel these things." The counselor's face was almost beatific in its wisdom. "It's different for them."

Different.

Samantha stood up. "I want detention. If I violated school rules by—by violating the letter and the spirit of our school community charter, I want detention. Just like anyone else."

"Samantha, Mr. Stagnita does not feel it's a necessary—"

"I want to be sent to Mr. Stagnita. I used profanity. I stood on a table. If there's a punishment, I want it." Samantha spoke through white hot rage. The macramé had stopped trying to communicate with her, thankfully. But while she only dimly understood the contours of the world she saw at those odd moments, she understood it was one she had been inhabiting, reaping the benefits of, even. And it wasn't fair.

This much was clear: if she broke rules she was a rule breaker. Not a patient. Not unless they were all patients, together. Standing up for herself was not a cry for help. Screw them for treating it that way.

Samantha folded her arms. "If I broke the rules, I get sent to Stagnita."

On a chair in Mr. Stagnita's office, though, Samantha felt smaller and more female than she had in the counselor's beige cocoon. No one looking at her now, she realized, would see any powerful woman mixed in with the frightened little girl. And Mr. Stagnita knew it.

Given what she'd said about guys and spanking at lunch, Samantha couldn't very well play the girly innocence card that worked so well with men.

But she had no idea what card she could play. Because Mr. Stagnita was not looking at her like an opponent. Mr. Stagnita was looking at her like she imagined she looked at Skinny Nowlin. An irritant, a bug that should be brushed aside or squashed but demand no further effort. Except—not quite.

He looked something like that, but he also looked bored.

"Miss Ward," he said in a tired voice, "we've never had any trouble with you before. We're not interested in punishing you. If that hurts your vanity, I'm sure you'll find plenty of ways to build it up again." He sighed, and leaned back in his chair. "Let's save the punishment for those who really need it."

There was something in his voice there. Anticipation. And Samantha, suddenly shorter and smaller than she had ever been in her life—she was sure she hadn't been this short when she was five years old—felt a shudder of pure fear. Because here was a man—her *bones* told her—who liked hurting children. And she was a child.

The same instinct, though, told her that she wasn't what he wanted. He wouldn't hurt her if she kept out of his way. She was not the kind of child he preferred.

It didn't matter. "I want everyone to get ..." She hated that her voice was shaking. She took a deep breath and continued, "the same punishment." She looked down. The dark gray flecks in the light gray carpeting were very, very distinct. She closed her eyes, then looked up again, steadier. "Jason Devlin got jumped under the underpass. It was the jocks. The burnouts were hiding just in case. That's what everyone's saying. Everyone knows it."

Samantha saw a flicker of pleasure behind Mr. Stagnita's impassive gaze. But he spoke evenly, he sounded fair, uninterested. "That falls outside of school jurisdiction, Miss Ward. And that's not the story Mr. Watson told the police."

"It's the story he's telling everyone else."

"It's hardly your affair. Now. If you want detention so badly, go ahead and have one. Dismissed."

"It *is* my affair—they were fighting about me!"

Shaking his head, he didn't even look unkind. "Not really, Samantha. Again, your vanity will recover, but it wasn't about you. Boys fight. It's what they do. We know who starts things, and who finishes them. We know who provokes whom."

Struggling to control her breathing, Samantha stood up. "I know some things too." She looked straight at the man behind the desk and put all her force behind her next words. "I want you to leave Jason Devlin alone."

On a dime, Mr. Stagnita's entire expression changed without one muscle on his face moving, from boredom to malice, all shifting behind the eyes. "Just who do you think you are, Miss Ward?"

The adrenalin rush was making Samantha giddy and sick, her limbs heavy. Stupid instinct. How was that supposed to help her fight? She folded her arms and spoke carefully.

She did have power—even if she didn't agree with its source. Her name meant something different from what the boys were using it for. "I think what you mean is who are my parents? *I* don't have a dead father, and half the school board golfs with my mother. Or *aspires* to. Ask around."

"Delusions of grandeur, yet." His gaze did not flinch or flicker. "I'll have to speak with the counselor about you in greater depth. Just how unstable are you, I wonder, Miss Ward?"

"Jason Devlin isn't no one to the Wards." Of course he was, but the words were just flying out. As her mouth formed them, Samantha knew that she meant them, that she hoped she could back them up, and that Jason must *never* know. "And if you don't know who the Wards are, I respectfully suggest you find out."

Stagnita looked down, rifled through some papers, paused looked up again. "Oh, are you still here? I said dismissed. And make sure to report to your detention."

Samantha felt a shiver run through her as she walked down the hall. The steel gray lockers reminded her of Stagnita's eyes, locked, holding messy secrets about teen boys. Teen boys shoved and pinned against them.

Bad boys get spanked. The words from a song had seemed such a joke before, so daring and racy.

A joke that wasn't funny. Another joke she wasn't in on—even when she was telling it.

She'd seen it in the hall the day before and she'd known it wasn't okay but she hadn't dreamed how not okay it was. She could *see* it now, how it fit into the spaces between, going on all around her, around all of them. And what else? What *else* was there?

Each day, layers kept getting peeled back all around her, and she couldn't help but look. Right now, more than anything, she wanted to smooth some of those layers back in place.

It was, she realized, what lipstick was for. Another coat. Maybe even pink. Samantha headed for the girl's room. She was late for Social Studies anyway. An extra minute wouldn't hurt.

15. I CAN'T STAND WHAT YOU DO, I'M IN LOVE WITH YOUR EYES

Heading to his great new class, Whining American Pinkos, or whatever the hell it was, Jason remembered exactly why he didn't get wasted, and even more exactly, why he didn't get wasted in school.

He had no idea what was going on. He hated it. He was slow, and fuzzy, and whatever high had been there was gone now, leaving him to deal with the world through cotton wool. Which was why he'd wanted to smoke, to ditch that feeling that the world was just a little bit too sharp. Problem was, the world *was* a little bit too sharp, and now he couldn't tell who was carrying the knife. Or planting it, he remembered, as he saw Diangelo down the hall.

Usually, Jason could read bodies and faces better than books, but with the cotton wool stuffed between him and the world, he had to look longer at things.

His former teacher was standing with some girl, the girl had her back to Jason but the hair looked like someone he should know. Something looked off. Instead of knowing the situation without a second glance, though, Jason stared. Too long. Diangelo caught him and the man's face went white and then red. Exactly the kind of thing Jason had been at pains to avoid.

Jason knew pot made him paranoid. But he also knew he needed to be a little paranoid, sometimes, it was a safety measure, and now he couldn't tell which signals were which. *Excellent fucking move, there, Devlin.*

By the time he remembered where the hell Kanter's classroom was, he was late. He mumbled something about being lost and threw himself into a chair. A murmur went through the room before Kanter silenced them all with a glance and went on with class. All he wanted to do was put his head down on his desk and go to sleep.

The sad thing was, he'd been kind of looking forward to this class, as far as you could look forward to anything in this hellhole. Before lunch, he'd thought mixing it up a little with Samantha and the other kids could be good for a laugh. For sure there'd be all kinds of politicals and it was fun getting a rise out of them.

At this point, though, he probably couldn't win an argument with Bogart.

So, yeah. The problem with doing something to stop yourself from thinking was that you couldn't fucking think.

He hated this.

He hated it more when about fifteen minutes into class, Samantha Ward waltzed into the room with a hall pass and an attitude and a goddamn soundtrack from some geeky girls singing in the back of the room. The Pretenders. She'd quoted them at lunch, or something. Fitting. Samantha held up her hand to quiet them and took a little bow, all rebel rocker chick today with her Madonna wannabe chains and crucifixes and her cut-up sweatshirt. What a poser.

But. The way the sweatshirt was falling off her shoulder hit Jason through all the cotton wool that was keeping him from feeling everything else. All goddamn class, which could have been about the mating habits of ocelots, for all he knew. By the end, the fog and fuzz finally lifted and left a headache roughly the size of Kentucky, which meant his head now matched the rest of his body.

That morning had sucked. He usually didn't mind a good tussle, he liked showing jocks who was boss and there wasn't a kid in school he couldn't take. But if the fucking football dudes *and* the swimmers were going to triple-team him and more, he was going to have to rely more and more on other kids or worse. How they'd missed his face was a miracle, but some stupid class ring hit his rib so hard it left a dent, and that kidney punch he took hurt like a mother, every breath he took. He could still see their livid pink and white rich boy faces spewing shit about Samantha Ward with every punch. He felt sick on top of the hurt because of it.

Worse, he knew Stagnita would eat that shit up. He loved it when other kids hurt Jason. He was the generous type, who didn't mind sharing his candy.

Jason managed to beg some aspirin off a sympathetic-looking chick on crutches and worked a Snickers bar and a Coke from a girl he'd made out with at a party a couple of weeks back whose name he had completely forgotten. Luckily names didn't come up in their current transaction, either.

Laughter and whispers preceded him in the halls, stopped abruptly as he passed, then followed in his wake. It was like a chorus of little birds had learned the phrases "bad boys," "spanking," "Jason Devlin," and "Samantha Ward," along with a few others, and the birds were so pleased with their new words that they just couldn't stop repeating them. Everyone, Jason reflected a little bitterly, wants to improve their vocabulary.

Goddamn Pris—the thought of her throwing up her hands, of her back as she walked away. The curve of her smile as she spoke of her former friend, how cool she was to have dissed Jason in public—when he'd stepped up for Pris, on her side.

Did Little Miss London not get anything? That he couldn't turn on Skinny over the politics hang-up of some girl he'd met the day before? Over any girl? Skinny had his back to the extent that if he didn't have Skinny's, no matter what, Jason would be the worst guy ever, and that was just the way it was.

As for Samantha, though—he didn't mind that everyone was saying their names together. In Social Studies, he hadn't been able to avoid a few glances, after all, and each time her poser bad-girl clothes revealed different stretches of skin and leg, she looked better and better. Sure, she thought he was scum and goaded jocks into jumping him. She made fun of him in front of the entire school.

But. Sick as it was, he liked that better than he liked her looking right through him. A hell of a lot better.

So he didn't like her. So what? She was excellent to look at and if she wanted to get up in his business he would be *just fine* getting up in hers. He got a little dizzy at the thought of her in his face the day before, her lips slowly forming around the words "Not. Even. Close."

She had been close this morning, that was for *fucking* sure. Jason could feel her, *smell* her—even in his memory. He didn't know what she'd been up to, but he was getting pretty worked up just thinking about it. So worked up he'd better think about bowling or Skinny Nowlin or something because otherwise detention was going to be *way* long.

Maybe if he thought about Skinny and bowling at the same time. And Bogart, also trying to bowl. That was surely the least sexy cluster of ideas ever brought together since man first failed at writing porn.

These things could be kept in check. You just needed to have a system.

Of course, if, when, he walked into detention the first things he saw were the legs of the girl he was trying not to think about, the system was likely to fail.

Samantha Ward, including all, like, two miles of her legs, was twisted around on one of those torture-chairs, bending back to talk to some random guy who was clearly more interested in looking down Samantha's shirt than in anything that had happened to him in a long time. Jason's first feeling was total empathy—with you there, dude—but this empathy was quickly overtaken by a twisting feeling in the pit of his stomach.

Jason had felt jealous before—of other people's homes, families, lives—often, of their food. He'd even felt jealous of Samantha, the way Pris had admired her. But he'd never felt jealous about a girl. Not like this. It was never a problem—there was always another girl. Now, though, *he* wanted that view of her skin and his rage that someone else was looking made his hands clench into fists. Plus it *hurt* him, suddenly, that this girl he didn't even like would be talking so easily to some random dude in a way she would never talk to Jason.

Which was completely crazy. Because this was a girl whose very existence made Jason angry.

Liking to look at her was one thing, but *feeling* this shit was another.

Still. Her long body was curved around the chair, she was laughing and twisting for someone else and Jason thought he might lose his mind.

He could put a stop to this.

Jason walked up to Samantha Ward and stood over in front of her, looking down. Sure enough, the guy talking to her shut up pretty fast, not wanting to meet Jason's eye. Samantha twisted her body back around to face Jason and her sweatshirt shifted, exposing more and different skin. She wasn't wearing pearls now, she had chains and some kind of dangly earrings and her hair was bigger and curlier and wilder, but her skin, Jason thought, was like pearls.

Jason idly hoped someone would put a bullet through his head if he thought anything like that ever again.

Her eyes were on Jason, looking up at him, and Jason felt something clench inside him. Hell. His palms were sweating and he bet he looked like a total fucking idiot.

It wasn't just her eyes on him. It was every pair of eyes in the room. Jason hoped to God he looked at least a little threatening.

"So." The corner of her mouth turned up, triumphant. "Cat got your tongue?"

Jason didn't let up on his stare but he let himself smile a little. "Nah—my tongue just hides when you're around. Didn't I make that clear at lunch yesterday?"

Stifled laughter from the surrounding desks.

Saccharine sweet, Samantha cooed, "Jason. I know your interests lie elsewhere. You don't have to hide it anymore." She looked around at their audience, who were suddenly all very absorbed in staring at their desks, the floor, the clock above the door. "Didn't I make that clear at lunch *today*?"

"From what I hear, all you made clear was that Rebel Barbie comes with a script Mattel swiped from The Pretenders, and an outfit swiped from—looks like, *Flashdance* meets Madonna. I think Teen Princess Barbie was more original."

Laughter less successfully stifled.

Jason could swear he saw a slight glimmer of hurt behind her eyes. He guessed the whole rebel act was a little close to her heart. He guessed he was doing it, hitting her where she thought she was strong. Funny, it wasn't feeling quite as good as he'd anticipated.

She didn't let the hurt stop her. Flipping her hair back, she sighed. "I guess they just couldn't compete with the originality of *your* rebel uniform. Army jacket, ripped up jeans—how *did* you come up with that?"

"Yeah, well, not all of us rebel with our charge cards—would you believe, some of us rebels don't even *have* charge cards?" That felt a little bit better. He hated the idea that clothes were just a matter of choice—that cost never even figured into it.

At this point, the Ed Tech walked into the room and glowered at them. "Take your seats, books out, no talking or you go for the doubleshot. Let's get this show on the road, campers."

Jason folded himself into the desk next to Samantha. He took out his Shakespeare and started trying to read. This quickly changed to pretending to read while looking at Samantha's legs, incredibly long and very close to him. He entertained himself by imagining them tangling with his and the different situations that could lead to that state of affairs. He heard the echo from yesterday about how it was his face she'd see when she thought of *that.*

He was so absorbed in this entertainment that the notebook took him completely by surprise and he jumped slightly, taking the torture desk along with him and coming down with a loud clatter. The Ed Tech glared at him. Jason answered her glare with a panicked look on his face. "Spider," he said. "*Huge* one. Look out, it's heading right toward you."

He smiled in satisfaction as the large woman in front backed up and nervously eyed the floor.

As he looked down at the notebook, he was struck again by strange echoes of the other girl. Not like passing notes in detention was an original idea—but it seemed so close.

The note said: "I need to tell you something. It's more important than insulting me right now. Time out?"

Jason wrote back: "Insulting you isn't important to me. It's just a way to pass the time." He wondered if he was always this full of shit, or if it was just bothering him more.

"You're getting better at it," came back. Jason glanced over. She was looking down at her desk, her shoulders slightly hunched. He could sense the vulnerability coming off of her in waves. Pose, no doubt, but it made him give in. He wrote back. "OK. Time out."

"I know you think I am an idiot and shallow but I talked to him today and even I can tell he is not OK. Stay after a minute. I don't want to write it."

A chill ran through his body. He knew right away who she meant. Remembering the smile on her face from the hallway the day before, he didn't like the idea of Samantha talking to that man about him, for sure. But there was another feeling there, too. Like he didn't want Stagnita near Samantha for *her* sake.

Jason Devlin was very uncomfortable with this turn of events. He wrote, "meet me where we were yesterday" and turned his back on Samantha for *The Taming of the Shrew*. It was a completely eloquent comment on his day that fucking Shakespeare made a lot of sense in comparison.

16. I WAS ONLY JOKING WHEN I SAID

Samantha was already waiting for Jason by the time he got to his smoking spot. She was leaning against a dumpster, hair fallen over her face, looking intently at something on the ground. The little slump in her shoulders made her look small, somehow, tall as she was.

"So," he said, willing himself not to respond to what looked like softness. Didn't matter. "That whole innocent thing, pretty much an act, huh? Gotta say, you kinda had me buying it. Nice one."

Shaking her head, she shrugged, not looking at him. "No—not an act, but, you know—I go' bet'er."

It was like getting slapped. Goddamn girl echoes.

She spoke again, still not showing him her eyes. "Listen, if insulting me doesn't mean so much to you, couldn't you—give it a rest for a minute? A time out, like we said?"

"Right. I thought that's what I *was* doing. I forgot how sensitive you are. Okay." Jason held his hands wide in front of him. "Times! What's up?" He spoke as evenly as he could. "Why all the cloak and dagger? Stagnita, if that's who you mean, already knows he doesn't like me. So does everyone else."

Samantha nodded, not looking up. "Does everyone know—about the other part?"

"What other part?" Surprising, how fast his body could tense to alert.

"About—about how he enjoys it?" She raised her eyes cautiously, and there they were, bright blue and somehow dark at the same time. Every time he saw them, they were more of a kick in the gut than he remembered. The idea that he was being seen by those eyes made him almost dizzy—another reason he couldn't think about them right now.

Silent, Jason stared at the girl in front of him, steeling himself to see her eyes only as indicators of attitude, truth, lies. Because—Jason wasn't sure that everyone knew that. How Stagnita liked it, and in what way.

Play it cool. He could like to look at this girl, okay, but he couldn't trust her an inch, whatever her eyes seemed to say. Her mouth, he knew, said different things to other people.

"Yeah, well, big deal. So he found the right job. Nothing new there. I mean—I'm the last person you'd have to tell, right? Why are we here?"

Not that he minded an excuse to be alone with her. Not really. Especially not after that long detention hour when he hadn't been able to think about anything *but* getting alone with her. But he minded her mixing in parts of his life where no one came.

"I just thought—given how he—is, I didn't want you *not* to know that I—that he and I had a conversation."

In a flash, the chill Jason had felt before was back like the goddamn Arctic. This wasn't funny and he didn't care what she looked like. She needed to stay the *fuck* out of there. He got up in her face. "What did you say to him? What the fuck—have you no clue how much of a bitch you are? You're gonna use *him* to get to me?" His voice was trembling, he could hear it and feel it.

"No. I'm not. That's not the conversation we had." She spoke very quietly, but with a firm tone.

Jason kept staring at her, right into her eyes that were looking at him without challenge but without flinching. They made him want to believe her.

Was she that good a liar?

Jason stepped away and leaned with his hands into the rough bricks. This was too much for him. He could take checking her out, he could take not liking it when other people were checking her out, although that part was harder, and very confusing. He could totally take sparring with her, trading insults. He had a feeling he might like swapping spit with her even better—though how he would pull that off he had no idea.

But. He could not take having this spoiled rich crazy girl running apeshit through his life, showing up in places where she could really hurt him.

Then her hand was on his arm. Tentatively. Like the hand itself couldn't believe it was there. It left, as quietly as it had come, but she was still close. He wanted to look, but he couldn't risk it.

Without looking at her, he asked through clenched teeth, "Just what conversation did you have, Samantha, with the man who gets off on messing with me? Did you discuss how much you have in common in that area?"

"This is supposed to be a time out," she said, her voice faltering.

"Trust me. It is." All the Arctic cold had migrated to his voice.

"Trust you. Funny."

He didn't look at her but he could hear the hurt. Again, he didn't like it. Fuck.

"I told him that I knew—about him."

"Bullshit." Jason shot her a glance beneath his stretched arm. She looked serious.

"It wasn't—exactly like that, but I can—communicate pretty well. He was totally uninterested in me, and then—he heard me, and—he changed." She was speaking very fast but halting, somehow, at the same time.

The Arctic waters in Jason's veins quickened and he felt slightly sick. Adrenalin. And hell if that protective feeling wasn't back. No. Not for the rich girl who'd thrown him to the dogs. "Samantha, what the hell do you think you're playing with? Who do you think you are?"

"Funny. He asked the same thing," she whipped out, "Maybe *you* are his kind."

"Don't push it." He could hear his voice. Cold and sharp. A total fucking lie. He was feeling anything but cold.

He heard her swallow. Hard. He was scaring her. Her voice was lower and softer when she continued.

"I don't think Stagnita can really touch me. My parents—anyway, it's— safer for me to say something, maybe, than for someone else."

Jason shrugged uncomfortably, not liking the mental image of Stagnita touching Samantha, but also jealous of parents who would protect you if a crazy principal was trying to hurt you. "Don't count on it."

Scrubbing his eyes, Jason tried to stop his spinning head. "You didn't see enough to make any difference." He turned toward her. Her eyes now were big, a different, quieter blue, looking at his steadily. Jason sighed. "He doesn't do anything that bad to me. He's careful. But—stay out of his way, okay?" He barked a short, thin laugh. "I mean—listen to you—you figure you have nothing to fear from a grown-up—professional sadist, but you're like, cringing in agony when a kid you won't even look at makes a joke at lunch? You seriously think—he can't hurt you, but I can?"

Samantha looked down, flushing. "He doesn't enjoy it like you do. Not with me."

Jason was silent at that. It wasn't a picture of himself that he wanted.

"Well, anyway. That's all. I just thought it was—fair if you knew."

Fair. *Fair.* Something in that word clicked on the switch and opened the flood gates to the rage that never left him. It had found its object.

Samantha Ward. His champion. However pretty, however even sweet she might seem right now, he remembered his morning, and he remembered what Pris had overheard the day before.

"Fair? That's fucking beautiful. Is that why you got ten guys to jump me before school? To be fair?"

Her face turned pale. "You think I did *that?*"

"There's no think about it." Jason turned and spat on the ground at her feet. "That's what your fair is worth."

Samantha looked stricken. She licked her lips, began speaking, then pressed them together. In the purple-red haze of his anger, Jason guessed she was pissed to be caught in the act. Fine. The rage was colder than the Arctic now, burning at the same time. It was everything, everywhere. It would help him take her down.

"You don't know what you're talking about," she said, not meeting his eyes.

"The hell I don't. 'Oh, Dave Watson, thank you so much for protecting me from that scum Jason Devlin. He doesn't know his place. You reminded him. Thank you so much for being like my big brother.' Sound familiar?"

Jason's entire body was shaking, he could taste bile. He couldn't believe he'd been going soft on this girl, again, just because she was pretty. Like he didn't have enough pretty girls, each of them worth ten of this one.

Samantha looked like he'd hit her and he wished to God he could.

She was shaking, too. "I had to say those things, but I didn't mean for him—you would never understand, but—you put me in the middle—you started this! I had to—other people were affected."

"Other people were traumatically affected by my joke. Give it up. You're pathetic." Jason's head was throbbing and his bruised body was aching and the rage was making them worse. He wanted nothing more than for this stupid girl to leave and take her accusing, hurt blue eyes with her. But they kept looking at him, reproachful, sad.

Her voice was like her eyes. "You expect me to believe that you're friends with Skinny Nowlin but you don't know what it's like to have to—to swallow something, to say or not say something, out of loyalty?" She was still talking quietly, trying to get through, as if she cared.

That caring sound put pain to the rage because it was such a lie, a lie that was personal between her and him. A lie no one else was even bothering to tell today. Not Pris, who walked away, leaving him Skinny, his best friend he didn't even like. And Skinny—Skinny was Ding Dongs and punches and bile, so many one-hits that Jason could barely stand up after. Skinny was all he had and it wasn't enough. It was too much for this girl to be dangling it, jerking it away. Jason could feel himself go for the throat.

"You think you have something to teach *me* about loyalty? You're—you're the most ridiculous excuse for a person, a plastic doll trying to play human for a day—and you think that?" He watched for the reaction. She flinched, her eyes teared up. He was doing it, going for her strength—what she thought it was. Pris was right. This way was a *high*.

He kept going. "You had to be loyal to Dave Watson? Are you dense? You know what he was saying about you this morning? 'Don't you ever talk about that pussy, scum, that shit is ours!' That's what your 'big brother' said. Nice pick."

Silence. Then, as Jason watched her, he saw his last move was a misstep. Instead of pain, he saw contempt. He'd got it wrong. It made him wonder what else he'd been getting wrong.

This time when she spoke, the tone was venomous and cold. "For God's sake, I'm dense? The only person I hate more than Dave Watson is you!"

Fine. Back to normal. That right there—that was the kind of caring he could take from her.

As fast as it had come on, his rage vanished. Only the pain was there, lonely on its own, and so was he, already missing the thing he'd just made sure to crush. "Well then why the hell do you need to be loyal to him by screwing me over like that? If I hadn't been smart, they would have put me in the hospital!" His voice sounded petulant, childish. He hated it.

Hers still sounded cold. "You have no idea who you're talking to and why I care about that, or you, or anyone being awful to you except to be glad about it—I don't know."

"Yeah, I think you'll get over it pretty quick," Jason muttered.

The fight had just gone out of him. It was like he'd become a spectator, his life some old-fashioned melodrama of a movie and this beautiful girl he'd been fantasizing about had reached out to him, toward his shadows from the light world of the screen, trying to be human. He saw her hand, saw it on his arm, and then he saw himself bite that reaching hand like a rabid dog—but worse. Rabid dogs lash out blindly. Jason thought about it first, where and how to hurt.

Now, he heard her voice trembling, raw. "All I know is that however much I hate you, I've been—trying to treat you like a person and you won't even—honor a time out. Fine, you're the Devil, like everyone says. So go to hell!" And she turned away.

Slumping into the wall, he let himself fall down it, the bricks scraping at his army jacket, maybe tearing it in places. Good. As he hit the ground, he said, more to himself than to her, "Where the fuck do you think I am?"

He sat there, looking at nothing, waiting for the sound of her footsteps on pavement, taking her away. Hearing them, he stared straight and hard at his boots and the crumbling asphalt beneath them. If he could just find that blank, feel the moments edging on, maybe the tension would ease and breathing would feel less like knives.

But the footsteps were going the wrong way. They paused in front of him, but he was done moving. In a moment, he felt her lower herself to the ground next to him, back to the wall.

He was barely breathing, and she didn't say a word.

For the first time in as long as he could remember, Jason Devlin felt shy.

He heard a soft, dull thud, the sound of her head falling back against the brick. "That's what talking to you reminds me of," she said, conversationally, as if she'd finally thought of something she'd been trying to remember.

He nodded. He couldn't look at her, afraid if he did it would break the spell.

"If I did it harder, you know, so it bled a little," she finished, in the same tone. Jason cringed. He didn't know if it was noticeable.

Then he felt her hand on his arm, tentative as before, but a little more like it meant to be there.

Usually, when Jason felt like he didn't deserve something, it wasn't going in this direction.

Aching, just this once, to say sorry, Jason was cut off by the endless loop of his mother playing in his head, screaming, sobbing, spitting the word that changed nothing. It wasn't something he said.

He felt his hand move across his body, grasp the fingers on his arm, hold them tight in his.

In his hand, her fingers felt soft, a little chilled in the fall air, but warming to his touch. Her hand, in his hand.

She let it stay.

17. BOYS MAY COME AND BOYS MAY GO

After two days spent looking at everything just a little bit too clearly, Samantha was trying her damnedest to look at nothing at all—here, where nothingness had all the flashy packaging. Total mindblock. Like her afternoon had never happened. Most of it, anyway. The other parts she wanted to keep pure from the rest of it, frozen, locked, but the contrast made the rest hurt worse.

Confused wasn't even the word for it.

Some people in her position might have been hammering shots or sucking down bong hits or cutting line after line on pocket mirrors or their parents' glass coffee tables. Some people in her position were absolutely doing that, guaranteed, right in Highland. Some people might go clubbing, slam-dancing, crank the Metallica, cut into their flesh slowly with razor blades or broken glass, pick fights with gangs of jocks over girls they didn't know.

Samantha Ward took Michelle and Jessica to the mall.

Everything was shiny there, jewel tones and shoulder pads, leg warmers with tinsel woven in, blue thickening mascara, free gift with purchase. Strobe lights for the brain. Samantha bought Giorgio perfume, she didn't even like the smell. She wanted the yellow box, the yellow bag, the beautiful vulgarity of it. She wanted to spend that much money on something her mother would hate.

More than anything, Samantha Ward wanted to *be* the girl Jason Devlin saw when he looked at her with his cold, sneering eyes. She wanted to *be* the plastic doll he called her.

It wasn't like he was seeing something that wasn't there. Samantha Ward could go Material Girl with the best of them. And like it.

It was decided Michelle should get a pink streak in her hair. She giggled. She did what she was told. Jessica insisted they get chocolate mousse and then puke in the bathroom. They did. They rinsed their mouths and chewed

Lifesavers and smoked cigarettes after, crowded into a single stall, Samantha feeling green as she always did at smoking, disliking the taste of the smoke but not as much as she disliked the taste of mint layered on vomit.

The things you did for friends. All of them better than thinking.

She bought a new blazer. Brocade. A ruffled blouse to match, as close as she could find to the one Adam Ant was wearing in the poster in the arcade. Samantha hated Adam Ant. She didn't care. It was new, different, cost money. It would make her mother cringe.

Duchess Barbie. Total break from Princess Barbie. Totally effing new. There it was, his vision of her infecting her own. Good. Go with it.

If Samantha had been alone she would have been crying but she was not alone so she spent most of the evening laughing. Loudly.

Jessica and Michelle were working toward Michael Jackson faux-military piping but Samantha made them stop short of the gloves. Jessica intervened at The Limited, insisting that seven Forenza sweaters were enough for one season. "Samantha, the first step is admitting you have a problem. Back me up here, Michelle."

Samantha relented. Instead, she bought glitter mousse, frosted lipstick, pink notebooks with Prince on the cover, skirts and tops in lycra, spandex, rayon. Nothing in natural fibers, just to make her mother burn. She took one of Michelle's diet pills and washed it down with a Diet Coke. Buzzing, she beat her high score in Ms. Pacman but Jessica still won.

Jessica killed at Ms. Pacman. Michelle turned out to be amazing at Centipede and looked awesome with her pink streak. Jessica looked traffic-stopping, broadcast attitude, eyes and earrings flashing in the brash mall light. Samantha had no idea what she herself looked like because she was avoiding mirrors, but she didn't need them. Cute boys in the arcade were checking them out. The girls pretended to flirt, then dissed the boys snottily and ran.

On the bus ride home, Michelle was gushing, she felt happy and chosen and had more bags than anyone else. Samantha gently suggested that the green purse would not go with the pink streak because pink and green was preppy and preppy clashed with hair streaks. Michelle nodded like something really profound had been explained to her. Mission accomplished. The world would never understand its debt to Samantha, but good works were meant to be their own reward.

Jessica was complaining about the bus, whining that her father's car service was so much better and what was Samantha's problem with money anyway. Samantha argued in favor of finding more people to laugh at. Jessica relented. She would be sixteen soon, her parents had promised her a car and she wanted a Corvette. Their days on the bus were limited.

It was true that on the bus, everyone looked stupid. Men in mullets and Magnum P.I. mustaches. Tight shirts. Gold chains. One had plastic pants with zippers and Jessica claimed extra points for spotting that one.

As always, women who shouldn't were wearing leggings with leg warmers. Girls stretched bright pink lycra miniskirts over opaque white tights, finishing the nightmare with all the wrong shoes. No one knew the first thing about applying blush, and all the hair was dyed to death and teased up, curling ironed back and frozen in place with more Aqua Net and Dippity-do than should ever come together in a single enclosed space.

The more fashion crimes Samantha catalogued, the harder, and higher, and better she felt. The world needed Jessica and Samantha to shop for them, Michelle explained. The bus, she said, was so much fun.

It wasn't, but Samantha didn't care. It wasn't thinking about Jason Devlin's hand on hers, holding it like a lifeline, all while he wouldn't look at her or take back a single one of his stinging words. It wasn't thinking about how his hand had felt on hers, how it had been more than skin, how it had touched her right on her feelings, where no one touched.

How incredibly, incredibly messed up that was.

How he'd made her feel beat up, how he'd seemed to enjoy it, how she'd gone back to him anyway, how he'd made her feel soothed, how each feeling seemed a betrayal of the feeling before it and of herself.

No one, she steeled herself back to thinking, should wear fishnets with penny loafers. Or a muscle shirt without muscles to go with it.

What were they thinking?

See? Everyone betrays themselves.

The conversation turned to Samantha's blow-out at lunch. Jessica was still incredulous and Michelle was torn between expressing admiration and disdain, clearly uncertain how it would all play out. Samantha shrugged her shoulders. "It's like this, if guys wanna fight over me, they have to, like, at least take me out once beforehand. I mean, dinner, a movie? *Then* they can have their stupid boy hard-ons for fighting each other and drag my name into it. But they will have spent money on me first. I mean, I have standards."

She eyed a girl at the front of the bus, "Like, for example, standards that would make sure I never wear flesh-toned nylons with a skirt that short unless I intend to get paid for my services—more than dinner."

As far as pain went, bitter was such a step up from sharp.

Jessica snorted. "I don't think Jason Devlin has any money, but I bet he'd pay up if he did. He has a hard-on for more than fighting when it comes to you. Maybe he could rob a bank."

"Maybe he could rob Skinny Nowlin—he deals weed to middle schoolers, I hear," Michelle sneered.

"Lovely," said Samantha. "Did I not mention the part about the standards?"

"Oh, come *on*, Sam, Jason Devlin is a walking sex machine. Burnout or no. And just because he hangs with Skinny—I mean, you and I hang and we're different people, right?"

Samantha looked at her friend like she had six extra eyes. "You think I should go out with Jason Devlin? That's a big change from yesterday, when you didn't even want Johnny and Chip polluting our airspace with his name."

Jessica shuddered. "Go *out* with him? Hell, no! Enjoy the thought of him rolling around in the dirt with other boys, over you? Why not? The boy as physical specimen is *fine*. And he might be more decent than he lets on." The last words sounded more reflective than was usual for Jessica.

Samantha was beyond uncomfortable. No one knew of the time she had spent with Jason Devlin behind the dumpsters. She'd rather die than tell anyone. She wanted the reason to be that she was ashamed to have anyone know. She was sure that's how he'd read it, he who was determined to take anything remotely good about her and see it in the worst possible light. He who would hold her hand after, but not look her in the eye. Where there were now *tears*.

No.

She would not look at this, would not feel this, would not ache this way.

Samantha snapped at her friend, "Jason Devlin thinks we're scum." She tossed her hair, fluffing it out behind her. Bigger was better, stronger. "If he looks at me, it's because he's trying to figure out what's wrong with me—and if he likes it, it probably pisses him off. Next on the agenda. Any ideas on how I can murder Dave Watson?"

Rounding her lips into a silent "O," Jessica shook her head. "Any ideas on how Vanessa Segal can murder you?"

"Isn't that a given, now that her boyfriend was fighting over me in some dumb rumble?" Samantha took out her new perfume and contemplated it. Maybe Giorgio could double as mace. Maybe she could trade it to Vanessa Segal for not murdering her in cold blood.

Michelle giggled. "And after you, like, outed him as a closet fag at lunch?"

Softly, Samantha corrected, "I did do that, kind of—to piss those guys off. But I actually think it's more of an insult to anyone gay, suggesting they're somehow like Dave Watson. And I don't call people fags. Ever."

Jessica assented easily. "Yeah, well, you're probably right. I mean, Monty's gay, right? And he's a total sweetie. Plus he loves the hell out of Madonna and can moonwalk, so why would you not wanna party with him? Anyway, if they're all gonna die horrible deaths like Rock Hudson, I guess the least we can do is not call them faggots."

Samantha felt cold on the inside. "What happened to Rock Hudson?"

"Oh *my* God. Do you, like, *never* listen to the news? He totally died of the gay plague. Maybe two days ago." Now it was Jessica's turn to look at Samantha like she was from Mars.

"But he had a wife!" Samantha's hands started twisting a receipt she'd found in her jacket pocket.

"*MacMillan and Wife* was a TV show, doofus. They're not *real*. Do you think Peter Falk always wears a raincoat?"

"No, I don't know, maybe—but—McMillan always seemed—Rock Hudson was gay? Did anyone know? And I thought—I thought they were saying with AIDS, it was like, bath houses and, I don't know, gross people, like, so it was not because they were gay but because they were gross, like, not everyone gay screws half of San Francisco, so it was, like, slutty gay people and then hemophiliacs and people who shot drugs. I mean, no normal people got it. I mean, I guess hemophiliacs could be normal but—"

In what could have been an act of mercy, Jessica cut off her increasingly panicked-sounding stream of babble. "Um, Sam? Newsflash? We don't have to call them fags and like I said, I like Monty fine, but gays aren't normal people. I mean, that's kind of the point, right? And who knows where Rock Hudson took baths?"

Michelle nodded. "Really. Anyway. Are you more worried about Jason Devlin or Dave Watson getting the gay plague?" She was trying to lighten things up. Funny strategy.

Samantha wanted the entire world to disappear and take Michelle with it. And Jessica. And anyone else who was not forced to understand, suddenly, not having been paying close enough attention before, that something terrible was killing people other people might love. The only people some people might love.

And the thing was, you couldn't talk about it, any of it. It wasn't your thing to say.

"I'm just sad about Rock Hudson," Samantha explained, swiping tears. "He was just on *Dynasty*. He looked *fine*. He was kissing Krystle, remember? They were lying in the leaves. He named a boat after her. He looked fine." Samantha sniffled and turned from her friends.

It was much too fast. How could anything go that fast? But it was the pace of things, suddenly. Like everyone on TV explaining how girls wanted to grow up too fast because of Madonna, but that was just stupid. It wasn't, she thought, so much that they *wanted* to. But how did you stop it once it starts? If you tried to dig in your heels, you'd get swept away by the current.

Staring out the bus window as the red and white lights of cars streamed by in darkness, Samantha found herself wishing herself back to the silence by the dumpsters, where someone had—without speaking—given her what she now wanted more than anything—a time out.

18. I'LL BE YOUR MIRROR

So they'd had a time out. Jason was not going to look at it, think about it, or ruin it in any way. Things that came in close contact with his life got spoiled and mangled.

Often by him. More often than he ever fucking liked to admit, but—a couple of times in the last two days, he'd had to take a good hard look at himself. It wasn't something he wanted to repeat very soon.

She'd come back anyway. Despite Jason's best efforts to be the worst guy ever. Then it had been simple. Her fingers in his. No eyes, no lips, no words, no school.

He was going to carve that moment out of time and wear it around his neck like one of those golden hearts made out of frozen tree sap. It didn't matter what it changed or didn't. It was just his.

Maybe hers, too, but he didn't know if it was something she would want to keep.

Before Jason even knew it, he was home, having somehow spaced the entire trip between the school and the store and his house, his skin tingling from the touch of the girl he didn't like.

Time to put that the hell away. Couldn't have it out here, getting lost. He'd wear it under his shirt where it wouldn't be seen.

The small white house sat in a row of other similar houses with neater lawns. A lot of the neighbors worked for Highland families and Jason guessed you wouldn't want the gardener's yard looking like shit. Jason's yard was unkempt but not insanely so. Jason had done it with his dad for years and he still hacked through it from time to time. The physical labor grounded him and brought his dad back, just a little, in a way that didn't hurt but felt good.

Inside was another story. Stuff was just in piles, empties never rinsed, stale-smelling, ashtrays overflowing onto random school papers, bills paid and unpaid scattered on surfaces from the unused dining-room table to the food-encrusted kitchen counter. And that crust was old, not much got cooked here. Sometimes Jason heated some junk from a can but it didn't seem like the kind of place you'd want your food coming from.

In the hall by the front door, piles of magazines whose subscriptions had long run out lay untouched, still in their years-old sealed wrappers. Screwdrivers abandoned by the hinge they'd once tightened, bread bags poking out of boots in sizes no one had worn in years. Thick dust covered books on shelves hemmed in by cobwebs. The family pictures on the mantle included nothing from the past four years. There were few insects, no rats, but nothing was clean or put away or cared for—it was a house where everything just stayed where it was.

It had never been a show home. But now it was just—less.

Jason didn't like coming there except to sleep, but fuck if he wanted to be around anyone else right then.

He took the can of powder with the little chick on it and the new sponges and trudged up to the bathroom. He'd clean that up, then take a bath and soak his sorry-ass muscles that were so much sorer from having sucked it up all day, looking like nothing hurt when it hurt like fuck. Physical pain might be preferable to other kinds but that didn't make it a walk in the goddamn park with ice cream.

Leaning over the tub scouring was not helping. Jason had wanted to get the little bubbles that talked to you while they cleaned or at least the gay-looking bald guy with the big arm muscles, but both of those cost too much. The chicks were cheap but required a lot of help from his own muscles, which were complaining about that arrangement. He'd take some aspirin and lie down, give the pills a chance to work.

His hands were on his button fly the second he was in his room, he didn't bother to turn on the lights but at about the third button he heard a strangled sound coming from the vicinity of the bed and froze. He flicked the switch and looked.

Yup. It was really true. He moved his eyes from her, collecting words.

Slow. Cold. Fine.

"Pris. What the living fuck are you doing in my bedroom while I'm stripping?"

"I don't know, the stripping wasn't my idea! How was I supposed to know you were a goddamn nudist?"

"I don't know, Prissy, how was I supposed to know you'd be in my bedroom where I don't even bring girls I'm screwing, let alone crazy chicks who ditch me at the drop of a hat to run back to their bitchy little friends?"

Considering he'd spent the better part of his afternoon eviscerating and then holding hands with the bitchy little friend in question, Jason vaguely recognized this might not be entirely fair, but he was so stung by Pris's defection that he didn't care.

"So, what, is it 'later, maybe' o'clock already? How time fucking flies," he snapped.

Pris was sitting on the corner of his bed, hunched against the wall, knees folded up to her chest. The way his grayed and rumpled airplane quilt twisted around her ankles didn't do much for her toughness factor, that was for sure. As Jason looked closer, he could see smears on her cheeks and her eyes were all red and smudgy.

Must be his week to make girls cry. That felt pretty much like shit, actually. Although, come to think of it, she'd been crying before he got there, so he didn't know what the hell he'd had to do with it. He just figured it had to be something.

"I brought you a book," she said in her intense way, as if he'd said nothing assholish. She reached under her knees, took out a book with a kind of blurry black-and-white photo on the cover, and held it out to Jason.

Jason stared at it. No one had ever given him a book before. Not since they had pictures in them, anyway.

"It doesn't bite, Devlin, just take the goddamn book."

So Jason walked over and plucked it from her hand, still feeling pissed and now guilty, too, his body still sore as hell. It was maybe the longest day in the history of the world. The book thought so too, since it was called *A Season in Hell*.

"You didn't have to come all the way over here to tell me to go to hell," he said, darting a glance at her. He didn't mention that her ex-friend had already sent him there.

"It's my favorite book, jerkoff, and why would you get so pissy when someone's doing something nice for you?"

And that right there was the six thousand-dollar question, thought Jason, turning the book over in his hands. He supposed it was, in some weird alternate universe, "nice" to break into his house where he never brought a living soul to give him something that meant a lot to her.

It was maybe even nicer to take a stand for him against Stagnita. Well. He didn't have to fuck this attempt up quite as badly. "I guess the book's not a comment on this hellhole since you had it with you when you got here," he mumbled.

"So far as I can see, you have heat and flush toilets, so it's a big step up from the last place I lived in London," Pris shrugged, emphasizing the casual. She knew it wasn't fucking casual. Jason was starting to get that warm feeling back. Pris just got him.

Jason opened the book and looked at the first page. "Pris, it's in fucking French. I'm failing French. Are you making fun of me?"

"No, but I should fucking start, apparently. The English is on the opposite page."

So it was. He glanced down the page.

One evening I seated Beauty on my knees. I found her bitter. And I cursed her.

So that was pretty close. It was maybe poetry or some bogus thing like that but it sounded eerily dead on the money. He read a little more, shook his head slightly, then turned back to Pris, who was biting her lip and looking so nervous it might have been her poems he'd been reading.

"Okay, so this totally rocks." Unbelievably, he felt shy. Again. Poetry. What a weird-ass up-and-down day. Who would have ever thought poetry would be one of the ups? It was beyond *Twilight Zone.*

Her face lit up. "Rimbaud is like, the total shit. I mean, he was so radical and, like, his poems say exactly what your soul says, you know, when it hurts. Or when it feels beautiful. And do you know he wrote all his poems before he even turned twenty? Like, he seriously quit writing poems when he was nineteen. And my favorite punk band, Crass, they broke up but I got to hang with them in London? The drummer is named Penny Rimbaud after him, he's a poet too, and they don't just play music, they resist with actions and protests, I was in one, and—"

Pris was sounding more and more like breathy little Prissy except she was going on about punk rock and poetry and protest and Margaret Thatcher, who was apparently the root of all London evil. The contrast between the tone and the tough clothes took care of any lingering resentment so fast Jason couldn't even cling to it.

Jason lay down on his floor, propped himself on his elbow and listened. She was just starting in on some punk commune outside of London and as far as he could tell, she might have kept talking until morning if the sound of the door slamming downstairs hadn't made her catch her breath.

That wiped the smile off Jason's face pretty fast.

"Shit, Pris, sorry." He got himself up off the floor. And fuck if he hadn't said that bullshit word, like his mother was just a magnet for it. He swore some more. Pris looked at him steadily, not saying a word. Jason mumbled something about being right back.

Before he was even out the bedroom door he heard it, "Jason, you little piece of shit, it better not be true that you're home instead of at work."

"It's cool, Ma, it's no problem, they didn't need me, I called." He shut the door behind him.

"Oh, 'they didn't need you?'" Her voice was high, shrill and mocking. "Listen to you. If you're knocking up some girl in your room, it's not gonna be me who bails you out. No one bailed me out!"

Last night it had been all sweetness and light or at least orange juice and Snickers. You never knew who was going to walk through that door.

"I know, Ma. Lemme get you a drink, okay?" Jason hurried downstairs, just wanting to get her quiet. He reached up into the cabinet by the stove and got down the plastic jug of vodka with the e-z grip handles. He stuck some in a glass and threw some ice in it. "Relax, Ma. I've just got a friend over."

Jason's mother turned to face him. Orange make-up and stripes of rouge, blonde hair piled on the top of her head with plenty of roots, skirt too short and blouse too open—but he guessed, in a way, she looked like a passable secretary. Maybe she didn't look so bad, in a used-up party girl kind of way. She looked a lot like some of the wives at the bowling alley.

She was like the house, probably, worse to him because he remembered her different.

She took the glass, downed half of it, then smiled at him as if the yelling had never happened. "So who's your friend, Jase? Anyone I know? Guy? Special girl?"

"No one."

"Well, if no one is in my friggin' house I wanna meet them, okay?" On a dime, she was back to spitting. She slammed the glass on the counter and stormed up the stairs, Jason right behind her.

"C'mon, Ma, gimme a break, that's embarrassing."

Shit. Wrong thing to say. His mother whipped around, teased blond strands flying from her head like tiny, angry fists. "Oh, so I'm embarrassing?" She was screaming again. "You're ashamed of your own mother, now?"

Jason could feel his voice rising, whining. He couldn't stop it. "No, Ma, that came out wrong, I just mean, you don't need to meet a girl just because I hang out with her a minute. I mean, I'm just a little old for that shit, Ma, please."

Smack. Her open hand caught him in the jaw before he could deflect it. It didn't hurt much, she wasn't that strong, but he had to put his hand out to the railing to keep from losing his balance, which allowed her to catch him on the other cheek. And that was just too many times to be hit in a day.

"Yeah, it's Prissy fucking Hines, Ma, you might remember her because you worked for her father back when you could hold a goddamn job. So I'm sure she'll be really fucking pleased to see you. Who isn't, you know? You look like a million bucks." The anger was clenching and churning in his stomach and he was choking on his own nasty voice. Everything could break now.

He needn't have worried. It was as if he had never said the words at all, except for the one piece of information he'd conveyed.

"Little Prissy's back?" she squealed, girlish, turning on her heels as if nothing at all had happened. "Just let me freshen up a moment." And she went into the bathroom. The door locked.

Christ.

Jason made his way back down the narrow hallway and opened the door. Pris was still sitting on the bed, face blank. "Check it out, Pris, you wanna ditch? She's kinda crazed right now and she remembers you and shit. You can get out while she's in the john."

Pris was a study in casual. "Why would I not wanna say hi to your mother, Jason? I may act rude as hell but I was brought up right." Her eyes did that narrowy thing and Jason wanted to spin her around and hug her.

Then he wanted to hurl because his mother was in the doorway, talking a hundred miles a minute, not even noticing his muttered "Ma, you remember Prissy. She goes by Pris now."

He did his best to tune it out, how his mother sped from Pris's blue hair to her clothes, to how her wonderful father was, to sorry about the house, it got away from her, it had been such a busy time. Her voice extra bright, eyes dancing, a different person from any of the ones he'd been talking to just minutes before. The edge of her finger kept skimming the bottom of her nose, her nerves, she'd always say when he used to call her on it, her allergies.

Pris was the model of friendly and calm. Jason felt more naked than if she hadn't stopped his accidental striptease.

After what seemed like hours, his mother let them alone with a suggestive eyebrow wiggle that made Jason sick to his stomach. She said something about a girls' night out and was gone.

When Jason finally had the guts to turn to Pris, she was reaching into her pocket to get something, chew, probably. He reached into his own to grab his smokes. Maybe he could smoke three at a time. If he could mainline nicotine, he'd do it.

Instead, Pris held out a wallet opened to the picture sleeves.

"I'll see your mother and raise you one lover," she deadpanned.

In the picture, Pris had even spikier hair. She was curled tight around this young-looking black dude with a Mohawk and many piercings. They were both wearing torn-up denim jackets covered in patches and medals and chains. Very tough and cute. Boyfriend seriously looked more like a girl than Pris did, but Jason didn't say anything—some kids took a while to man up that way and Pris was clearly overcompensating for years of being Prissy.

Boyfriend also looked seven different kinds of into Pris, probably important if you were going to put up with all that relationship crap. The next photo showed them sucking face a lot closer up than Jason wanted to see. At least someone was getting the sex vibe from Pris. Nice for her, anyway.

Pris had her knees hugged to her chest again and had that nervous look. Jason decided that he totally loved that look, like she cared so much about what he thought. He decided he didn't even mind her on his stupid airplane quilt.

"Very cute and tough to leave looking. So dude's black. You said that before. That what the shitstorm with your parents was about?"

There was something a little odd, a little sad, about Pris's smile then. "Kind of," she said, pausing a minute, shaking her head, and then continuing slowly, "Sisulu is half black, half white, but in South Africa, that's more of a problem."

"But you weren't in Africa so—dude's African? South Africa's where white people keep black people in, like, separate towns? And the religious dude named after a ballet costume, and that famous dude in prison that everyone's jacket pin wants to free, and that other dead dude Peter Gabriel sings about?" Jason was hoping at least to get a little smile out of her, even a sad one.

Which he got. But hell if enormous tears weren't streaming down her face. That was definitely not the vibe he'd gotten from the picture. Maybe Pris just missed the kid.

But the words coming out of Pris's mouth were telling a really different story, one that veered the conversation even farther away from Jason's experience than puppy love took it.

"Yeah." The tears were running into her mouth as she spoke. "It's also the country where all my family's money comes from, where it was made by keeping people like Suly down—literally. In diamond mines. The worst. Everything I've ever had. I never thought about it, where it came from. Where it *still* comes from. And I couldn't even tell them no." Pris scrubbed at her face with her hands and then as Jason watched she bit into the palm of her hand, pretty hard, it looked like.

She looked up, eyes blazing and tearing at the same time. "So that's one thing I'm ashamed of, Jason Devlin, and it's a hell of a lot worse than anything you can put up." Her body started shaking in little sobs.

Hell. Hell on wheels. Crying girls. At least this time, Jason hadn't set her off himself. He went over to the bed and sat down next to her. This was, after all, something he was good at, holding girls. He wrapped his arms around her, unhitched her arms from around her knees and pulled her torso into his lap. Pris buried her face into his shirt and he felt her tears making it wet. Rubbing circles into her back, he rocked her slowly.

"C'mon, tough as nails punk rock chick, it's okay." His voice was gentle.

She kept sobbing.

"Pris, you have fuck all to do with your parents' money, okay? You can— you can use it as a weapon, you know? Steal shit and give it to those dudes in prison."

"I stole some diamonds from my grandmother's house. No one even noticed." She sniffled. "I'm joining the ANC out of college and giving them the money."

"That's right, you do that. That'll show 'em," soothed Jason, wondering what the ANC was.

Pris went back to crying in his lap. Jason wondered if he could convince her to take a cigarette break.

"Um, Pris?" Jason moved her head a little to one side, "your weeping girlish wetness is moistening my manhood."

Total stillness. Total silence. And then, convulsion. Bingo. Pris rolled off the bed she was laughing so hard. "Devil man! *Harlequin?!* Samantha and I made our own Sex Ed course on that stuff!"

Whoa. That was information Jason was probably better off not having. Agonized, crying, book-giving friend be damned, his mind and all his other parts were flooded with the image of Samantha Ward, a too young version of her, cuddled up on a sleeping bag reading vanilla smut, maybe over matching ice cream.

He muttered something about living Harlequin so he didn't need to read it and hoped the way his heart had totally stopped and his pants were getting all tight and funny-looking was not going to get noticed.

No such luck. Pris's tear-reddened eyes narrowed, the smeared eyeliner accentuating the usual effect. "Huh. So, Devil's bargain, just how bad do you have it for my ex-best friend that you hate?"

Jason found a hole in his jeans suddenly fascinating. "On what fucking planet?"

"Oh, I tell you my biggest shame and you can't cough up a stupid crush? Some friend you are."

"I don't crush. And if I did, it wouldn't be on people I didn't like. I don't like her."

Pris rolled her eyes, then her body, kicking her feet up into the air, then crashing them down at the end of her sentence for a full-body exclamation point. "Jason Devlin, if you think you are the only person to ever be into someone he thinks he shouldn't be into, it's possible that you are wrong as fuck."

He wouldn't meet her eyes.

"Okay, so, for the love of the Velvet Underground and all that is holy, just how bad do you have it?" She gestured toward her boot. "And don't make me kick you on your own bed."

Jason flopped backwards and pressed the palms of his hands into his eyes. Hard. "Only a little bit fucking bad, okay? But what's not to like? She set me up to get jumped and told the entire school that it was all about our spanking man crush. I act beyond evil to her and my palms sweat looking at her and I hate guys that talk to her almost as much as I hate guys who look at her. I am so unbelievably fucked and have become everything in the world I despise. Okay?"

"Sure," said Pris easily.

Jason moved a hand away from one of his eyes and glared at her.

Pris reached over and ruffled Jason's hair. "I don't know if it helps," she said, slowly, "but that scene in the hall? All the tension was between Sam and that Vanessa chick. Swim boy was just kinda there. So I think it was—girl stuff. Not like it wasn't heinous to talk about you that way."

An echo of what Samantha was saying as he was ripping her to shreds flitted through Jason's mind, but he didn't say anything. For whatever reason, he wasn't telling Pris about his little talks with Samantha.

Pris leaned against his bed, her fingers tracing over the shapes of airplanes as she spoke. "And by the way, Devil's bargain? Samantha was spot-on at lunch. I know you don't want to hear it, but it *did* start with the guys. She just walked into it and you know that's true."

Jason stood up and went over to his dresser for an ashtray. He took out another cigarette, the first one having gotten wet from Pris's crying, and lit up. "Did you not catch the part where I said I was beyond evil to her?"

"They do call you the Devil."

"Yeah," he said darkly, taking another drag. "Fuck it. At least I won't have to worry about why she doesn't dig me."

Pris took a pinch of Skoal and reached over into her backpack for an empty juice bottle. Jason tried not to think about the spitting, and for a moment, all was quiet. But something about Pris's own confession was tugging at Jason's thoughts.

"Pris? Why would you be ashamed of things your grandparents and parents did? What does that have to do with you?"

"Right back at you."

Hell, no. Not there. Jason fought for an even tone. "I'm not fucking ashamed of her. She has fuck-all to do with me. But I don't talk about that stuff. Off the fucking table."

"Holy profanity, Batman! You are so fucking tough. Nothing gets to you, does it? I wish I could be that tough." Jason didn't have to look at Pris to know how narrow her eyes were getting.

Jason showed her his middle finger.

"You shouldn't give your mother liquor," said Pris, suddenly simple and serious.

Clenching his eyes shut, Jason gritted out, "Not that I know what the fuck it has to do with you, but she doesn't drink that much. I give her a drink sometimes to try to calm her down. That's the least of her fucking problems, seriously."

"Jason. I know what her fucking problem is, do you?"

"Pris, FUCK!" Jason pushed himself off of his dresser and started pacing. "Listen, you little know-it-all freak. You break into my house and my fucking life and cry all over my pants and that's fine but I don't fucking TALK about this shit, it fixes nothing—and it's none of your fucking business if I give her a drink!" He made to run his hand through his hair, forgetting the lit cigarette in his fingers. The smell of burning hair filled the room. "Fuck." He took another drag. "Listen. It's only gonna be a year. I'm almost seventeen. I just have to get through—I only came here today because I wanted a bath. Because I got jumped this morning and I'm sore as fuck. Which by the way I knew was going to happen. You're right. Samantha didn't set me up. I fucking did it on my own. That way I can see it coming." He kicked the dresser, rattling the contents of the drawers and knocking the ashtray to the ground. "MotherFUCK!" he yelled again, and gave the ashtray a kick too, scattering more ashes.

"Right. Got it. Nice try at changing the subject 'cause you know I love to be right, plus the spilled ashtray is an excellent distraction." Pris's tone hadn't changed a bit. Easy, simple, serious. "Two things and I will never say another word if that's what you really want."

Jason nodded, almost imperceptibly. "Given the stuff we're not going to talk about because that's so goddamn helpful to you, it's possible alcohol could stop your mother's heart. So I don't think you need to go through life knowing you were the one that gave her that drink, even though it would be on her for taking it. Right?"

Silence. Another nod.

"Two, I didn't break in. Door was wide open. So even if this is a fine neighborhood, it might be on the decline. You never know when druggies might move in, and you never know what desperate people who need to get high like they need to breathe might do. Not everyone squatting in London is a doctor or a straight-edge punk, so I know what the fuck I'm talking about, okay? That's a very nice stereo you have there, I'd say it's hands down the most valuable thing in the house, and you work hard for your money. So let's you and me go to the hardware store and get you a lock, okay?

"The lock on the front door works fine. I'll just tell her to be more careful."

"Brilliant idea since she clearly values your opinion. The lock is for your room, shit for brains. For your room. So what she does or doesn't do—with the goddamn lock—can't take anything more from you than it already has."

Pris was staring at him hard, impassive, no attitude. No softness there. Nothing to hit. No easy shot.

"Store's probably closed now," he said miserably. He hated this more than life. More than anything, he hated this. Someone seeing it made it so much more real, so much harder to put away.

"K-mart's open. I have my dad's blood money car outside."

"I want a bath."

"I'll clean out your tub when you get back."

"The fuck you will." The cigarette cherry crumbled as he ground it into his ashtray, burning the tips of his fingers.

"I moistened your man parts with my girlish wetness. I gotta do something."

He managed a leer. "Over the bra and we'll call it even."

"You're lucky I didn't bite them off while I was down there," she snapped, flipping him off and shrugging herself into her jacket. "C'mon, Devil-may-care. Grab your coat."

In the car, Jason asked how she'd found him. To his surprise, she'd talked to Skinny.

"Yeah, I told him we didn't need to pull you apart between us since we both had your back." Pris sighed as she explained, sounding defeated in a way Jason didn't understand or like, but he kept his mouth shut about it, since it was clearly something she was doing for him.

"Okay. So it is totally fucking surprising that you did that." That by way of a thank you.

"Tell me about it. So we agreed that he would not say that shit about girls and gays in front of me, and I would stop threatening to cut his balls off, and he told me where to find you as a peace offering."

"He doesn't come to my house." He looked at Pris pointedly. "No one does."

"Yeah. Well. I don't back off."

"Apparently fucking not."

"Yeah," she said grimly, "so never doubt the extent of my love because you have no idea how hard I had to swallow for that Skinny stuff to go down."

The hell? "You sucked his *dick?*"

"NO! Metaphor!" Pris sounded suitably horrified. "Pay more attention in English class or something. You're lucky I didn't just barf all over you."

Jason grabbed at his ears with his hands. "Jesus. Don't talk about love *or* swallowing and Skinny at the same time, or I'll ralph all over the blood money car."

"Oh, that's right," Pris kept her eyes on the road, "I forgot for a minute that you are so fucking tough that nothing in the world pierces your surplus store armor unless it's to make you puke in disdain." Jason caught a little smile creeping up the side of her face though, and he could feel one of his own join it.

"Yeah, well, don't forget shit like that. It's careless."

IN BETWEEN DAYS

How had it come to this? She moved the towel a moment, checking for shock. His hair, the back seat, her lap, all of it sticky with blood. It was what everyone said about head wounds, that they bled a lot. It was what everyone said when they were covered in blood. She brushed the sticky, dark strands from the face beneath them. The face itself was chillingly pale, but the hand in hers squeezed back.

The ones who weren't bleeding downed NoDoz with cans of Coke, cranked Suicidal Tendencies on the car stereo. When anyone's voice shook, none of the others mentioned it.

"I got a bunch of money. And some jewelry."

"Did you tell anyone what was going on?"

"How could I? I don't even know. I just said it was for me, that works better anyway."

She knew enough about money to know it was better to have it than not. So she'd spent the day telling stories: she'd dented her dad's Jaguar, lost her mom's pearl earrings, spilled rum and Cokes down her cousin's couture dress, torn her own couture dress in the backseat of whoever's car. Her father/mother/cousin/designer would kill her. Murder her dead.

Everyone liked to help out with problems like those.

Little Jah Rubenstein hadn't needed any stories. He'd counted out ten hundreds, no questions. "I know some shit been going down."

Everyone in the car was holding back something, you could feel it in between the words that actually got said. This was hers: It wasn't just money Jah gave her.

She had an ace up her sleeve for a high stakes game. "Rain." Jah wrote the name on an empty nightclub matchbook. "Not nice, but professional, A reference my father gives to clients when they come through town. They were childhood friends. You mention Pa-Jah, whose other name is Simon, and Rain give it to you straight." Jah pressed the bit of cardboard into her hand. "This club. Don't call ahead. Don't say this name loudly, even there. Don't play this card unless the stakes are blood itself. Jah Love protect you."

She sincerely hoped it would.

19. BRICKS IN THE WALL

Samantha had been up half the night baking chocolate chip cookies, removing all traces of crumbs and batter from the kitchen so as not to make more work for Ernestine, the maid paid to clean up her crumbs. The cookies needed to be all from Samantha so that the love talisman would work and keep Stephen safe forever.

Or something.

She'd mailed the package this morning, covering the brown paper wrapping with shiny, girly paint pen hearts.

In her new mall clothes, she looked like a birthday cake, she thought. Frosted lipstick and shimmery eyeshadow. So much for tough girl.

Keep 'em guessing.

Or something.

Vanessa Segal was glaring death at her and someone had written "Burnout Whore" on Samantha's locker and someone else had washed it off and someone had written "Swim Slut" and someone else had washed *that* off and the ghosts of the words blended and blurred together in the gray.

People she swore she'd never seen were giving her high fives in the hall.

Samantha warned Kim Sato to keep her distance in public. Kim should put her cheering first. Kim looked hurt. "I'm a better friend than that, Sam," she'd said.

"I know, buttface. Just not in the halls. We're not messing up all that hard work."

Kim on cheer was the one good thing Samantha saw at Highland. She was proud she'd helped make it happen, and she wasn't about to let it go sour because of *her* dumb problems.

It had started this way. Kim was Samantha's lab partner in Earth Science freshman year and the two of them took turns prodding Jessica awake.

Samantha studied with Kim and when they'd both do well, the teacher would thank Kim for helping. Kim would look down, embarrassed, and say it wasn't like that, and the teacher would smile indulgently.

But it was true, the blonde girl was the brain and the Asian-looking one was kind of a ditz, even though no one ever imagined that was how it worked. Kim was shy and a little mousy, always running off after school to some activity, but Samantha had remembered her from ballet, and Jessica knew her from gymnastics, and then one day they'd seen her watching the cheer practice from behind the bleachers, hidden but jumping along with the squad.

Samantha and Jessica began to have an idea. They'd conferred, they'd plotted, and they'd ambushed Kim Sato, made her confess her secret over ice cream. Because when Kim had played teenager as a little girl, she'd always been the one with the short pleated skirt and the matching sweater who jumped higher than anyone in school. But when Kimmie finally *was* that teen, no one saw her in the part she'd chosen. Soon enough, not even Kimmie herself.

Samantha and Jessica thought that was dumb. So they'd made Kim an offer she couldn't refuse: be one of us, and you can be one of *them*, too. And sure enough, a few trips to the mall, a haircut, a blush lesson, and a cheer clinic later, Kim made JV hockey squad that year and varsity football the next. The math and science teachers grumbled that Kim Sato wasn't living up to her potential, which made Samantha snort, since Kim had roughly the math potential of an olive. But cheer was her *calling*.

Samantha made this point, strongly, hissing between clenched teeth. Kim shook her head, her mouth growing small and stubborn.

Now Samantha was almost shouting. "Cheer squad was your effing dream, it's the whole reason you're friends with us!"

"Survey says? Zero!" Kim folded her arms. "Try again."

"What*ever!* We are not turning your dream into *The Nightmare on Elm Street* over some dumb swim jock! You have lunch with Richards anyway, we'll still have class and the phone. We just don't need to shove it in your captain's face."

"Whatever," muttered Kim, "I'm still cleaning your locker."

Samantha shrugged. "I'll come to your funeral."

As for the rest of school, Samantha counted on Jessica to take her side, and that was, in fact, a given. Everyone else got a choice. And maybe there would be no sides to take. Maybe Vanessa Segal would think it was beneath her dignity to take on a sophomore.

Crazily enough, Samantha didn't care. About any of it, as far as *she* was concerned.

All she cared about was someone she *wasn't* going to care about, thank you, because she had more self-respect than that.

Or something.

But she *was* getting to Social Studies early so she could talk to her teacher about an important issue in a purely ethical, impersonal way.

Ms. Kanter was sitting at her ever-messy desk, going over a folder full of newspaper clippings and sipping a cold cup of coffee. She looked up when she saw Samantha hovering.

"Are you fidgeting there for a reason, Samantha?"

"Yes, I have an ethical question. About ethics, and—theory. Ms. Kanter, hypothetically speaking, if you knew that someone—like, one of your peers— was doing something bad, do you think you would have an obligation to speak out?"

Mrs. Kanter looked over her glasses at Samantha, instantly serious. She spoke clearly and carefully about moral versus legal obligations, how knowledge of a crime committed could force even hypothetical hands. "With all that in mind, is there anything you need to tell me about, Samantha?"

Crime. No, maybe not? Probably Stagnita was more careful than that. Samantha tried again. "What if it was—more of a—gray area. Like the person doing—the bad thing—was careful to keep it more borderline." Samantha chewed on her lower lip and her hands were shaking. Theoretical ethics could be very stressful. "And what if—in this hypothetical case— there's an institutional element, like we talk about in class. Like, the person doing the harm could be within his job description, but, like, is pushing the limits."

Mrs. Kanter laid her hands flat on the desk, closed her eyes, and took a deep breath. Samantha realized—perhaps too late—that Samantha might be putting her teacher in a bad position.

God, this was complicated.

Samantha distracted herself with a wall display depicting the separation of powers through a series of stylized buildings—Congress, the White

House, the Supreme Court—each with lightning bolts leaping out of them. Something about this struck Samantha as slightly off.

Her teacher reclaimed her attention. "Samantha Ward. This conversation, I take it, is not about girls picking on girls or students here engaging in small-time drug-related activity?"

Samantha shook her head, not meeting the teacher's eye.

"You are not talking about a hypothetical me."

Slowly, Samantha shook her head again.

The poster made her think of electric chairs or electric shock.

Samantha knew she was paying a weird amount of attention to walls, worrying over them as if they held some kind of message beyond what they should. Mallards. Macramé. Even Adam Ant in the arcade.

Brick behind the dumpsters.

None of them seemed quite right to her. Maybe it would pass.

"Samantha. Do you want to tell me about it?"

"I don't know," Samantha said miserably, abandoning the separation of powers. At Highland, they all seemed to be concentrated in one person anyway. "I don't know if it would put you in a bad position, or why—"

Janine Kanter took another deep breath and let it out slowly. She repiled a pile of papers and moved them to the other side of her desk, then spoke. "I should explain, perhaps. In continued hypothetical terms. If I have reason to suspect any maltreatment of a minor child, a category that covers the vast majority of Highland students, I am bound to report it to the Department of Education. There will be an investigation. Hearsay is insufficient for many things, but it is sufficient to require an investigation. But I need to warn you, those can, without concrete evidence, go badly, and then vulnerable people can be left more vulnerable. Now. Again. Is there specific, non-hypothetical information you are giving me?"

Samantha managed to shake her head. "I barely even know—I just saw someone enjoying something that ... shouldn't be enjoyed. And this class makes me think and—"

"Samantha, keep in mind, enjoyment is not a violation." Ms. Kanter's voice was sharper, but not unkind.

Jason had said the same thing. "That's why, no one does anything?"

"No one like me, you mean."

"I didn't say that."

"Samantha, students are always free to speak out."

Samantha rolled her eyes. She couldn't help it. Could someone as smart as Janine Kanter really think that was true? Her next words exploded out of her. "But only some of us get listened to. Only some of us are someone."

Ms. Kanter pursed her lips. "Surely, Samantha—if that were true, you would be one of the—"

"I know. So I told someone that—the student—wasn't no one. Not to me and to my family."

"Your family. That's a little different than who gets to eat at your lunch table." Ms. Kanter's eyes were interested. "Your father who went to Yale with the Vice President's son?"

Samantha blushed beet red. "They were just frat brothers. I thought you'd think it was funny that Bush's son was such a partier. It's not important." Samantha looked down. She didn't mention the family stops for shore dinner in Kennebunkport as they sailed up the coast to Bar Harbor. "Don't tell anyone. It's not the kind of thing you're supposed to talk about, I guess." She paused. "I guess there's a lot of those."

Janine Kanter smiled a little wryly. "It would be nice to know that by saying something we'd at least do no harm. But don't worry, Samantha, your secret decency is safe with me."

The bell rang and students started filing in. Samantha took her regular seat by Kim and concentrated hard on not watching Jason Devlin or noticing where he sat.

It was far away.

It was unclear to Samantha how long she had been occupied by not noticing Jason Devlin when Kanter announced new group work.

"Group number five, Kim Sato, Kwame Bartholomew, Samantha Ward, please welcome Jason Devlin," intoned the teacher, barely pausing to squash the resulting murmur with a single look.

20. HELL IN A BUCKET

Elation was a curious emotion to feel in Social Studies class. Jason Devlin recognized it, named it, and tried to shove it away. He failed. He settled for hiding it and sauntered over to his new group. Someday, sometime, he would do something really nice for Janine Kanter.

Kanter was explaining the assignment: something social blah blah Highland blah blah discussion. Jason had no idea what she was talking about and didn't care.

Because there she was, the girl he'd been dreaming about all night long, and there it was, the only moment he'd really been thinking about all day—despite jocks, and coke dealers, and punk rock chicks, and mothers—let alone school or work.

One evening I seated Beauty on my knees. I found her bitter. And I cursed her.

Okay, so maybe no knees had been involved, but his hand still tingled where it had held hers. He met her eyes and it felt like stars were exploding in his skull.

Or something.

It wasn't even like he'd been dreaming about her tits or legs or anything normal. Just a strip of pale skin on her arm that he'd noticed the day before and had stared at by the dumpsters when he hadn't been able to meet her eyes. He was sure that in the dictionary of guydom, dreaming about someone's arm was a primary definition of totally fucked, and not in the way that would make you high five each other, either.

It was a really pretty couple of inches, though.

Today she was dressed up like some kind of a pirate pop star. Ruffles and brocade. Shimmery everywhere, even her skin. It was fucking beautiful. Stupid, but beautiful as hell.

There was really no doubt, here. He was in plenty of trouble.

He wanted to take her hand again and draw her out of class, out of school, out of town. He wanted to be romantic and poetic and win her with his words.

It pissed him off to no end he wanted any of those things. Not as much as it would piss her off, though, if she knew.

Better to be a dick to her in front of a lot of people. Because that was something he was fucking stellar at.

"Duchess Barbie," he nodded. Barely. Samantha looked down, coloring. Damn. She smiled, just a little. Excellent. "I knew you were going to say that when I bought it," she murmured, shaking her head. More than excellent.

She was thinking about him. When she bought clothes. Was she thinking about him when she was trying them on?

Jason threw himself into the chair next to her, considering how to proceed. Other group members. Right. African dude. Football. Stayed out of fights, not a big partier, kinda boring. But the Asian girl—Pris said she'd been in the hall when Samantha had sold Jason out to the jocks. He had to say, he didn't love that about Asian girl.

"African Ken, Chink Barbie," Jason nodded curtly to each.

The dude ignored him, and the Asian girl curled her lip, but Samantha whipped around, eyes flaming. Bingo. "You idiot, Kim's not even Chinese." She sounded tense, disgusted—and maybe disappointed. Interesting.

Jason smirked. "Wait, so, you're saying, if she *was* Chinese, it would be okay for me to call her Chink Barbie?"

Samantha looked incredulous, "No, I'm not saying that!"

"But I want to use the correct terminology." He turned toward Kim, "So, what kind of Barbie are you?"

African kid glared at him. "You're more of a jerk than you need to be, aren't you, man?"

Jason shrugged. "I don't know. I go for just enough of a jerk. It's a delicate balance." He turned back to Kim, interested in spite of himself. "So, did they forget your voice box when they made you? Do you always let your friends speak for you?"

Kim stared at him. "Only when I'm talking to racist pigs who pick on my best friends in disgusting ways."

Jason raised his eyebrows. "Okay, voice box apparently intact. Interesting policy, by the way, but it shouldn't include me. I'm not racist. Your friend I was disgusting to…" He gestured toward Samantha, who was boring acid holes in his head with her eyes. "…is as white as I am." He looked her up and down appraisingly. "Maybe even a little paler. Under all the makeup, of course."

Kim didn't bat an eye. "I meant sexist, racist pigs. My mistake."

Samantha spat out, "Jason means he's one of those equal opportunity jerks that insults everyone in the grossest way possible and thinks that makes him some great servant of equality."

Jason smiled broadly, nodding. "You got it, babe."

"Sorry to break it to you, but being a pig to everyone doesn't make you a prince." Samantha was practically hissing now. This was so easy.

Much harder to figure out how they'd ended up holding hands, or how to ever get back to doing that again.

Jason's gaze was now full on Samantha, its burn not acid but slow. "Well, I guess you'd know, Princess, how would I go about going all Prince? Dress up like you are? Shrink a few feet? Sing about masturbating?" He lowered his voice and looked at Samantha a little more seriously. "Or maybe just get a princess to kiss me?"

Samantha looked down. No retort. Wow. Her hair hung over her face, so hard to tell, but he could swear she was blushing. Beyond interesting. Stirring, in fact. Harlequin vanilla smut echoes stirring.

Hell on wheels.

The kid Kwame chuckled. "I think sometimes the frog just stays a frog."

Jason shook his head slowly, lips forming their soundless whistle. "Maybe the frog'd be cool with just getting kissed." Just the thought of it, actually, was making him feel something…unfroglike.

"Frogs don't get kissed by princesses," Peppy the Asian snapped, "especially if the frog is all *slimy*."

Oh. What an opening—so to speak. Jason licked his lips—so to speak. Innocent girls should *not* to try to get into it with him. "Don't knock the slime, in the right places, a little something slick—"

Peppy the Asian cut him off. "*God*, why don't you just save it?"

"Too late for that, sweetheart. But your friend here," Jason lowered his voice to a stage whisper, "I think *she's* saving it."

Kim exploded. "Nice try, but you *don't* get out of being racist just by being a dick to everyone!"

Ms. Kanter glared sharply at Kim, then said to the whole class, "Of course, these issues can cause tempers to flare, but I expect the school's rules on language and civility to be respected. You can *discuss* offensive language—but not use it on each other. C'mon, people."

Jason smirked again. He imagined the teacher had not caught his Chink comment. He noticed Peppy's mouth get a little smaller, a little tenser, before she spoke again.

"Anyway, face it, Devlin, confusing me for Chinese? *Is* pretty racist—I mean, Japanese grandfather, Filipina mother—how do you get Chinese out of that?"

Shrugging, Jason looked at her steadily. "Does that bother you? Do you not like Chinese people? Is that, like, an insult for you?"

Samantha at last looked up and narrowed her eyes at Jason, ready to pounce. "Lay off her," she commanded through gritted teeth.

Jason turned to her, wide-eyed innocence. "Why? I'm not going to hurt your favorite toy."

"She's *not*—"

"And I'm interested!"—a side glance at Kanter had him raise his voice slightly—"in social ... institutional ... things. We're supposed to be talking about the stuff, right? That's the point of the class? So I think it's *interesting*"—he paused as Kanter moved on to the back of the room—"you know, in an academic, schoolboy kind of way, that someone would be less upset I called them a stupid racist name than that I got the friggin' country wrong."

Even as he spoke, the thought came to Jason that a commanding princess would be a main character in a series of fantasies he'd be having soon. She could be the sister of the blushing princess, they could take turns.

Hell in a bucket.

Kim's mouth was small and her voice was shaking. "Take back 'toy.'"

So they were still on that. "Why? I hear she dresses you. Isn't that what girls do with their dolls?"

"Devlin, man." Kwame sounded dead serious. "You should *know* better, man, even you. Maybe *especially* you."

Jason was quiet a minute. Kwame wasn't a big talker, he knew that much. "Fine." He turned back to Peppy. "I will never again so much suggest you are a toy—Barbie."

Kim leaned forward, intense. "Seriously, have you considered professional help?"

Jason leaned forward, mimicking her. "Seriously, do you not like Chinese people?" He raised his voice. "Let's have a cultural encounter. For the *assignment.*"

"Kim is *from* your effing culture, dickwad." Hissing Duchess Barbie. An Exciting Playtime Experience from Mattel.

"It's fine, Sam, whatever." Kim sighed. "Look, Devlin, I don't even know any Chinese people. I just think it's stupid the way everyone assumes, like, everyone with eye folds is the same." She shrugged. "I'm a total mix, I've never been anywhere in Asia, so it's annoying when people think I'm some kind of expert on Chop Suey, or whatever. And if you could get out of your own head for one second, you'd understand. But I don't expect miracles."

So maybe Peppy had a point, but how the fuck would Jason know the ins and outs of Asian features? His last world tour? He leaned in. "Right. How *ignorant* of people. So. I'd get this perspective on the rich variety of Asian chick—where exactly? there's what, five Oriental kids in the whole school? And guess what? Not one of them lives in my neighborhood."

Kim raised her eyebrows, but African Ken jumped in, pointedly addressing Kim rather than Jason. "I get what you're saying. I mean—even my parents, I'm from Eritrea and when they adopted me they named me Kwame. Turns out it's Ghanaian or something. They just wanted something African, like it's one big country instead of all these people who look and talk totally different and fight each other in wars. I could get annoyed. But I just figure,"— he nodded briefly in Jason's direction—"how would they know? They're from the Chicago suburbs. They meant well."

Kim murmured that she liked the name Kwame and suddenly seemed unable to lift her eyes.

Great. They'd gone from UN hour into the middle of some United Colors of Benetton love story. It was a little nauseating.

Plus, their cutesiness made it more pronounced how he couldn't talk to Samantha except to hurt her, when really, he wouldn't mind it if she couldn't look at him in a *sweet* way, while whispering things she liked about him.

Instead, Samantha was actively not looking at Jason in a decidedly unsweet way, muttering something about not everyone meaning well.

Jason eyed her. "Would it matter if I did?" he asked, softly enough that he was pretty sure no one but her would hear.

But Kwame was still talking to Asian Barbie and apparently that was much more fascinating to Samantha than any attempt at actual human communication Jason could offer.

Kwame was saying he thought Kim was a Korean name. Riveting stuff.

Kim blushed furiously as Samantha answered for her once again, giving Kim a playful shove, "Yeah, unless your grandmother from Iowa is named Kimberly."

Kwame smiled wide. "That's beautiful." Kim looked at him shyly and smiled back. Benetton wedding bells were no doubt ringing. Kwame turned back to glare at Jason. "Just watch it with the Chink comments, got it? They're messed up and they make you look ignorant."

Jason felt that burn of rage starting up again. Samantha had blown off his attempt to connect a little or whatever, and on top of that this Ken doll was holier-than-thouing in his face, trying to make him look bad.

Not like he needed any help with that, maybe. Sure, Chink was a jerkoff thing to say. But really—as if Jason was the one in this group who *really* made snap judgments about people based on appearance or made them feel like shit for where they came from.

Jason smirked, not nicely. He leaned back in his chair and stared at Kwame. "Fair enough. Pan-Asian-Iowegian Barbie it is. 'Cause we wouldn't want to use any slurs—like, I don't know, scum? Loser? We're above that, right?" He turned directly toward Kim. "People who talk like that are messed up and ignorant, right?"

From Kim's expression, he was pretty sure she knew *exactly* who and what he was referring to. He didn't even try looking at Samantha.

Instead, he raised his hand.

The teacher nodded permission to speak.

"Ms. Kanter—we were wondering, there's racist, right, and sexist—but what do you call it when people look down on people based on what neighborhood they're from, or what their parents do, or what clothes they wear, or whatever?"

"That would be classist, Mr. Devlin. And classist behavior is a huge problem in many schools—Highland being obviously no exception. Excellent question, thank you."

Kanter opened the question out to the class as a whole, asking them to look for instances of class prejudice at school. Of course people had a lot to say—Jason Devlin had started a big, serious discussion.

It wasn't lost on Jason that Ms. Kanter was making an effort to show him some respect, and in public—it had been kind of a basic question, not that excellent at all. He thought this was pretty decent of her.

In fact, Jason Devlin couldn't believe a teacher had kind of taken his side against the Barbies and the jocks—or at least named the feeling that gnawed at him. He didn't know what the hell he could do for Janine Kanter, but he would think of something and when he did, it would be something pretty nice.

And he would do his fucking homework, too.

He stole a glance at Samantha, who was looking down. Again.

God, she was pretty, though. She'd looked good all tough and sexy yesterday and she looked good all shimmery and duchessy today. And here he was, sitting next to her.

So Jason was able to ease back into a good mood. At the very least, he had a whole new classroom full of people to rub the wrong way, maybe make them think a little about how things went down at this stupid hell-hole of a school. And, from the looks of it, a second halfway-decent teacher in exchange for a tweaky cradle-robbing scumbag.

Yep. Janine Kanter was definitely the tits. Well—he glanced briefly upwards—in a manner of speaking, only. So she was flat as a board and none too pretty. She still kinda rocked.

And Samantha Ward, no matter what else she had going on underneath all that crazy pretty hair, sure as hell wasn't looking through him anymore. And as for *her* tits—

Jesus. He had to stop doing that in class. It got so uncomfortable.

All in all, though, things were looking up.

Maybe he'd hang with Dylan Dougherty after school, blast some bootlegs with his Deadhead crowd and just chill. Play some hackey sack, crack a beer. Dylan could spill his guts about his massive crush on Pris and Jason could keep his mouth shut about his massive crush on her ex-best friend. It would all be, what did those kids always say? Copacetic.

It would be like Jason was any other kid, hanging in some basement, chilling to tunes, crushing on a girl who wouldn't give him the time of day. Mothers and door locks and principals be damned.

Then he'd head over for his Wednesday night veggie special.

Jason's mind drifted back to class, Kanter deep into a wrap-up lecture. He'd paid enough attention in class for one period, though. Instead, he listened to the song looping through his head that would get louder whenever he glanced at the grouchy princess next to him.

I may be going to hell in a bucket . . . The white ruffles by her throat made her skin look creamier, a contrast of pale on pale. Jason wondered idly if her skin beneath her jaw had ever been bruised by a mouth, sucking and biting while she . . . probably not. Jason shifted in his seat.

But at least I'm enjoying the ride . . . Yeah, that was one ride he would definitely enjoy the hell out of.

Christ, man, he chided himself, *can you cut that out?* Jason looked around quickly. One of these days he was going to say something like that out loud. He had to get a grip.

Suddenly, a pen clattered to the ground by his desk. Samantha reached down to pick it up, and Jason almost fell out of his chair seeing that she'd left a tiny crumpled paper on the floor where the pen had been.

And fuck him if his heart wasn't in his goddamn mouth. He could feel it pounding in his throat and weirdly behind his lungs at the same time. He felt a little sick, too, like he'd just smoked a filterless cigarette way too fast. Idiot body. Adrenalin rush from a crumpled maybe note from a bitchy rich girl.

He waited a minute. The last thing he wanted to look like was eager, for Christ's sake. He also didn't feel like anyone else in the room needed to get the idea that he was even halfway interested in picking up whatever scraps Samantha Ward deigned to drop at his feet.

But he motherfucking was. More than halfway. More than all the way. He was gone. He moved his foot over the piece of paper and gently drew it further under his desk.

The clock on the wall had the slowest second hand known to man, or Jason was caught in a time warp, the only things in the room him, his note, and Samantha Ward just outside his field of vision. In his field of vision there was just the stupid clock and some even stupider cartoons of buildings getting destroyed by electrical storms or some shit. What fucking ever.

When he judged a reasonable interlude had passed he bent down to adjust the tongue of his boot and grabbed the wad of paper. He fingered its torn paper edges as he shoved it in his pocket. He could feel it there, small as it was, pressing against the skin of his thigh through the thin cotton of the pocket lining.

No way in hell he was getting hard from a fucking piece of notebook paper. No.

No way in hell he was looking at it in front of people, either. He'd keep right on with the stupid buildings and their lightning bolts.

Except then, because he was clearly a fucking idiot with not one tiny shred of self-control left in him, the paper was in his hand again, under his desk but in plain sight of anyone, say, sitting next to him who would have put it there and wanted to watch him make a fool out of himself. He could have played it cool for what, five more minutes? But no. The paper was in his hand and he was uncrumpling it, slowly but with idiot hands *shaking*. He was sure he looked cool as hell.

The girly handwriting was rounded but not bubbly in that junior high way, a little grown up, actually really pretty, even on a crumpled, stepped on scrap of paper. It said, "Yes, it would matter."

The buzzing spread through his body like a swarm of happy bees. He felt one side of his mouth turn up despite his best efforts. Then he reached up and put the paper in the pocket of his flannel shirt, counting himself lucky that he'd managed not to nuzzle it or something.

If Jason had looked back, he would have seen Kim Sato's eyes on him, a different, thoughtful look on her face. The gaze shifted from Samantha to Jason and back, and her smooth brow showed a little furrow.

But Jason never looked.

21. HOLIDAY IN CAMBODIA

For the second time in twenty-four hours, Samantha Ward was in her kitchen late at night, trying to right massive wrongs through food. This time with carrots. And maybe mushrooms, or cabbage.

God. How could she have been so stupid?

It had been such a relief to go off with Ernestine. School was still a game, but these days, she was the chess piece they all liked moving. The worst of it was, Samantha didn't even care.

Would it matter? He'd asked. He'd *asked.* As if it mattered to him.

It had made her scribble out an answer to drop on the floor, not daring to breathe as he read it. He hadn't looked mad, but then, she wouldn't know, because he left without so much as a glance in her direction

In the hall, *he* was always surrounded—three, sometimes four girls at once *fawning* on him. He played with their hair. When he kissed one of them on the neck, the others just giggled.

As if he'd give her the time of day when he was getting anything a guy could want before he even had the chance to want it. And exactly what time of day did she want him to give her? Samantha couldn't, could not *even* believe, that she was thinking these things about Jason Devlin.

So simply serving hungry people had seemed like a balm. For once, in the florescent glow of a church basement, Samantha hadn't felt her presence as an insult to the people she was feeding. All the servers weren't dressed like her mom. Most of the women wearing aprons beside her were black while many of the hungry people weren't, and Ernestine's easy, joking way had helped Samantha's manner ease as well.

People smiled back at her like they meant it.

She joked with a mother who had several children in tow, assuring them that vegetables would in fact make them grow as tall as she was one day. They looked impressed and let her pile their plates with green beans and squash. She flirted with a tall, battered but still good-looking man old enough to be her father. The flirtation earned them both a *look* from Ernestine, but the man just winked as Samantha prettily shrugged her shoulders, and then they all laughed.

No one here, Samantha reflected on her way to the soda machines during break, thought she was plastic.

Getting lost in these thoughts made her distracted, unprepared for the glare that met her as she looked up at the person she'd bumped into.

Whose body she had pressed against in uncharacteristic clumsiness. Whose arm she had grasped to keep from falling. Who had jumped back from the contact as soon as he'd seen her face, as if her body burned unpleasantly. Who was staring at her with an expression she couldn't name. Although she could name the face that went with it well enough.

Samantha felt all the blood in her body rush to her face. Beyond flustered, she could not fathom what had brought him here. She was in a soup kitchen in *Ernestine's* neighborhood. But there he was, tormenter, tormented, annoyingly beautiful handholder, in the middle of a Baptist church basement.

She was stained with green beans, smeared with gravy, and probably smelled like pork.

And that look on his face—there weren't words for it.

She fought for control as she all but stammered, "What brings *you* here, community service hours or something?"

Under the bright lights of her own kitchen, Samantha cringed at the memory. She chopped garlic furiously, the fine German steel blade moving fast in pace with her heightened pulse. The small, slippery cloves, the too large knife, the tears clouding her vision made the slice into her finger inevitable.

"That's right, Princess Barbie. Why else would someone come here?" He'd spat the words, as sure as he'd spat on the ground at her feet the day before. It felt like he wished his words were a whip.

And then he'd stalked away, rage seething out of him in visible, toxic waves.

Samantha had run to the bathroom, curled into herself on a toilet seat, beyond thought. It was beyond thought that anyone could hate her as much as that sneer had hated her. It was beyond thought that she could have deserved it.

Wincing at the memory, she brought her cut finger to her mouth, sucking red and salt and copper.

"Just a flesh wound," she muttered out loud. A ghost of a sad smile crept up her face.

Perched on the toilet, knees scrunched to her chin, Samantha had thought herself back to middle-school sleepovers, huddled in sleeping bags between Stephen and Prissy Hines. Memories she kept for the bad times, hugs from the past she didn't want to get used up.

The plaid flannel of the sleeping bag linings clashed with the plaid of their matching pajamas. Samantha and Prissy insisted on having pjs just like Stephen. They'd burned their flower print, lace-collared nightgowns in a campfire down by the tennis courts and slept naked until they got their way.

They could all of them recite every line of every movie in the Wards' library, even *Harold and Maude,* accidentally mislabeled as *Lady and the Tramp.* Monty Python was weekly, they held hands tightly as their mouths moved to the words on the screen.

So that years later, alone in the strange church basement, in the silence of her bathroom stall, Samantha could whisper "Come back here and get what's coming to you. I'll bite your bloody leg off." And it was enough.

She squared her shoulders and returned to the serving line. She could give the semblance, at least, of the ease she had truly felt before. What was she *for,* if not keeping up appearances? It was her family's life work.

But inside, his voice in her head echoed her own. *Stupid. Stupid. Plastic. Pathetic excuse. Playing at being human.*

She would not, *would not* cry.

Just then a low, flirty voice—a tone she'd never heard, but a voice she knew—said the words, "Hey, gorgeous. Looks like I just couldn't stay away from you."

The small choking sound came from Samantha. As she opened her eyes, she saw Jason Devlin, his lips curving up further on one side than the other and his eyes looking warm and teasing.

At Ernestine.

Ernestine looked like she might be *blushing.* Wow. Samantha hadn't really known black people did that and this thought made her squirm. *Stupid. Stupid. Plastic.*

"You're late, Mr. Movie Star." Strong, unflappable Ernestine sounded like a little girl playing grownup. "I thought you stood me up."

Jason shook his head. "Like I'd miss out on seeing you."

Ernestine turned to Samantha. "Ladykiller here will have all the vegetables you can pile on his plate." She simpered. *Simpered.* Ernestine. Samantha's world was undone. "Don't ask him why, he'll just tell you he packs his own meat." And the world's most unflappable housekeeper dug a knowing elbow into Samantha's side and giggled. *Giggled.*

The effect on Ernestine was shocking, but this scene meant something else, too.

Samantha felt the walls becoming distinct again. The barest glance revealed stains, smudges, a bulletin board boasting posters of Alcoholics Anonymous meetings, youth group, Bible discussion, various musical events. The cork behind these notices was a rich brown, darker than your average corkboard, really.

He was a regular. He came here every week. Jason Devlin was here because he was hungry.

It was just her own voice scolding her now, the way she might have taken down some interloper at school. *Duh, Samantha. Way to pick a fair fight. Plan your battles over a game in the billiards room. Or a spot of tennis out by the courts. Or maybe Daddy could take you back to the family shooting range and go a few rounds there.*

Ernestine nudged her. "Now, Samantha, close your mouth to keep the drool in and don't let Mr. Movie Star here distract you from your job—though you wouldn't be the first. But give the boy some food."

Which was, after all, what she was there for.

So, Samantha smiled up at Jason Devlin, who was looking straight at her, plate outstretched. If she wanted to see walls, she didn't have to look any further, because they were tall and stark all around him. The smile froze on her face.

Samantha gave him as many vegetables as a plate could possibly hold. "Enjoy your meal," she said, inanely.

It wasn't like she hadn't known that people went hungry. She just didn't know they went to her school. The image of Bethany complaining that her father had replaced her broken Sony Walkman with a Panasonic flitted unbidden through her mind. "He did it just to punish me," she'd whined, "Like who has *Panasonic?*"

Ernestine had laughed at Samantha's supposed reaction to Mr. Movie Star all the way home, and Samantha just took it. There was no amount of discomfort she didn't deserve.

The oil in the wok was a perfect temperature.

He was going to hate it that she brought him food, but she was going to hate herself if she didn't. If you had as much as Samantha did and your enemy had nothing, you had to feed him. Maybe. What *was* the proper response to seeing your high school enemy in a food line? Did Emily Post cover that?

And if it was an enemy you also secretly held hands with, so secretly it was as if you didn't want your own selves to find out? Where was the etiquette manual on that? Maybe the next time the Wards stopped off in Kennebunkport as they sailed to Bar Harbor, they could work with Bushes on an educational campaign.

"This is drugs," Samantha told the wok on the stove. "And this is your vegetables on drugs," she said out loud. Samantha stirred the ingredients and listened to them sizzle as their colors grew bright in the pan.

IN BETWEEN DAYS

Thank God they changed the music from the whining and pounding. Now, a gravel voice and mingling cellos filled the car. He knew the song, but the voice was different, soft and very close to him. He knew it, too.

It made him want to be less ugly on the inside.

Shame, then, that he seemed to be lying in a pool of blood by a dumpster in an alley.

Was that where he was? It was warmer, then colder, and the ground was rough, then soft, and there were streaming trails of light.

Maybe he'd just slip away.

Wave. Pain. Every breath a knife. Head hurt, hands in his hair, stroking. The lightest touch, nice through the pain. Maybe his mother, back from the store. Maybe she'd brought cookies. She almost always did.

Rich 'n Chips. His sister's favorite. He said he liked them too, because he loved it when his sister smiled. Really, he liked the elves on the package but he thought the chocolate tasted like plastic. Mom knew. She knew he secretly liked Hydrox best, liked breaking them apart and licking the white from the black and saying Hi to a Drox like on TV. On paydays, she bought both kinds and smiled her secret smile at him and ruffled his hair and called him big guy.

And at night she'd come, take the rings off her fingers and stroke his hair, even when she got home late. And he'd slip away, back to sleep, warm, and safe. It was like that, but now the night was grayer, like his rocket ship nightlight was burned out.

22. SHE DON'T LIE

"I don't know, man. That just fucking sucked." Jason Devlin blew smoke rings into the predawn air. They floated ghostlike up against the line the trees made in the sky above his head. Everything around him was gray.

"All the soup kitchens in all the towns in all the world, right?" It was worse than anything.

Another drag. His body ached with cold already, his fingers frigid. The gas station coffee in the Styrofoam cup was long cooled. He leaned up against Mr. Studebaker's stone and felt the ice bone cold against his back.

The battered watch in his hand told him it was 5:30 in the morning. The sun would be out soon. He turned around to pound Mr. Studebaker's gravestone gently with the fleshy part of his fist.

"I like it how you don't feel like you have to talk, you know, man?"

He ran his hand through his hair, this time careful to transfer the cigarette first.

Jesus. Samantha Ward in a goddamn church basement, dishing pork to the poor. And there he was, plate in hand, competing for the pathetic pansyass pussy of the year award.

What a bad goddamn day for Jason and the world of green food.

"A salad, Jase? A fucking *salad* you're bringing me now?"

Jason flinched. The memory was too clear. Out here in the open, the familiar stones and trees offered no cover. The words played and echoed around him in the cold, as loud as if they'd been spoken there.

He'd known that salad wasn't going to go over well. They'd never sent a salad before, and it wasn't all sealed up like usual.

Of course, she barely even ate the food anyway, but one thing about his mother, she really liked to know what to expect. Jason must have looked nervous because Harry had boomed from behind him. "Don't worry, kid, chicks love salad."

"It's, um—thanks Harry, but—should we, you know, tape it up, like usual?" Jason was shuffling his feet, aware he sounded like some twelve-year-old loser trying to make good with the big kids.

"Doesn't need taped up," Harry boomed. "Isn't warm. Tell her I sent it and if she wants different she can see me about it." The tone of Harry's voice was for sure not announcing a question and answer session—and it *was* fucking charity, after all. His mom could suck it up.

It was what you did when stuff sucked and you were hungry. You sucked it up, whatever it was that went along with the food. Jason closed his eyes and saw Samantha's shocked, frozen eyes but found that they weren't, after all, the worst thing. And they couldn't bring him out of the next scene's replay.

In the dim light of their filthy kitchen, his mother's voice had been scratchy, crow-like. "Wait a just a minute, you little twerp. Are you trying to mess with me?" She looked at him sharply, it was not a version of her he knew. "It's like that filthy little bitch was back again, do you hear me?" she muttered. It wasn't even clear who she was talking to.

But it was clear who she was talking about. He'd punched out half the school for less than what he'd just heard, but in his own house he was paralyzed.

Jason hated looking but he couldn't stop. His mother was pawing through the iceberg lettuce and bits of turkey and tomato like a fucking animal, her hands greasy, shaking, blind. Then she threw a handful against the wall by Jason's head. Lettuce crawled down the wall like those sticky rubber spiders that come in cereal boxes sometimes. Tiny drops of dressing prickled on Jason's ear. He didn't move.

He'd known she wouldn't like the salad.

He hung his head, waiting. She was screaming again. He wanted to leave, but that shit Pris had said the other day about hearts stopping was still bouncing around the back of his mind, casting shadows.

"Don't you think you can pull this shit on me!" Her face was right in his, she was spitting as she spoke and the parts of her face were twitching independently like they all had lives of their own. "Enough of this bullshit. Where the *fuck* is my *coke,* Jase, huh?"

And then Jason was at some distance from himself, jittery and calm at the same time. It was like watching his body do stuff he wasn't telling it to do while words he hadn't thought of came tumbling out of his mouth. Like someone had hit play on the Jason game and he was watching the show.

"God, ma, calm down. Harry said you'd like the salad. He said you could talk to him about it, okay? I mean—it's not like he has to send it. And I'll go get you some drinks, okay?"

The loser twelve-year-old had taken over Jason's body and was using him for a mouthpiece. But Jason didn't even care this time.

Babbling like that, he backed up to the door. He ran out of the house to the convenience store around the corner, shaking and sick, flying that adrenalin high and still feeling like a video game version of himself.

He knew what was happening but it was like he didn't know it at the same time. It was probably the split between him and his body that made everything look a little weird around the edges.

So weird that he got lost in the drinks aisle, confused by lines of sodas flashing under an old florescent bulb. You'd think it would be simple, regular or diet, but there was the question of bottles or cans or even the soda fountain, so he bought one of each, balancing the fountain drinks in a little cardboard tray and carrying the different cans and bottles home in a bag. He spent all his money.

She was barreling down the stairs, hair combed, make-up fixed. She looked at Jason standing in the kitchen carrying half a dozen Cokes and barked at him, her voice hollow and scratchy and mean. "I suppose you think that's funny," she sneered. "Well, *you'll* learn." And she was gone.

In a minute, so was he. He shoved the drinks in the empty fridge and ran up the stairs three at a time to grab a change from his clean clothes pile. He made triple sure to lock his room on the way out.

Jason couldn't stay the night at Cindy's, though, he realized soon after she'd let him in at the window and he'd removed her hands and mouth from him. No matter how good it might feel to bury himself in someone warm and caring and soft, it hadn't even felt right in the *hall* nuzzling up with Tracy or whoever the hell it had been.

It was a hard, fast rule. When Jason was with a girl, he was with *her*. Even if the girls didn't know the difference, *he* did. He wasn't with one girl while thinking about another, ever.

And he couldn't stop thinking about Samantha Ward to save his life. She was *far* out of his league, as the rich variety of his evening had made clear as fucking crystal—and still, he couldn't stop for anything.

This was his league, right here. His league and a step up. Cindy's room was small and unassuming, tapestry on the wall clashing with the Snoopy and Woodstock comforter and the Loverboy posters. The poorly hidden dragon-shaped bong clashed with the cut-out Tiger Beat heartthrobs pinned around her girly light-up mirror.

It looked like someone *lived* here, though. Unlike his house that at best looked haunted by stale ghosts. Jason fingered a Cabbage Patch doll on the bed.

"It's my little sister's," Cindy blew a plume of smoke into the air above her bed. "She leaves it here when she's over at her dad's so I don't get lonely." Her smile was sad.

Jason knew he wouldn't have to feel ashamed telling anything to Cindy, she was a friend as well as a sometimes ... whatever it was girls were to him, when they did stuff together that a lot of people probably thought friends shouldn't do.

But Jason *was* her friend, too, and as such he had to get the hell out there.

So he got warm in Cindy's room instead of in Cindy, bummed a couple dollars and a few cigarettes, kissed her cheek and was back out on the street.

He'd tried to stop by Skinny's but he wasn't home. Kid kept no kind of hours and for all Jason knew, he was still at Del Lanes, which was the very last place on earth Jason wanted to go. It was beyond bad to run into his mom on a "night out." And as for any other guys from school, he'd had enough looking like a pussy in public for one night.

So Jason had killed time wandering around the closed-up shops and brightly lit bar-restaurants of downtown Highland. The cutesy fake-looking white buildings with the big black beams on the outside and gold letter signs made him want to smash things.

When the last yuppies stumbled out of the wine bars into their waiting cars and cabs and the air got colder, Jason found a foyer. It kept him out of the cold, but the tile was clammy and hard enough that he was well into regretting his Cindy-inspired decency when a cop showed up to move him on toward a coffee from the Shell station. From there he walked to pay a visit to Mr. Studebaker.

Jason supposed he should be grateful how the cops mostly knew his mother and so didn't bother hauling him in to the station or taking him home if they found him sleeping out. Didn't happen often enough to create a public nuisance or raise any prominent Highland eyebrows that were tired of being raised at stuff anyway.

At six, Jason's "graveyard" shift ended and he spent his last change on rent at a table at the diner where he finished Shakespeare paragraph number seventeen hundred and twelve and nursed a butter roll and bad coffee for another hour.

He pulled out the book Pris had given him. "Life is the farce we all have to lead." Damn straight.

It was enough to get him to school, anyway, early so he'd be spared any chance encounters with Miss Young Charity. But since Rimbaud was right on the money about the farce of life, apparently, Samantha was there early too, waiting on the steps.

Her hair was pulled back in one of those low ponytails that Jason usually hated but on her of course looked excellent like every other thing she put on that would look stupid on someone else. Offered not one tiny bit of cover from her eyes, though. He barely looked at her, and was about to walk right past her but she called his name, and then he *had* to look.

Sure enough, they were big and blue and knee-numbing like usual, but also every bit as pitying as he'd feared, and on top of that they looked extra dark and strained, like she hadn't slept much. On top of *that*, they look like they were having trouble meeting his and she looked all slumped and—*tamed.*

Fuck this. Fuck Shakespeare. Who wanted *tame?*

"What?" He snapped, hoping for at least a rise but too tired to come up with anything clever. Feeling like this was probably how arsonists got made.

"Look," she said, pityingly, a nightmare his sleepless night had spared him. "I don't want to fight with you anymore." And Jason felt something sink into his stomach and rise in his throat at the same time.

Of course she didn't. Highland girls don't play with soup kitchen boys. "Well, fuck off, then," he growled, at least finding the strength to stalk off without looking back.

But the day just wouldn't let up. Twenty minutes into first period he got called to the front office, for what offense he had no clue. His feet felt like lead in the hall, but the lead was no help in steeling himself for what was coming. Maybe he would go to fucking child welfare. Maybe he would see if someone, anyone, could help him.

Then he remembered Skinny's stories about foster before he got placed with his gran, who might be a drunk but at least didn't beat the shit out of him or rob him blind for dope like some of the homes had.

Jason tried to square his shoulders but they still hurt bad from Tuesday's fight, worse after his night of cuddling cold tiles and tombstones. He closed his eyes and saw Samantha Ward's pitying blue ones staring through the dark. Stagnita, he decided, was better, and he swaggered into the office.

But Anthony Stagnita practically shied away from him, his face almost furtive. He went straight into his office and slammed the door, hard, shaking the little white letter S so hard it fell down at a slant across the beige.

Fucking weird.

Someone had left a paper bag with Jason's name on it. He asked where it came from and the secretary shrugged. "I don't know, your mother? We checked it out, don't get your hopes up. No knife, no pot."

"Why didn't you just save me the trip then?" Jason growled. He grabbed the bag and looked inside to find a Tupperware container. Vegetables.

Seething, Jason waited after class where he remembered seeing Samantha Monday morning, a scene now seared into his brain. She walked by him as if nothing had changed. As if he was still no one, nothing to her. She didn't spare him a glance. She just opened her locker, replacing a book and looking for something inside.

Jason's hand slammed down hard on the locker next to hers, flesh on steel clanging loud metallic anger, his arm and his rage blocking her path.

Jason shoved the brown lunch bag crumpled in his other fist in Samantha's startled face. "What the fuck is this?" His voice nearly contained its rage but his hand around the bag was shaking.

Samantha looked at the bag, then at Jason, then the bag again. "Well," she said, "if it's anything like who's holding it, I'm guessing it's full of shit." She smiled widely and fakely. "Do I win?"

"Don't play cute with me. It's filled with *fucking vegetables.* I'm not a charity case, Samantha."

She grabbed a notebook from her locker, laughing. "Listen, Satan spawn, let's get this straight." Then she lowered her voice and looked into his eyes and Jason felt it in his stomach and lower. "You think that because you have some stupid burnout scam going, where you fake out the nice church ladies so they'll feed you when you're stoned or whatever, I'm going to feel *sorry* for you?" She shook her head, overcome with fake concern. "You're doing *way* too many drugs."

Her eyes were cold blue, beautiful, alive with scorn and not a trace of pity. He didn't really have words. He had butterflies in place of words.

Hell. She kept talking as he stared at her like the biggest fucking idiot with a bag full of vegetables the world had ever seen.

"Jason Devlin, you must have an ego the size of that lake over there. I mean, you have *how* many girls following you around, hanging on your every word and ... appendage." All hint of that blushing girl from the cafeteria Monday gone. "And I'm sure any one of them would *swoon* at the thought you might eat something they cooked. So you get some secret lunch Santa elf and your best guess is me?"

She tossed her hair again, it was down now, out of the pony tail from this morning and she was wearing more makeup, shimmery pinks and purples, her eyelashes were blue. "Why would I do that for *you* when you've never done or said ..." She fixed her eyes on him. "... even *one* halfway decent thing in my presence?"

Jason swallowed, wondering when his words were ever coming back.

"I don't think you know who you're talking to, Jason Devlin," she sniffed, and turned from him, every inch the teen princess once again.

He felt his *palms* sweating. Jesus. "I fucking *want* to, though," he mumbled to the air where she'd been standing.

Samantha whipped around, an odd look on her face. The endless stream of kids in the hall seemed to part around them, curious but not wanting to get in the way, which looked like it could end up painful.

"What was that?" Samantha asked, tilting her head to one side and looking at Jason in a way that made him want to die or write poetry or do both at the same time and which he therefore found all kinds of distracting. Shelving the death and poetry after some struggle, Jason decided she looked like she really wanted to know what he'd said. Like she hadn't heard. But somewhere, despite eyes and exhaustion and anger and despite the vegetables clutched in his hand, he managed to find his cool.

He leaned back against the locker, looked at her, raised an eyebrow, and smiled. "Damn if my rewind button isn't jammed," he drawled. No one looking at him would know about the legion of butterflies fluttering and apparently humping each other under his skin.

IN BETWEEN DAYS

"Swear." The word was slow.

"What? Oh my God, that was him. He's awake."

"Keep him that way."

"I'm trying. Okay. I'm here. What do you want me to swear to? You can trust me."

"No."

"N-no?"

"No, I mean." His voice was slurred, as if coming at some great distance. "Jus' swear. Fu-uck."

"Does it hurt that bad?"

"Kills. Don' be ... thick. Just. Swear. So fuckin' hot. C'never sleep through it."

"I don't get it."

"He wants you to swear. Like, curse. He thinks it's sexy."

"That's perverted. And he's bleeding."

"Have you two met?"

"Okay. Fine. Piss. Shit." She grasped for his hand. "If you want me to keep going, you have to squeeze my hand every time I say the eff-word."

"Say it."

"Fuck."

"Again."

"Guys," she sighed, "are so weird."

23. THE TASTE WAS NOT SO SWEET

Sometimes, a girl had to draw the line.

It's not as if there wasn't enough to swallow that felt bad going down. But if Samantha had to stay home from a party so Vanessa's slime of a boyfriend couldn't hit on her, then fine. She would swallow that right down.

Not that it was *her* fault that the disgusting weed of the century Dave Watson thought her speech in the cafeteria was *cute.*

In the end, it was almost Biblical. Samantha had made up an excuse, and her words had been made flesh. Samantha would in fact play hostess that evening to the client's offspring that Samantha had herself invented.

Samantha didn't even know if the offspring was a boy or a girl. Her father had just smiled, murmuring something about uncertainty being the spice of life, and to be home by six.

Whatever. It wasn't like she had anything better to do—although to be honest, even if she *did,* there were certain tones of voice possessed by Lincoln Ward that could not be said no to.

Client's offspring. Friday night. Fine. Samantha would swallow that right down too.

Eew. Not that way. Everything had gotten so much *grosser* since her burnout-inspired Sex Ed. Just one more reason to hate Jason Devlin instead of bring him lunch and pretend she hadn't. Which was either selfish or really nice of her, and she had no idea which.

Thank God it was a long weekend.

The bus wound its way through the treelined streets, the world a gold and brown and orange blur. It should have been clearer, she still had her contacts in from hockey practice, but her eyes kept tearing up.

He was infecting her. Without even trying, He'd barely looked at her since they'd spoken in the hall over vegetables and Samantha had *thought* they'd had a tiny *something*. It didn't matter what she had thought, though, because clearly she'd been mistaken.

In class he was himself. Just without looking or talking to Samantha. At least he still baited Kim. And Kim was baiting back, even though Samantha would have said that Kim didn't have a baiting bone in her body.

On Thursday, Jason Devlin had badgered Kim about making him lunch because it was stir-fry, and wasn't that Chinese? And then Kimmie sniffed and said she'd thought about it and yes, it was unreasonable to expect a boy from *Highwood* to be able to distinguish among Asian peoples and cuisines.

Which had been very funny.

But fine. He could have a plain vegetable pocket sandwich. She wasn't going to cook for him if he wasn't even going to be mean to her about it.

So Jason quizzed Kwame about whether pita was African bread and if Kwame was trying to woo him with food.

Kwame said he didn't swing that way, but that if he did, he wouldn't swing toward Jason. He also said he hadn't set foot anywhere in Africa since he was two years old, but he was pretty sure pita bread was Middle Eastern. Kim slapped reprovingly at Kwame's arm and told him not to expect that kind of knowledge from a boy from Highwood.

Then Jason's hand was in the air, asking if the Middle East was not partly on the African continent?

Then Jason told Kim he wouldn't expect that kind of knowledge of African geography and cuisine from a girl from Highland.

Kimmie explained that was irrelevant, because she lived in Highwood.

Which was true, of course, and the main reason Samantha and Jessica bought most of Kimmie's clothes.

Jason just looked down and didn't say another word the rest of the period. Which for another person wouldn't have been at all strange, since the rest of the period was lecture, but it was strange for a bigmouth like Jason.

But there was more. Jason had looked awful the past two days, stupid scruffy movie-star factor notwithstanding. He had dark circles under his eyes and they were red in a way Samantha wasn't sure was from pot, because he didn't seem high or slow. Maybe he had some kind of more serious drug problem.

She was upset that he looked awful and upset that she noticed.

She noticed every move his hands and jaw and mouth had made every second she was in class with him. So she knew exactly how many times Jason had so much as glanced her way, a number which was zero.

At least he was getting lunch out of it.

The only thing Samantha was getting out of any of this was, according to her very happy coach, a suddenly inspired attack in field hockey.

But that was where she drew the line.

Actually, here, right where she stepped off the bus. Here, where the tasteful gravel of the long driveway stretched to meet the crinkling fallen leaves raked into piles by gardeners whose names Samantha didn't know.

Maybe she could have the same gardeners edge the line with an attractive autumnal border. Samantha was sure that if her mother knew the line was to keep her from thinking about a boy like Jason Devlin, she would be happy to have it landscaped.

The crunching sounds of her feet on gravel renewed her resolve. Tonight, the secret inner world that showcased wall décor in disturbingly distinct detail would be left behind in the wake of a school bus.

Which was in fact what happened.

Because Lincoln Ward was waiting by the door, drink in hand, gesturing toward the grand staircase and shouting, "Surprise!"

There, on the bottom stair, stood a shorter and slightly stocky girl wearing black Dickies rolled up over thick combat boots and an Iggy Pop t-shirt pinned together with safety pins. Bright blue hair hung down in her face and stuck out in other places and Samantha just stared, because there was something so familiar about the girl and so strange at the same time.

The girl was looking at Samantha, too, she looked guarded and worried and this look didn't match her outfit at all. Her hand strayed up to the studded collar around her neck, and twisted it, but there wasn't enough leather to twist and it dug into the skin of her neck and finger.

Samantha shrieked, dropped her bag on her father's foot and lunged at the girl, squeezing hard. The girl's face at last broke into a smile.

The Wards and the Hineses rested their highballs on attractive coasters featuring images of Early American antiques not owned by the Ward family. They regarded their daughters with an amused if distant affection. Lincoln

Ward even tolerated the enormous hug his daughter insisted on wrapping him in with more good grace than usual.

Samantha thanked everyone, again and again. Because Prissy was here, or Pris, as she corrected Nancy Ward politely if through clenched teeth. And nothing else in all the world mattered.

Later, the basement floor was littered with record jackets. The club-like room was all brown and gold, wood paneled walls, full bar, stereo. The television was so big that the screen wouldn't fit in Rhode Island, Gran said, so she made Grandpa Ward send it to them. "Mommy hates it," Samantha giggled. "So osten*tat*ious."

Samantha didn't have to explain about her mother. She and Prissy just knew those things about each other.

At least, they always used to.

Now, though, Samantha couldn't stop talking.

"So I totally don't know anything about the British punk since, like, the Sex Pistols and The Clash, but … " Samantha was pulling out album after album and shoving them at her friend. Pris sat near her but not quite close, her legs pulled up to her chest and chin resting on her knees. Her eyes never left Samantha, but the gaze felt cold, which made Samantha speak even more.

"But there is totally great punk in the Midwest. Check it out, here's Hüsker Dü, then there's sort-of, semi-punk, like the Violent Femmes, and Stephen just sent me these guys, The Replacements, it's totally funny how Stephen's out in Connecticut but he's sending me the Minneapolis bands, which is, like, so much closer to me, but he's always been the one— "

"You don't have to hide your Madonna just 'cause of judgments you make about me because of the way I dress." Pris's voice sounded cold, too.

Samantha dropped the album she'd been holding like it had stung her and the words came out of her mouth with their own bite. "Stupid me, making judgments about what music you'd listen to based on your look." Samantha raised an eyebrow. "I wouldn't have thought you'd be interested, but I've also got Duran Duran, Loverboy, Wham!, Michael Jackson, so, you know, go wild, punk rock chick."

"Punk isn't just a look, Samantha."

"Oh, sorry. Based on your uniform."

"I wouldn't expect you to understand. Just skip it." Pris looked down at the albums strewn at her feet and shook her head. "So, no Bowie anymore?"

"All of it." Samantha's eyes narrowed. "Every single thing, bootlegs, Japanese pressings." She looked for Pris's eyes, forcing them to meet her own. Then she tossed her head. "*Let's Dance*, which he did to make your boy Iggy some money, so don't even start with me."

"Yeah. Sorry about that."

Samantha wanted to imagine that Pris was talking about more than just David Bowie's "Modern Love."

"It's not like it's a bad album. I mean, it's *good*. But it's hard if you loved him—before he was, like, top forty pop candy."

"You got that right."

Now Samantha didn't want to imagine that Pris was talking about something more than Bowie. "But I still love him because people might change here and there and get more popular but they don't become, I don't know, different people."

Samantha cringed at the sound of her own voice. This couldn't be happening. It couldn't. "I guess if Bowie was going to sell out, I'm glad he did it for a friend." She paused. "I guess I'm glad that for *some* people, old friends might even be more important than new fashion, or ... musical tastes." Now her own eyes dropped and her voice got much smaller. "Or whatever."

"Sorry," Pris muttered through a faint smile. "Hard week, Sammie."

Sam nodded. "Tell me about it." Silence. "No, seriously." She looked at Pris and saw confusion. "All about it. Like we always did."

Maybe Pris was jet-lagged. Or hurt Sam hadn't written in so long.

Or maybe her parents had just made Pris come here because Lincoln Ward was an important business contact or Nancy Ward belonged to the right clubs.

"Just a minute." Sam got up and put her hands over her burning eyes. "My contacts are killing me."

"You never used to need glasses," said Pris, her voice weirdly accusing.

Samantha smiled, it hurt a little. "Three years is a long time. All kinds of stuff, you know." She gestured vaguely at nothing.

"Ch-ch-chaanges," Pris nodded, trying. "So, my favorite punk band in London, they took their name from Ziggy Stardust. 'The kids were just crass,' you know ..." But she trailed off.

The silence was thick and made the air feel awful inside Samantha when she breathed. She pressed her eyes again. She didn't want clear vision. Didn't want strange messages from newly distinct walls telling her about *Pris*. She didn't need messages about Pris. She was Prissy. She *knew* her.

Samantha began talking fast again. "I'm not even supposed to wear contacts much. But I will die before I wear my glasses in school. So I'm blind half the time. Which basically improves my high school experience. Everything just a jewel-toned blur." She went into the bathroom, calling behind her, "No need for drugs."

"You can't see, like, at school?" Pris asked, her voice funny.

"Nope," called Sam from the bathroom. "If I hadn't been coming from field hockey, your head would have been a blue smudge."

"Don't you bump into stuff? Why wouldn't you want to see?"

Pris sounded panicked about Samantha's eyesight after not seeming to care very much about anything else. Samantha hoped Pris wasn't all into drugs or something. "Why wouldn't I want to see? Are you kidding? High school must look way better in London. Anyway. I wear contacts for sports, or until my eyes freak. And I can see if I concentrate hard enough. It just gives me headaches."

Pris didn't answer. Samantha came out of the bathroom and went right on talking, keeping that thick, choking silence at bay.

"Yeah, so now? Blue blur. I would never have recognized you. I almost didn't anyway."

Samantha tried to say the whole truth, but couldn't get it out. So she didn't say that close up, she could see fine, but that she felt so far away from Pris, it felt like she would need a telescope to see her eyes.

"You look so cute, by the way," she said instead.

"Cute?" Pris didn't sound sure that was good.

"Oh my God, yes." A little more truth pushed through, a tired little fish swimming in aspic. "You look like the best thing ever."

Samantha put on her glasses. They were wide and covered half her face, she always felt under water behind them. The little gold S she had stuck to the bottom corner of the left lens was starting to peel off. She covered her shaky breath with a sniff.

"See, I must wanna see your face bad to wear these." She hoped Pris would think the red eyes were from contacts or drugs or something.

She hadn't needed to worry. Pris was not meeting her eyes.

She didn't speak. It was Pris's turn to brave the silence.

At least she got that much. "So, you're kind of like a mall rat now, Sammie?" asked Pris.

"Um, not kind of, Pris. I'm a mall rat to the nth degree. I am," Samantha paused, "the queen of mall rats."

Pris was boring a hole in the sole of her boot with a pencil.

Samantha spoke like she was unfolding the secrets of the universe. "I have seven sweaters from The Limited. From this season alone. I have the complete outfit to become any pop star in the charts." She paused, waiting for effect. "Mostly, though, I mix and match. This week, Madonna, Prince, and Chrissy Hynde. Oh. And Adam Ant, a little. Given enough time and temporary hair dye, I can do Cyndi Lauper." She furrowed her brow. "You would not, seriously would not, believe the glitter involved with my position."

Silence.

Pris slowly looked up at her, her face a question. "Nancy must love that," she said, her finger twisting her choker into the flesh of her neck.

"Totally." Samantha met her eyes. "So how does Saskia Hines feel about, you know—" and she gestured toward Pris, her hair and outfit.

"Tip of the iceberg, Sam." Pris shook her head, her mouth blowing a silent whistle. "You have no idea."

"You could give me one," Samantha whispered. She began fiddling with the penny in her loafer, smoothing the brown sheaves of wheat she'd carefully placed facing up.

Pris pulled out a wallet from the tattered backpack at her feet, and as she leafed through the pictures, her eyes softened. Then she nodded slightly, hard and closed again. "Well. Fine. Here's one idea." Her voice cut Samantha to the quick, all over again. "For starters," she spat.

Pris's entire body tensed so tight it was a miracle she managed to move enough to thrust the open wallet forward. As soon as Samantha took it, Pris's arm retracted into her stone-still body like a fishing line onto a spring reel, wrapping tightly around her knees and pushing them into her chest as her chin bore down hard against them.

The pose did not match the voice. The pose was all Prissy, while the voice was new and hard and belonged to a person Samantha realized she did not know.

Samantha felt something like stage fright as she took in the pictures in the plastic sleeves, peering carefully over the wide, ugly glasses she did not need at close range. As she looked, she felt one kind of tension leave her body and another take it over.

Because she saw the answer to what was going on with Prissy—Pris—plain as day from the photo in her hand. But Samantha was at a loss for how to say the right thing, or at least the thing that would not be wrong.

"So," she said, willing herself to look at Pris and her fear, her anger. "She looks pretty, you know, under all the Mohawk and metal."

Pris turned her eyes at her, guarded, staring. "She looks pretty," she echoed, her tone mocking, incredulous.

Samantha held the gaze. "That's what you say when someone shows you a picture of their girlfriend, right? What did you want me to say, oh my God, she's a dog, I'm so effing sorry!"

Pris suppressed a giggle. It sounded more like choking. "No."

"I mean, she is wearing a collar. And you too. Sorry. She's a dog. You are too. Better?"

Pris pulled her legs back up to her chest and buried her face in her knees.

Samantha's voice was softer. "What did you think I was gonna say? You know Stephen is too, right?"

Pris's sudden intake of breath and wide eyes said she hadn't.

"I mean, not that he's dating some black punk rock chick. I mean that he's, you know."

"Can't you even say it?" The judgment in Pris's voice was back, clear and cold.

Samantha felt herself caving under the pressure. The little girl inside her was whining that friendship shouldn't have pop quizzes.

And Samantha's patience snapped.

"Oh, please. Yes, I can say it. I helped Stephen say it, actually. But when we started saying it, my parents shipped him off to school!" She sniffed. "And Stephen never blew me off or was mean or cold to me just because he was and I wasn't. He never assumed I'd have a problem with him before he gave me a chance to not have one."

And the silence between them was thick and long and wide.

Pris broke it, but carefully, like she was worried about breaking something else. "Sam, you don't know what it's like. What people say in school. Even you, like—I heard." She stared hard at Samantha's loafer.

"In school, in London?"

Pris looked up. The taunting was gone now, her eyes black smears. She licked her lips, but said nothing.

Samantha shook her head. A trembling numbness spread through her veins. "How did you hear about me? When did you get back?"

Silence. Pris folded in on herself entirely.

Samantha's voice was small. "Prissy? Were you even going to call me at all?"

Pris's voice was smaller, muffled by her knees. "I went to school. I thought it would be a surprise—I had a present, and everything. It's still in my bag, I've been carrying it everywhere."

"You were in school? *My* school? This week?"

Pris nodded.

Samantha stared at her friend and hurt.

"So, it's like I'm not even here? I mean, I'm not gay or punk or whatever, so you don't know me?" Samantha's breath grated in her chest.

"No! I wanted to. I wanted to *so bad*." Pris raised her head. "I was so freaked out to be coming back, but you were like, something to look forward to."

"You didn't even say hi?"

"I thought *you* didn't." Pris spoke quietly. "I didn't know about the glasses. And then you were—different, and I—was so different, and I just—" She wiped her face with the back of her hand, smearing the black and blue further down her cheeks. "I was scared, and it made me wrong." Pris's voice was hardly distinguishable from silence. "I got it wrong, Sammie."

Samantha still held the wallet, she looked at it again, then back at her friend.

She was *so hurt*.

But her old friend, the friend she'd yearned for, was back. Probably all her friends, the ones who knew her now, were across an ocean. Her parents were coldly sipping highballs among the antiques, and Pris needed Samantha to step up.

She tossed the wallet back.

"Yeah, well," she sniffed, "I guess I do look pretty effin' tough, compared to you and your little girlfriend there. No wonder you were scared."

Pris made another choking sound that sounded like it might be a giggle.

It wasn't that Samantha couldn't understand what it was like to have people hate you without knowing you. Or to like to the very last person in the world you thought you would or should. In fact, though she knew it was not so simple, she felt like she'd give whole worlds to be secretly crushing on a girl instead.

She took a deep breath, then gathered one knee up to her chest, prodding her friend with the toe of her other leg. "So what were you more afraid of, besides my tough-as-nails penny loafers messing up your combat boots? That I would get all grossed out? Or that I would be jealous of her?"

Suddenly, she felt a hand on hers, squeezing. "Both," said Pris, her frightened, shy blue Prissy eyes peering out at Samantha from the bottom of the black smudge. "Sammie, I am so sorry."

"Yeah, you should be." She squeezed the hand back. "Gy, that was so gay of you."

Pris kicked with a combat boot. Samantha shoved with a penny loafer. "You think you're so special. Just wait until I tell you about the horror story of my painfully wrong crush. You like some girl, which makes perfect sense because actually, guys are totally gross. Talk about against the laws of nature. Jason Devlin is against the laws of nature. Black punk rock girlfriend? Child's play."

IN BETWEEN DAYS

The fluorescent light of the downtown ER showed the distraught girl was covered in blood. She choked back sobs as she told her story to the tired-looking woman with the wire-framed glasses and the clipboard. They'd been mugged, the thieves took everything. They didn't even know where they'd been when it happened, they'd just given the cabdriver the name of the club they'd heard about.

No, they weren't from around here. Not at all. They didn't know the city, they were just here on a layover. Thank God those kids had come along and helped them get here.

Yes, they'd need to file a police report. But she had to reach her parents right away. She needed to get money wired, cancel her credit cards, like that. No, of course all their ID had been stolen. Nineteen. Her brother was nineteen, March 27, 1966, yes. Yes, she was eighteen, just turned in September. Yes. She ticked off names and addresses. Rhode Island, yes.

She'd fill out all the forms and make all the calls. But she needed to check on her brother first. They'd taken him back already. He'd lost a lot of blood.

24. ONE LOVE

Saturday night. Jason wasn't up for a party. Skinny was. Jason wouldn't crash Danuzio's the night before, and Skinny wasn't having it tonight. "C'mon, man. One Love. Jah's a funny guy, free booze, those high-class chicks all grinding up against you."

Jason shook his head, stared at the pool table. Everything was so fucked.

Skinny came closer, his sour breath in Jason's face as he hissed, "C'mon. Jah put out the fliers this afternoon. Everyone's gonna be there. It's *One Love,* all the hippie chicks you can swing your dick at. And I can get rid of some party favors. Get those Artie guys off your back."

Get my mom off my back, thought Jason. *Get my mom off* her *back.* He curled his long frame over the pool table. He had no shot. He couldn't get clear. "Off the nine," he muttered, and missed.

"You're off your game, Devlin,"

"I had no fucking shot."

"So take your fucking shot at this party C'mon, man. One Love, mon." Skinny spoke the last words in a falsetto with a fake Jamaican accent and swooned around the pool table like he was dancing. "Jah Love mixing drinks. We'll hijack the turntable." He spun on a dime and started shadow boxing. "For Anthrax!"

"Dude, Jah'll *play* Anthrax for you if you want. That's the point—whatever, man. I'll go, I owe you. But no party favors. We're not mixing with Artie, I'm not, and you're not unless I say so."

"Geez," whined Skinny. "I'm my own goddamn man, Dev."

Jason shook his head and looked Skinny in the eye. "No, dude. Not to Artie Fisher, you're not. Far as he's concerned, anything you do, it's on me."

"Fuck *that* shit, man."

"I'm with you. But sometimes, you don't get to choose the shit you fuck."

Skinny's Caddy was covered in spray paint and duct-taped together, one door was from a different model and didn't quite fit, but his cousin whose junkyard the whole pile came from had wired it together so it stayed put. The car was beloved by Skinny and the cousin and it ran sometimes.

Jason Devlin watched the low-roofed bars and gas stations whiz by, letting his eyes drift out of focus so that the lights made trails against the night. But it was no use. Every time he relaxed the past few days, he was right back *there,* with his mother spitting and cursing and throwing slimy lettuce at his head. Or *there* Friday morning, when he'd stopped back home after two nights to grab some stuff and *there,* coming out of Jason's own front door, was Artie Fisher.

One pants leg was caught up on the top of his motorcycle boot and he was tucking in his shirt.

"You—you lookin' for me?" Jason had stammered.

Artie had just looked at Jason and shook his head. "Sorry, kid. Not this time."

Jason's body and brain were frozen because Artie Fisher was coming out of *his house* but not for him.

"Your old lady, man, she wants to talk to you about that *arrangement.* She's in favor."

"Uh," said Jason, rubbing his head. "Then I guess I'll hear about it."

"Seems that way," nodded Artie, and he looked at Jason with something almost like sympathy. Which made Jason's blood run even colder than it had been. Then Artie swung his skinny leg over his motorcycle and strapped on a helmet. "Later, kid," and he held up a hand. The sound of the BMW revving was loud as it sped down the street but it came to Jason like an echo through water.

Now, though, the sound of Skinny revving the Caddy was loud.

Loud was good.

It drowned out his mother explaining how good it would be for the family if Jason dealt coke at Highland Central. How proud his father would have been if Jason finally stepped up. Jason had kept his eyes focused on the grease stains where the lettuce had hit the wall. And then the screaming started.

Luckily, Skinny liked to be plenty loud on the roads where the rich kids lived. He cranked up the metal and rolled down all the windows in the car, fist pumping the air as he pulled up to Jah Rubenstein's house.

Jason smiled. The party was loud.

A few kids were out on the lawn, plastic cups in hands, swaying to the Bob Marley blasting from the backyard where things were obviously going full swing. A couple was making out in the bushes, hidden from the house but pretty much on full display to anyone on the street. Skinny gave them a whoop. The guy held up his middle finger but kept his other hand on the girl's ass and his mouth firmly suctioned on to hers.

Which made Jason realize he was more than a little overdue for some of *that*.

Tonight could be simple. He could worry about things like whether he could stand to hear *another* reggae song or if Michael Jackson was *always* worse. He could watch all the little Madonna wannabes gag when Skinny got his Anthrax played.

And then, maybe one of those pretty hippie girls who liked to hug would lean up against him. Maybe Jason would slip his tongue in her ear and play with the hoops and studs there, tugging. Then maybe he'd slip his tongue in her mouth and then—he could stop and look around and see if Samantha Ward was there.

Because even in his fantasies he was now an enormous pussy-whipped douchebag.

But even that was all right. Because it would have fuck all to do with his mother or Artie Fisher—for all that Fisher was probably the source of whatever lines kids were cutting and snorting in bathrooms while desperate drunk girls pleaded outside the locked doors. Whatever. Those lines at least would have fuck all to do with Jason.

He closed his eyes to the little blonde girl by the lake, screeching with laughter as Jason chased her up the beach.

Jason Devlin was not dealing cocaine. No way, not now, not ever.

Instead, he'd blown his whole paycheck. Train into the city and back that afternoon, hardly staying an hour. Certain kinds of stores were always near train stations, convenient for desperate measures. Security measures. Duane from Del Lanes had told him where to go, not saying it out loud, writing the address in block letters on a scrap of paper.

Security measures and also some stupid thing he'd wanted. He'd gone looking in three pawn shops before he'd found one. It was a little chipped but that only made it seem more true.

He barely had any money left over for food or bills and tried not to think about lunches, because they confused his heart and mind.

His fingertip rubbed over the smooth, hard surface of the small thing in his pocket. He liked the way the slight chip dug into his fingers, not as hard as the broken watch.

Jah started blasting the Hendrix and Jason got a little happier.

One thing was sure, little Jah Rubenstein knew how to throw a party. He'd strung tie-died sheets all over and thrown cushions for little outdoor smoking dens—even built a stage. Jah himself was spinning stacks of records in his own personal DJ booth. He'd wrapped his white-boy dreads in glitter and wrapped his scrawny arms in hippie chicks. Boy had it made.

Everyone loved Jah. Because the One Love rules were, love everyone. And give them drinks.

Pa-Jah was loaded, worked for record companies and who knew what all, he traveled a lot and Jah had the run of the place to himself half the time. Pa-Jah underwrote the parties. And the music collection. And the well-concealed bedroom greenhouse. Of which Pa-Jah was the best and biggest customer.

Yeah. Jah's dad bought from him. But it was different. Jah thought marijuana was from God and the pathway to Him from Earth and the answer to all the world's problems. No one thought cocaine was going to solve the world's problems. No made special trips downtown to keep themselves safe from Dylan or Bogart, that was for sure. Worst danger they posed was that you might trip over them, as Jason almost did on his way to the keg.

"Dudes. Be less like rotting logs," drawled Jason, righting himself.

"Whoa, Jason, Jah's got, man, this shit, it doesn't just have purple threads, it has, like crystals. Like, in the *buds,* man." That was like a lyric poem for Dylan Dougherty.

Bogart made a joke. Sort of. "Dude, Devil makes his own smoke. Be scared, dude, stop rotting." They laughed hysterically until Bogart pointed at a tapestry. "Oh, Dylan, dude, that one, the Not-Fade dyes, with the caterpillar, man. It, like, *moves.* Sick."

Jason chuckled. Reefer fucking madness. Run, run while there's still time.

He poured himself a beer and drank it down. He wasn't getting drunk, not with what he now carried and who might show up in his house and God knows where else any given morning. But he could slam one beer just to jolt his head and he could nurse another, because the thin pale liquid tasted bitter and cheap and that was Jason's flavor, too.

Tie-dyes, stoners, mall girls giggling into wine coolers. A jock with a beer funnel. A metal head girl—Amanda? Althea?—banging out to Marley somehow, hair teased higher than the Sears Tower. Jason was pretty sure she'd had her tongue all over him at some point. He hoped idly he'd returned the favor, couldn't be sure, there were so many girls and they'd begun to run together in his mind. Maybe he should offer tonight.

Except his mind—or other parts—had divided the entire girl population into two categories, Samantha Ward and Not Samantha Ward, and only one of these was of any interest.

Didn't mean he couldn't give a little, he supposed. He had to fucking get over this. Had to think about other things.

Like, that cheerleader girl Vanessa's amazing chest. She must be a colossal bitch to have Dave Watson so eager to stray. Didn't stop him staring daggers at Jason, of course, but Jason just held his beer up and Watson raised his in return. Fighting at One Love meant a lifetime ban, a price not worth paying. Still. Probably enough time staring at any dude's girlfriend's tits. It was never One Love the next day under the underpass, and there was always another girl.

JAP Barbie Jessica, for example. So much attitude under all the makeup. She could be in a magazine, except her face was more interesting than that. Plus she had these legendary perfect tits that had their own appreciation area on the locker room wall. They could be in a magazine, too—a different magazine.

That had been a totally enjoyable train of thought until Jason noticed Jessica and her skinny friend were clearly amped on coke and that was the least sexy thing in the entire world to Jason right then. Not like he had a shot with either, he was just trying to find something to *think* about. Not including cocaine.

Thin arms snaked around his waist and gave a gentle squeeze, then hovered, as if they'd snake lower if he let them. Jason smelled patchouli and THC and nicotine. He looked down at the hands. Snakes and cats. Silver. "Darlin' Nikki," he drawled, wrapping his arms around her back and bending over so her feet left the ground and her body pressed into him through thin, sheer cotton. Over that shirt would be as good as under, just a little texture. No bra. Hippie chicks. Made a boy's life so much better. Jason tucked Nikki into his side where his jacket fell open so he could feel her better against him.

He had to get the feel of something else besides *her*.

He could barely look at *her* at school, he wanted her so much.

Plus Jason had begun to notice things. Things like nothing made her madder than when he ragged on her friend Kim. It made her breath change, because of him. He would rather that happened for different reasons but he would take what he could get. Things, too, like she was sharp as hell when she wasn't hiding it, so sharp that he had no idea how anyone could be so smart and still not see what was right in front of her face. It was a puzzle he thought more and more he would like to spend serious time with, trying to work it out.

But the more Jason noticed these things, the more he'd see his mother or his house or Artie Fisher. He'd see that with each passing moment, his own life was pushing him farther and farther away from where he started Monday morning, when Samantha Ward had already been miles out of his reach. Before he'd even *wanted* to touch her.

And the farther out of reach she was, the more he felt like she was the *only* thing he really wanted to touch.

He *had* to cut loose from this thing. Nikki. Against his hip. Nuzzling his chest with her pretty brown hair. Natural soft the way Jason liked it, not so much smelly sticky stuff. Nikki. Maybe he could. Jason caught Jah's eye and gestured toward the girl on his chest. Jah nodded, laughed and turned back toward his booth.

Jah cranked the Prince and Nikki giggled, all her soft parts trembling against him.

"How'd you like 2 waste some time?" she breathed, her hips brushing his in time to the music. But even in the dim light, Jason could see her pupils were like black saucers.

Jason froze. Wasting time. Story of his fucking life. And with her eyes like that, and him thinking about someone else, using some tripped-out girl to jack off to—not his scene.

He bent down to breathe in Nikki's ear, "You go dance to your song. Check out Jah's taps while you're doing it. They're gonna look great. You're gonna look great, I wanna watch you."

White lies. Jason's stock in trade with girls these days. Better than white lines, anyway.

As Prince trailed off, Jah mixed in the opening strains of that song that now followed Samantha Ward around like she was on TV. The wistful notes rose above the crowd as everyone turned to look. Because she had a *theme* song now when she got to a party. Because that was how much she fucking mattered.

Jason wondered how long she'd been there, wondered if she'd seen Nikki pressed up against him. And if she'd give one half of one tenth of a shit if she had.

25. SUCH A DRAG TO WANT SOMETHING SOMETIME

Samantha high-fived and hip bumped her way to Jessica, who pulled her to where she and Skinny Girl were dancing. Then *every* guy at the party was watching because three of the best-looking girls in school were dancing together, hair and hips and pretty arms in the air, grinding and bumping and shimmering in the low lights. It was a high point of the evening whether you liked those individuals or that style of girl or not. Because they were gorgeous and rich and young and they just sort of sparkled with it, and some of that sparkle landed on every person there.

Skinny Girl was too skinny to have much in the way of chest but Jessica had chest to spare and the shirt to make that clear. Samantha Ward didn't need to borrow any though, she didn't need to borrow anything from anyone because she was achingly fucking perfect. Jason couldn't even see parts of her distinct from other parts, he just saw all of her and she took his breath away.

Her shirt was deep fucking sexy even though it wasn't low cut but it only had one sleeve and that wasn't even attached, and so these *shoulders*. Hell.

"Maybe tomorrow," her stupid theme song mocked him. "Maybe someday."

He dug the rough chipped edge of the thing in his pocket into his finger, a reminder.

"You've changed," she mouthed to the song, swaying her hips, coaxing someone in the crowd.

Pris looked shy from her place on the sidelines. She looked fucking shy, *Pris*. And all the eyes at the party turned toward her, because Samantha Ward was looking at some weird punk rock chick like she was the Second Coming and that was against all the laws of nature, even the laws of One Love.

It was breaking his heart, somehow.

They just stood there adoring each other for a minute in a way that must have made the whole goddamn party feel like intruders. It sure as hell made Jason feel like that. It was also kind of beautiful, though, so it was pulling his heart in two different ways at once, which was uncomfortable.

A voice at Jason's elbow took his attention. "Looks like our little punk rock chick dumped us for Barbie love after all," said Skinny.

"Whatever. Who cares? Girls are girls," Jason lied. He had never felt that to be less true.

"Yeah, good point," laughed Skinny, punching Jason lightly in the ribs. "So, you're not getting in on that, huh?"

Jason snorted. "Pris? Nah, man, we aren't like that. But dude, I gotta warn you, I don't think you're getting in on that either."

Skinny shuddered. "Well, I'm so fucking crushed because she was my first choice after a rusty pipe infected with the clap, y'know?"

Chuckling in spite of himself, Jason shook his head and kept his eye on Samantha.

"Not Pris, man, the Ice Princess. I swear she's got a thing for you, and that is one girl who needs to learn a lesson about who the fuck is not a fag, you know? I'd be all over that pussy if I were you, man."

Jason suddenly wanted to deck Skinny Nowlin more than he'd wanted anything in a while, except Samantha. But since a) he'd never called Skinny on talking that kind of shit before and b) it was One Love, that was out of the question. Plus Skinny had his back at all times. It would be wrong as fuck for Jason to deck his best friend for talking shit about some Barbie, whatever secret crush Jason might be harboring.

So, as Samantha had foretold, Jason swallowed that down with a shrug. "Yeah, well, that's probably the reason no one gets us confused for each other, man. 'Cause I got no fucking interest in teaching her a lesson that way."

"Yeah, I guess you made that pretty clear Monday." Skinny snickered, then lit a cigarette and they stood a minute in silence, smoking and watching the popular girls swarm on or sneer at Pris, depending on where they were taking sides on the Samantha Ward issue.

That Vanessa girl whispered loudly to one of her friends, "No surprise Psycho Ward brings some foreign freakazoid to a party, right?" The minion agreed, of course, then they switched to even bitchier fake sympathy. Samantha had shown so much promise, but not everyone could take the pressure.

It made Jason want to deck *them*. Which also, of course, wasn't happening.

Once again, though, Jason found himself distracted by Skinny's voice in his ear. "So, you got no objection if I wanna get in there, man? Break the ice?"

Jason felt his stomach turn in several Skinny Nowlin-shaped knots. But he said only, "Yeah, man, you just ask her. I'd fuckin' pay to see you try, actually."

"Who said anything about asking?" Skinny laughed and Jason had to get away from him.

"You're a sick fuck, y'know that, Nowlin?"

"Aw, sweetheart, you're makin' me blush."

"And you're makin' me retch, so we're even. Check it out, chill on the Barbie lust, okay? If those jocks jump me again over some Barbie I'm liable to kill someone and then my beautiful future will be for shit."

Skinny wandered off to do some drugs, leaving Jason to wonder if everyone spent a lot of time kind of hating their best friends. He made a resolution to call Skinny on his shit the next time he started talking that way, like forcing yourself on a girl was some kind of joke.

Skinny didn't understand, he didn't have a sister, had never come home to the aftermath of that. He'd call Skinny on it, and that would be the end of it. Just not at One Love, and not in public.

For now, just party on.

So Jason let his thoughts and wants wander in a whirl of mismatched sparkles and tie-dyes, big hair from Mohawks to headbanger to mall girl clashing oddly on the dance floor. Bare arms, bare shoulders, twisting hips and thrusting chests, the air rising and pulsing with patchouli and perfume and different kinds of smoke.

When the writhing mass of girl and gaze revealed Samantha to him, her hair was swinging and her arms were around different girls and she was laughing, but he noticed she stiffened whenever a guy tried to move in.

Some of the dark cloud the week had gathered over his chest lifted. Then twice, for many seconds each, her gaze met his. Jason had to close his eyes, tilt his head back, and breathe just a little deeper. It was beyond electric.

Jason felt high. It could've been a contact high, enough people were sparking up around him. It wasn't, though. Jason Devlin was buzzed because he was looking at the girl he liked looking at, and she was looking back.

Until Jenn from English plastered herself on him and started licking his neck. He guessed the whole goddamn world knew he had a thing for that, but right then, it was doing nothing for him. Instead, he saw those eyes he'd been looking at darken, and the lips beneath them stopped curving up in the same way. They got thinner, and straighter, and seemed to smile at other guys instead.

And when some big football dude came up behind Samantha Ward and put his hands on her hips, pulling her ass to his groin, she let him. She put one hand up back to his neck, and wiggled just a little more.

Jason wanted to dismember him.

To make it worse, Jah was playing music that was too sexy to begin with and then the lyrics were about caged tigers eating each other for dinner. With cream.

Fucking pop songs.

Jason fell back quick. No fighting at One Love, and what would he say anyway, hands off the girl I publicly declared I would never lick?

"Goddamn The Cure to hell," growled Jason out loud.

He caught Pris's eye and his frantic look made her smile, but she shook her head. When he mouthed the word "Please" and held up clasped hands, though, she rolled her eyes and nodded.

Pris liked to make trouble as a kind of hobby, so Jason held his breath as she went over to the DJ booth and whispered something in Jah's ear.

Jah laughed, his head bobbing in that stoner way. Familiar chords filled the air, but they had a strange effect on Samantha. She stopped dead on her feet and her mouth fell open. She looked straight at Pris and shook her head violently.

But Pris hopped up on the makeshift stage. Her finger pointed, then made a little crook. Samantha held up her hands and shook her head again, but JAP and Pan-Asian Barbies shoved her forward, insisting with the song, *Oooh, yeah.*

It was the cutest thing Jason had ever seen.

They weren't dancing like normal. Instead, hardcore Pris and sparkly Samantha were dancing out a routine like little girls do, lip-synching the words and doing what they said. They screwed up their eyes, they screwed down their hair, and when they acted out "well hung" the entire party cracked up. The move for "god-given ass" got a cheer from every guy there.

Pris caught Jason's eye, and he blew her a goddamn kiss. She ducked so the "kiss" would hit Samantha. Jason made as if to flip her off, but he was glad he was in the shadows, this time, because he was actually fucking blushing.

In a few minutes, Samantha was back swirling with her little friends, and Pris was by his side, digging out her chew.

"So I take it you two made up."

Pris nodded and pulled out, much to Jason's surprise, a little silver flask.

"What was her excuse for, like, all week?" Jason could feel the scorn creeping back in his voice. He hated, *hated* when people turned their back on their friends. One more reason he couldn't deck Skinny Nowlin. At least not in public.

"Oh, that." Pris unscrewed the cap and took a swig.

"I thought you were supposed to be all straight-edge. And yeah, that."

"Schnapps. It's not a drink. It's a penance. I am the worst person in the world, and I have to atone."

"With Schnapps."

"It was my first puking drunk and I gag at the smell." She took another swig, her whole body shuddered.

"What the hell, Pris?" Jason tugged at her sleeve.

"She doesn't wear her contacts."

Jason took a minute to process this fact but found himself unable to.

"Because Samantha Ward doesn't wear contacts, you are the worst person in the world?"

"Yep."

Swig. Shudder.

Pris was starting to slur. "So, you know, when she looks blankly at a person across the hall like they're not even there, like she's looking *through* them . . ."

"Yeah."

"It's because she can't motherfucking *see.*"

"Oh."

Jason lit a cigarette, and let this knowledge percolate a moment. He kicked his heel into grass and dirt. "So why doesn't she wear her fucking contacts, then?"

Pris shrugged, swigged, and gagged.

"She even made me come here tonight, so everyone would know I was her friend. 'Cause I spent the last half a year running around the worst parts of London learning how to use a knife, so I need protection at goddamn Highland Central. And the thing is, she might have a point."

A smile twitched on Jason's face, he remembered how Samantha said she'd warned Stagnita off him, Avenger-Barbie style. He thought of how he'd treated her then, and the smile faded.

"And those *bitches* are calling her Psycho Ward because of it. It might look like she's just partying, but she's putting it all on the line. For me. I know how these girls work." Swig. "But me," Pris continued, "first thing I do—"

"You come to me."

"Yeah."

Jason blew out a puff of air from his mouth. "Y'know, every time I think I know just how much of a dick I've been—"

Pris passed the flask.

Jason drank, but spat it out. "Jesus. I think you're atoned. Anyway. Seems like she's a forgiving sort."

But Pris hadn't told her everything. Yes, that she'd been at school, yes that she'd known Jason back in seventh grade. But not, as Pris bitterly put it, that when Samantha was in the nurse's office because Jason had made her feel like such crap, Pris was egging him on to do more.

Pris put her head in her hands. "You cannot imagine how much that conversation sucked. I mean, if there's one thing my girl is, it's loyal, you know?"

Jason nodded. Because he had been thinking the same thing himself. But the ease with which Pris now said "my girl" set off a pang of want in his gut and throat that was strangling him, one breath at a time but from more than one direction.

They'd edged back deeper in shadows. A beam of light glanced off the silver cap of the flask like a tiny moon. Jason tried to focus on that instead of on the mess inside him. After a minute, Pris went on. "Listen, I told her I told you to back off. 'Cause I had to say *something*. She said it seemed like you listened, because you don't even look at her now. At which I did my best not to snort."

"You tell her anything else?" Jason kept a cool eye on her, interested in the answer, but more interested in questions he wasn't asking.

"Like that you're apeshit over her?"

Jason swallowed the urge to put both hands around Pris's neck and squeeze hard. "For example," he said instead, tone even.

He looked up into the sky, because sometimes, a view to the stars could make his worst problems feel small. But the party lights kept the stars at bay, and Pris put the silver flask back in her pocket. Jason turned his gaze back to his friend. He wanted answers without having to ask the questions, so he waited.

Pris wasn't buying it. "Listen," she said again, "I'm not doing that for you, that 'he said she said' thing. If there's something you want to know, go to the source."

"Did I ask?"

His voice sounded flat, bored. His voice was a lie.

Pris rolled her eyes and ruffled his hair in that weirdly girly way she had.

But Jason had gotten the answer he was actually looking for, he felt certain. Samantha Ward hadn't said anything to Pris about—dumpsters, hands, soup kitchens. Jason was both elated that these were still private and also crushed that Samantha was so ashamed she wouldn't even tell Pris about it.

He sighed. "Okay, so when Samantha Ward and I have our next deep heart to heart, I won't tell her about your shit either."

"Maybe you *should* just talk to her, Devil man, you ever think of that?"

Jason laughed, not happily. "Like she'd fucking talk to me. Highland girls don't play with Highwood boys." He closed his eyes not to think of vegetables.

"On the other hand, maybe she doesn't play with you because you are totally effin' horrible to her."

"Then there's that."

"You *could* say you're sorry."

"I don't say that shit. Ever."

"Oh, yeah, I forgot how fucking tough you are."

"Bad move."

They sat for a while in silence. Some kind of Deadhead spacey stuff was playing, and everyone was chilling in little groups—the hackey sack on the lawn, the smoking circle under the trees, even what sounded like an intense conversation about Sammy Hagar that had one big dude in tears, blubbering, "It's not fucking Van Hagar, man. It's Van *Halen*. Forever. Y'know?" He sounded desperate. "Y'know, man?"

Pris grabbed Jason's hand and pulled at him. "C'mon. Truth or dare. Samantha's playing. Never know what you might find out."

Suddenly, Jason's tone was far from flat *or* bored. "Are you outta your friggin mind? We were just saying how you *weren't* gonna tell her shit." Jason had been fine, more than fine with that idea. Truth or dare—you couldn't lie during that shit. That was *heinous.* And he was not up for truth at the moment.

"C'mon," Pris narrowed her eyes and flashed a smile. "Live dangerously."

26. SWEET-TALKING, NIGHT-WALKING GAMES

Wisps of smoke played in the colored lights and shadowed tree branches. Samantha liked how it swirled with the perfume her girlfriends wore, how in her lungs and throat it mingled with the sharp October air that smelled like leaves and must and cold coming on.

Samantha and her friends sat cross-legged by the edge of the lawn. It being One Love, kids who either despised her group or normally wouldn't measure up sat with them., It added a sweet or bitter flavor to some of the secrets, a crueler edge to some of the dares.

Some kids almost always chose truth, like it weighed heavy on them but they needed an excuse to get it off their chests. Jessica Levin always took the dare. Samantha took whatever seemed most advantageous or least damaging, keeping a running toll of what would benefit friends or shame enemies. Tonight, for example, someone had to dare Kwame to kiss the cheerleader of his choice, because Kimmie told her when they'd gone off into the dark together, they'd just talked the whole time. And there were limits, she said, to the amount of just talking that even a nice girl could take.

Samantha looked across at Kwame. Rugby shirt, white collar looking kind of dazzling against the dark skin—rumpled only enough to look like he didn't care *too* much. Beer in hand but wasn't drinking it. It was kind of hard to tell what got him going besides football, but Samantha hoped it might be Kim. He was maybe too mellow a guy to ever prefer anything, even something exciting, to a pleasant situation that was already in place.

After the week she'd had, Samantha could sympathize, but she couldn't let it stand. He needed to kiss Kimmie and that was that.

The sweet in the smoke had thickened, bongs out in force in another circle. Samantha laughed as she told the truth about what color all her hair was. Blonde. Really. *All* of it. Someone dared Jessica to kiss her. People were always daring girls to kiss other girls. It didn't mean it would be okay if one of the girls really liked it better.

Still, Samantha paid close attention to anything different that happened with Jessica compared to boys like Adam Kowalski or Scooter from the yacht club. If she really did like it better, it would explain some things. Of course, it would complicate some things too.

Duh.

Kissing Jessica. Concentrate. It didn't gross her out like Scooter had, the way he'd shoved his tongue in her mouth and wiggled it like some sodden, panicked garden mole trying to find a new home. Even his hands on her had been mole-like, as if he could dig his way right through her shirt. It was awful, she had always liked him fine and now she had to avoid him like the plague. The mole plague.

Jessica was unrodent-like, her lips were soft and tasted faintly like pop— Orange Crush, maybe, and something sharper. She smelled like Jess and Johnny Walker and it was fun that people were watching, but there were none of the strange rushes or tingles or trouble with breathing that she felt when Jason looked at her. Let alone if she thought about kissing him, which she tried hard not to do. A kiss on the lips from Jess was not solving any of those problems.

All night, girls had been whispering about Samantha. The girls who usually went with Jason Devlin at parties had noticed how he looked at her.

Samantha had noticed, too.

He was always dancing with other girls, but when his hand brushed against Samantha's once or twice she felt it in every single place there was to feel something. Then he would smile like he forgot for a minute anyone else was watching him, and it was dazzling in a way that could not be blamed on colored lights.

He looked so *at home* in his body, while Samantha felt like hers was something she needed to grow into, clothing bought for the next year's season.

But girls plastered themselves against his chest and legs like it was territory they had held before. Girls who would do *anything* for him, and ask nothing in return. Or ask for the kinds of things Samantha couldn't even say.

After that, she did not stop the boys from rubbing themselves up against her. She wanted to show Jason how other boys wanted her and she could want them too, but when she felt the hard lumps in their jeans press against her, she felt sick, and bad, and slutty, while the girls who ground their bodies on Jason were bold and experienced and sexy.

Before, she would have dismissed those girls as sluts and mocked their broad-lined lips and eyes, but now she felt like they had something she was missing.

Those girls whispered about Samantha, putting thoughts and words in her mouth and mind that could never have got there on their own. It wasn't just them, either. Vanessa and her friends laughed poison behind their wine coolers. Samantha was happy Pris remembered their dance, but the timing couldn't have been worse.

Jessica got it. She was so sharp like that, drunk or no. She'd gotten Jah to play "Safety Dance" and soon half the party was doing a line dance, even rockers and hippies who would never admit to liking the song at school. But everyone knew the words. Everyone knew the moves. Jah caught on and started playing "YMCA" and "Stop in the Name of Love" and any song he could think of that people would have made up a dance to when they were nine years old.

So Samantha was trendsetting instead of dorky. Jessica was a genius.

Samantha checked back into the game in time to shout out, "Can someone dare Jess to kiss me again? I miss her!" at the precise moment Pris and Jason Devlin showed up. They were walking really close and sort of slamming into each other and if Samantha hadn't known better, she would have thought they were a couple. They sat down together on the opposite side of the circle from her, looking like they'd gotten a two for one deal on the same smirk.

A different kind of jealousy, double-edged, both dull and sharp, twisted in her chest. They were clearly so much closer than Pris had made it sound. Jason stared at Pris's boot, knocking at it with his own. He pulled at the grass with his fingertips. Samantha watched as one of the metal girls looked at him, then at Pris, then frowned and whispered to her friend.

Samantha didn't understand. Jason was with a different girl every five minutes, usually more than one. They never seemed to care, but that girl cared about Pris plenty, and the whispers already going around about Jason and Samantha were like vicious tiny knives.

Samantha shook it off.

She'd been getting distracted.

What mattered was Pris, who raised her eyebrows and wore the look that said she was up to something. Samantha got a tickly feeling, excitement and a little bit of fear, like when they'd burned their nightgowns by the tennis courts or sneaked peeks at Samantha's father's *Playboy* collection. Samantha raised her eyebrows right back.

She might not be able to show Jason Devlin that she could play like other girls. But she could go shot for shot with Pris even though she might never touch a drop of Cuervo or Jack or Johnny.

So Samantha waited. Jess got dared to do another shot of Jack and Samantha made a note to be careful who she took dares from. Bethany gave Kwame the cheerleader-kiss dare and he picked the right one—Kim looked like she might float to Mars. Vanessa Segal dared Bethany to straddle Jimmy Nordstrom right in front of his jealous girlfriend, and then Jimmy had to confess he'd gone to second base with his first cousin. "Whatever," he mumbled, "it's not like she could get pregnant that way, and she's really built." Now the girlfriend was crying softly, but Jimmy was too drunk to care and was clearly hoping that Bethany would come back for another ride.

Soon enough, play got to Pris. After she'd belted out "Girls Just Wanna Have Fun" complete with girlie preening and prancing in her combat boots (her musical tastes were clearly less pure than she let on), she turned to Samantha.

Her smile was a little naughty. "Okay, then, Sammie. Seems like everyone goes easy on you."

Samantha raised an eyebrow pointedly and looked at Jason.

Pris rolled her eyes. "Yeah, well, with a few notable exceptions. So, Truth or Dare?"

Samantha tossed her hair. "Dare. Did you forget who you're playing with?"

"No, did you?"

"I never forget anything," she said quietly. "You might want to keep that in mind."

A little chorus of murmurs underscored the number of eyes on them. Including Jason's. Pris kicked out her feet in front of her, crossed them, leaning back on her hands all casual, then spoke. "So in the spirit of One Love and peace in our time, I dare you to—kiss the biggest burnout in school. With tongue."

Samantha stared at Pris. Peace in our time, It sounded familiar, but she couldn't place it. Three years ago, she would have known Prissy's every nuance, but now she was a little lost. She could feel Jason's eyes on her. Was it a set up between Jason and Pris? Samantha shook her head slightly, willing the thought away. Maybe Pris was just giving Samantha a chance kiss Jason without it meaning anything.

Maybe Samantha was thinking way too much into a party game.

Although in her experience, you could never overthink a girl game. Girls were always thinking more than you even thought they were, just like guys were almost always thinking less.

Pris caught the slightest shake of her head. "Backing down, Sammie?"

"Pris." Samantha was careful to call her friend by her new name. This was girl chicken, no blood, no cars. "I don't back down."

Jason's mouth made a little "o" and he shook his head.

Samantha stood up and crossed her arms. "I was just considering the candidates." She eyed every boy in grubby denim or army pants or tie dye she could see. "The biggest burnout. What does that even mean? It totally depends on if you wanna go for size or performance."

A week ago, Samantha wouldn't even have gotten the joke.

"Why not go for both, Barbie?" It was an obvious comment, and of course he made it.

Samantha Ward looked at Jason Devlin steadily for a moment. "Well," she said, "this could be the beginning of a beautiful friendship," as she walked towards him, and then veered toward his friend, "Bogart."

Samantha was very careful to get her tongue in Bogart's mouth for only long enough that he would verify she'd done it. He tasted like bong water. Well. Not like she'd know. But she was pretty sure that after tonight, if she ever drank a bong, it would be a familiar flavor. Before and after tongue she lingered a little, for the benefit of anyone who might be watching. She'd had worse.

Bogart fell backwards and said, "Whoa." And then he said "Dylan, man, you gotta try a hit off that Barbie."

Samantha eyed them. "Actually, if any of you comes near me when I'm not on a dare, you'll get a different kind of Barbie hit."

"That so?" said a voice from behind the circle. The voice made Samantha's blood run cold. "Like the Devil himself said not long ago, I'd pay to see you try."

"Skinny Nowlin, are you playing?" Pris's voice was suddenly like Samantha had never heard it. "You wanna dare me? I dare you."

Skinny's high laugh sounded even thinner and higher than usual. "Nah, you're just too sexy for me, Pris. I'll come in my pants if I get within five feet of you.'"

"Then maybe you should back off before you embarrass yourself."

Wow. Samantha Ward would never in five hundred million years have believed little Prissy Hines could sound like that. You could take that voice with you down any dark alley in Chicago and no one would come near you.

"C'mon, guys, not in front of the children," drawled Jason, who'd been staring stone daggers at Samantha ever since she turned toward Bogart. But his voice was cool and amused as ever.

Pris gave him a little shove. "That's more messed up than you even know."

Samantha ignored the cold clenching inside her chest and made a show of putting her hands on her hips. She looked at Pris. Pris looked back, and it was like a circuit was completed, buzzing electric. "All right, punk rock chick. Let's do it up. Truth or dare?"

Everyone was watching, like they could leach off the energy of the two of them.

"Truth," said Pris. "I've already taken all the dares this crowd could come up with."

A taunt. Child's play.

"Oh, God, I could do better than that," Samantha sang in her best Bowie voice, eyebrow raised. Someone on the sidelines air-guitared the opening licks of "Queen Bitch." Samantha smiled at that and took a little bow, shaking her hair back. "I might not be who you think I am."

"No," said Pris, and she narrowed her eyes. It was like the whole rest of the world dropped away. "I know who you are. Truth," repeated Pris. "I don't back down, either." Their eyes met and Samantha saw Prissy looking out, pain that flickered and hid.

Samantha closed her eyes, shutting out Pris's now arrogant, black-lined face, its ghosts of Prissy peering through only to her.

Pris had given Samantha her secrets—most of them, anyway. Did she want Samantha to make her tell? They'd always pushed each other to do what they couldn't quite dare to on their own. But they'd always been alone, or with Stephen, safe as parents' houses. Samantha stared again at the eyes that stared back at her. They gave nothing away, except maybe a slight lack of focus.

It was up to Samantha, then, to focus on what was clear. And that was, whatever set-up Pris had in mind, Samantha Ward was not going to out Prissy Hines as a lesbian at Jah Rubenstein's One-Love party.

Highland kids used "Queen Bitch" guitar licks to refer to a certain kind of girl. But they didn't even know what the song was about. Samantha knew. And Pris did, too, they'd talked about it that day. Bowie had written it for Lou Reed, who'd been sent for electric shock treatment in his teens for homosexual feelings.

Samantha never betrayed a friend, even if the friend was literally asking for it. She *could* do better than that. She never betrayed a secret, either. But she was not above trying to find them out.

"Okay, Pris, tell me this. All seventh grade, you had a secret crush you talked about *constantly*. You cast him in all the movies we ever watched, in every football game you made him quarterback—you even wrote poetry about him. You never told me his name."

Pris shook her head. "Oh, Sam, I think you kinda took the dare by acci-dent." Samantha couldn't help notice how Jason's head dropped into his hands, dark bangs falling over his pale fingers.

Then Jason looked up, his eyes unreadable. As if Samantha had entered some bizarre mirror universe, he sang from the same song, "It coulda been me," repeating it like Bowie did in the song. Then he shrugged.

Samantha stood stock still and stared at him. She shook her head no.

Then the smirk was back, and the sneer, and the snap of a different song entirely. "Pleased to meet you. Hope you guessed my name." He laughed, but it didn't sound happy.

Sympathy for the devil. Right.

Pris elbowed Jason in the ribs. "Now Jason, people who live in glass houses shouldn't throw Stones."

That was funny. Pris was a funny girl. Samantha wanted to kill her, but she was a funny girl. Samantha's shoulders and then her whole body started shaking. She sat down hard on the ground, holding her sides to keep the laughter from splitting them. When she was able, she looked up at Pris, who was laughing just as hard. Word had got round to Jah, though, the congas and the samba beat snaked up through the crowd and got everyone singing along and dancing.

Skinny grabbed Jason and dragged him off somewhere to the party's edges, where he and some other boys in torn jeans and leather were pacing in tight circles. Between convulsive giggles, Samantha could see the serious lines drawn between them as clear as if they'd been outlined in marker. They were talking about boy things, probably business.

He was so the wrong kind of boy.

27. I WON'T SAY IT IF YOU WON'T

It was that time at a party when everyone was suddenly more buzzed than they had been. Wasted, even. Jessica was so drunk, she was talking to Skinny Nowlin. Jason had stalked off somewhere, Skinny yelling after him, something about cars. Samantha made a note to walk in the opposite direction.

Pris was still on her back, laughing. Some hippie stoner was lying next to Pris, trying to lick her arm. Pris wasn't even stopping him. And she'd said she didn't party like that. Whatever. No one really smelled like a Schnapps factory by accident.

Not Samantha's problem. She looked back on her night, and then on her week. She thought about everything that hadn't been mentioned, and should have been. And contact lenses and gayness and London be damned, Samantha was hurt all over again.

Pris had Jason now. That was more than apparent. And Samantha didn't want to deal with a drunk Pris, or Prissy, or with anyone else in the world.

So she walked away.

It was time to leave anyway. Even Samantha could see people were pulling out mirrors, right there in public. Kwame had taken Kimmie home, but one of his friends was wearing some girl's underwear on his face like a mask and drinking beer right through the crotch.

Samantha liked parties before they got to this point. She always had an exit strategy, though, a plan. This time, her plan was that she lived nearby.

Jason Devlin being Pris's old crush wasn't part of the plan.

Of course it had been Jason Devlin. Of course little pink Prissy monogrammed sweater Hines, soon to be a London punk rock lesbian, would have fallen for baby bad boy Devlin in seventh-grade homeroom.

Of course Samantha would have dressed up in her brother's football jersey, pretending to take Prissy to the movies, to score touchdowns for her, pretending to kiss her in the car, pretending—

It was beautiful. Samantha might be a Barbie now, but she'd started her career as a Ken.

Maybe Jason knew she used to pretend to be him. Maybe Pris had told him. Maybe this whole farce had been *their* plan, together.

Through a gap in the bushes, Samantha saw Jessica Levin getting into a red Corvette down the road, its engine running. She didn't know the car. It could have been from the private school. It could even have been from the college. Samantha knew Jessica did things with boys Samantha never thought of doing. It was an understanding between them.

It reminded Samantha that just because Jason looked at her didn't mean he cared. That these things were very separate for most people.

Walking home would be no problem. The neighborhood's sprawling lawns were well-lit, had private security. Parties were tolerated. Assault and robbery weren't. But first she'd find one quiet place, a piece of sky that would not mock her, and put herself together before the short walk down the road.

She ducked back behind the blind of tie-dyed drapery to find an empty space of grass, and night, and quiet. She made sure to stumble enough to look drunk if anyone was watching, but only enough to make it look like she was off peeing or puking rather than ready to pass out. There was always someone who saw "passed out" as "please crawl all over me."

You could never stop thinking, really.

But then, you did anyway.

Because the smell of smoke was in the air, and the tone of the voice was sharp, and bitter, and familiar as it spoke to her when she'd been expecting the silence of the sky.

"So, you and Bogart, Barbie?"

This smoke had no perfume or drugs to cut the bitterness. You and Pris? She wanted to echo. Instead, she matched her tone to his. "Yeah, that's right. We couldn't fight it anymore."

"That's very interesting. I'd have to say—" Jason paused for a smoke, then an exhale. "Not the popular choice, as far as burnouts go. So it's a surprise, you being such a popular girl." He made "popular" sound like some really shameful disease.

Samantha shrugged. "It was a dare. Different rules. And really—if I was curious what it was like to kiss a burnout—" but Samantha found she could not pull it off, whatever she'd been trying for. "Oh, whatever."

Samantha could feel Jason Devlin closing the space between them. "Oh, I don't think so," he said slowly, "I think I might be curious. I wouldn't have thought kissing burnouts was something you'd let occupy your designer mind."

Even the cold air around her felt hot and his voice was on her like a tongue. She closed her eyes and tried not to go too far with that feeling.

She used to pretend to be him. It threw her off. "I don't. I wouldn't—I mean, it's a dare." Cover. Collect. "It's supposed to be, you know, gross, or scary or something."

Jason's body was really tall and big and really right in front of her. "Scary," he nodded, in his condescending and threatening and mocking way that enraged and undid Samantha. "We might bite," he said, "is that it?"

The thought made her dizzy. Usually she was not as aware how connected speech was to tongue and teeth. This was a terrible time for these insights. She had meant to go home.

Instead, words came out of her mouth. "I just mean, for *some* burnouts, it's written up on the bathroom walls or on display all over the halls—or dance floor. I mean, with *some* big burnouts, I wouldn't have much to wonder about." She felt her own tongue and teeth as they formed those words. She felt Jason watch them, too.

Now his voice was acid, closer. "Maybe you wouldn't have to, but do you wonder, Barbie?"

She closed her eyes. It was like he undressed her, but didn't waste time on superficial things like clothes.

"Why don't you just leave me alone? Since when are we even talking?"

They shouldn't be talking. The Devil was in league with words and mouths, and they were winning, the tremble in her voice said so.

"It's One Love, remember?"

"So Jah Rubenstein throws a party, and all of a sudden you can look at again?" She didn't even bother to hide the hurt.

Jason Devlin did a double take. He literally stopped dead and stared at Samantha as if she'd sprouted antlers or something. But then he shook his head. "Oh, for Christ's sake. I look at you plenty. Everyone does. You're there to be looked at. You know it, I know it."

"No—I've been, you *totally stopped* speaking to me or looking at me. For days."

"Maybe I was doing you a favor."

"Look up 'favor' in the dictionary. It's on a different page from 'totally rude.'" She tried, but Samantha's voice could not get rid of the tremble. She fought to at least to toss her hair in a dismissive way.

"Nice try. But that line was a little strained." After a silence, Jason sighed. "Whatever. Maybe—if I just, you know, backed off, it seemed better than the alternative."

"Yeah, well, I guess it was an improvement."

Jason's eyes darkened. "Yeah, so stop complaining. What do you care if I talk to you or not?"

Samantha was silent for a moment. There was no true answer that could be spoken.

This was so absurd. There was an entire world of ways that they were to each other that for whatever reason, just couldn't be said. It was impossible. So she didn't say, um, remember how we pass notes and meet to yell at each other and hold hands after? Remember how I bring you food and obviously lie about it to spare your feelings? Remember how we don't even tell this to our best friends, some of whom seem curiously to be the same person?

Instead, she said, as if it were a new philosophical idea, "Couldn't there be, I don't know, something in between ripping me to shreds and ignoring me, like maybe saying hi—I mean, at least for Pris's sake or something?"

The music from the party drifted over. It was like a curse. Samantha hoped and prayed that Jason would not catch the words of the song that said, again and again, "I might like you better if we slept together" in a sneering voice that sounded like the soundtrack of Jason Devlin's own face if his face had been sung by a girl.

Sometimes Samantha hated pop songs.

Jason scuffed his foot on the ground and folded his hands into his jacket. "So maybe I have a hard time finding an in between with you. Maybe it's better for people like you not to know people like me. I just get pissed off, and then you're right there in the line of fire."

"Oh," said Samantha, and hoped the disappointment she felt, a deep, crushing disappointment that made no sense compared to the incredible amount of sense Jason Devlin was making, was not audible.

Then she got mad. "Wait, people like me? Who is *like me*, exactly? I'm not *really* a plastic doll. You can't just buy one in the toy aisle. And if I'm so much like all my friends—why me? What did I *even* do to you that you are *so mean* to me all the time?"

In the silence that followed, Samantha found Jason Devlin, head thrown up toward the stars, shaking his head. "I don't know," he said at last. He rubbed his face with his hands. "You're—" and he broke off.

Samantha thought she might never breathe again. He looked at her, all up and down her face, the collar of her shirt, her throat, her eyes, and then turned away as if in disgust.

"You're just so *fucking* pretty."

Oh.

"Oh," she said out loud, her voice finding the ghost of a joke. "I guess that is pretty harsh of me."

Between the moonlight and the shadows of tree branches and the lights of the stars trying to break through, Samantha watched the face before her for the smallest smile.

"Yeah, you should really watch that," he muttered, not meeting her eyes.

"You know," Samantha said, hesitantly, fingering her glittery ropy shirt like it was the Braille key to a map of an undiscovered country she was about to enter, "other people might have noticed, you know, or thought, maybe, that, I was, what you said, but—they don't necessarily take it as, like, something I did against them, you know, personally." It would have gone better if she had known Braille. Or any language fluently.

And sure enough, bitter was back full force. "Believe me. I would never for one fucking minute think you took the time or effort to do something against me personally."

He pushed his hands out into the world and walked away. Samantha followed, it didn't seem possible not to. Their path took them farther from the party to an area of lawn flanked by trees and gentle slopes that slowly, over a wooded rocky incline, would lead them to the lake, if they were to walk that far.

Samantha's sense of injustice was churning with shock in her mouth, garbling words. "Do you literally not even see anything about me? How can you think I'm pretty when you're obviously *legally blind?*"

"Very cute." His lip curled. "But not all of us forget to wear our contacts. Yeah, Pris told me. She feels bad. But this is between you and me. Oh yeah, and your audience, your watching friends." Jason spoke to the air, as if mad at it as well. "But I'm not blind to see you'd rather kiss fucking *Bogart* on a dare than—so you can show everyone that even *Bogart* was better than me. And I'm not blind to how hard you laughed—at just the idea that a cute little rich girl not so different from you, might have *really liked me*, not just noticed me and then felt dirty because she did."

Samantha saw he wiped his face once, like his nose was running. And she wanted to hit him hard in that face and then she wanted to touch his cheek right where she wanted to hit him.

"You're crazy," she said instead. Her voice was still shaking, now with rage. "Like you're someone to judge. *I'm* the one who tries—*anything*. Even though it probably means I should be in therapy for the rest of my life, because you treat me like dirt. How dare you be mad I kissed your friend. You told the whole school—that your tongue hides. That I'm cold, and shallow, and not worth the effort."

Samantha waited a minute, staring at the same place in the grass where Jason's eyes seemed fixed. Some old dandelion stalks were bent over a broken piece of twig—nothing so fascinating that it would have prevented Jason Devlin from apologizing or correcting anything she said.

The shuddery breath she took hurt her lungs. Breathing, in general, had come easily to her before she'd met him. In fact, there wasn't anything Jason Devlin didn't make more difficult. But once she caught her breath, she kept using it to talk. She couldn't stop.

"So okay, maybe you think I'm pretty. But that just pisses you off because I'm so plastic and worthless. And you're so above that, usually, because you're *poor,* and only wear t-shirts, and make out with girls who aren't as pretty as you, which proves you're not superficial like popular kids. So you punish me, because I made you as superficial as you think I am. But you know what? Even after all that, I still try and—"

"You still try and what? Oh, that's right. You try to help. You're a fucking angel of mercy. I get that. Help the poor—but don't fucking *kiss* them— not even on a dare." His eyes were back on her. "But maybe you feel different without all your friends looking. That why you came over here? Curious after all?"

"Jason, you know what?" And now, Samantha was just tired. "Not really. I wouldn't have come if I'd known you were over here. I don't actually *like* being hurt." And she turned back to the party glow. She'd check in on Pris and call it a night.

"Samantha." He actually used her name. "Samantha Ward. Time out."

28. I'VE WAITED HOURS FOR THIS

"Time out?" An echo. A changed voice. A name. It made her pause. Samantha turned, swiped at the mascara she knew must be running down her face. "Why?"

Jason ran his hand through his hair, roughing it up a little. He looked up, looked down, as if he might have the answer written down on some tree or piece of sky. And then he just exploded into words. "Because I need one. I want to not fuck up, just for five minutes. You gotta understand, my life—it doesn't fucking stop. All week, it just got worse—I can't talk about it—not to anyone, but it's—it's serious grown-up shit. Like it makes Dave Watson laying for you under the underpass look like—selling Girl Scout cookies or something. Like I can't even tell if Stagnita laid off me or not, because the rest of this stuff is so much worse."

Samantha listened, transfixed. Because somehow Jason had found a way to break through to some of those unsayable things.

Jason Devlin wiped his face again. "I know from the outside, maybe it looks like I don't try so hard, but," and now it was Jason's voice shaking. He clenched his fist, then unclenched it, then ran his open fingers through his hair again. "Maybe you don't really know, what trying looks like, where I come from, you know? Maybe you're right about some things, what you said. But maybe there's some stuff, that you can't even imagine."

Samantha remembered the food line, and the hunched look, and the principal's smile. She thought of her father's billiard room in the basement of their house, his Yale ring, her mother's special book that recorded the fact that her family mattered in ways that shouldn't, but somewhere, somehow, still did.

"You're probably right." And as she spoke, she looked him in the eye, and saw his eyes look right back at her, suddenly serious, and troubled, and sad.

He shook his head. "See, part of me knows, that I shouldn't even be looking at you, much less come near you—*that's* the really fucked-up thing I'm doing to you. 'Cause I'm like a fucking bomb waiting to go off. But even though—I know that's true, and I know you don't owe me a goddamn thing, I feel like I just gotta—*be* here, just me, for a minute, with just you. And the stars and trees and stuff, that can stay—but without *any* of that other shit."

Samantha swallowed. "Like behind the school." She watched as his pale, bruised hand fingered a small object, rubbing it back and forth. She thought at first it was a dime, but it was the wrong shape and color. She looked up, and his eyes were on her.

"Yeah," he whispered, putting whatever it was back in his pocket. He looked shy and unsure of himself.

This look made Samantha want to lick Jason Devlin's neck from his frayed shirt collar up to his jaw. Wow. She hoped it wasn't visible on her face or anything. It wasn't really appropriate given all the difficult things he was trusting her with and trying to say. In fact, he was still talking.

"...so I get pissed because it's like, I don't have a shot. I swear, I take every shot I get, bank shot, English, you name it, I can make a shot when it looks like no one could sink that fucking ball but—but usually, you don't want a *particular* shot so bad, you just want a shot at *something.* Now, though, it's not only like I don't have a shot, it's like all I want is the fucking striped ball and I'm playing solids."

As it happened, Samantha knew a thing or two about pool. She took a deep breath, chalked up the way her father had always taught her, and took a shot of her own. "Maybe you have the game wrong. Maybe you're not playing stripes and solids. Maybe it's just straight pool." She raised an eyebrow. "So you might have a shot at a ball you thought—you know, was off limits."

Silence. Samantha was more than a little afraid of what she had just said.

"That is not something I ever for even one second considered."

Samantha half-smiled. "Well, don't get all cocky. You might still be disqualified for bludgeoning the poor striped ball with a baseball bat."

"At least then it would be my own fault." Jason shook his head back. "And not just the fucking rules of the game that shut me out." He looked at her for a moment. He spoke slowly, casually, but his voice was shaking just a little. "I swear to God, though, if I would've thought I had even half a shot—" and suddenly his eyes were much closer to what they had been on the dance floor. "I'm very good at pool."

Samantha looked up at Jason, tilting her head as she said, "I'm better than I look."

"That's not fucking possible."

Suddenly, Samantha was grateful for tree trunks. Her knees were not being as supportive as they should have been, but she also thought leaning back would make her chest and neck look good.

The idea that her prettiness troubled Jason Devlin was delicious to her. It probably would be okay if she distracted him from some of the terrible problems he was talking about. She twirled a strand of hair around one finger and let it go again.

Jason's eyes got very wide.

She twirled her hair again. "So, what else do you want to talk about, Jason Devlin?"

Jason came a little closer. His eyes got that cocky, mocking look again, but it was different now. Warm. "Actually," he said slowly, "I'm very interested in your shirt, Samantha Ward, not in taking it off, which is the unjust conclusion you probably jump to, but more as a fashion statement."

Samantha always found it surprising that in addition to swearing more than she would have thought was possible, Jason had this way with fancier words than you'd think a boy like him would know or care to use. She found it tended to unhinge her. To be perfectly honest, the swearing could sometimes have the same effect.

Clearly, she was losing her mind. And Jason Devlin was talking to her for the very first time as if he liked her.

"I mean . . ." He fingered the shirt's ropy edge Samantha had traced earlier. "This unusual piece is very different from what most of the girls are wearing this season." He paused, making a point of looking up the length of the shirt without lingering at her chest. "I mean, I get this—" he ran the back of his knuckle down the bare place on her shoulder. "It's crazy sexy, without showing anything that should be sexy. But it's also all, 'Rebel, rebel, you've torn your dress.'"

Jason Devlin had touched her, and said "crazy sexy" at the same time. This was actually happening. Something was coming undone between them. "You want to talk about fashion, and you're quoting Bowie at me," Samantha whispered. "Did Pris put you up to that? Did she give you, like, a guidebook or something?"

Jason shook his head, a half smile playing at his lips, half shy. "I told you, if I have even half a shot, I can figure the angle." Then he got serious a minute, looked Samantha in the eye. "Listen, Pris won't talk to me about you. Not like that."

Samantha breathed a sigh of relief. "Prissy and I—you know—"

"No," he said, softly. "I don't. Tell me.

Samantha stared.

"Not like a secret—just—anything." He smiled again. "Like how you made the Spiders from Mars cuter than puppies and kittens."

Samantha looked up at the stars to avoid looking at Jason Devlin's face so she could breathe well enough to continue speaking. "We made up the dance together," she began. Her mouth was moving, and words were coming out, but if her pulse could talk, it would be repeating the fact that Jason Devlin had touched her.

She thought if he didn't kiss her soon, she might die, but the slow and the talking was also just—dizzying.

She took a deep breath, still a little shaky but for a different set of reasons. "We were on a sleepover, baking cookies and making out with my album covers. Pris liked the weird pictures like *Aladdin Sane*. I liked *Changesone, Heroes*, you know, more normal. But then we didn't want to ruin the albums by kissing them with chocolate mouths, so we just—danced." She smiled. "I had these sparkly platform heels. I hid them in the bottom of my closet under my sticker collections so my mom wouldn't find them. My mom only ever wanted me to wear Mary Janes. With white stockings. Like with the pearls now. Whatever. I know I have dumb problems. So anyway, at Prissy's, we'd play dress-up. Sometimes we'd be back-up singers David Bowie was in love with, and sometimes we would both be David Bowie."

"You could have worn this on one of your sleepovers. It's very Ziggy Stardust." Jason traced his fingers over the bottom of Samantha's shirt again. "Hand-made? I wouldn't have pegged you for the crafty type."

Her own hand traveled slowly down to her waist so that approximately one tenth of one part of her finger was touching Jason's. The two of them ignored this fact and went on talking.

"Oh, you're so right. I couldn't hem a stupid triangle scarf in Campfire girls," Samantha babbled, shifting so an infinitesimally larger portion of her finger touched his. Her pulse didn't ignore it. Neither did his. "I'm hopeless with my hands."

She blushed at mentioning hands. She talked even faster. "Prissy—Pris—she got it from a vintage shop in London. It's like, a do-it-yourself thing from some '70s teen zine. The pattern came pinned to it. So some Samantha-like girl, but one who could sew, made it for herself, back in the day. I guess Pris figured, whatever happened, I'd still like Bowie."

A note of sadness crept into her voice. Anxiety flickered under her skin—cold, distracting. Contagious. Did Jason even like her? He always made out with different girls at parties. Was this just that to him? Did she care if it was?

Probably, but not enough to want to stop. He was very good. It was what all the girls said. Samantha was just going to enjoy it.

Jason moved his other hand up to the tree, so he was leaning on it, too. Samantha's body was between him and the trunk. Not so their bodies were touching, but you could feel the not touching in every single place it happened, which was everywhere. They never covered this in Sex Ed. Maybe she could think of something else to say about her shirt.

But it seemed like Jason wanted to tell her something else, something important. "You know, sometimes Pris, she sits like you, or you say, like, exactly the same things. I noticed it all week, and it totally freaked me out, 'cause on the surface, you couldn't be more different."

"I guess it's not just on the surface." Samantha sighed. It was probably the one topic that could really distract her from the touching and not touching right now.

Jason just nodded. "Pris, she takes that punk stuff pretty serious. It's not just an outfit to her."

Samantha took her hand away and slumped against the tree harder. "Yeah, she's so unsuperficial. But when there was some question, about whether we were going to be friends again because of how we looked, it wasn't—" Her voice broke. "It wasn't me, you know, who thought that."

"Hey, me and Pris are definitely tight," he blurted randomly. "But not in, like, a sex way, not, like, at all, okay?"

Did Jason know why? Interesting minefield to be navigated later.

"You know, she's so fucked up about coming back here, it's like she's coming down hard off of some pure London dope or something."

Samantha's forehead creased. "I don't think she's into drugs. Like, when you were so—weird in class—I thought maybe you were, but—it's not like I would know."

"Right. I was *trying* to use a metaphor. Or maybe an analogy. Something too complicated for Highwood boys."

Samantha rolled her eyes. "You are so full of shit. You're one of the best—talkers in the history of time. You know it, too."

"Did you just say the S-word?" Jason made his eyes go ridiculously wide. "You're a bad influence."

"Obviously." Jason ran a finger down Samantha's arm and she shivered. The bark of the tree dug into her back a little as she moved, reminding her of the rest of the world. She should have been getting cold, but there didn't seem much chance of that. With some effort, she brought her attention back to what Jason was saying.

"So—the other day in class, you were trying to figure out what was wrong with me? Like you cared, or something?"

"Oh, my God. Did it never occur to you that maybe I was bored? Or just curious?"

Jason trailed his finger down her other arm and she shivered again. "I thought we established that you had no reason to be curious about me."

"We did," Samantha tossed her hair, causing one of tears that had built up from thinking about Pris to spill down her cheek.

Samantha sniffed and wiped her eye on her sleeve and the mascara made a smudge on the vintage fabric. "Sorry."

"Don't say that." Suddenly his voice was steel anger.

"What, sorry? People should say it more." Anger flashed out of Samantha's eyes, too, a clear telegraph about which people in particular she meant.

Jason's eyes darkened. "People should never say it. They should just stop doing the things that made them feel that way, and shut the fuck up."

There was a long silence. Samantha *wanted* him to say he was sorry. That he'd been wrong about her. That he noticed her trying, too. Then she wanted him to kiss her.

Instead, he lit a cigarette.

Samantha hated smoking more than she ever had. But Jason only took one drag before he stubbed it out beneath his boot. He reached into his pocket and took out a Lifesaver instead, put one in his mouth. "I hear smoking is hazardous to your health."

"I've heard that too."

"Mint?"

Samantha giggled in spite of herself. "It's only wafer thin." The mint chalky whiteness felt cool, and solid, and familiar against her tongue.

"That's one of those lines from those movies, right? Like what Pris is always quoting?

"I remember that one. Right after the dude says that line about the mint, the other guy explodes in vomit and it is the most disgusting thing I have ever seen, including stuff from the boy's locker room I don't talk about because it would pollute even my mouth. So thank you for the romantic interlude."

"Thank you for the mint." Maybe he wasn't going to kiss her, after all.

"Hey, have you been drinking a lot? Tonight? You don't seem wasted, but I saw—I mean you always had a drink."

Samantha frowned at the sudden weird question. "A little buzz," she lied automatically. It was her standard response at parties.

"Enough to blame this on an extra wine cooler?" Jason laughed, a little bitterly, and gestured between the two of them.

Samantha shrugged, her own bitterness hovering. "I guess. I mean, you've still never done one decent thing in my presence."

"Yeah, well, pleased to meet you, hope you guessed my name." More bitter.

Samantha tried for cool. "How about you? High?"

"The usual. But you're not, like, wasted, right? You don't seem like it."

"Why?"

Jason shrugged. "I've got rules."

"About my being wasted."

"Yeah."

"That's really strange."

"Yeah, you're probably right. Anyway. Listen." Jason put his hand back by Samantha's head and leaned toward the tree. "There's a few more topics we need to cover and a time out only lasts so long."

The heat was back, but with a little more of that angry edge. His eyes had that burn.

"For example, I'm really gonna wanna hear about why the hell you would pick Bogart out of all the burnouts in the world, because that's such a fucking interesting choice, I feel I could learn a lot about the human condition from it."

"Yeah?"

"Yeah."

"That really bothered you?" Samantha liked that this was true.

"Yeah. You wanna know why?" He moved in close to her ear so she could feel every move his lips made. It set off something like insects moving their legs under her skin, like every part of her was alive and moving. Except she couldn't move herself. This was crazy. He was just talking. He even sounded mad. "The reason, it's also very interesting."

"Oh."

"It's because I saw you think about it. I saw in your eyes, which by the way keep me up very late at night because they are fucking beautiful, that the thought of kissing me had crossed your mind, and did not make you spit in disgust—so I got pissed off when it didn't happen." Every word he spoke blew differently across her ear, or neck, or hair.

"Oh," she breathed again, not meaning to say it out loud. "You're the one who spits," she tried to laugh. It came out like a shudder.

"That is very true," he said, his lips even closer to her ear without touching. "At you, as I recall. Because I am a total fucking bastard to you every chance I get. This is one of the reasons why your kissing me seemed unlikely."

"Yeah, there's that and—"

"And?

"Well ..." She closed her eyes. Why would she not just shut up? It was like Jason had stopped torturing her so she had to step in. "Well, Pris would know—that I don't—really like the whole choking on other people's tongues. So kissing anyone would be, kind of, a dare. For me."

Jason let out a low whistle. "Well. That might explain a few things."

"What, like I really am frigid?"

Jason shook his head, then moved his mouth even closer. "Jesus, no." He let his lips touch just under her ear, and she felt her whole body shiver.

"Obviously never called anything so wrong in my entire life. No, like you've clearly been kissing the wrong people."

"Duh. I just kissed Bogart."

"By the wrong people, I meant everyone who isn't me." And now Jason brought the tip of his nose gently across her jawline.

"I'm pretty sure you're a poster boy for the wrong people." It was getting so hard to talk. Everywhere he touched sent ripples somewhere else, like her entire body was liquid.

A low chuckle from Jason into her neck sent more ripples. "No, I'm the right people, because I'd trade third base with any other girl at the party to just stand near you and insult you for a while."

"Huh? Why?" Jason seemed to be able to talk through anything. Samantha couldn't form words.

"Because," Jason brought his hand to her hair and fiddled with it, getting lost for a moment. "Jesus," he whispered. "Because," he continued, bringing his mouth back to her ear, "trading insults with you is way hotter."

"Oh," she managed.

"Maybe not quite as hot when I make it so you can't really talk." He moved his finger over about an inch of skin on her neck. "And that's kind of incredible, because watching you talk when you're all pissed off is one of the sexiest things I've ever seen in my life."

"That's so messed up," she breathed.

"Pleased to meet you."

Samantha wanted to wipe the smirk off his face.

She summoned all her nerve and took the edge of Jason's t-shirt between her fingers. She let her fingers brush underneath it. "Do you know that a really worn t-shirt shows way more of a boy's body than a new one? The way it drapes over the muscles and stuff." She ran a finger down from his chest to his navel. "Huh," she said, not quite pulling off nonchalance. "You can really feel texture through it, too." When their eyes met, it was so intense it was almost funny.

"Huh," he said, a little shakily.

"Cat got your tongue?" she asked sweetly.

"I guess we'll find out," he mumbled, and then he kissed her.

Never, in all the imagining of how Jason Devlin might kiss that Samantha had done while trying not to, did she ever imagine anything gentle and sweet.

She had imagined tearing, and thrusting, and biting, and wet, things she had feared and wanted at the same time.

But he went slow. He even seemed nervous. He kissed one side of her mouth, and then the other. He whispered "Ohmygod" before he put his mouth on hers. She would have thought that if any niceness made it in at all, it would be laced with mean and bitter like everything else about him, but this kiss was just—sweet. Like he *did* like her.

All over, baby insects were opening their wings.

Once she had gotten a little past the shock of how good something so simple could feel, and how relieved she felt that he might actually like her, she managed to get her own lips to move slightly. And she kissed him back. She could feel his lips start to smile at that, but then they changed their mind and kissed her again.

So they just did that for a while, traded kisses instead of insults, not even any tongue. "Fuck, that's so sweet," he murmured, and then kissed her on the cheek, then the lips again. His hand traveled slowly back to her hair, which made the insects flutter.

She didn't know what to do. She loved the sweet, but she wanted him to touch her in more places, and was afraid of those feelings and what she might do. Her plan had been to leave the party. She started to panic. She froze, her lips froze, she was failing.

"Hey," he whispered, hand soft on her cheek. He spoke little words into her lips. "I know I've been a total bastard. But I'd never hurt you like this." Mouth to her ear. "Never."

Of its own accord, she felt her hand reach up around his neck, but it still felt a little like a claw. "Relax here," he whispered, then brushed his fingers over her lips and jaw.

So she did, instead of puckering or tensing for a fight. She felt his mouth open against hers and she felt his tongue against her lips. And all of the insects fluttered their wings and began to move their legs. Some of the legs seemed to have tiny lights attached to them. The lights went out when Jason's tongue went away. And so she opened her mouth, and licked Jason Devlin's lips, just to see what it would be like.

He groaned.

She tensed again. "Was that wrong?"

"Oh, God no."

He put his forehead on her forehead and shook his head. "It's just—I might have thought about this once or twice. And I don't usually ever want anything this bad, so I'm not used to what happens when I get it."

In addition to all the strange insects and their various wings and legs inside her, Samantha felt some outpouring of sweet, achy *like*. There was, there really *was* something she could like in this boy and not feel frightened or mentally ill because of it.

Which was also a relief.

She really wanted to kiss him again based on this new insight, but she was too shy to actually reach up and do it. She couldn't kiss him, but she found the nerve to look up at him, and her new thoughts and feelings made her smile.

Jason rolled his eyes. "God, that's pretty, when you smile like that. I'm going to stop you now, though."

This time when she felt him pushing slightly she let him in.

Not down there, just the mouth, but it felt like more.

Jason Devlin's tongue was in her mouth. It touched her own tongue and this was like nothing else. In a good way.

She tried to touch back, worried she wasn't very good at this sort of thing.

But Jason's throat made sounds and his hand slammed onto the tree and something in Samantha seemed to take that as encouragement enough. Because while Samantha Ward would have still been trying to figure out if it was okay to push back a little, or if that would be slutty or lame or too forward, this other thing that lived inside her grabbed on to the hair at the back of Jason's neck and pulled his face down harder on to hers and reached up between their bodies and grabbed a fistful of his t-shirt and pulled that, too. And then before she had time to think about it, her tongue was in his mouth, twisting and playful, like a kissing pro, and suddenly Jason's hand was gripping at her hip, hard, and there was another sound from his throat, this one more like a growl, Samantha's hand in his hair gave a little pull and she pressed up against him and his hand snaked around her waist, up her back, and pressed her tighter.

She pulled back and bit his lower lip slightly and then his jaw, and then licked his neck from his shirt collar to his ear and bit that too.

She leaned her head against the tree again, panting, but also taking in the delicious sight of floored, kissed to stupidity Jason Devlin, and thinking it was a view she could get used to. She smiled triumphantly. "Whoops," she said. "I slipped."

"Fuck me raw."

Samantha shook her head. "Not happening."

"Course not," panted Jason. "Expression. You know. Figure of. Something. What was that?"

Samantha shrugged her shoulders. "Beginners' luck?"

"I'm not a beginner. Shit." He leaned over into the tree, one hand on either side of her face, and just stared at her, panting. "All fucking night, is how long I wanna hang out with you, but I'm gonna have to go. Excuse me a minute." Jason dove at her neck and began doing things there with his mouth and teeth and tongue that Samantha had not considered could be possible. Her eyes were closed but she didn't think they'd see anyway.

He stopped as suddenly as he started. "Any more men's fashion tips you wanna give right now?"

She shook her head dumbly.

"Well, let me know when you do. I enjoyed the hell out of that last one. Listen, I gotta go face down the maw of hell, is there somewhere I can drop you?"

"I'm good," she murmured, but when she pushed back from the tree, she stumbled a little. "Whoa," she said unevenly. "Maybe I'm drunker than I thought."

Jason looked pained. "I guess that'd explain a few things."

They kept their distance from each other as they walked. It hurt.

"Gotta find Pris," Jason muttered. "She could be passing out or getting sick, and Dylan—he's not that much help."

"He was licking her arm."

"Aw, shit, I told him to fucking keep an eye on her, not a goddamn tongue. But I didn't think I'd be gone this long. This was kind of surprising."

Samantha nodded. "Yeah, I didn't really plan for that."

Then Jason pulled her behind another tree and started kissing her again, muttering about one for the road, taking several. He took her head in both hands and *looked*. "I've got a shitstorm to deal with. I'm not sure when we can get back to this."

"You wanna get back to this?"

"Hell, yeah. But I gotta 'time in' again, you know? Like, hardcore. I might be in a place where, really, you have to stay away from me, okay? There's some fucked up shit, some paths are crossing that shouldn't."

Samantha felt her heart sinking. "Like ours?"

"No, not like fucking ours. Jesus. Just—" He kissed her again, harder, deeper. Kind of desperate. "Listen, when you're beating yourself up later about kissing the wrong kind of boy, just remember—it was the right kind of kiss, okay?"

29. LOVE IN THE MIDDLE OF A FIRE FIGHT

Jason Devlin took the time with the stars and the moon and the trees and the girl, the whole fairy tale sweetness of it, and he put it in an empty matchbox in his pocket. He kept it separate from the other things there. That hour had no place in his life, no place for sure in what he was heading to that night. He knew, though, he'd carry it with him for years.

It wasn't like Jason never felt good, because he did. All kinds of ways—girls and food and music and sports, mouthing off, fighting—these days even reading—he liked the hell out of all of that. In fact, Jason thought that if parts of his life didn't suck so hard, he'd be a pretty happy guy most of the time and he wasn't sure that was true of everyone.

But.

That kind of sweet, weird-ass fluttering had made his hands tremble when they touched her—that kind of thing was just not in his dictionary. It only felt familiar when the hints of bitter edge crept in, an edge he'd come to need, probably, like a cokehead needed that line.

And that right there was why he shoved it in his pocket. He didn't want to get it mixed up with *that*. It was more than bad enough he had used a kiss to distract her while reached into a hollow tree to get the gun he'd ditched earlier.

Jason might've been "legally blind" to certain signals. Recent evidence did seem to point to that effect. Still, he'd been pretty sure he was the last dude who should be walking around with a loaded gun in his pocket feeling the way he did about Skinny Nowlin and life generally. So he'd ditched it while he tried to find the calm he'd need to figure his next move.

Found something else he wouldn't trade.

But. Next move still needed, and coming on fast. More reason to bury that hour deep down in his pocket. Because once he started thinking about it, he'd be on another planet spinning way higher and faster than the ground he had to walk on.

He couldn't afford it. And neither could some other people, whether they knew it or not.

Because. There had been a hell of a lot going down that Jason Devlin should have been paying attention to instead of girls. Skinny had hit him with it while Jason was still reeling from the gutwrench of a sucker punch it was to watch Samantha Ward put her tongue in Bogart's cesspool of a mouth. Not to mention the heartwrench of her laughing her ass right off her body at the idea that one of *her* friends might have crushed on Jason, even a long time ago.

Devil. Right. Beat up by his own hope. For a party game kiss. For a dumb mall girl drunk on wine coolers. He'd go kiss someone else or seven and be done with it. And then punch something.

But while Jason had been busy making a total idiot of himself, Nowlin had made plans without him. Fix up some little foxes with their fixes, he said. Public as all hell, four or five guys standing right there, Skinny acting the big man. Dropping Artie's name. The wrong order of things.

Girl that liked to play cat's cradle with Jason's entrails still laughing, Pris too. Rich girl crushing on Jason was the funniest thing they'd ever heard.

Funniest thing he'd heard, too. Joke over, though, game on.

Skinny's going on and on. He's got that *skeeve* in his voice. *Intro's all they need, man. Pleased to meet you, hope you guessed my name.* Snickering, elbow in Jason's ribs like they're big men together.

Skinny doing too much coke, thinks he really is that high.

These guys wanted to buy from the back room, from Artie or a level below, not just the street cuts out front where kids could cop, high price, low risk, low quality. That was Skinny's scene, where he was tolerated, where he was safe—and where Jason was safe having him. Instead, he was trying to make a move. Like standing next to Jason made Skinny a big man too.

Skinny had it all wrong. Talking to Artie Fisher in a men's room did not make Jason a big man. Jason was just a kid to them, tolerated or useful at best until the second he stepped out of line. Jason knew his place, Artie and his crew knew he knew it. Kept him safe so far. Could be the end of that ride, now.

To be fair, though, the end of that ride had come and gone. Going downtown and buying a gun was not something you did when you felt safe. And it wasn't something you did and then let yourself get all twisted and distracted by a stupid girl playing party games when all this other shit was at stake.

Grow the fuck up, Dev. Time to man up.

Jason lit a smoke with the last match in the box, swatting away a lighter in some girl's hand. If he could right then, he'd burn the match straight to his lung, bypass the cigarette altogether. He watched the flame burn the wood down to his calloused fingers and rubbed the scorched skin to black.

Skinny. Jason tried to speak low. "Not cool, man. Too many people. They can buy small from the dudes up front like anyone else. Not on my fucking name, man. It's not shit I do, you know that. C'mon."

"Chill man, it's gonna be chill. Like ice, man," and Skinny laughed again. He sang out of tune, "No one guess your name." Flying.

Then that other friend of *hers*, that Jessica girl, she's up there twitching and edging around Nowlin. One of those girls who thinks she's got it figured out. One of those girls who thinks she's up for anything but really, she's in for it.

Everywhere kids playing with what they don't understand.

Like buying a gun, for example. Right. Like that. But Jason could not watch something happen to his mother like what had happened with his sister. He wouldn't be some punk kid in an alley, watching helpless. Not this time.

Not that Jason had ever said a thing after. Del Lanes was the only place he had to go but home. So whoever the Artie was back then when it happened made sure Jason got extra burgers for a month. Had one of his guys tell Jason no one meant to go that hard on his sister, and that in the beginning, it was her idea. And even at fourteen, Jason knew that to be true. But something had twisted and burned inside him, because no one on the jones could say yes the way a sixteen-year-old girl needed to before someone shoved their prick into any part of her.

That was when Jason started beating on anyone at school who said a word about Heather. Because it wasn't his sister who was a whore, it was the coke. At Del Lanes, though, he ate his burgers and kept his mouth shut when it counted, and this was part of what his name stood for now. Someone who could keep emotions and business separate—his own and other people's.

Skinny didn't *get* that he could say his own name 'til he was blue in the face, but if he said it down there, it'd translate as "Devlin" or dirt. Skinny was high, smelled money and pussy, and Jason was off his game.

So Jason started bullshitting, gathering the boys around him like he really was the big man they thought he was, giving times and names of people who didn't exist. Warned that going in too high or too jonesing was like wearing a big neon sign that said, "Please rip me off." Everyone, Jason told them, should chill a minute, maybe go down and shoot some pool. Words were just coming out of his mouth, buying time till he could figure the scene and how to play it.

He was pissed as hell which was scary to Highland kids, but it wasn't scary enough. Plus, the one thing Jason knew better than he knew his own name was that you can't keep people from the things they come to need. You could only watch or walk away. So he did that, walked past the tie-dyes and the dancers and the giggling girls, to the edge of the lawn where the dark was winning against the party lights.

They got cars, man, Skinny yelled after him. Top of his fucking lungs. Chill as ice, man, he said.

Nowlin was out of hand.

In a little while, Jason would go down there. Set some things straight. Chill everything the fuck out. First, though, he had to cool down himself.

But really, if Skinny fucked up—

Jason shook his head. A gun made a strong point. At least he hoped so, because Jason barely knew how to take a safety off. He knew, he *knew* he was just a kid grasping at straws—this one with a slightly higher caliber.

Standing in the rich kid's big lawn, with the music, and the party lights, and the girl somewhere under them, laughing at him—Jason wanted to stay. He needed to pretend, just for a few minutes, that *this* was his life, that he could have some more beers and stumble home drunk and get chewed out for it. Go to bed with the room spinning and maybe cry that the girl didn't like him.

Or maybe find the girl and tell her, actually, that he knew she kind of did, even if the thought of it made her a little sick to her stomach.

He needed to pretend that he was *not* being drafted by slimy idiots who passed for friends and his own goddamn mother into ruining the lives of pretty girls with tons going for them—not to mention selling his own future down the river.

Jason felt a tear on his cheek. He swatted at it angrily, and his hand stung his face, so he hit a tree, which hurt too. It just sucked, because really, he *was* that kid who was so hung up on a girl, he could barely see two feet in front of him. He *was* that kid, and he had no business doing anything in the world but sitting here, smoking, and sighing, and thinking about her, because he wanted her, and a life that would let him have her, so fucking bad he wanted to pound his fist into trees or cry in a mother's lap. A different mother, obviously, from the one he had.

And then the girl was there. She looked tired and a little sad, as if maybe what she wanted most out of life was a hug.

So of course Jason said something cold and cutting and watched her flinch and adjust and parry. And then things had gone the same, and then things had gone different.

And then for the first time in he didn't know how long, Jason Devlin let himself name something he wanted, asked for it, and got it in spades. And now the whole fucking world had changed.

Except it hadn't.

So it was time in, in a big way, maybe for keeps, and shove that box down deep in the pocket. Girl goes round the other way, they don't go into the light together. Meet up back by Pris.

"I took her keys before, her car's down the street. I'm good to drive, I'll drop you," he stated, not daring to meet Samantha's eyes.

"Thanks for the warning, but it's cool, I bounce," she said with an attitude the size of Kansas.

"Good to know," he said, still not looking because he knew how lost he'd get. "Get in the car. Dylan, you too."

"Hey, homophobe buddy," slurred Pris, smiling up at Jason sweetly. "Didja know David Bowie and Lou Reed used to get each other off?"

"Jesus Christ, Pris, not fucking now. And bullshit. Lou Reed's married."

"Oh my God. Then there's no way he ever screwed a man, is there? Unless 'he shaved his head and then he was a she,'" she sang horribly.

He heard Samantha suppress a giggle.

"Shut up," he snapped at her. "I got no time for this."

"Well, don't let me delay you," Samantha hissed, flouncing away.

"Listen, Ice Princess Barbie, I told you to fucking GET IN THE CAR!" he yelled.

Samantha whipped around, fine blonde hair streaming.

"Oh my God, you totally did, but you know what? The time when I was taking orders from you? It was over…" She made a show of looking at her wrist. "Oh, that's right, about a BILLION YEARS before it ever started. So fuck off and die."

Jason still didn't meet her eyes, but he knew exactly how they'd look because his dreams were full of them. Eyes of pure ice goddess rage. Led Zeppelin could sing about them.

"Out-of-character obscenity duly noted, you must be so serious," he started right back, but then he did it. He looked. And really saw her. Her eyes, makeup slightly smeared from tears he caused, the fresh hurt in them so visible through the anger that sprung to cover it, lips still swollen from getting kissed so hard by him. He teetered at the edge of a swirling vortex of absolute adoration and shame. He closed his eyes. Then he took a breath and as he took that breath everyone was quiet and he could feel their eyes on him because people watched when Samantha and Jason talked, it was what happened.

Jason steeled himself for the next moment of looking at the eyes and the next hour and the next days of his life when he couldn't, and then he looked at her right in them and saw her look right back, and for a split second the other people and the world fell away and it was just them again, and Jason said something he didn't much say.

"Samantha. Please."

He saw just the briefest nod, and then she was on the ground by Pris, rubbing her back and saying sweetly, "We gotta go."

"Don't wanna. Sammie, he wouldn't even like me if he knew," whined Pris. "Not gonna."

"But Prissy, if you don't, I'm going to keep calling you that, and if I do, so will everyone else. It's how it goes."

"You are such a bitch," grumbled Pris, but she got up slowly.

"Don't call her that, Pris," growled Jason automatically.

"Oh, is that just for you?" Pris whipped around.

"That's right," answered Samantha. "He's got the market cornered on that one. Now just walk, don't talk."

"I got a lot to say, Sammie, I'm so fucking sorry, you have no idea how fucking sorry I am, I'm not the only one, I swear—"

Jason felt himself cringe but then watched in a kind of awe as Samantha just kept walking Pris calmly to the car. "Ssh, Pris. I know. But you shouldn't say that right now, for some reason it really upsets Jason."

"I think know why," started Pris. "It's because his—"

"Pris, shut the fuck up!" shouted Jason in desperation, because if she didn't, he thought he might die.

"Pris," Samantha said in the same even tone. "You're not wrong. I can be a real bitch. But I never was to you. And you know you can trust me, right? You know I have never, ever, let you down?"

"Well," sniffed Pris, "except in Loverboy and fashion sense and supporting the status quo."

"Right," said Samantha, as if this made perfect sense. "Except in that. But that has nothing to do with the fact that if you don't shut up right now, you will really, really hate yourself, and other people will too, and on top of that, I will call you Prissy every day for the rest of your life in an extremely public fashion. On that, you can trust me. Okay?"

"Okay." Pris pouted, and was silent.

Jason wondered if Samantha Ward would marry him if he asked, and then realized the box in his pocket must not be shut all the way.

After what seemed like several decades, they were all in the fanciest car Jason had ever driven in his life by a factor of about three thousand. He dropped Samantha off a couple streets down from Jah's, and as she got out of the car, she muttered, "I told you I could walk, genius."

"Just being a gentleman as always," said Jason directly to the steering wheel.

"I wouldn't have expected anything less," she said lightly. "In the Opposites universe." She leaned into the car. Fuck. He just couldn't have a moment with her. Couldn't. He wouldn't be able to drive away. But instead she just dropped a slip of paper in his lap. "Not sure where you're all off to, and for sure I don't want to know, but that's the address of the car you're driving."

"Fucking blood money car," groaned Pris from the back.

"Prissy—" said Samantha in a warning voice.

"Not saying anything."

"Thanks for being decent," said Jason woodenly, wishing the earth could swallow him whole.

"Don't thank me, it was really a weapon. I had hoped the shock might kill you."

Samantha turned and walked up the beautifully lit path to her gray stone mansion of a house that was big but not shiny or screaming "We have money" but simply taking it as a given. Jason was stuck between trying to memorize details and not look at it because it might make him sick all over the blood money car.

He shook his head to clear it, shoved a tape into the tape deck. Iggy Pop. Thank God. Raw Power. Mood music. Heartful of napalm. And then things started moving very fast.

30. THERE'S A DARKNESS ON THE EDGE OF TOWN

Near Del Lanes but down the street from the parking lot, Jason passed a Corvette idling, lights off, and it wasn't empty. He slowed and stared in the driver's window as best he could, but all he could see was a leather jacket with its collar turned up and the shape of sunglasses in silhouette.

But Jason had seen those shapes before. He knew. He *knew* who the fuck that was. His mind flitted back to a scene in the hall—the way a teacher's body had curved down to a girl whose face he hadn't seen. The alarm bells, the stoner haze that had kept him from *seeing* what he'd seen. The curve, the stance—it was the wrong angle.

His jaw clenched. If he lost his mind and went out in a shooting rampage, that Corvette driver would be number one—with a bullet. Jason felt a smile twist his face, then shook his head. It wasn't the matter at hand.

He woke Dylan who was sprawled out across Pris's lap in the back, snoring, and told him to keep an eye out, seriously, for anything that looked bad. If it looked too bad, he should lock all the doors and honk, then drive—but just around the block. Keep circling 'til he saw Jason. Otherwise, his job was to stay with Pris and if it looked like she was gonna puke, he should help her do it out the window.

Jason ran toward the door and then cut from a run to a walk and, summoning all the gods of cool and collected, strolled into Del Lanes. Technically it was after hours, so the front beer signs weren't lit, but everyone knew what went down there at night and he had to assume the cops were on the take. As usual, people were playing pool and drinking at the bar, but the lanes were closed and it didn't seem to him like a big business night. Low level counts and whatever else you could sell in dimes and quarters clearly available in the front but he didn't see any of the faces he associated with bigger size.

No Artie, no Skinny. Good sign? Maybe. No girl either, but her ride—he'd bet it was her ride—was still waiting.

Anxiety in his gut like a wringing fist, Jason sauntered over to some pool players. "Seen Nowlin?" he asked casually. "Wasn't he gonna meet ..." And he looked around, registering a couple of faces from the showdown at the party. "... you guys down here?"

"Yeah, but I guess—his guy wasn't here or something. He got antsy and took off."

Bet he did, thought Jason darkly. *Coming down, he'd know for sure I'd be pissed as hell.* "So that's all off for tonight?"

"Well, not necessarily." Edgy, twitchy, playing at cool. "Some other dudes said they'd talk, but just to that one girl from the party. Said they only did business one-on-one and not, you know, out here, so she'd need to come with them. Said they knew her, had seen her around so she'd be the best one."

The clenching fingers in Jason's gut turned to ice.

"Yeah, so we're just chilling, waiting to see if she cops."

"Right. Great idea. Keep talking about it loud. Harry loves that."

Jason made for the back entrance, not allowing himself to think of the two—or no, three—guys who were more than happy to send a fifteen-year-old girl off to a back alley with a few coked-up midlevel dealers to score for them. He did not think of the last time he had done this. He simply moved.

The brown walls he passed looked strange and alive, faces playing in the wood. Behind the door he would see brick, smell smoke and piss. He would breathe and not feel sick. He would look and see shapes and shadows only, angles and motion.

Girl pressed up against the wall, raccoon eyes streaming, glazed in the low light from the main street. Glazed from other stuff too. The look of a girl who's put herself out of her body. Panda bear rag doll.

The three dudes, they turn sharp at the sound of the heavy door. One with a shaved head and skull tattoos adjusts his pants. "Hey, kid, alley's taken. Back off."

"You back off."

Ugly laughter. "Says who?"

"Says Artie if he was here. You think Harry wants you raping some Highland surgeon's daughter in the back alley?"

"Chill out on the rape talk, she wanted to buy."

"She's got money."

"Yeah, we know, little of that, little trade. It's late night. Did you see her goddamn chest? We won't even fuck her pussy. Just her goddamn chest and mouth. It's not like she's saying no. Don't you get that? They're not *saying* no."

Racoon-eyed Barbie nodded and shook her head at the same time. Her hair was flattened now, matted against her head and against the wall. She turned to Jason with her blackened, empty eyes. He wanted them to be saying please help me, but for all he knew, they were saying please go away.

"Listen. Dude. Fifteen-year-old girl can't *say* yes to you. Law says it's fucking rape."

"Then I guess the law never met your big sister, huh?"

Hand out of pocket. Point. Shoot. Bang. Small hole in the wall and some reddish dust. Nowhere near where he was aiming. Lucky as hell he didn't kill someone just then, given how hard his hand was shaking.

"Jesus, fuck, kid. You really wish you hadn't just done that."

"Yeah, I do. Hands in the goddamn air. Turns out I'm a terrible shot. I could aim at your legs and take out your junk." Jason backed up to the door. Shots might bring backup, the door behind him would give him a warning. Cold metal gave him something to lean on. We all need something we can lean on. People in glass houses shouldn't throw Stones.

He could feel the sick rising in his throat, taking the stiff from his legs which felt like they might melt in a puddle beneath him.

Swallow.

"Now you listen," he said, still pointing the shaking gun. "My sister, before—she had no one. No one but me and I was half the size I am now, and you could *see* that on her. You think this looks like a girl who has no one? Look at her clothes. Look at her fucking *skin*. That *costs*. You think she looks like no one notices? You think her doctor dad won't see it, won't *test* her if he does? You think you'll be some kind of hero to Artie if they shut this place down over some coked-up rich girl?"

"Fuck it. This blows." The biggest one, long greasy hair with a scar on his lip and a bloody knife tattooed onto his forearm, grabbed Jessica by her pulled-down shirt and shoved her over to Jason. Her body hit hard and soft at the same time. Jason tucked her into his arm, she was shaking pretty hard. It made the gun shake more.

Breathe. Swallow. Steady.

Big dude coming toward Jason. Hands up, but coming down slow. Like he's conceding—a point, not a whole game. "All right. Even Highwood cops might turn out for gunfire. This sure as hell isn't over, but for now, here's how it goes. Wipe that shit off her face, she goes in with you. We go out the back."

Jason gestured with the gun in his hand, "Back the fuck off, I'm calling the shots for another minute here."

They'd go in together, cool as hell. Tell the kids in there waiting to for her to cop that it wasn't happening. Harry wasn't cool with that much size going out to underage kids. It wasn't happening on Jason's name, Jason's watch, he was ditching with the girl and everyone else could work the rest of their business as they wanted. Jason wasn't doing business, but if he ever did, it wouldn't be big and loud with underage kids, some of them clearly buying for older idiots Artie'd already cut off.

Jessica whined in a way that sounded like protest and the bald dude in a torn denim vest just like Skinny's laughed.

Jason shoved the girl up hard against his hip and she shut up. He hissed in her ear. "You're drunk, you understand? So you lean into me, staggering, and no one sees your shirt. Wipe your face some."

"You think you're coming out of this whole, kid?" Bald dude snickered, hands in the air bobbing with his shoulders. It even seemed like the dude was having fun. It was like a time warp, like Jason was looking right at Skinny five years from now. Jason felt the sick in him again. It would be good if he could get out of there before it blew.

"Don't know as any of us are. If I was Artie? I'd be pissed as hell at the four of us—waving guns and what, half-kilos in front of untested kids who saw everyone's faces? An underage girl whose father does crime scene consulting for the goddamn Feds?" Jason wondered idly what Jessica's father actually did. He thought he might be a heart surgeon. "Let's not make it any worse."

"Hope that pussy's worth it, you won't have long to enjoy it." But they went in through the door he opened, he followed them, hand back in his coat pocket, grasping what was there. And that was that. The way through

Del Lanes, the walls were still brown, the carpet still red. The kids from the party looked none too pleased to see Jason walking the girl past them. Jason expected to be jumped every step he took, but it didn't happen.

When they were out the door, Jessica made to push away from Jason. He held her.

"Let *go*," she said, "I gotta go, I got—someone's waiting." Her voice sounded shrill and frail and completely unlike herself.

He kept holding her, pulling and dragging her along.

"How are you better than them if you won't let me go when I want to?" Now she was hiccupping, shuddering she was shaking so hard against him. "They were right. I told them they could touch my tits. What do I care? They're just fat. They're not, like, inside my body."

He shoved the girl in the front seat and climbed in the driver's. Kids passed out in the back. He cranked on the engine and peeled out of the parking lot. Sirens wailed in the distance and he wondered if they were heading toward him. Girl whimpering all the time how someone was waiting, he loved her. She was doing it for them, it made things so special between them. When he touched her it felt like something. Those pricks couldn't touch her, she started repeating, over and over.

Then he couldn't take it. Jason drove behind a closed gas station and turned off the engine and all the lights. He turned to the girl and grabbed her face. Got his own face up right close to hers, then screamed.

"ARE YOU OUT OF YOUR FUCKING MIND?"

That woke the back seat up some, but no one said anything.

The girl stared at him, nodded. "Yeah," she whispered. "Yeah."

Jason gunned the engine again and took off, checking his windows and back mirror. Couldn't believe he'd stopped to scream at a girl who'd just been felt up rough in an alley trying to cop for her history teacher.

Feeling like an asshole and more than a little sick, he glanced at the girl, who was still just nodding her head and shaking. He took her hand.

And then he just drove, up and down and in and around until he could be sure he wasn't being followed, between and around the bars and gas stations and banks, up the drive near the lake and back down again. He pulled into an overlook where you could see the water in the moonlight, wide enough it looked like an ocean but he'd learned that was a lie.

He turned off the lights of the car, got out, and puked his guts out in the grass. In a minute he felt a hand on his back, rubbing up and down. He shoved it away, but it came back, rubbing tiny circles.

"You wanna talk about it?" Pris sounded calm, sober.

"No." He retched again. There was barely anything in there.

"Okay." Pris spoke slowly, but not slurring. Thinking. "Dylan's asleep. We can drop him and take the girl to my place. You can crash there, too."

Jason grimaced. He hadn't even thought about sleep and where to do it, home obviously not an option. "Right. I'll just crash with you. Your folks'll love that."

Pris snorted. "It's kind of a big house. In which 'kind of' means 'obscenely.' I have my own entrance. Besides, if my parents even notice, they'll be thrilled I brought a guy home."

"Funny."

"Not really. Skip it. Listen, does she need a doctor?"

"I don't know. You better ask her, okay? 'Cause I'm seriously afraid I might belt her. I'll stay here, watch the road—you—just take her. I'm done."

He heard the sounds of Pris getting the girl out of the car, then soft speech, then sobbing. All the while, he kept his eyes on the lights of the cars passing along the roads, watchful for the slightest slowing. All kept going at the same pace, no thought for him or where he might be.

Later, Jason learned it had been just as he'd known it had to be, the second he saw the car and driver. Jessica was getting high some, and starting to feel off when she didn't. But that wasn't so bad yet in itself. The bad jones was for the man in the Corvette, who told her he loved her, who told her the coke made the sex so good, it hurt him to give her less than what he'd had with other women. When what they had was so much more. But his hands were tied, he couldn't buy, he was already risking so much to be with her. He knew he could trust her, it was what made their love so special.

His hands were tied.

The men in the alley had roughed her up some. Bruises, but not on the face. They knew better. Pris said she'd looked carefully other places, didn't see any skin broken. They hadn't gotten to the point of putting anything in her mouth. One had jacked off in front of her and wiped the semen down her cheek and neck and breast. She swore, swore he hadn't gotten to the mouth.

At first, Jessica had bridled at these questions, which started as soon as they'd dropped off Dylan. Pris said okay, they could go to the hospital, but Jessica blanched and said her father was on call. She said she was totally fine.

Jason spun around. "What, you trusted those guys to stick to your tits but you can't trust us to see if you're safe?" He could feel bitter words bubbling, bursting through, spit and bile burning for a target. Pris silenced him with a punch to the shoulder.

More calmly, but still with an edge, Pris asked, "Do *you* know what safe means these days? Because I spent the last year living in squats filled with sick junkies and prostitutes and I'm not sure suburban Sex Ed covers the whole story." And Jessica had started shaking again.

Pris explained she was just trying to make sure about the broken skin, that it wasn't clear how much contact had to happen for—

"AIDS?" Jessica had actually snorted. If they were gay, she wanted to know, would they really have so much interest in her tits? Pris kept talking, explaining how some people just got off on power, or on whatever way they could. How intravenous drug users were at high risk, that was how her lover's mother had gotten sick, and it seemed possible that skeevy dealers might shoot up.

Jessica was quiet after that. Pris asked if she thought Diangelo shot up, and she shook her head, then asked softly like a little girl, "How would I know?"

Jason just drove, working hard at not listening. He hadn't known any of that, what it might mean for his sister. Then he began to wonder if he'd just get beaten by Artie's crew, or if it would be worse, and the sick came back in his stomach despite the huge, yawning emptiness inside.

Before, as he'd watched the night for cars coming after them that never came, Jessica had made her way over to him. Her voice scratched with tears and coke dripping down her throat.

"I guess I wasn't really thinking clearly."

He nodded, surfing the great wave of understatement.

"And, I—I mean, thanks—for that, but—" She took a deep, hiccupping breath. "Why? You hate us."

Jason shrugged. Some things could not be explained by speaking.

"Is there anything I can do, you know—?"

Jason turned, and looked at the girl straight on. Not a rag doll, but not yet quite in her body either. The fight and snap that made her stand out so much at school was gone, there was an older girl and a younger girl taking turns in her place, turning and rotating with the twisting of her fingers.

"Someday," he said. "Not now, now you gotta keep quiet, but someday, you tell your friend I did a decent thing."

IN BETWEEN DAYS

Squeeze, she said. His line, he thought, but it didn't matter. He liked being with her. There was always an upside. You just had to know where to look.

He closed his eyes and he was back in the alley. He'd shown up, like a goddamn date, because he knew they'd find him and he didn't want them looking and finding anyone else. Kid had stiffed, taken off. Of course. He'd known that was coming. He'd made it happen. His need for atonement was stronger than Schnapps.

Word was they were supposed to leave him standing. Said they'd be back every twelve hours 'til their boss got whole, and if he went home, he'd get worse. Boss was grim, his mouth a thin line and nothing else.

Dude who'd done most of the kicking, though, grooved a kind of rock and roll beat. Dude was humming. Saturday night's alright for fighting, Saturday night's alright, alright. Dude seemed to enjoy his work.

Fists first. Stomach, ribs. He fought back. To the jaw. To the eye.

And then slam. Head against the dumpster as he fell.

Then the grainy started. He thought he heard word come to lay off, they'd been going at it long enough.

Find your friend. Get it. Don't fuck around.

He'd have to be able to stand up to do that. But the guys didn't get the message. Or started having too much fun. Hard for some people to stop partying once they started.

To the chest. To the back.

And one of them said the teacher'd pay double if he didn't walk.

The ground beneath him was hard and cold, he didn't know why he was lying on it. He got up, but the alley swayed and came to meet his face all sudden and unfriendly. And then it wasn't gray. It was black.

Car running. Voices. Fright. You could smell it. Hands. Tears. Car moves closer. That girl. The one he liked. Blue. He had something to tell her but only broken bits got through. Hands. On him, pulling, twisting, pain beyond mind. That word. Again and again, he'd say it. If he could ...

The sound of a body hitting pavement. Not his own. The world coming a bit more into focus, the knob on the TV twisted just right. A voice crying and yelling at the same time. "Just close your eyes and help me get him to the goddamn car. We've gotta get him to the hospital."

"No hospital, not here. No."

But he was in one, it seemed. Time was all weird. Girl saying something about her brother. The voice didn't match. The dates didn't match. The facts were wrong. It sure as hell wasn't any goddamn mugging. Plus she was talking about parents, like there was more than one.

Confused wasn't even the word for it.

31. I SEE THE GHOSTS
OF MY CHILDHOOD

After a night of tossing and turning with the restless ghosts of the right kind of kisses—she wanted to tell Jessica she'd finally liked it, but she was afraid to even say it to herself—Samantha Ward, to her own surprise, spent most of the next two days with another boy.

Because when Samantha got home from church (where one went) on Sunday, instead of bracing herself alone among the cold stone and ivy, she found Pris standing on her front porch. Her hair was down, not teased or spiked or ratted, and she was doing a sort of hardcore version of a little kid's Christmas morning dance.

And Stephen Ward was sprawled casually at her feet.

Samantha's mouth worked and no words came out. The other two stared at her. She stared back. Finally, she managed, "You missed church."

Pris covered her mouth in mock horror.

Samantha's fear was more genuine. "Does Mom know?"

But Stephen grabbed his sister in a hug and whispered. "It's fine, Sam. Paternal pass from quarantine."

Samantha took a moment to just be perfectly, perfectly happy to see her big brother, however it had happened. Then she stared at Pris again, hard. "Since when did you know he was coming?"

Pris shrugged. "Yesterday."

Yesterday. Samantha's eyes widened. Even after the party, the drinking, the Truth or Dare, the ... Devil himself ... Pris hadn't breathed a word.

Pris said quietly, "I got good at keeping secrets, Sam." A shadow seemed to pass over her face as she looked at Stephen. "Goes with the territory."

Then suddenly Stephen was out on the lawn with a football, shouting at them that the huddle was over. "Out for the pass, Sam!" And Samantha went, Laura Ashley dress and white stockings and pearls be damned.

Yes. Pearls be damned. *Please*, she thought. After all, she was consorting with the Devil. There should be some practical application.

But then the football was spiraling towards her. She caught it in a satisfying thump and had to run fast before Pris took her down too easily. By the time they all collapsed in a grass-stained heap on the lawn, it was like three years had disappeared. Almost.

The rest of the weekend had gone by in a blur—a cuddly, flannel-encased blur of blue hair and Stephen slouching *just* so. There had been highlights even before the rest of the family had left them to themselves. Like Pris still killing at tennis despite refusing to let any white clothing even approach her body. Or the priceless look on Nancy Ward's face when someone wearing all black— except for the purple high tops—beat her son in straight sets on *her clay courts*.

"The blue hair, it's psychological warfare," Stephen had laughed, then he'd ruffled it and told Nancy he might try it himself for baseball season.

Dinner had been a quasi-formal Sunday afternoon affair for which Pris agreed to wear a dress to appease Nancy for her son's surprise visit, a visit secretly sanctioned by her husband, but planned and paid for by Pris. Complete with car and driver. Pris's grandmother, Samantha now learned, had left her a ton of money. Blood money, as Pris called it, loudly, to everyone.

In fact, as if to make up for the dress and blood spending, Pris talked politics the whole meal, causing veins to appear prominently on Lincoln Ward's neck and Nancy Ward to stifle many smiles. She also offered to donate to the students protesting apartheid at Northwestern University without Pris even asking. She even insisted her husband look into divested-only mutual funds for their own investments and watched placidly as he squirmed.

It was, the children agreed later, Nancy Ward in top form.

Splayed out on the sloping back yard after dinner, Stephen and Pris serenaded Samantha with Velvet Underground songs, swaying back and forth with upraised eyes before, in a sneak attack, covering her face and hair with silly string they'd hidden in their sweatshirts.

"It matches your sweater!" shrieked Pris. "It's an accessory!"

Then Stephen and Samantha had wrapped Pris in a blanket and tickled her feet until she confessed her love for Cyndi Lauper.

When Pris had mysteriously run home Sunday night—she had to check on something, something that involved stealing a large quantity of dinner leftovers—Samantha was able to have a serious talk with Stephen about "Rock Hudson" that nearly killed them both with its extreme awkwardness. Furthermore, Samantha was left with the unwelcome knowledge that, faced with an incurable wasting disease attacking people like his son, Lincoln Ward had sent his cousin Pip to take Stephen out to lunch.

"Cousin *Pip?* With the *ascots?*" repeated Samantha, incredulously. "Did he bring his *wife*, Lacey?"

Stephen shook his head. "Lacey mostly lives in France, Sam."

"In France?"

Stephen nodded. "That was pretty much the extent of his advice. Get a wife, have her live in France. And then he gave me a box of condoms and said they'd work wherever I wanted to stick things."

Samantha's jaw dropped. "He did not."

"Did so."

"I'm going to kill Daddy."

"No you're not, he was trying to help."

"He doesn't have a *speech impediment.* He could have talked to you about it himself!"

There was a pause while Samantha and Stephen contemplated this possibility, and then a cacophony of gasps and strangled laughter at the image it created. They were like this when Pris found them, sitting cross-legged across from each other with their heads together, holding on to keep from falling over giggling.

When they explained, Pris shrugged. "Obviously Nancy should have done it: 'When one places one's willy anywhere except one's own hand, as one does, one wears the appropriate latex *attire,* it's very *simple,* Stephen, blah blah blah.'"

At that, Samantha and Stephen *did* fall down then. It got serious later, as Pris told about the sick people she knew in London, and Stephen explained how he'd been too scared to do anything when he'd found someone interested.

But even that conversation was not as serious as when they all sat down with David Bowie's *Tonight.*

"*Let's Dance* is genius by comparison," sighed Samantha. She glared at Pris. "I blame Iggy Pop."

Pris stuck out her tongue. "I blame shopping malls."

Stephen rolled over. "I blame lesbian vampires."

"Hey! That movie was *hot!*" Samantha and Pris spoke in unison, looked at each other, nodded, and insisted they watch *The Hunger* before switching to Monty Python.

Stephen said the lesbian sex scenes were way hotter than David Bowie.

Pris snorted and said Stephen totally failed as a gay man. Samantha said *she'd* make a better gay man than Stephen, but that she agreed, the lesbians were way hotter.

Pris raised an eyebrow at Samantha, who kicked her. "Don't get any ideas just because we used to practice making out on each other and Catherine Deneuve is a babe."

Steven put his hands over his ears and shouted "LA LA LA" as Pris repeated, "Little sister, making out, little sister, making out!" at the top of her lungs.

And so it went on all the rest of the long Columbus Day weekend. As if by secret agreement, neither Samantha nor Pris ever said a word about Jason Devlin, not to Stephen or to each other. But as Monday afternoon rolled around and Stephen had been driven off, Pris turned to her friend and asked in a strangely small voice, "Was that a better way of saying sorry than getting drunk on Schnapps, Sammie?"

Samantha nodded. It *was* better.

But not all the way.

Prissy wanted forgiveness without having to say what for. Samantha didn't even know herself what it was. Which made it difficult. And so their weekend faded into some limbo between childhood and the present—closer to how they'd been, but not quite the new thing yet. And not, Samantha feared, something you could hold on to on a school day.

Samantha needed *someone* to talk to, though, at least about what to wear to school after making out with said school's most infamous boy slut—she said it out loud in her David Bowie-lined closet—and your own sworn enemy. And liking it.

It was the kind of question Jessica excelled at beyond all others, but Jessica did not pick up her phone all night or morning. She must have had, Samantha thought, one hell of a Saturday night. She supposed she'd hear about it, but for now she was flying solo.

Fifteen outfits later, it was decided. Dark eyes, big curly hair, high ruffled collar, purple satin jeans, chains, and a frock coat. "Queen Bitch."

Okay. So the song was really about transvestite prostitutes. Samantha knew that. But you could pick and choose your lines and your meanings, your guitar licks and your wardrobe. You could put things together as you saw fit.

Some days your outfit was more than "just fashion." It was armor, disguise. And the song you hummed to yourself on the way to school? It was a battle cry.

The weekend was over. Vanessa Segal was on the warpath. Time to round up the pawns.

On Tuesday, Samantha started whispering with Michelle and Bethany and the freshmen girls before she even got up the main steps to the school. Things could get ugly, she said. Wait for a sign. She motioned to other girls, politicals and theater types, even the girls who didn't quite fit in any group at all. She told them Vanessa Segal was going to try to take her down—for Dave Watson, for being friends with a punk rocker, for speaking out about stuff that didn't get said.

"Why are you worried about her taking you down?" The girl who spoke seemed aggressively devoid of make-up. "Is it really so great 'up there?'"

"That's not the point," Samantha tried to explain. "If you don't fight back, it's like lying down and taking it."

"So why don't you bring that spirit to politics, you know, bring it where it'd count for something *real*."

"Duh." Samantha rolled her eyes. She couldn't help it. "This *is* politics. Are you in or out?"

Samantha needed bishops and knights. But it looked suspiciously like the best candidates had been captured, or at least disabled. Because when Samantha got to the girls bathroom to put on her contraband chains, she found the *two* of them, Pris and Jessica together, talking earnestly in a corner and both looking red-eyed, contrasting shades of eyeliner smudged under their eyes.

Wordlessly, Samantha handed them a bottle of eye make-up remover and tissues and waited to be briefed.

"Hi, Sammie," sniffled Pris.

"Sam," wavered Jessica, "I heard you called."

Only eighteen times. Samantha just nodded, looking back and forth between them.

"I was totally crashed last night. And then this morning I left way early. I, um, I walked."

"Jess, that's like, four miles."

"Yeah, like I said, it was early."

Pris met Samantha's eyes briefly, and it looked like she was begging for something. "Looking swishy, Sammie," she whispered.

"Pris, Sammie has left the building. She doesn't go to this school." Samantha folded her arms and shook her hair back. "So I take it you two know each other?"

Pris wiped her eyes. "Yeah. Saturday, remember?"

"Well, glad to see you're hitting it off." She waited a minute. No one was looking her in the eyes. "What the hell, guys?"

Both girls just shook their heads. "It's complicated," whispered Jessica.

"Right. While you guys discuss that, I'll just go live my simple little life." Samantha turned on her heels to head out the door in the flounciest flounce she'd flounced in a while, but instead ended up bumping into a cheerleading friend of Kimmie's who'd come running in.

"Hey, Sam. Can we have a minute?" Cheer Girl glanced at Jessica and Pris. "Tell anyone I was here and I put Nair in your hair gel, got it? Nothing personal."

It was very simple. Vanessa and her friends were amping up. They had a plan. They'd be expressing their concern about Samantha's mental health to the counselors—maybe even Stagnita, if he'd listen—all week long. Coming in teary-eyed, halting, worried.

Samantha was pretty sure he'd listen.

The idea was to get a note on her record, a call to her parents, and of course counseling. Samantha was vaguely impressed.

Cheer Girl was telling, because Stagnita was a step too far. Plus Kim was being kept out of the cheer loop, and Cheer Girl was for squad solidarity. Information delivered, she was out of there fast.

Samantha turned to her friends.

"Vanessa Segal is toast," Jessica said.

"No, she'll win," Samantha sighed. She didn't even look at Pris. "Jess, I swear to God, I don't even know why I care. But if Stagnita calls my parents, I'll be at Miss Porter's School for Girls by lunchtime. I should at least go out with a bang."

Pris hopped off the sink she'd been sitting on. Her make-up was fixed, too. "I'm in."

Samantha turned to Pris. "Really? You? Girl war with the cheerleaders?"

Pris shrugged. "Hell, I live here now, right? And going to Stagnita is heinous. I agree with Cheer Girl. Plus."

"Plus what?"

Pris kicked at a cracked tile on the bathroom floor. "One of the reasons they call you Psycho is that you hung with a freak like me in public, right? Least I can do is fuck with them a little."

Jessica grabbed Pris. "C'mon. How out of it are they? It's 1985. Punk is so mainstream it's not even funny. I mean, it's not my thing, but it's not like none of them ever jammed out to Billy Idol."

"I feel so much better now," deadpanned Pris.

Jessica was already planning, "I'm totally going to pretend to make out with Dave Watson and smear inky hand prints all over his back."

Pris looked at her sharply. "Really a good idea?"

"I can make out with anyone," Jessica said firmly. "I just tune out if I don't like it."

"God, I have tried so hard to do that," said Samantha, "I'm kind of jealous."

"Don't be," said Pris and Jessica in unison.

The three girls walked out of the bathroom, plotting. Samantha threw herself into it. This, at least, was something she knew. And something to think about other than the fact that Jason Devlin was not looking at her except to shake his head slightly in her direction. Speaking not sexy, but stay away.

32. THERE'S NO WAY OUT OF HERE

Jason Devlin realized he'd managed to fuck up a lot in the past few days. But probably nothing more thoroughly than he'd managed with Pris. There, he'd taken something great and make it shitty, as opposed to taking shitty things and making them potentially worse.

He looked for her first thing Tuesday morning, but he couldn't find her.

And if he did find her, he wasn't sure what he'd say, since the thought of her kind of made him want to throw up.

Shit just kept taking him by surprise. Girls, especially.

The worst surprise, though, was getting paged to the principal's office out of second period. Well, that wasn't exactly the surprise, considering it was a more or less daily occurrence.

It was what he saw there.

He'd been ready to blow off school—didn't think he could deal with seeing Samantha, because then he'd definitely think about her.

Didn't think he could deal with seeing Pris, because it was like looking in a funhouse mirror that spread his soul in ugly directions.

In a regular mirror, he still just looked like a regular dude. He'd checked. So he'd wanted out of the funhouse.

Sure he'd wanted different. But not *that* different.

He also didn't think he could not strangle Jessica if she looked like she'd been doing blow. Or if she showed up within two feet of that prick Diangelo. And he didn't think he could see Diangelo without putting a fist through his skull or, worse, ratting him out, which was the last thing he could afford to do.

He doubted he could see Skinny without using his ugly bald head for a cueball, and he didn't have a *clue* how he was going to handle all those other girls, or rather, not handle them, because girl skin and tongue—with one exception—kind of nauseated him now.

So for all those excellent reasons, he'd been dead set on blowing off school. Then, after a night of smoking himself to death in the cheapo motel room he'd snagged from guilt-ridden Jessica, he got the bright idea that school was the safest place for him.

School was the one place, he figured, where whoever else he had to see, he didn't need to be looking over his shoulder every two seconds for an angry coke dealer.

Because school, apparently, was the place he could look right in front of him, in the Vice Principal's office, and find one.

There was a kind of rushing in Jason's ears. He grasped the door frame to keep steady. Stagnita was at his desk straightening some papers that didn't need it, saying something about a stepfather, a mother, and worry.

A stepfather.

Artie Fisher twisted his lips into a smile-like shape. "Yeah, kid. The old lady's been worried sick about you. No one's seen the least part of you since Saturday night. And you just know it's not 'cause they haven't been looking."

Stagnita's hands were shaking.

Holy mother of fuck.

Jason tried to run his tongue over his lips, but they were so dry it got stuck. The thought occurred that it was lucky he'd just taken a piss or he'd be standing in a puddle.

Artie's lips curled a little more. It wasn't really that much like a smile.

It was more like in a horror movie, the thing that scared the scary monster.

"So, Tony here—okay if I call you Tony?"

Jason couldn't look at Stagnita but the very fact that he said nothing was enough.

"Tony here's been good enough to lend us his office so we can talk this out. Your mom and I want you home, buddy."

Tony. Buddy. Home.

Stagnita couldn't get out of there too fast, and Jason found himself in a chair, his mind leaving out whole chunks of time and movement. He should be sharper. Now was the time for that sharp, that smooth.

Artie's face hardened into a carved glass version of itself. "Now, no bad words, kid. I figured I could find you here, but we're not stupid, right?"

Jason nodded. He still hadn't spoken.

"You're probably wondering what I need you for, if I can just waltz in here like this." Artie chuckled. It was not a nice sound.

Jason nodded again.

"I'm just your step-dad. Step-dad with a fine photo collection of all his kids and their friends. Some of those kids, they're your spitting image. Tony was amazed at the likeness when he first saw them. Know what I mean?"

Jason swallowed, glad he hadn't had much for breakfast.

"Step-dad?" he repeated, his voice a rasp.

"Well, nothing formal. But I'll be around, kid."

Jason could not imagine what could possess this man to be interested in his mother, but he also hoped to God he would not press himself to push his imagination further.

"I'm not mad, kid. I worked hard on getting some straight answers from my people, and I gotta say, you weren't wrong, what you said. That was some bad shit, and if it had just gone down a little different, I'd probably be thanking you."

Jason felt his jaw drop. He hadn't been expecting *that*. Maybe this would be okay.

Artie went on, not expecting a response. "Course the way it *did* happen, I can't let it stand. Not some punk kid. Not at my crew. Can't happen. Not with the—" And he made a little trigger of his hand and pulled it.

Stones began to form in Jason's stomach again. "So—so you gotta let me have it, right?" He tried to swallow but couldn't. "But not my mom, right?"

Frowning slightly, Artie shook his head. "Nice of you to think of her." He seemed genuinely to mean it. "Not to worry, she takes care of herself—in a manner of speaking. Anyway, it'd be you. Wouldn't be pretty."

"Harry—" Jason was grasping. "Since I was a kid, he's been—"

"Harry doesn't see much, these days, without his glasses. But listen, kid, I've been trying to tell you—it'd be different, see, if you were working for me. That'd be a whole different story. If you were doing business—at the shop, you know what I mean. You'd've just been doing my leg work. Like I said, you weren't wrong. But you stepping in, just you, it messes with the order of things."

Jason looked at the shit-brown paneled walls of the principal's office that he knew better than the walls of his own living room at this point, and felt they were coming closer, like that scene from *Star Wars* with Artie starring as the creepy garbage monster and Jason about as articulate as Chewbacca.

Jason shook his head. It was a good movie, but it wasn't really going to help him now.

He didn't want the kind of beating that would say to angry cokeheads that Jason had been taught a lesson for shooting at them.

And he really *didn't* understand why, if Artie had so much dirt on Stagnita that he could commandeer his office, he couldn't just deal himself here on campus.

Probably put his time in dealing coke at a high school in high school. Graduated, so to speak.

The walls were closing fast. If Artie had his home and his school and his work—what was left? Jason could run, but this was where and what he knew. He sometimes went to Chicago—but not much. And as to what happened to runaways—Artie had pictures, and some of them already looked like Jason.

Plus Artie was the big man at Del Lanes pool hall, but probably no more a big man outside of it than Jason was the big man outside of Highland Central. The kind of counts Jason knew moved from that back room, that kind of supply wasn't based in Highland. There was a whole food chain behind Artie, and that food chain was not going to let stand some punk kid shooting guns off at any part of itself. Artie was right on the money with that.

Kid who'd been groomed, though, who'd already been a runner for years, which was the case, as Jason knew in the pit of his stomach when he looked at his meal deliveries for his mother—that *was* a different story. That was an up-and-coming kid looking out for business, protecting his deal and his turf.

What did he really have to lose? Jason closed his eyes.

He closed his eyes to the images of Jessica, raccoon eyes streaming, his sister raiding his room time and again for *anything* to steal. He closed them tighter to the image of Pris who he didn't have now, thanks to himself, and even tighter to the image of Samantha, who he'd never, ever have, not if he did this thing, not ever.

Insane as it was, it was that thing, the thing he didn't even have, that was beyond bearing. He wished he was valuing all his principles and his future and his freedom more. But it was the thought he'd never get to kiss that girl again that did it.

Because really, he was just a dumb punk kid, when it came down to it.

He opened his eyes but kept them at the floor. "What about, you know, the step-dad thing, if that got around? Wouldn't that take care of it? If I just lay low after that? Family, and all?"

Artie shook his head. "Do I look like Marlon Brando to you, kid? No godfathers here. Business is business."

Jason sighed. He grabbed a pad of paper from the desk and started writing.

"They'll be watching me now. *He'd* like to get out from under your thumb. It's not safe." He drew a little arrow, pointing at the office door.

"Anything happens to you, kid, he goes down." Artie spoke out loud— much louder than he had been, and jabbed with the thumb in question toward the door.

Swallowing, Jason wrote again, feeling like he might as well be signing his own death warrant. But no, not that. Signing the sad compromise like that dude they'd talked about in history class, dude that signed over some sad little country to Hitler to try to keep the peace.

That hadn't worked out so well. But probably that country hadn't been begging to be signed away. Not the way Skinny Nowlin had.

And anyway, Jason had gotten kicked out from history last year for getting the whole class to call that sad dude Chamberpot. Which Jason had thought was perfect, since the guy was full of shit. Sold out the country with the funny name and Hitler was bombing the shit out of London within a couple of years anyway.

But Jason hadn't been allowed to take the final exam, so you couldn't really blame him if he didn't draw on the lessons of history.

So he wrote, "I farm it out. One week, it's on me, I vouch for him. He works out, score's even, week's up, I'm out. For good. He doesn't, take it out on me like you have to."

In a week, maybe he could figure out another plan. Maybe his sister could help. Maybe his new rich girl friends and enemies could help him get to Mexico. Maybe Samantha would come. A week was so much better, anyway, than nothing at all.

And Skinny was clearly headed toward this anyway. Jason was only pushing the inevitable one step closer, maybe helping Skinny do it smarter, so he wouldn't get killed in the process. Give him the in.

Jason could talk his way into almost anything, even in his own head.

Artie read, paused, considered. "Do you feel like you can come home now," he said loudly, "now that you know we won't let anything happen to you if you just follow house rules?"

Jason teared up at that. Because he would have given his right arm, suddenly, for some *real* parent to say something like that to him.

While he spoke, Artie wrote one word. "Name."

And when Jason wrote it, Skinny was one step closer to having his own.

"It means a lot that you would say that, thanks," Jason said out loud.

"Five percent off the top to you." wrote Artie. "Well, you better get back to class," he said out loud.

Jason shook his head. He didn't want any of that money. He wrote a zero on the paper. "Can you get Stagnita to give me a pass?" he asked.

"Not a problem, I'm sure," Artie said out loud, but shook his head, pointing to the zero.

Jason understood. He had to take something. It was business. His mind flashed back to their conversation in the men's room what felt like ten years before, then cut to the Corvette outside the pool hall, engine on.

He wrote on the page. "The prick I told you about gone from here."

Artie spoke out loud, getting up. "We'll see what we can do about that a little later, when things have settled back into a routine. Glad we had this talk, kid. Your mom, she'll be relieved. You'll see. She'll get off your back now. She just likes things regular.

He stuck out his hand for Jason to shake. And, because there wasn't anything else to do, Jason shook it.

Peace in our time.

Now all Jason had to do was find Pris and tell her that he hadn't meant to dry heave in the bushes outside her pool house when she'd told him that her boyfriend was really a girl. Simple gut reaction. But he probably shouldn't have offered to cure her with his special tongue talents afterwards.

That was after he yelled, "What the fuck, Pris, I *hate* that shit! You *know* I hate that shit!"

Her eyes had been running black—he was seeing a lot of that lately, why the hell was he surrounded by crying girls all the time? What was wrong with hanging with dudes?

Aside from the fact that his best friend was a skeevy, disgusting coke dealer wannabe he'd planned to beat some sense into but instead was promoting from wannabe to partner in crime. Aside from that.

When Jason finally saw Pris, her eyes weren't running, they looked right through him. Funny. She caught on fast. She and Jessica were whispering and looking daggers at a cheerleader and Jason thought bitterly how Pris was finally getting into the spirit of high school. Bull Dyke Barbie. Excellent.

It was true the idea of two girls getting it on made him sick. Not as sick as the idea of two guys, maybe, but sick. Thing was, none of it made him feel as sick as when he remembered the look on Pris's face when he'd said that.

Like she'd just lost her best friend. The colors beneath her eyes ran more blue than on other girls.

Stupid girls shouldn't smear that stuff on if they were going to cry so much. Jason felt the mean settling in on him, digging in its claws.

Samantha's eyes were cool, dry, perfectly lined, every time he stole a glance. *She* wasn't wasting any tears on him, that was for sure.

At least Pris's eyes had gone back to flashing soon enough. Even that night. Jason's mouth twitched at the memory. "Yeah, well, I don't like the idea of sucking cock, either, but the fact you let half the fucking school suck *yours* didn't keep me from letting you crash in my room!"

"That's different."

"Damn right that's different. Because I think of you as a whole human! Not just one part of what you do that I don't wanna think about!"

He did like a girl with a mouth on her, but in Pris's case, he really wished he didn't know where that mouth had been. If she was so proud of what she did, why did she lie about it? He'd asked that too, genius that he was.

Her eyes were tiny, rage-filled slits when she answered. She'd thought about this one, plenty. "I never lied. I just didn't say. You assumed. Even when you saw her picture. I didn't correct you because I *thought*, that if you got to know me first, it wouldn't matter. I *thought* you were prejudiced because you didn't *know* any better. I didn't realize that you were just a dumb-ass parochial asshole who doesn't *want* his world to get any bigger! Good luck with your goddamn coke dealers, Jason. I'm done making you sick. It's my turn to be sick, now."

Thanks for asking, Pris. It's going great with my goddamn coke dealers.

The way Jason's life was fucked up in every direction possible echoed like reverb in every movement of his mind and body.

He hated the hurt look in Samantha Ward's eyes as he hadn't spoken to her. He also hated how quickly that hurt look had vanished.

She shouldn't be hurt. He'd warned her, and that was before coke dealers were after him.

Now, of course, he was a coke dealer himself, so that was no problem.

He had become his worst nightmare.

As if to prove it, he shoved some freshman up against a locker because the kid had dropped a book on his own toe and it startled Jason.

And if Samantha Ward really thought he was dropping her without a second thought, why wasn't she *more* hurt? Shouldn't he be harder to get over than that?

At least every other girl he kept putting off his body all week had the decency to look hurt. Which felt pretty much like shit, actually. It wasn't like any of them had done anything wrong.

Jessica Levin was steering clear of him at school, just like he'd told her. At least she also seemed to be steering clear of the sleaze who made "Don't Stand So Close To Me" sound like an anthem of child friendliness.

If there was one good thing to come from this whole thing, it would be that Diangelo would go down.

Skinny, on the other hand, thought all kinds of good things were coming from it. He was ecstatic with his new position. Jason told him they shouldn't be seen together all the time, given everything, made it clear it was just the week and he was out.

Skinny said sure, they could go out for burgers and pussy when it was over.

Jason had a new understanding for why girls might want to be gay when he thought about dudes like Skinny. He told Skinny if he traded coke for skin, Jason'd drop him. "Cash and carry, man." Skinny's scowl had gotten a little darker.

"It's easy for you, man, but we don't all look like the goddamn heavenly choir."

Jason *ached* to tell him off with fists and feet, but that had to wait now.

Tuesday night he slept at home. His mother made macaroni and cheese out of a box and called him honey, sweetheart, big guy.

Artie Fisher came by. Jason cranked Pink Floyd very loud. He switched it for Sabbath after a while.

On Wednesday, Jason wrote "Sorry" on a piece of notebook paper and shoved it into Pris's locker.

In Social Studies on Wednesday, Samantha Ward handed him back the paper. It was way more crumpled than before, but had been folded up again. "Pris said you dropped this. She said she tried to tell you, but you didn't listen."

Jason just nodded.

Samantha Ward spoke bright and airily, as she did to everyone except her girlfriends. To them she whispered urgently. Clearly something was going on all the girls mistakenly thought was important.

On Thursday morning, Jason was called to Stagnita's office because Vanessa Segal's underwear had mysteriously ended up in the front trophy case.

He said he didn't do it.

Stagnita just nodded. "I hope you understand. A teacher saw you waiting around near the girl's locker room, so I had to ask."

I hope you understand? That was one of the scariest things he'd ever heard come out of Stagnita's mouth.

Stagnita smiled at him. *Smiled.*

"I think it's the girl they're calling Psycho Ward," Stagnita continued. "Your friend. Cheer girls have been coming to me all week concerned for her welfare." Stagnita's smile got a little wider. "Let me know if she gives you any more trouble."

"I barely know her."

Stagnita shook his head like he was sad. Shit. That might have been the wrong thing to say. Who knew what Samantha Ward really said to this crazy-ass motherfucker? Maybe she really was psycho.

The mean in Jason had dug deep and sharp.

"Mental illness can affect even the first families," Stagnita said slowly, lips still twitching. "Look at the Kennedys."

Jason folded his arms. "Look, this has been real, but even if I knew anything about Pantygate, I wouldn't tell you, all right? No matter who it was. I'm no nark."

It seemed like he could say what he wanted now. Not like he didn't anyway. In fact, with this new freedom, he even toned it down some. He had nothing to prove, nothing to lose.

Stagnita met Jason's eye for a long, difficult moment. "It's my job, Mr. Devlin. That's all."

33. SHE'S LOST CONTROL

Pris didn't waste so much as a glance at Jason until Thursday lunch, when she shoved him hard in the chest and asked what the fuck he was doing there. By his locker.

Jason looked at Pris. Stared. Stock still. He shook his head, confused. "What are you talking about? I get it that my existence pisses you off, but I still go to school here."

He glared at Pris harder, the sight of her still made him feel like shit about himself. And even though that was true, the whole lesbian thing creeped him out, too.

"Shit for brains, you're supposed to be out meeting Samantha."

"Again, what are you talking about? I haven't said a word to her all week."

"You think I don't know that? But I also know, because I know who the hell you are, that you're *dying* to, and that's why, despite your bullshit with me, I told her it was fine to go. That you wouldn't try to hurt her, not anymore." Pris shoved him in the chest again. Hard. "God, I have *never* been so wrong about a person."

Something cold and slimy started creeping up from Jason's gut toward his chest.

He grabbed Pris's shoulders and shook her slightly. She made to punch his arms away but stopped short when she looked at his face. "Pris. For the last time. *What.* Are you talking about?"

Her face crumpled in confusion. "The note. The note you wrote her."

"I never wrote her any note."

"Don't *pull* this shit, Jason. I saw it, she showed it to me. She was afraid to go if no one knew. I told her you wouldn't set her up. Because I SUCK!"

The cold, slimy hand started tugging at Jason's lungs. He fought for breath. "Pris. I didn't write anyone any note."

He let that sink in, and then realized maybe they didn't have time.

They spoke at the same time. "Well, if you didn't," and "What did it say?" canceling each other out, a little chorus of panic.

"C'mon, Pris, what the fuck did it say?"

"Field house. Lunch. Important. Spelled wrong. And your name. But Jason, who would think she'd go there for you—how would Vanessa have any idea—hey, wait!"

Jason was already halfway down the hall. He slammed into Dougie Douglas, who looked for sure like he'd have something to say about that, but Jason just shoved the quarterback out of his way like he was nothing. Another jock came toward him, but when he saw Jason's face, he just backed right off again. The scattered kids in the hall just scattered further, ready to trip over themselves to stay out of Jason Devlin's way.

Jason himself was only dimly aware of any of this, he was aware of nothing but speed and the amphibious fist clenching at his heart. He passed Janine Kanter, caught a look of alarm off her but kept running. He had to. It registered that Kwame Bartholomew had been talking to Kanter, and that Kwame was running after him, and he could maybe catch up. So Jason swung around.

"Get your girlfriend. Something is fucked."

"Hey, slow down, what's going on?"

Kid was fast, but not fueled by turbo panic. Plus Jason didn't really know the kid, didn't know what he'd find when he got where he was going, though he had a bad feeling he knew who.

Jason kicked open the steel door that led out to the playing fields and held to it just a second. "Just tell your girlfriend," hissed Jason, barely sparing the breath. "Tell her Samantha, trouble, Field House, but keep it quiet." He took off, but turned to see the kid was still standing there. "NOW!" he yelled. "No time to fuck around."

He'd never run so fast in his life. The colder air was like a knife to the chest and he cursed cigarettes for maybe the first time ever if they were slowing him down even a fraction of a second. He cursed the heavy boots he always wore, because every second could be one too long. Laughter echoed in his ear with the sound of his own silence when he should have been talking. Loudly.

The field house was looming, yellow brick and metal siding. The sun shone cold in the icy air, the warm spell over. The brightness just gave everything a sharper edge

Jason knew, he *knew* this edge would cut deep.

He rounded the corner, there was nothing by the side. He heard a low, strangled whimper. He ran faster.

Around the back, there was an extra set of bleachers, old and rusted in places, shoved against the side of the building. You couldn't really see anyone back there—for this reason, it should have been more popular—but it was too far away for most people during lunch, stoners not being big on sprinting, plus the field was long and exposed, and there was no other way out. For smoking, making out or even sex, the main bleachers were better.

So people didn't really go to the field house, but since Samantha didn't go in for any of that stuff, she wouldn't know.

He couldn't see anything through the folded, sagging bleachers, but he could hear.

Jason was afraid he wasn't close enough to stop it, He had to run all the way around, trying to go quiet until he could see.

The bald head. The hair splayed against a wall. The hand on a mouth, exposed because she was taller. The bright autumn sun glinting off metal at her neck.

The threat. The shaking head. The hand moving from the mouth lower. He saw these things at a closing distance, they became clearer as he neared.

Her eyes were closed.

Skinny heard him, turned. Smiled. "Dev. You're late for the party."

Her eyes opened. Jason was close enough to see the frozen, hollow horror in them.

"Skinny! Drop it!"

"Yeah, that's not your style, and I guess the both of us can handle even a Queen Barbie." And he actually chucked it. "You want in on this after all, Dev?"

But then Jason was on him, yanked him from the girl and threw him away. "What the FUCK, Skinny? What the FUCK're you doing?" Skinny staggered back, but didn't fall. He was a small guy, but a hell of a fighter.

Now, Skinny was just laughing. He was still fucking laughing. "What the fuck is wrong with *you*? I *asked* you, man, you said it was cool! You said you had no interest in her."

Jason heard a sound behind him. He couldn't bear the crumpling girl he would see there.

Skinny laughed again. "Yeah, can you believe it? I *told* you, man, she had a rich girl thing for you. But that stuck-up bitch doesn't get it that you're too good for her."

He was fucking high, coked out of his mind.

Jason was so winded from his run and his panic, he could barely spit the words. "I'll kill you."

"Dev, what the *fuck*? We're *partners*, man. I wasn't gonna cut her, I was just partying. And it's not like I'd do it to a real girl, but this one? She's plastic, she's not even *REAL!* You said it yourself, a hundred times."

Jason lunged toward him, but Skinny had a head start, and Jason hesitated, remembering the girl. He turned, and Skinny took off fast toward the school.

Samantha Ward had slid down the brick wall and was sitting, hunched over, arms around her knees, shaking. Her lips were swollen and her stockings were torn. Shredded. She had a hand to her throat.

Jason was down on his hands and knees. He had no idea what to say or do. The words that came to him so easily were gone. She was broken, it was his fault, and he wished more than anything in the world it had been a knife at his throat, even if it had gone in.

He looked for blood and saw none.

He put his hand out toward her, but she flinched.

"Did he—?" Jason didn't know what to ask.

She got up from the ground, wobbling. He darted a hand out to steady her, but her voice was awful as she growled, *"Get your hands off of me."*

She stepped out of her shoes, reached down and pulled the remnants of her stockings off. "Did you pay him? Or was that going to be later?"

"What?"

"He said. You'd pay to see him try."

"I never said—" but he stopped. Because he had.

"Don't bother," she rasped. "I knew it was true the second he said it."

"Samantha, *please—*"

"Don't say my name. You don't get to say my name." Samantha walked over to the knife that lay in the grass where Skinny had chucked it. She put it in her jacket pocket. She zipped up her jacket and adjusted her skirt over her bare legs.

Samantha tried to fluff her hair, then took out a compact. She opened it, looked in the mirror, winced. She started dabbing gently at her face, at the puffiness and finger-shaped bruises, with a little sponge.

"It doesn't matter—what you—I mean, we've gotta get you seen. The nurse—"

"That can't happen. Anyway, I'm not hurt." She paused, dabbing some more. "It's just a flesh wound," Her eyes teared at that, at *that,* and then she gasped, holding her hand to her mouth, and doubled over, like a sharp pain had overtaken her.

Jason reached, made to go to her again, but she went into her pocket and pointed with the knife.

"Nowhere near me." Her voice was so hoarse, it sounded blood-laced. She leaned against the wall.

"Samantha, we'll get Pris—she'll know—something."

"Pris!" Samantha's laugh was like a bark, animal. "You don't think Pris has helped me enough? Your friend, he told me—how she explained me to you. Both of you. Like, first thing."

"It wasn't *like* that."

"Yes, it was."

Again, Jason couldn't speak. He wanted it not to be true. But the fact that it was kept him from denying it, even though these cold, hard, simple truths left out so much of the feelings that had driven everything, and those feelings had truth of their own.

The fact that the feelings had done nothing to keep finger-shaped marks from Samantha Ward's face kept him from speaking of them now.

Samantha, though, kept speaking. She sounded almost thoughtful. "You started it. You and my best friend. You made it open season on me. And then on Saturday—you told *Skinny* you'd pay to see him try. Was that because I was pretty, too?" Her voice was barely a whisper. He wasn't sure she was even talking to him, or if she was just saying the words, as if getting her mouth around them would help her do the same with her mind.

Jason was just shaking his head, no. But he couldn't even say the word. Because he knew, that judging on words spoken or unspoken, everything she said was true.

Samantha took out a little tube and began dabbing cream on bruises at her throat.

"Police," he managed to get it out.

"Please. I'm not hurt, and do you know what they'll ask me? What they'll ask my parents? Do you see how short my skirt is?"

Jason rubbed his hands over his eyes. He felt like sobbing.

"And I may not know exactly what goes on, but I do pay attention to some things. So do you *really* want Skinny Nowlin picked up by the police right now?"

Jason just stared at her. He found her voice so painful, he could barely hear the words it strained to speak. And worse than her voice were her eyes, all cleaned up now, but dead and glassy. And still beautiful, but like a painting, like some haunting painting of a girl who'd died. Somewhere on the outside of her eyes, the little words "Skinny" and "police" prickled at his thoughts.

He shook his head. "None of that matters."

Samantha laughed again. It was the worst sound that Jason had ever heard. "Every single thing. Matters. It's something I've learned."

She shook her head again, the hair fell forward, covering. "I knew stuff was going on all week. But I didn't get it."

"No."

"I get it that you just stopped him. I do, I do get that. But what I don't get is, why?"

"Because I would *never, ever* let him do that, no matter what!" Jason felt if she did not know that, nothing mattered, and the police could pick up whoever, Artie could do whatever. He didn't understand how she could be saying true things about him, and still be saying what she was saying.

"Oh, obviously, that's what I'm supposed to think. But I'll never know for sure. Was it all just, like, a set-up that went too far? Was kissing part of it? Is your showing up in the nick of time like the movies, you know, part of it, too? Do you meet later to laugh?"

"Samantha, please, I swear to God, you have *no idea* what's been going on!"

"Right. Which is so strange, given how much everyone keeps telling me." She put on lipstick, gently, as if it hurt. It was all shiny, though, just like usual. "Look. Don't worry. It's not like I'm going to try to get back at you or anything. I'm a lightweight. I could *never* hate anyone enough to make them feel like this." She put her compact and lipstick away behind zippers. "Maybe because I'm plastic," she added quietly, and walked, straight-backed and chin high, off toward the school.

Jason watched from the side of the field house, gauging bodies and distances and speed. No trajectories neared her. When he judged she'd put enough distance between the two of them for her own comfort, he followed, trying to stay within sprinting distance.

A figure approached her; Kim, Jason judged by the dark hair and bouncy step. They hugged. Jason felt a tightness in his chest ease a little. He thought he saw Kim look toward him as she put her arm through Samantha's and headed her toward the parking lot.

34. IT'S SO COLD IN ALASKA

Kim Sato didn't ask Samantha about her voice, or the bruises, or what she wanted to do. Kwame was just waiting in the parking lot, his car running. They knew it was bad.

They took her the lake. Kwame had a blanket in his trunk, he spread it on the shore and motioned for both girls to sit on it. Then he sat in the car. At a distance.

Samantha was glad of the quiet. She felt beaten on the inside. Her throat hurt from screaming before Skinny had got the knife.

She was glad he hadn't cut her throat or raped her.

But the fact that Skinny Nowlin had had her up against a wall, his fingers digging into her flesh and tearing at her stockings, stymied by her legs that were stronger than they looked—that wasn't what was making her feel beaten. At least, that wasn't what felt the worst.

Samantha felt strongly that it *should* have felt the worst. She was mad at herself for feeling hurt worse by Pris and Jason than by a slimy pervert trying to force his way between her legs.

Her feelings compensated by retreating even further beneath her skin than they had when Skinny's hands were on her.

She was bruised down there. It hurt some to walk, but it hurt to sit, too. It was better to look at the lake.

The lake stretched wide and blue before them, its shades deepening as the afternoon wore on. Its surface was not as smooth and placid as it sometimes was, nor as sparkling as it could be in late sunlight. About what went on underneath, its surface gave little away.

Kim drew the blanket up around them and hugged her. Samantha thought it would feel the same to her if Kim had hugged a nearby tree. Her outside and inside felt so disconnected.

Kim seemed to get it. She let go, put some inches between them. "Can you tell me? It's okay if you can't."

Samantha sighed. The words didn't matter. She could say them all day. It wasn't a long story, so she told it.

Samantha didn't need to look at Kim. She could hear the shock.

"But Jason was there, behind you, when I went to meet you. I *know* it was him. Was he *watching?*"

Samantha shook her head. Then shrugged. "I don't know," she rasped, her voice faltering again, badly. "He stopped it. But he started it, too, even last Monday, he started it. Maybe even Pris—she said it was okay to go. I don't know."

Samantha felt a huge, burning lump in her throat that was pressing harder than Skinny's hands, and from the inside.

Kim frowned, looking down. "I'm so sorry. I even thought you kind of liked each other."

The lump in her throat put pressure behind her eyes. Samantha felt welling and burning in there as the lump squeezed out the words "So did I" in a thin little moan. She grabbed her knees to her chest and pulled them in tight.

Kim asked about going for help, or parents, or police. Samantha said she'd have to keep talking about it forever, and not in some therapy way, and besides girls had been saying she was crazy all week, even to Stagnita. Who knew who else they'd like to tell that to?

Kim said she'd only just heard about that. She would have been mad that Samantha hadn't told her, but getting attacked at knifepoint was a major get out of jail free card.

Samantha tried to smile.

Kim brought up that telling someone, like the police, might help other girls, later, but Samantha said she cared more about herself right then. And she'd rather never talk about it with her parents because they didn't know about it, than never talk about it with her parents because one didn't.

Kim nodded. "It's totally up to you, Sam. You're one hundred percent in control."

"Cute," said Samantha. She flinched at how hollow and bitter she sounded.

"I wasn't trying to be cute," Kim whispered sadly.

"But you can't really help it," sighed Samantha, and smiled a little, even for real.

Then she faltered again. "Kimmie, I didn't mean—"

"I know," said Kim. "I know you."

Samantha nodded. It hurt her throat to do it.

A little later she said, "Kwame's kind of awesome."

Kim nodded again.

Samantha wanted cold on her throat. She wanted cold all the way down to her bones. She wanted normal on the outside. She wanted calm.

"Do you think Kwame would take us for ice cream?"

Kim smiled a little, even for real. She stood up, helped her friend off the blanket. She held her arm for Samantha to grasp if she needed to but didn't put it around her or make any moves to touch her. The two stared at each other a moment, then Samantha put her hand on the offered arm. "You're awesome, too, Kimmie."

"You, too," said Kim lightly. "It's why we rule." And she walked her friend slowly to the waiting car.

35. THE BOY WITH THE
THORN IN HIS SIDE

Skinny was nowhere in the school. Jason checked under closed bathroom doors and all the other places people might meet a scumbag to pick up their coke. It was after school, but there was a weird kind of quiet. The vice principal's office door was shut tight, the faces of the office ladies strained. They didn't even give him any shit.

Jason Devlin was in a daze, sick to his stomach with his life and the lives of others. He could think of nothing but the feel of fist plowing into cheek and bone and gut.

When he closed his eyes, he no longer saw hers. He no longer saw anything, reaching or stretching toward him. He saw his own fists, and then he felt the blows that would be coming for him soon.

He might kill Skinny Nowlin. And then Artie might well kill Jason if he couldn't get the coke back—or fuck him up so bad he'd wish he was dead. But anything, *anything* would feel better than this.

Jason left the school and headed towards Highwood. He figured he'd stop by the bowling alley, see if he could find Skinny there, then check some other places he knew to look. Worse came to worst, he'd be waiting under the underpass come morning.

But now someone else was under the underpass. Jason tensed, on auto pilot, although a punch to the gut would suit him right now. Throw one, take one—didn't matter.

It was Pris. Pacing. She looked like an animal in too small a cage. And then she was flying at him, in his face. He brought his hands up to block her.

She grabbed him by the hair, reaching up, threatening as hell despite his having a good half a foot on her. She looked like she could cut into someone, even with just her teeth. "Where the fuck *is* she? I got hauled in to Stagnita's office because of stupid cheerleaders, I couldn't get there!" Pris pulled his hair tighter around her fingers.

It wasn't enough to rile him, to ruffle his dead, horrible calm. Jason reached up and took her hands. "Pris. Calm down. I'll tell you."

She wrenched her arms away. "If anything happened to her because of you, I will *end* you!"

Jason just said the words. "Skinny always thought she had a thing for me. Figured she'd come if I asked. He was right."

Hands back on him, grabbing his shirt, twisting. Spitting in his face, slit-eyed. "*What? Did? He? Do?*"

Jason didn't even draw back. Spit in the face was maybe too good for him. "He tried. He had a knife. I got there."

Punch to the gut, then head to the chest. Jason staggered back. Girl was stronger than she looked. She was yelling. Bastard. Cocksucker. She shoved him again, really hard. "I fucking *sent* her there! Jesus *CHRIST!*"

And then she just stared at him. "Why aren't you fighting back, you *prick?* Fight back, you don't think of me as a girl, so why pretend to treat me like one?"

"You wanna get hit, Pris, is that it?" Jason looked at her face and didn't need an answer.

"I *sent* her there. I made *peace* with him."

"Pris." Jason took her shoulder, she swatted him off. He took it again. "You told him you'd cut him if he called her bad names. You warned him off on Saturday."

"I still talked to him. I did it for *you!* And don't fucking touch me, you think I'm disgusting!"

"I can't hit you without touching you, genius!"

The two of them just stood, staring, a face-off. Then Pris looked down, muttering, "Yeah, well, if you're gonna split hairs."

"Pris, I'm not hitting you."

"I hit you."

"I had it coming."

"Yeah, you did. So do I."

"No, you don't." Jason shoved his hands in his pockets, awkward. He looked down at their boots, both pairs, scuffing in the grimy dirt. "Pris, you're the best person I know."

"I sold out the best friend I've ever had, because I didn't like how she dresses and I wanted to hang out with my tough-guy crush from seventh grade. Because I was cool enough for him now. I talked her down to the scumbag who tried to rape her. If I'm the best person you know, that's fucking pathetic."

"Thought's crossed my mind. Still. You're the best friend *I* ever had. Even if who you sleep with grosses me out."

"Are you afraid I'd forget, or what?" Pris's slit-eyes widened, and in front of him, for a second, stood a little girl who looked like she'd just been slapped. Jason closed his eyes.

"No. And it was true. It's *still* true. But if I had a fucking *soul,* I would probably try to do better."

Without touching, or looking at each other, they turned toward Highwood, black boots falling heavily on the dusty sidewalk. "Did you get Samantha to a safe place? Is she getting help?"

"Samantha Ward hates our guts. She thinks we planned it. Skinny told her every shitty thing we ever said. Just so you know."

"I'd hate us too. But is she safe?"

"She's with Kim. She wouldn't go to anyone, you know, grown-up."

Pris nodded. "Stagnita's out to get her, and her parents would just pack her off if they knew. And anyway," Pris sighed, then wiped a tear that was falling down her cheek, sucked it from her own finger like it was frosting or something. "Pretending like things didn't happen is in her blood. I'll talk to her later."

"Not sure that's gonna happen."

"It'll happen."

"How do you know?" Jason wondered how a person had faith in good things happening.

"Because she loves me best. And you don't stop loving someone just because they let you down in horrible, painful ways."

"Pris."

"Yeah." Her voice was clenched so tight, it was amazing it still had room for sound.

"Your fucking veiled references are beyond me because I'm just a tough-guy crush, but if I could feel anything besides the desire to smash Skinny Nowlin's face into a bloody pulp, I would, like, probably love you, too."

"The idea of me disgusts you."

"Yeah. But I would love you anyway, if it was the kind of thing I did." Jason kicked a stone into the road very hard. "Instead, though, I'm gonna go beat the hell out of my ex-best friend."

"Cool," said Pris. "I missed doing stuff with you."

When they got to Del Lanes, Jason stopped at the door. "Listen, you can really fight, right? I mean, I can take Skinny, and normally I'd think it's shitty to double team."

Pris parted her feet and folded her arms, looking solid. "I can handle myself. Plus I have a blade. Which I won't use if you're in the fight."

"You carry a knife in school?"

"Nah, just a blade. Easier to hide. You should hear some of the shit people like you say about gay people. I like to have something on me."

"Fuck, Pris. I'm—Look, I got your back, from now on, okay? I'll make it fucking known."

Jason didn't mention he might not make it past the weekend. He hadn't mentioned about Artie, Skinny, and the coke, in part from shame, in part because he didn't want Pris talking him out of doing Skinny.

"I don't need goddamn protection. This guys fighting over girls bullshit. It's *archaic*."

"Right. Enough with the vocab, okay? I'm not in the mood." Jason pushed Pris toward the brick wall by the door, not hard, but enough to show her he meant business. His voice was low, but he made every point a little stronger with a finger to her shoulder. "Listen, Miss High Horse. For your information, it's not just 'cause I like her. That makes it triple shitty for me, but I would do this if he'd done it to *anyone*. And even if it wasn't on me. But it is, okay? I've known the kid since kindergarten, and he doesn't fucking know how much I would hate that. It's *on me*. I'm the only person he ever listened to in his life, and apparently I said fuck-all that mattered."

"Jason, I shouldn't have said—it wasn't your fault."

"I don't care what you think. All I know, he had a knife to a girl's throat and thought I'd want to *party* with him on her. So that? That's on me. You get that?"

Pris looked him in the eyes, hard, and for a long time. "Yeah," she said. "I get it."

"Good. So you want in? Fine. You go round to the back alley. If he's here, I'll bring him. If not, we keep going till we find him, and we fuck him up. Because it has to happen. But we don't kill him."

"Of course we don't!"

"No. Not of course. You didn't see her. He bit her neck and put a knife to it. He tore up her stockings, I don't know how far he went down there. She has his goddamn *fingermarks* on her face from where he wouldn't let her scream. Pris. I've been called the Devil for a long time, but I swear to God, I am in *hell* now."

Pris put a hand on his arm, tentatively enough to remind Jason of another hand, another time, different bricks. He shook it off.

"I thought you said she wasn't hurt," she whispered.

"There's inside hurts," he muttered. "C'mon."

36. IT'S CARDS ON THE TABLE TIME

There were some things ice cream couldn't make better. You could pretend for a while, though, and the cold would feel good. Later, Samantha had pressed ice to her face in the bathroom, reapplied makeup, as Kim looked sadly on.

But when Samantha got home and pleaded sore throat to her parents, she had no one to pretend for. She went to bed. Not in flannel.

Pris called. Samantha asked her mother to explain she'd lost her voice.

Her mother brought her soup. She'd heated it herself. She put a hand briefly on Samantha's forehead and murmured that she didn't feel warm. Samantha said it was probably just a cold.

Her mother said her face looked puffy. Her brow furrowed a fraction of an inch. Samantha said it must be allergies, then, and asked if the gardeners hadn't just done some new fall plantings. Her mother's brow was smooth as she murmured she'd speak to them about it.

Samantha's father stopped at the drug store to buy cough drops and cold medicine and popsicles. The sore throat was true enough. The horrible swollen ball of hurt was still there, swelling every time she thought of Pris or Jason.

She must have drifted, in and out of pale silks, smooth sheets, cool drinks brought on a doily. When she woke up, Jessica had called.

And Pris was at the foot of her bed, just sitting.

Samantha turned and faced the wall. The sight of Prissy squeezed the lump in her throat. Like aliens might burst out of it and if what was in there left her, she wouldn't survive.

Pris was talking, but Samantha couldn't hear it. "I can't, Pris."

"I would ten times rather it happened to me, Sammie."

"I wouldn't," Samantha said. "No matter what."

She shut her eyes.

Samantha slept and did not dream. There was a distance between her and the world, and she felt she would like to maintain it.

She did not go to school. She spent the morning wandering around the house, "like a ghost," complained Ernestine, half concerned, half disapproving.

So she went downstairs and watched soap operas and glared at her record albums. The problem with experiencing a lot of your feelings through music was that it wasn't really available when you wanted to avoid them.

Every time she thought about Pris or Jason, the alien bulb in her throat threatened to hatch. When she thought about Skinny, though, she just felt angry. *General Hospital* made more sense than she did.

When Ernestine made her way downstairs to tell her that she had a gentleman caller, Samantha was surprised. Chip or Johnny, maybe, checking in? Or Kwame?

"White guy?" She asked absently, following Ernestine up.

Ernestine stopped short before her on the stairs. "You know some other kind, now?"

"Ernestine? That wasn't very nice."

Ernestine chuckled. "I don't know why not. Anyway. Yes, white guy. That narrow it down for you?"

"Very funny."

Apparently Ernestine thought so, because she kept laughing. Something a little different had gotten into her. Back at her stove, she relented. "Nice looking. Very clean cut."

"Like *that* narrows it down," Samantha sighed, disappointed by something she would not have allowed herself, under any circumstances, to acknowledge.

"I plumb forgot to get his name. But he said he brought homework for you, some weekend project. He's out front."

Samantha wondered why, if he was going to say all that, he didn't just *say* his name.

She figured it out pretty quick when her heart stopped.

He looked amazing. He always looked amazing. Now he looked *preppy*. She had no business thinking any of that. He had set her up. Maybe. His hair fell over his eyes. At least over one of them. It was still long at the front. The sides were short. He had a haircut like her brother's. The eye she could see wasn't meeting hers.

Right. Jason Devlin was wearing a button-down collared shirt and khakis and the world had clearly ended, it was an apocalypse. She worried she might be happy to see him. She had no self-respect. She would end in a battered woman's shelter. He had stopped Skinny from hurting her. He had kissed her. He had said horrible things. He had put on *penny loafers*.

It was too much.

"Costume party nearby?"

Jason just shook his head.

"The neighborhood doesn't actually enforce the dress code, you know."

"Yeah, I just—um, I didn't want to cause you any trouble."

"Right. It is completely hysterical that you just said that," said Samantha, not laughing. The shock was wearing off a little.

"I mean more trouble. Like with your parents, or whatever. If they thought you knew someone like me."

His eyes were all but fixed on the ground. Every so often they would dart toward her face, but not make it there.

"You weren't at school," he said, still not looking at her.

"You missed not looking at me at school, so you got all dressed up to come to my house and not look at me?"

"I wanted to know if you were okay."

"Afraid your friend didn't finish the job?"

Jason just winced. He didn't fight back, not at all. It was weird. Weirder than the Oxford shirt.

He managed to get his eyes up to around her hand. The eye hidden by hair looked bruised. "Can I talk to you a minute? I have to tell you something. Like, really have to."

"I don't know. I kind of hurt." It wasn't quite true. She felt numb.

Jason swallowed. "Kim said—that it might help, my coming here."

"You talked to Kim?"

"Yeah, and she, um." He gestured to his clothes, his hair. "She did this. In case your mom answered the door. Or whatever."

It seemed extreme and unlikely. But it seemed more unlikely that Jason Devlin would manage that outfit on his own. And since Kim was currently the only person in Illinois she trusted, Samantha went with it.

She sighed, "Alright, Burnout Ken, there's a bench over under that tree."

They sat at opposite ends of the wooden bench. Jason spent some minutes staring at his hands. Samantha looked too. One knuckle was cut, another swollen.

When he finally spoke, it was very loud in the afternoon air. "So, Skinny's even uglier now. I mean, I definitely broke his nose."

"Well. Thanks. You know how I love guys fighting. I thought you'd call next time. Do you *never* mean what you say?"

Again, Jason Devlin just winced and took it, then went on. "I beat the crap out of him. He was my best friend since forever, and if Pris hadn't been there, I would've put him in the hospital. Or worse."

He paused, staring at his hands.

"I let Pris help. So he'd know, it wasn't some honor thing. I double-teamed him. With a girl. I held him down, Pris spat on him and kicked him in the groin."

There weren't any more smart-ass comments coming out of Samantha's mouth. She tried to register any of the familiar house, and yard, and world around her, but she could not.

She spoke slowly, as if giving words more time might allow sense to catch up with them. "So, you got dressed up to tell me you broke up with Skinny, and it's not just guys fighting over me now?"

Silence. It was interesting watching someone struggle so hard. Without his even moving his body, it seemed physical.

"It wasn't about you."

Somehow, these words placed a crushing weight on Samantha. "Right. I was just there."

"No, I mean—I would have done the same if he'd done that to any girl."

"Oh."

Jason buried his head in his hands, then picked it up again.

"There's something else."

"Okay?"

"I am—" Jason looked at the sky, then at his hands. He held his hands before him, as if there might be something there he could grasp for support.

"So sorry." He took a deep, shuddering breath, as if the words hurt him, physically. "I am so *fucking* sorry. I'm sorry for last Monday, I'm sorry for Barbie, and plastic, and anything I ever did or said that got you there. I'm sorry I didn't deck Skinny every time he talked shit about a girl. I'm sorry I came between you and Pris. I'm sorry for being the kind of person you don't *know* wouldn't set you up for that. I'm sorry I didn't get there sooner. I'm just—I am so fucking sorry."

Jason waited for the horrible sick weight on his chest to lift. It stayed put. He was afraid to see her face, marks on it still there, maybe, bite marks on her neck, probably hidden, but he knew about hiding bruises.

"I thought you didn't like saying that." She sounded slow and far away.

"Yeah. Well." Jason scuffed on the ground with his stupid loafer. Shoes for rich people to pinch pennies. The grass beneath them was plush and green, even in October.

He'd said what he'd come for. In a minute, he was going to say goodbye, and she was going to let him, and he would want to die even more than he did right now. And he'd never even get to open that box in his pocket and let all that happiness wash over him again, because it would be tainted and gone, lost, tossed and trampled on.

"Jason?"

He closed his eyes. She said his name. It was almost like a touch, it felt that good.

"Are you sorry about—all of it?"

"No." It was out of his mouth before he could even think about it. It was shocking to him, in fact, that some of it he wouldn't have taken back, even considering where it led.

"Was there, you know, *anything* that *was* about me?"

At that, even more shockingly, Jason got mad. And not at himself. He got up, walking till he stopped needing to yell.

But of course, Samantha Ward would follow him.

"Excuse me?" she said, folding her arms over her chest. "I must have missed your totally important answer in all the stalking off moodily you were doing."

"I didn't fucking answer your stupid-ass question." Jason couldn't believe how fast his blood was pumping. Anything about her. Jesus Christ.

"Oh, excuse me for wondering if anything about my attempted rape actually involved me, and wondering if, when the skeevy rapist wannabe's *best friend* was kissing me at a party, he actually noticed who he was with!"

Jason grabbed at a fistful of bushes and pulled off leaves, throwing them to the ground. "Jesus, am I not fucking groveling enough for you? Or what? I dressed like a total asshole just to get you to listen to me snivel!"

"You're *dressed* like my *brother!*"

"Then your brother dresses like an *asshole!* You wonder if I noticed who I was *with?* Are you blind *and* deaf, or are you just totally sadistic?"

"Ooh. SAT word. But why can't you answer the question?" Her hands were on her hips now. She was wearing some turtleneck with little kittens all over it, and she still managed to look like an avenging goddess.

"Why are you *asking* the question?" As if she didn't know. This was *bullshit.* "Pris knew before I did—and the Afro-Asian Accord *kidnapped* me, for Chrissake, because Kwame said no dude who looked at you like I apparently do would want other guys looking, let alone doing—what Skinny did. And every girl I've ever gone near wants to kill you. And none of *those* people were even there, you know, with me ... when there were trees, and stars, and stuff."

A breeze came up and rustled the bushes near where they were standing. Jason realized he was 0 for 2 in the "not yelling at girls who'd just been sexually assaulted" category.

"Shit," he said. His hand made for his hair, but it was so different now, it threw him off. "Plus I have this stupid hair."

Jason stole a look at her, not quite meeting her eyes, but her lips, at least, looked less angry. Maybe even twitching upward.

"I kind of like the hair," she sighed.

"Yeah?"

"Yeah."

Well, that was probably a good sign.

"Walk?"

That was even better.

"With you?" It just seemed so unlikely.

Samantha shook her head, but it didn't look like no. "Isn't that usually what someone means when they ask you that?"

"That, or a long walk off a short pier."

It made her smile a little.

37. HERE YOU ARE

Jason and Samantha walked down past tennis courts, and more little clumps of bushes, and what looked like shooting targets set up a long way past that. It seemed like the yard was bigger than Jason's whole neighborhood.

He was glad of it. The farther they walked, the farther they were away from anything in his life.

It was insane. She was *talking* to him. She was okay enough to get pissed off at him for stupid reasons. And she sort of smiled when he acted like a total dickhead. It was fucking fantastic.

Samantha took him to another bench but she sat differently, this time, knees turned towards him. This bench was set up to give a view of the lake, all sparkly in the late afternoon sun. The air was chilly, though. Jason idly hoped her turtleneck was warm enough. It was funny, kitten prints. So not her style—even though she had, like, ten styles. But now, even after everything, it made her look like someone you'd want to hug a lot.

Then Jason grimaced, realizing what the little shirt was worn to hide.

"What's the matter?"

"Your shirt. I just remembered why you were wearing it."

Samantha's hand went to her throat, she fiddled with the collar a moment, pulling at it nervously. It looked like habit.

Habit exposed a line of purple teeth marks.

Jason just stared. He couldn't look away. Suddenly it seemed like Artie and his crew couldn't get to him soon enough.

He'd remembered thoughts *he'd* had, about bruising her there—different, maybe, but the overlap was awful. He remembered having his mouth there, her breathing, arching—maybe an hour after he'd told his friend he'd pay to see him try.

"I know it looks bad." She sounded apologetic. It made him say the thing he hated.

"I'm so fucking sorry. You will never know how sorry I am."

"Hey," she nudged him gently with her foot. "You didn't do it."

"Doesn't matter. You said you hurt. You couldn't go to school." The horrible, knifing weight was slashing at his throat where his voice was. Shit. Shit. He was going to lose it. He was already losing it. She didn't need this.

"Of course it matters, don't be dumb. And I am sore. But it's not like—I mean, it only went so far."

Jason just nodded, looking down. Miserable.

"You stopped it."

"Yeah, I'm a real fucking hero." He thought he might explode. "He asked me, Saturday, if he should stay away from you, or if I was—you know." He put his knuckles to his eyes and felt like driving them clear to the back of his skull. "He never would've gone near you if I'd just said—"

All the other things in his life just slipped from focus when he remembered, how Skinny had asked for permission, how he had given it. For what? Why?

"But I just fucking lied."

It was tearing him to pieces. He felt his fingers, twisting.

Then her hand was on his. She took it in hers.

It felt so amazing. Like it just soothed all his rough edges. He felt himself relax into the bench a little, his head fell back, his eyes closed. "Jesus." There weren't any more words that could make their way out of Jason, but he did manage to hold Samantha's hand. So they sat like that a moment, looking at the day's last sun on the lake but not each other.

She gripped her hand on his a little tighter. "Who doesn't lie about their feelings? It's like, crazy not to." Her voice sounded tiny then, and she took her hand back and twisted it in her lap. "So, were you—lying, like that—when you said you thought I was pretty?"

"When I said you were pretty, what I meant was," he paused and took a deep breath, which was hard to do. "In a way that makes it difficult to breathe."

"Oh."

The lake was so big, stretched out before them, its glints and shifting currents a map of changes without pattern.

"So why don't you look at me?"

"Because—" Jason thought about Rimbaud, all those words that flamed and flowed together. It was a lot harder to pull that off, maybe, when you were sitting with the girl, you were shredded and ecstatic, and there was sun and water and she had *kittens* on her shirt, covering over teeth marks. "Because if I look at your eyes I'll lose my shit."

"But—if you don't," and she hesitated, shy. "If you don't, then I can't see yours."

"You want to?"

"Yeah." It was a whisper.

Well, then. That was a no-brainer.

So he looked. Lost, kind, warm, blue. Little girlish in her kitten shirt. Shadows giving that look the lie. Looking back. Late sun on the lake, clouds over trees, a wind that streaked the surface with dark tones—right there in her eyes. Everything he'd ever dreamed of getting lost in, right there.

Lost.

It could have been hours.

Unbidden, Skinny's face floated before him, the look of rage and absolute hurt on his face *before* the fist connected. *Over a girl, Dev? Over a fucking girl?*

Yes. That, over any girl. But the whole world over this one. In a heartbeat.

She was saying something, smiling, looking wounded and soft and pretty and telling him she was tough and in his corner. And the bruise peeked around her collar like a knife.

He laughed and knew it sounded bitter. "Now's when I should tell you to should stay the hell away from me."

"Oh." She turned to him, and narrowed her eyes. Now, her voice was the knife. "Keep talking like that, you'll make it easy for me."

"It looked easy enough earlier in the week, thanks."

Samantha was incredulous. "Wait, you're nobly blowing me off for my own good, and pissed off that I didn't look devastated enough the last time you did it?" She shook her head. "That's . . . impressive."

Jason took her hand back, hard. "Listen. I wasn't done. For sure it's *not* healthy to be around me right now. But I'm no goddamn hero. So I'm going tell you some reasons you should stay away, and then probably beg you to ignore them, later, if I can get clear." He kept holding her hand, but the fierceness eased. "Listen. There's a lot you don't *wanna* know."

"You're wrong."

"We'll see." He closed his eyes, opened them, looked at the ground, and began. "My mother—she's a fucking cokehead. Not just a little. A lot. Just like my sister, they were always stealing from each other. And from me. Now, though, it's worse."

He told her, from his mother and the solid milk, to watching his sister in the back alley, to the "meals" he'd been running from the bowling alley. How he'd tried so hard just to live through it, how talking about it made it worse, because it didn't change anything. How he'd had "sorry" screamed or wept or spat at him so many times just the sound of the word turned his stomach in knots.

Samantha held his hand. But other than that, she just listened, her eyes getting wider and wider, squeezing his hand when it seemed to her that he might need it. She was right every time.

He didn't give details, because he said that wasn't safe, but he told her things had gotten messed up, and that scary men would be after him soon, that they would find him, and he didn't know how to hide.

"Do you get, now, why I would say not to come near me?"

Samantha nodded, completely serious. "Let me think how to help you," she said, at last.

"You. *Don't. Help.* I *know* you are weirdly fearless. I *know* you got yourself in trouble with Stagnita over me. This isn't something you can fuck with. It's *why* I don't talk to you or look at you in public, got it?"

"I can send you somewhere. I'll get the money. Just leave."

"I leave, they'll take it out on someone else. Like my mom, or—someone else."

"They could *kill* you, Jason."

"Nah."

"Yeah, they'll clearly cut you a break, they sound nice." Samantha sighed. "I know there's stuff you're not telling me. But whatever. I have to get back to the house. You have to do your secret boy things."

She stood up and started back to the house, and he followed.

"So I can call you when it's over, though?"

Suddenly, Samantha turned fierce, in his face, eyes narrowed and *on his.* "Jason Devlin. You think you can waltz over here, turn me into *goo* with your haircuts and apologies and eyelashes, dump your scary coke men into my lap, and then *leave me out?* Like I'll just, I don't know, cover up my bite marks and get my hair done and have drinks on the patio?"

But Jason narrowed his eyes right back. "I'm not having you in this. As if I can't see your goddamn bite marks. So me, all that shit I told you—you gotta just put it out of your pretty mind. And yeah, get your hair done. Whatever it is that you do . . . do." He folded his arms.

Samantha Ward made her eyes go wide. "Oh my God, you were rude and made me mad. I'm so totally distracted now, I think I'll just go have a pedicure." She folded her arms, too.

Something changed behind his eyes. They still looked angry, but there was a different edge to it. "You want me to stop making you mad, you should work on looking a *hell* of a lot uglier when I do."

"You can't distract me just by telling me I'm pretty, either."

"Sweetheart? Pretty isn't the word I was thinking, trust me. And if you weren't hurt, I would have *no problem* coming up with other ways to distract us both."

At that moment, Samantha realized how beaten he'd been looking since he'd come, dressed up in someone else's clothes, hardly meeting her eyes except to dive into them, struggling to occupy as little space as he could hunch himself into. That look had made her melt one way, but this—this made her melt in another.

She was glad Skinny hadn't broken the part of her that felt that.

But then Jason crumbled again, eyes fixed on the ground. "Jesus. I am such an asshole. *Jesus.*"

Talk about not seeing was in front of your face. So she went up to him, took a little of his shirt in her hand, and rubbed it back and forth between her fingers. "You know, this is okay. But I kind of liked that old t-shirt thing, too."

Jason's breath sounded sharp on the way in. "I remember, believe me."

"Really? Doesn't seem like it."

"I put it away. Where it wouldn't get broken."

"Tidy of you. Funny how even memories of me are fragile." The Oxford cloth felt rough in her hands.

Her eyes were back on his. "I don't break so easily, Jason. They're just bruises." She brushed his hair from over his eye, grazing purple. "You have some, too." She took his hand again, smoothing over the swollen knuckles.

"Yeah," he said, his eyes locked on hers.

Samantha knew around them there were bushes, and some trees, and a lake not far away, darkening with evening, but she couldn't see anything of it.

Jason's eyes darkened with evening, too. "Maybe you should make them better."

The skin of his hand against her lips was rough.

"Better?"

"Fucking fantastic."

And then they were walking up the long, green lawn growing cool and damp with evening. From time to time he would take out an empty match-box, opening and closing it in his hand, even though he'd never had a cigarette, not the entire time.

Samantha brought Jason by the kitchen so Ernestine did not murder her in her sleep, and sent him off with leftovers that looked suspiciously fresh and a mutual promise not to do anything stupid.

It was a promise neither of them kept.

38. OURSELVES, UNDER PRESSURE

Blood loss. Fluids, plasma. Stitches, obviously, for the head wound. Ribs cracked. Multiple contusions. Blunt trauma. CT scan needed, how would they pay or was it charity? The woman at the desk looked skeptical.

It took a while for that concept to filter through. Samantha had gotten stuck on the word trauma, thinking really, it was more sharp than blunt.

Charity. Someone was asking about charity. The ER didn't have any rooms, just sheets hung in little white rectangles of crying, yelling, bleeding. Nothing in the hospital looked very clean. There wasn't soap in the bathrooms. But charity. Sure, her dad could make some donations to Chicago hospitals, targeting soap if possible. Samantha was sure she could swing it.

No. She didn't say it. That wasn't what the woman had meant.

Samantha swallowed hard. "No. Not charity. We can pay." She paused. "I mean, as soon as I can, you know, reach someone." She paused again. "Because of course our wallets are gone. I'll go out soon, use a phone. I just ... need to make sure someone's with my brother in case he wakes up."

It was best if you didn't think too much about it. It was best if it could just flow through you, like you really were the person you were pretending to be.

Jason looked like he was sleeping. She asked the nurse if it was okay. The nurse barked they were monitoring him, he was stable, there were people who weren't, and did she mind? Samantha would have said in the car he was as white as a sheet, but pale against one now, she could see, it was not true.

Pris was in the bathroom, punching things. Because they knew now.

In the car, before Jason had woken up, Dylan had lost it. Gone on and on about auras, and how no one had seen what was really going on. How Jason's aura was off all week. No one listened to Dylan, no one even noticed he was *there*. But *he* could see. How Jason had pissed off the wrong dealers trying to help some girl, and then Skinny had too much coke. How no one would ever trust Skinny with that much, and Jason had gotten meaner and meaner. And Jason had *wailed* on Skinny, and Skinny was madder than Kirk yelling Khan, Khan, but Skinny's Khan was *Jason*. And that was against the order of the universe. And then Skinny was gone, Dylan had gone looking for him, but he was *gone* and so was the cocaine. "And I'm telling you, Skinny was holding for Jason. I don't know why, 'cause it's no secret Jason hates coke, but that's what was going down. Skinny was holding for Jason, and he stiffed the wrong people."

And Pris had yelled at the near-comatose Jason that he was a stupid sui- cidal cocksucker, and he had mumbled sorry, and Samantha had started cry- ing and so had Pris. The tears had made their hospital story more believable. It was great when you could make your own costume.

Samantha had known what hospital to go to. It was always on the news when really bad things happened to poor people. It was not a world Samantha had ever imagined would come closer to her than the screen. But it was also a world that had more things to worry about than holes in the stories of a few lost teens from the suburbs. She had known this with the same video game sharpness she'd seen in her room just hours ago. It had left her, now. Now she didn't know anything at all.

Plasma. Cracked ribs. Blunt trauma. Cocaine. Words bouncing around her pinball-machine brain, taking root nowhere.

Samantha tried to track the clear fluids slipping into Jason's arm, trace a rhythm in the beeping of the machines they'd hooked him to. The walls were plain, and gray, and gave nothing away.

She looked at the red-eyed, tear-stained hippie hunched over on a metal fold-up chair.

"Who even are you?" she asked.

"I'm Dylan. Dylan Dougherty. You've seen me every day for the last two years." He whispered, since as far as the hospital knew, they'd just met when he rescued her from a fictional dark alley. He wiped his eyes. "I'm in love with your friend."

Samantha smiled wearily. "Which one?"

Dylan shrugged. "Doesn't even matter. They're both in love with you anyway."

She shook her head. "It's so much more complicated than that."

Dylan wanted to know what to tell the hospital people when they came and Samantha and Pris were gone. Samantha silenced him with a glare and said in a loud voice. "I told you, I have to call my parents, wire them for money, and get a little cleaned up so I can pick it up. It might take a while. I'm so grateful to you both for helping out total strangers like us. And thank you so much for staying with my brother while I'm out."

Dylan wanted to know what to tell Jason when he woke up and Samantha and Pris were gone.

"Tell him I'll be back."

He'd laughed, called her the Barbinator, and told her to make it soon.

The Barbinator. Fine. It would be fine if she were a little plastic now, Samantha thought, making her way to the soapless restroom where she could still hear Pris cursing out the empty towel dispenser. Too many thoughts and feelings wouldn't do her a bit of good now, when so much of what she was doing would feel bad if she thought too much about it. In fact, if she thought about it much at all, she wouldn't do these things.

Samantha pushed open the bathroom door. Pris turned around fast, startled. She had some dried blood on her hands from Jason and some fresh blood on her knuckles from punching things. All around her, the walls crawled with anguished graffiti. Black pen, gouged tile, grime, anguish, threats.

Samantha blocked it out. Background noise. Not needed.

Pris started swearing again. "That stupid cock*sucker*. What if I don't get a chance to fucking kill him five times because those coked up assholes killed him first?" She kicked the sink.

"Calm down. I came to tell you. They said he's stable. They did a scan, no hemorrhaging in the brain." Samantha took a deep breath, rolled her eyes. "And anyway, you totally showed that towel dispenser. It is never going to bother anyone, ever again." Her voice was calm. She carefully checked the doors of the stalls.

Pris stared at her. "Don't worry," she said, her hand twisting her collar necklace. "I scared everyone away." Her face was still jagged and angry but behind it flickered Prissy Hines who'd been shy and awkward on the outside, astonishing and brazen on the inside, in places only Samantha could see. Pris had flipped the equation, but Prissy still peered out.

"Truth or dare, Sammie?" Prissy whispered.

Samantha smiled. It wavered, but it was definitely there. "Dare," Samantha said. "Duh."

Pris smiled back. "I thought you might have had enough. Daring, you know. For one party."

Samantha took a deep breath. It came out shuddering, but she shook it off. They'd always pushed each other to do the things they'd never dared to do on their own. "Yeah. Like the truth has been one big picnic tonight, right? And anyway. I don't back down. Did you forget who you're playing with?"

Full-on serious, all hardcore and punches and blades, Pris stared at her again. "Samantha Ward. I never forget."

Samantha tossed her head. "Good," she said, opening her bag. "Then you still remember how to play dress-up."

39. EVERYBODY'S QUEEN FOR A DAY

Later, Samantha's concern was that the black tank top she'd cut and shimmied down her thighs was plenty short, but it looked like a maxi-dress compared to what the club girls were wearing. Pris had taken some extra safety pins from her shirt and folded and pinned Samantha's black turtleneck above her midriff. She'd cut fine strips from the top of the chest with her blade, leaving the turtleneck intact. Pris said it would distract from the shoes, which were not clubwear. "You're good at this," Samantha told her.

Pris narrowed her eyes. "It's for a cause." She'd cut more strips from the back of the shirt. "That would distract anyone from anything. Trust me." Then she smiled. "Can you believe I'm having fun? Sick, right?"

They'd washed up as best they could in the soapless hospital bathroom and ratted Samantha's hair out wide. Pris said the bloodstains on Samantha's black clothes just looked goth. They stopped for lipstick at an all-night drugstore. Samantha wore red. Pris wore black. Pris insisted Samantha buy nylons but Samantha balked at the flesh-tones. Pris stared at her, flinty, and told her not to question her stylist's judgement in a crisis situation. Samantha held up a No-Nonsense black mist. "More goth," she explained. Pris rolled her eyes and bought both.

Back in the car, Pris explained through clenched teeth what the stockings were for, and Samantha felt stupider than she'd felt in a while. But she made the best of it, and on this count, did exactly as she was told.

They had several thousand dollars in cash between them. It wasn't enough, but it helped them feel dangerous and grown up, counting the money in a dark corner of the well-lit pay parking garage they'd found. They rolled the money in brown paper and put that in the trunk. High five. In the bag were also pearls. In the bag were also diamonds.

"South African," said Pris in a low voice as they'd walked toward the club. "Blood diamonds. I swiped some to give to the ANC. I'll have to make it up to them somehow."

"Well," Samantha said thoughtfully, "blood diamonds do match our outfits."

Pris stopped. "Thank God I have you to remind me what's important."

"I know, right? Everyone should have one of me. Let's hope Rain sees it that way. Whoever the hell he is."

Strobe. It helped Samantha's video game self to separate from the parts of her that were still scared. Because this was way hard. Not the getting in part, that was easy. Girls who looked like Samantha mostly got into clubs, even without the namedropping and fake IDs. Girls from Highland went clubbing in Chicago all the time. Girls from Highland probably went looking for Rain, too.

But Samantha was having a hard time not staring at Rain's coke nail. It was so disgusting. The *girls* were so disgusting. Some of them had skirts shorter than their bottoms, somehow. And she wasn't even sure they were the prostitutes.

She couldn't look at the walls here, because it looked like people might be having sex against them. Why had she put in her contacts *now?* Hadn't anyone at this club ever heard of AIDS? She missed fighting with cheerleaders. When she saw Vanessa Segal, she would probably give her a big hug.

She felt Pris take her hand and squeeze it, hard. Reassuring. But even Pris's eyes had gone wide when they'd first gone in. "No one gets it," she whispered. "People are going to die from stuff like this."

Right. Samantha came back to herself a little bit. This wasn't about cheerleaders. "Maybe they're counting on dying young. But let's not you and me do that," she whispered. Hips swaying as best she could in her definitely-not-clubwear flats, Samantha approached a man who looked to be about seven feet wide and ten feet tall, and who was just standing around, glaring. "We're looking for Rain," she said, hot and moist and close in his ear.

Unmoved, the man had nodded, gestured toward a much smaller man at a table towards the back. He was sitting alone, but a few girls and other large men hovered over him, several paces behind. Another man came up to him, shook his hand, whispered in his ear. Rain nodded, and the man went off with one of the girls behind him through an unmarked red door. "You found him."

"Thanks," said Pris loudly to the bouncer. She held her hand for a high five and got it, she thought—but the man held on, pinning her in place. Pris glared at him. He glared back.

"How'd you come by that name?"

"Let go of my friend," Samantha folded her arms and brought on the snotty rich girl. "It will work out better for you. You can tell him Simon. Just Simon. If that's not enough, tell him there's other places we can go." The man dropped Pris's hand and nodded them over toward Rain, like Pa-Jah Rubenstein's first name was a kind of magic password. Pris grabbed Samantha and swaggered over to the table as if she'd been swaggering through sex clubs to buy drugs all her life.

Now, at the table, Samantha was struggling to keep her eyes on the very important man sitting across from her but not on his coke nail, and definitely not on all the gyrating bodies in the flashing lights around her. Her own voice drummed in her head. *Get it together. It's just sex. It's not you up against a wall, hand fumbling at your underwear while you try to scream. You have a gun chafing between your bruised thighs that is held there by torn drugstore nylons. You are meeting a big-time coke dealer whose help you really need. Get it together.*

Rain was looking at them, amused. Samantha wasn't sure amused was good. He was very tall and thin. Warm skin, cold eyes. Striking.

Gamely, she tried smiling, nodding once when Rain asked if since they were from Simon, they had a record coming out.

"What label?" he asked.

"It's, um, secret."

"Right." He looked back and forth between the two girls. "So you're looking to party?"

Pris scooted closer to Samantha and licked her neck and jaw, pulling down the turtleneck to expose the still purple bite. "Only with each other," she said, putting her arm around Samantha possessively.

"You know it, baby." Samantha smiled, catching the game. She felt better when she knew what the game was. "The last connection wanted to f-fuck me. Just so you know. We don't do that." It was true.

Rain smiled a slow, unpleasant-looking smile. "So you're not up for size, then?"

"Very funny," snapped Pris. "We can pay."

"Good to hear, but I wouldn't expect any less from a client from Simon. Come into the back, then."

Samantha and Pris exchanged a look. It didn't sound good.

Rain just smiled again at the worry in their faces. It crinkled one side of his face more than the other, as if some scar held the other side down. "I wouldn't risk business for unwilling underage pussy, little girls. I have willing pussy of all ages. Follow or not, as you will."

"We don't have the money on us."

"I can see that. Where would you put it, in your girlfriend's bellybutton? If terms are agreeable to everyone, we'll make those arrangements."

In the back room, a tall blonde in a leather dress and stiletto heels offered them drinks, which they took. It took all of Samantha's acting ability not to gag on the vodka.

Next, the girl started patting Pris and Samantha down all over their bodies and removed a blade from Pris's pants pocket. Samantha could barely breathe. Even if they found the gun, wouldn't they just take it? Samantha and Pris for sure weren't the only people who'd ever tried to buy coke while armed. It had to be kind of a regular thing. But why had she even brought it? Did she really think she'd shoot her way out of a drug den?

But Pris shoved the girl off. "Hey, it's just a blade, what the fuck do you think we're here for? And you can stop touching my girlfriend, or I'm out of here!"

Rain made a hand signal. The girl stopped. He motioned to Pris and Samantha to sit down around a large mirror-topped table in the center of the black-walled room.

"So. You'll try the product." Rain did not ask. He told. He rolled a new hundred-dollar bill, slowly, watching the girls' reaction, then scooped small piles of white powder from a black, diamond-shaped box. He cut lines with Pris's blade, motioning first to Pris. She shook her head.

"I told you. Only together. We don't do *that* with men, either. It's only for each other. Just for sex. It makes it ... so much more."

Rain folded his arms and shook his head. His cheekbones were incredibly sharp. He looked like a bird of prey. "Aren't you a little too young for Vice?"

"Isn't it a little hypocritical, *you* worrying about *our* vices?" Samantha did her best to keep her voice even.

"Sam! It's not what he means."

Rain did not look impressed. "You have less than an eighth on the table, nothing on me. I don't know how you got Simon's name, but I assure you, you have nothing on my music business associate, either. There is simply nothing to have."

"He thinks we're cops." Pris hissed.

Samantha leaned forward. "Really not."

She met his eyes, brown with green flecks, and they stared each other down a minute. Samantha decided dare was not going her way. She opted for truth.

"Look, okay, we're not up-and-coming pop stars. But I do know Simon. I went to his son's Bar Mitzvah. I was at his house last week. One of our friends is in trouble. *He's* friend's with Simon's son, too, that's who gave us your name. Because he knew the trouble was bad. Can I level with you?"

Rain frowned, considering. The blonde woman went up and whispered something in his ear. The frown deepened, then he spoke.

"It is possible that I myself am not overly fond of some other ... business-men from Highland. But I am also not running a charity for wealthy high school girls."

"We need help, but we didn't come for charity." Pris's voice was one notch down from you'd-run-from-it-in-a-dark-alley, but it was the kind of voice any-one would believe meant business. "I told you, we can pay." She slowly put her hand in the pocket that had held the blade and pulled out a small paper packet. She unwrapped it. "That there will cut lines into your fancy table fast as you can cut lines on top of it."

Rain stared. "You need to do a line, first, one of you. So I know you're not police. Or if you are, I'll know you're dirty. You look young, but the light is low, makeup is magic, and there are special units."

Samantha looked at the powdery white lines on the table before her. She'd never done it before. She didn't want to. Unbidden and unwelcome, images form Thursday flooded her senses, she felt the bruising hands on her face, between her legs, probing, the taste of Hawaiian Punch sweet and sick in her throat. Everywhere, people wanting things inside her body she didn't want there.

But someone had been putting Jason's whole life, whole future, where he didn't want it. And now people were beating him, and wouldn't stop. She was out of her element, and out of time. She needed information. She needed trust. She needed help that nice people didn't need, and couldn't give. And she hadn't come up with even one thing she wouldn't do, in the car, when she'd worried he might not wake up. Without looking at Pris, Samantha just said, "Don't tell Jason," took the bill, and bent forward to the tabletop.

The blonde in the high boots spoke. "Wait, Rain." There was a note in that voice Samantha recognized, having heard it recently in her own. Restrained panic.

"What's it to you?" Samantha remembered thinking Jason's voice was like a whip. Rain's was more like one.

The girl stammered. "I just—I don't think she's done it before. I don't think—you should make her. It—makes me sad. I know it's funny coming from me—I love to party, I love to party with you, and your friends, and the other girls, and usually with whoever you say, but not—not with people who don't want to. And I don't wanna be sad, Rain."

Samantha looked at the girl who spoke, looked at her hard, then at Rain. Unflinching, Rain shook his head slowly and pointed to the table.

Samantha bent forward again. The piercing, cold feeling in her nose and throat made her sick. Her head was spinning. She turned quickly and sneezed, trying to keep it from the table. "I'm sorry," she said, miserably. "I just suck at this. I mean, I suck wrong, or something. Did enough get in to convince you I'm not crooked, or am, or whatever? I mean, I know I'm supposed to love this and be ready to sell my parents' house to get more, but I just hate it and if I do any more, I'm going to throw up." She bit her lip, looked from Rain to the blonde girl and back. "No offense. I'm sure it's, um, very good and all."

"None taken," Rain sighed, smiled a strange, almost sad smile, and gestured toward the coke, then the other blonde. The girl held her hair up to keep from sweeping the cocaine to the floor as she snorted it.

"So go ahead," Rain said, now turning toward his visitors. "Make my day."

By the time they left, the diamond Pris exchanged for information and tactical help had cut a scratch in the table that seemed to please Rain very well. He ran one finger over the scratch, smiling, and turned the diamond slowly in his other hand, watching it reflect and break the light. "South African," he said, "this pleases me. I have ancestry from there, it seems, and my forebears did not leave with any diamonds. I have other forebears," he said, "Sephardim who dealt in diamonds in Spain, and were forced to abandon their trade. So it pleases me I should take this from you, and that a girl who looks like you," he turned to Samantha, "should come to me for help."

Samantha reflected that anything that pleased Rain, at this point, was a good and a great thing, since it meant he was less likely to find the gun on her thigh, which now that the cold rush and panic had abated, was again incredibly uncomfortable. It was a miracle this had gone as well as it had, but she was suddenly very, very tired, and in a few hours, her parents were going to begin the grandfather of all freak-outs. Knowing her father, she probably had to figure out how to head off the police or at least avoid them so she could follow through on the plan she did, at last, have in place.

"You're tired and have places to be," Rain murmured. He stood and offered his hand. "I would send my best to Simon, but I agree it is best he knows nothing of our acquaintance. We'll keep those worlds separate, since we've decided I won't be entering into yours for now. But you'll keep in mind my other offers, should things prove more complicated than we've anticipated."

Samantha nodded. "It's always good to have options."

She turned to the blonde in the corner and hugged her.

"Thank you," whispered Samantha.

"Please, don't tell Jason," the girl whispered back.

"You, either."

40. ONLY DREAM IN RED

Jason Devlin didn't know why the hell he was in a tent. It was cold, and raining, and he was taped and sewn together like goddamn Frankenstein. So was the tent.

Everyone was going on about Africa, which was fine. He wore the Free That Dude button on his coat now like everyone else, but if one more college kid yelled at him for drinking his can of warm Coke, heads were gonna roll.

Well. They would if he could move his body without agony.

Still, he'd been so pissed off to wake up in a hospital to Dylan Dougherty passed out over a chair, he'd almost clocked the poor dude. Everything hurt like hell, and his memories were all messed up, blurred flashes and fog. He had no idea where he was or how he got there, and the fluorescent light above his bed flickered like a headache's nightmare.

In some of those flashing memories there were girls, but when he woke up in the hospital, there were no girls anywhere around.

Jason panicked. The guys who beat him told him they'd be watching the hospitals. He remembered that much. Every twelve hours, he remembered that, too. They'd beat him every twelve hours until they got Artie's money or drugs. Jason shouted to Dylan to wake up and get them the hell out of there, but a grim-faced nurse with a voice like his kindergarten teacher had told him to settle down and stuck a syringe in his IV bag, saying that would calm him down.

Jason had ripped out his IV, yelled at his nurse and tried to walk out of the hospital in his bare feet because no one would give him his shoes.

Turned out they really didn't want him to leave without paying.

And he didn't. Even after that fancy test that told them his head would stay on. Everyone was calling him some weird name, and his bill was paid. He didn't want to think about how. He kind of wanted to think about why, but he didn't let himself.

Because then girls were there, all faded lipstick and ratted hair and shadows under their eyes that weren't just running makeup. People were signing things and he had to sign, Pris shoving the paperwork in front of him and poking the name at the top of the page, hard.

"Against Medical Advice." He'd signed the name. He figured whatever trouble he could get in, it couldn't be worse than the trouble he was in already. And then things were foggy and then Jason was in a tent.

Dylan Dougherty was in the next tent learning about politics. Pris was braiding his hair. *Braiding his goddamn hair.* He sure as hell hoped Pris had told the dude she was—whatever it was she liked to call it.

And Samantha Ward was asleep next to Jason.

Not that they were in bed. More like in a pile of dirty sleeping bags. But still. The one clear memory he had was getting to the godforsaken tent city or shantytown or whatever, and Samantha saying, "I'll sleep with Jason."

He just wanted it on auto repeat. He knew what she meant. Jason, however, chose to think of it as a long-range prophesy.

There was so much important, scary stuff to think about, but *Samantha Ward* was *lying down next to him,* and what would be the point of surviving if you couldn't take a minute to appreciate a thing like that?

Jason turned to face her and got a kick to the gut. Well. Having had a few of those recently, he had to say this was a lot more pleasant and that wasn't the best metaphor or whatever. But her eyes were open.

"Shit."

"Nice to see you, too," she smiled. It sounded true.

Jason got nervous. His hands were sweating. He had no idea what she'd done for him, but he had a feeling it was a hell of a lot. He should try to get things clear. "So, why are we in a tent again?"

"Protesting Apartheid. Duh."

Jason closed his eyes, brought to the foreground of his brain a foggy flash of Pris yelling about blood and diamonds in the front of a car. It seemed like a weird time for political action but Pris was a weird chick.

"Right. I got that. Very bad African government, Pris's ... girlfriend's from there and so's her money and that feels bad but ... right now?

He was way too foggy to remember what Samantha knew or didn't about who was after him or why. He was not so foggy that he didn't know better that they couldn't talk about any of that here.

Samantha sighed. "I'm really bummed you're on the ground like this but——we needed a place to chill for a few hours. And, you know, there's probably some people we'd rather not run into right now, right? So Pris knew some people running this shantytown, they need bodies in their tents, we don't stand out on a college campus, and it's a good cause that means a ton to our friend."

"Oh. Right."

"I hope you like it. We have to come back to help her atone."

Girls. Were so goddamn complicated. "Jesus. I mean, I get it, she doesn't like where her money's from, but it's not like *she* earned it. Why does she have to feel so bad? No one has that much money without it being stolen from *someone*, right?"

Samantha was quiet after that.

Jason reflected it might not have been the best thing to say to a very rich girl who had probably just paid your hospital bills.

"Right," said Samantha slowly. "But I guess it's hard, once you start thinking about it. Or when it's not all——historical or something. I mean, my parents are always on about how you have to give back, and I guess——I guess I agree. I mean, it used to bother me, because I thought it was mostly to help them feel better about having the money in the first place but maybe, maybe it's still good, for people to *get* help and support, even if it's for——some complicated reasons."

Jason thought about how it felt a little bit fucking bad to be getting help and support. How it also felt bad not to get it. Then he thought about who was after him and how much he didn't think they'd look here. It was so much easier to care about *that* than politics, which always seemed like stuff people talked about when they didn't have to worry so much about getting hit or eating. But then he thought about how much it sucked to be beaten and know there was no way out, and he figured it probably happened to people in South Africa, too. He didn't know much more about it, and he didn't see how sitting in a tent could help, but he could see why people would want it to.

"But also," sad Samantha, "it's not just historical. Pris and I, we have to sell some stuff, and I guess she was thinking she was gonna give it to the cause. We have to go really soon and do that, actually."

Jason's head was swimming. "On a Sunday? How are you gonna sell stuff on a Sunday?"

"I'm not sure pawnbrokers visit the house of the Lord that often. But anyway, we have help. Friend of Jah Rubenstein's father, Jah gave me his name. Don't you worry. We're gonna get you out of here. Don't you even move."

"Pawnbrokers?"

"Don't worry. Rich kids, stolen money on trees. You're just like another accessory for us. You'll look way better than pearls."

Jason groaned. What the *hell* had girls been doing while he'd been passed out cold and useless? "Samantha, seriously. There's stuff you're not telling me."

"I can't imagine what that might be like," she huffed, and turned over.

Jason wondered what it might be like to not fuck up every good thing that ever happened to him, and if he'd ever get to find out.

But after a while, she turned back, her eyes all soft and sweet again. "I've never been in bed with a boy before."

Wow. Okay. There had been some really serious thoughts a minute ago, but now Jason just *really* wished he could move. "Well, um, I gotta say, typically, we'd be doing other things."

Suddenly her eyes were right back in his field of vision, and her head was looking down on him, her hair tickling his neck and face. "It wouldn't be typical of me, you know," she said.

"Have you done any atypical things because of me so far?"

She snorted. "Um. Only all of them. But Jason—" she sounded sad. "It's gonna be a while—I mean, a *long* while. For me."

"And I am probably not going to live the week out, but if I do, think how much time I'll have for waiting! And a guy can dream, right? In a someday kind of way? I mean, I haven't had a cigarette since Thursday. Miracles happen."

"You quit?" She sounded impressed.

"Shh. Don't say that, it'll make me smoke ten. I didn't quit. I just— haven't had a cigarette. I don't want to think about it." But it was too late, the crawling nicotine fingers were already threading, tickling, scratching under his skin. Shit. He wondered if anyone from the next tent would have one.

"Do you dream about me?" Samantha was still propped up on one arm, she moved a little closer so he could feel her warm in his space. And then she came closer, and he could feel *her*, just softly, all up and down against him.

"Yeah." He definitely wasn't thinking about cigarettes anymore.

"Good dreams?" She tangled her leg with his. That was sometimes how they started.

"Oh, yeah." He thought he could *hear* her blushing. It was unreal.

Except it wasn't. She was really here, with him. He couldn't get his mind around it, couldn't begin to know it, not really, not now, his mind still foggy from pain and drugs.

"Great dreams." He stroked the place on her arm he'd dreamed about once, what seemed like a long time ago. "But you're real." The leak in the tent confirmed it.

"Jason," she paused, then started again. "Is it bad if I'm—you know, close up, if I'm not gonna—you know."

Jason did know. Sometimes it was so hard and so important to say really basic things. Of course he knew. But he was so slow and stupid and they were hiding in a goddamn tent. Still. He was *not* going to fuck this up. Just this one time. He would not do it. He took a deep breath. "Samantha. One, I can't move, much less 'you know.' Two, if girls don't want it, it's wrong and not fun. And three, 'you,' 'close,' and 'bad' can't possibly be together in the same space."

Jason hoped that was an okay way to say it. He closed his eyes and waited to find out.

"Hang on." Samantha leaned closer, careful not to touch his ribs. She was barely touching anywhere on his torso and even through the ache that was goddamn exciting. "This part behind your ear isn't bruised." She was whispering close by it. "I want us to heal up because I do want to—" she kissed behind his ear. "Keep learning."

"You have no idea how much restraint I'm showing by not swearing a blue streak right now."

"I told you I liked the swearing." Her lips were right by his ear and her body was close to his but not touching anywhere that hurt and she was a bigger miracle than not smoking.

"I know," he managed to get out. "But you're gonna have to wait."

Samantha giggled and Jason could feel her body shaking on the damp sleeping bags next to him and Jason thought that maybe if he *did* die, it would be worth it just for that.

She reached out for the chain he wore now, her fingertips brushing his skin. Perfect.

"Amber?" She smiled and frowned at the same time.

Whoa. Where was she getting that from? "Hell, no, I haven't had anything to do with Amber since ninth grade, I swear. She's *crazy.*"

Samantha giggled again, her hair brushing against his chest. "No, that's—that's what it's called. But they usually give those amber hearts to little girls. Did someone give it to you?"

Jason shrugged, a mistake, given the state of his ribs. He was back to not meeting her eyes.

She sighed and let go of the chain. "Fine. It's none of my business. It's not like I don't know you have a billion girlfriends."

Hurt in her voice. And he found he really couldn't have that. He was being stupid. He was *wearing* it, after all. And she was wearing his goddamn blood.

He put his hand to it, feeling its smooth texture, its little chip. "I knew what it looked like, not what it was called. I went to like, three stores before I found one."

"It's what you had in your hand—last Saturday, I remember, right before we—"

"Yeah. But I only started wearing it—after Skinny—I was pretty sure you'd never come near me again, after that, so I didn't think you'd see it." He shook his head. "Fucking embarrassing," he muttered.

"Why?"

He doubted he could say this. "It's sap."

"Oh, sorry, forgot how tough you are."

He laughed again. Which hurt like *hell*. But it was like she and Pris shared scripts sometimes. "No, I mean, the stuff from trees." Sometimes he *ached* that the words that came out of his mouth only matched what was inside when he was all pissed off. "And maybe it's not that beautiful to start with, all bugs and stuff, but they get frozen, like, out of time. And they just get to stay there—and somehow, even if they came in ugly, they ended up—"

"Beautiful," she whispered. "Like behind the dumpsters."

Maybe he could say it all right. "Yeah," he paused, "And it's so old, it's close to forever, so, like, even if it was just one moment, and they never had more, it would always be ... that—" Jason scrunched up his eyes, "... beautiful."

That was closer. Maybe not Rimbaud, but close enough. He never thought he'd be this close, actually.

"Maybe they did, though." She propped herself on her elbow again, her fingertip sliding the heart along its chain and the skin beneath it.

"Did what?" Jason felt himself getting sleepy.

"Have more. Maybe they did."

The loud sound of the zipper did not mean what a healthier boy might have hoped "more" signified. Instead he looked up into blue hair pushing through the tent flap.

"Jason was right the first time, it's *sap*."

Jason groaned again. "*Please* tell me the head on the door is a dream."

"For future reference? Tent walls? Not soundproof. C'mon, time for girls to go shopping, and boys to sleep. And anyway, someone has to stay here, to atone for the goddamn blood diamonds."

"I'm not sleeping with Dylan," slurred Jason, already half gone.

"Me either, poor kid."

41. JUST FOR ONE DAY

They'd all agreed, Dylan had to drive and Jason would ride shotgun. The girls would sleep in the back. Jason promised faithfully to wake them. Then they'd drop off the money and head for the Satos, who'd been told the girls were helping a friend get out of a drug-ridden, abusive home. Which was true. And a good story. It even explained the bloodstains.

The Satos would tell the Wards and Hineses that their lost lambs were making their way home, so that particular hell could wait to break loose until they got there, Pris explained before dropping off to sleep. It was all arranged.

But when the Mercedes pulled into the Del Lanes parking lot late Sunday night, Jason didn't wake anyone. He whispered to Dylan to wait in the car. Kid protested, but he'd spent too long doing the Devil's bidding to change up now.

"They're not gonna like it," Dylan whined. "Fuckin' Blade Runner and The Barbinator. You got guts, man, they're tougher than they look. And Pris, she *looks* plenty tough."

"You think I don't know that?" Jason sighed, staring out a minute at the battered shapes of old cars, the shiny new ones, colors muted and strange in the flickering neon. He would've thought he'd had enough of this parking lot, but just now, he didn't want to leave it. Not to go in there. Every single part of his body hurt. "But they did their stuff. Now it's my turn. I don't want them known here."

They'd got the money. Jason would do the paying.

He felt bad enough about the money—diamonds and pawnshops and private accounts, he didn't know what all. Because they wouldn't tell him. In fact, they were obviously psyched as hell about not telling him. Whatever. Some rich dad's friend helping? That sounded pretty safe. And Jason didn't have any idea how much money they had, kids like that, or what it was like to have it. He'd always laid down whatever he had for his friends. Mostly his fists—and that had cost him plenty. They were probably doing what he'd do.

But he couldn't let them go farther down that road. Just as he didn't understand their world, they didn't understand his. And you had to play the hand you were dealt. You couldn't play someone else's.

It sounded good. But it hadn't gone as it should. He went in Del Lanes, but Artie wasn't there. Jason put the call in, waited by the phone by the wood paneled walls where people did, waiting for Artie to show. But then Skinny-in-Five's longhaired friend was whispering in his ear, complaining they'd missed him at the first twelve-hour mark, and now he was right on time.

Jason kept calm, said he had the money.

"Dude," Longhair whispered. "That's not *our* money. And it's not just Artie who's paying us. You want your girlfriends in the car out front to get the same as your sister?"

Fuck.

"That's what I thought. So you'll come with us now and take it like a man. We got instructions to take pictures. I'm not sure you're the teacher's pet, Devlin."

So that was why he was on his knees in the back alley waiting for the blows to start. Not what the doctors ordered, probably, when they'd said to take it easy. He straight-up wasn't sure he'd survive it. Now, when he really goddamn wanted to. Now, when he was so close to getting clear.

Fuck it. He just couldn't go down like that. Not without a fight.

Jason knew he'd be slow getting up but figured he could still fall down like a champion. So he put his hands out to catch himself and lashed out with his legs. He caught Skinny-in-Five in the knees, and headed Longhair in the groin on his way down. But then Jason was flat on his face. Worse, on his *ribs*. He was spinning, exploding in pain, and the air was filled with groans and swears and hisses. His goddamn ribs and head would keep him down, face to the dirt. Even more than the foot on his back now pressing his ribs into pavement. He knew that foot, that boot. He knew the hands that cable-tied his wrists together.

Then he heard the click. He knew that sound, too. It wasn't a beating after all.

He prayed to die with dry pants and wished that wouldn't be his last thought.

But the click was from farther away.

"Freeze."

Laughter.

No.

"Laugh all you want. But don't move."

"Dude, it's a *girl,* c'mon."

No.

"Honey, get out of here. You don't belong here."

"How do you know where I belong?" Samantha's voice sounded dead calm.

"Well, alright, sweetheart, maybe you do belong here. Maybe, was that one of your little friends we had out back here last week? She was partying up a storm. That your friend? Are you Jessie's girl?" Skinny-in-Five laughed.

"Wait, Jason?" Shit, the voice was trembling. "Jason, did they hurt Jess? She didn't answer any of my calls. Or Kimmie's. Jason, she's *gone.*"

Now Longhair laughed. And then he *sang.* "I want a skanky little Jewish princess ..."

Damnit. Soft spot. Strong suit. Both at once. Girlfriends, the very best way to get to Samantha Ward. Jason knew better than anyone. "No," he tried, "they're just fucking with you. Don't fall for it." He struggled to get to his knees.

Damn boot came down harder, pinning him.

"Get your foot off of him." Samantha's voice sounded even tighter, trembling. That wasn't good. "I have the gun here." That wasn't good either. Hell.

"Sure you do, baby. But you don't know how to shoot it." For sure he was right there. "Maybe you've got other talents, baby. Or merchandise. Now your *friend's* tits—her tits should have a goddamn patent. What you got?"

More footsteps. And a yell. "Don't come *near* her."

Pris.

Her voice sounded scarier than the goddamn gun.

"Sammie." But she was breathless. She'd been running. Samantha must have snuck out first, alone.

Maybe she really was crazy.

Pris kept talking. "Sammie, Last week. Jess. She was in trouble, you saw, she was crying in the bathroom. It was those two, they hurt her, they had her up against that wall, right there."

Shut up, shut up, shut up. Didn't Pris get it? That would bring Samantha *down*. She didn't need to remember what it was like to be against a goddamn wall. She didn't need to know her friend had got the same. Not now. Not when she needed to stay strong.

He struggled with the foot, now on his neck. It just ground down harder.

"So it all comes down to you, Sammie." Pris's voice sounded like a goddamn anthem. "They got Jess. They got Jason. But I know who you are. You show them."

"Yeah, baby. You show us. We wanna learn." Longhair made it all sound like such a big joke. He ground his foot a little deeper into Jason's neck.

"Get your foot off my goddamn friend before I blow your head off." Her voice was metal, but thin, and trembling. A voice like that didn't have a steady hand.

"Squeeze that trigger, you could off your friend here by accident. And the cops come for gunfire even in Highwood. Who the fuck do you think you are, baby?" The foot didn't move. "Put that thing down and get out of here."

Blood started running into Jason's eyes, mingling with the red rage.

"Who I am? Hard to say." Now her voice sounded weirdly ... conversational. "Spoiled rich girl, mixed up in something she knows nothing about? That's me. No idea how to fire this thing and too scared to do it? Could be me. Test it. Make your move."

There was no sound except for a motorcycle somewhere down the street past the alley.

"On the other hand, maybe I'm a spoiled rich girl, *and* my dad's idea of father-daughter bonding is a little target practice. Maybe I hate guns, but I play along because despite what a *pig* he is, I *adore* him. *That* could be me. You just never know."

"Show us, Sammie." Pris again.

"Okay, let's find out. Check out that beer bottle on that dumpster!" A twing, loud and metallic, a twinge, brown glass exploding, shards skittering across Jason's vision. "Oh, you're too late, it's gone. That father-daughter story's sounding better. I even have a silencer. They are not that easy to get, it turns out. Thank God I made some new friends in Chicago."

"Sweetheart, that's fancy work, but you gotta turn away. There'll be hell to pay for this already."

"Not by me. Don't you know? Girls like me don't pay like other girls. That's why we should sometimes be the ones to step up." *I don't back down,* Jason heard, plain as day.

Fuckin'. A.

"Don't kid yourself, *sister.* It doesn't matter who your daddy is. Girls like you are all the same when you're begging with your back against a wall. Trust me. You gotta walk away from this while you still can."

"No, *you* do. Good luck."

The shot sounded plenty loud. Scream. Sounded louder. Thud. Skinny-in-Five on the ground next to Jason, writhing. Blood. So much blood.

"Oops. Too late." Suddenly Samantha sounded like she might be talking about milk spilled in the school cafeteria. "You know, you look so much like the guy who tried to rape me last week, it's not even funny. And you. *Get your motherfucking foot off my boyfriend."* Voice was steel.

The foot was gone and by sheer force of will, Jason was up, his eyes on Samantha and his everywhere else screaming agony.

Samantha Ward was standing perfectly motionless, gun between two steady arms, her blonde hair streaming. Blue eyes hard and cold.

"Take their weapons, Prissy."

"Sam!"

"Oh, come on, think how they'll like being disarmed by a girl named Prissy. It's kind of worth it."

"Good point."

Pris pulled her blade and held it out as she approached them, keeping out of Samantha's line of fire. First she made Longhair stand with his hands in the air and feet apart, then she patted him down, took a knife. She went round to the back of Skinny in Five, who was down, clutching his shin, bloody and moaning. From behind, she put her blade to his throat. "Nothing personal," she said, "but give me your jacket and that gun in your boot."

"That crazy bitch friend of yours shot me in the motherfucking *leg!*" His voice sounded slurred, blurry. "I could bleed out, you gotta get someone, she's going down for this, I'm telling you ..."

Jason kicked him and he shut up after that.

Samantha flinched. "Jesus, Jason. He's *down."*

People picked funny times to have scruples. "Yeah, he is. You *shot* him. But before he was down, he put me in the goddamn hospital and he was taking money from someone at my fucking *school* to do it again. He was the one fucking with Jessica." He kicked again. "*And* with my sister."

"Fine. Pris'll untie you, and you can kick him as much as you want."

Longhair laughed, it sounded nasty as hell. "What a crazy bitch."

"I know, right? It's like I'm psycho. But take that jacket and put some pressure on your friend's leg, I don't much want to leave a body if don't have to." Just then the Del Lanes door moved an inch and Samantha's whole body tensed, whipped around and was poised, gun steady, as if she'd been doing this for years. Which in a weird way, Jason gathered, she had.

But it was only Dylan. "Artie's here."

"I thought I told you to wait in the car!" Jason was plenty glad to be alive, but it was like no one listened to him anymore.

Dylan eyed Jason nervously. "Um, sorry, man. Turns out the girls're light sleepers. And Samantha had the gun. Anyway, Artie suggests you all come in and play a little pool if you're done out here. And Samantha? you look scary as hell, could you not point that thing at me?"

Samantha glanced back at the men on the ground. One was passed out. The other was swearing, covered in blood, but seemed to be listening about the pressure.

"I hope they have good people on clean-up here," she said, and turned her back on them.

As soon as they were in the door, Samantha put the gun away, fluffed her hair, and put on some fresh lipstick. Jason stared.

"She's a complicated person," Pris muttered as they walked toward the pool tables. Jason nodded.

Dylan showed them over to the table where Artie was standing, grim and stock still. Jason felt his stomach clench. These were the worlds he had never, ever wanted to meet, and he was the one who'd brought them together.

"You must be Artie," said Samantha, apparently greeting guests at one of her mother's cocktail parties.

She turned to Pris and Dylan. "Do you mind taking the front and back doors and yelling if anything looks funny?"

Artie shook his head, spoke quietly as he racked the balls on the table. "From what I understand, you're here to play some pool. I got no need for anything or anyone outside to interfere."

Samantha smiled brightly. "I'm going with trust, but verified." Pris and Dylan took the doors.

And then Samantha Ward was playing pool with a scary, powerful man, like she'd done *that* all her life, too. Jason reflected it was possible she had.

Jason felt like he could watch her his whole life and not get bored. She was so many different girls, all of them her. *All* of them girls he wanted to know. He shook his head. He'd better tune in a little sharper and see how all the girls he wanted to know were handling his coke-dealing stepfather.

"The thing is? Jason doesn't want in. He wants out," she was saying to Artie, for all the world like she was talking about the weather. "So like I said on the phone, we'd like to buy that *car* his friend stole, at your cost plus twenty percent."

On the *phone? She'd* talked to Artie before they even got here? How? No matter how many girls she was, how would *any* of them have his number?

"You did say that," Artie said, in the same easy tone. "And I might agree. For now. But what am I finding out back? What I hear, it's a mess back there. Clean-up's not cheap, either."

"You're telling me. How about this? He had it coming. For *years.* And you know it. Get him a doctor pretty soon, clean-up shouldn't be too bad." said Samantha, sinking the five. "Listen. You don't want to mess with us. We know people. My dad knows one kind, and I know another, these days. I'm telling you, messing with me is pointless trouble." She lined up another shot. Three ball, bank shot, side pocket.

"Nice," said Artie. "You play well, I bet you're good at poker. But you're bluffing."

"Trust me," said Jason, "it's hard to tell."

"You see, guys, my mom makes me play bridge. Way harder than poker. She *kills* at bridge. But every now and then, I pick up a few tricks. If you know what I mean. But whatever." Samantha just missed sinking the seven. "Here, Artie. Your shot." She lowered her voice. "By the way, you know Rain?"

Artie's face suggested that he did. Jason, on the other hand, had no clue, but figured they weren't *actually* talking about the weather. And Samantha wasn't done. "Turns out, one of Rain's favorite girlfriends used to do business with you. She had a bad time. With my friend in the alley, turns out. So even though he wasn't really interested in this small-time location before I talked to him, he'd take it over now. He offered to help us cover, you know, to replace the *car* for cost. He even offered to deliver a new one himself, from his own stock."

"That right?" Artie sunk the ten in the corner pocket, straight shot, hard. Samantha had left him an opening. "So. Why'd you turn him down?" Twelve ball. Off the four.

Samantha shrugged her pretty shoulders. "Devil you know, I guess. Or Devil's stepfather. Plus we want out, not in deeper. I've got a Chem test on Wednesday."

"You've got balls, I give you that. *And* you know what to do with them."

Samantha shuddered. "Please, spare me. Maybe I'll get to that next year." She darted a glance at Jason. "You know, in Physics." Then all her attention was back on the game. "But also? Rain sent you a message."

And Samantha Ward went up to Artie Fisher, put her hand on his shoulder, and whispered in his ear. He shook his head and whispered back. Samantha nodded, then spoke out loud. "You see, Rain gets that you can force people's hand in business. But you can't force them to *do* business. That's not Kosher, he said. You wouldn't think it to look at him? But he's half Jewish. So he's really not a fan of your skinhead friend out back, either."

Artie shot at the four and missed. Wide.

Samantha sunk the seven, and then the eight-ball.

Jason was watching Artie Fisher's face like a hawk, and one thing was clear to him. Samantha had found Artie Fisher's scarier monster. And apparently made friends with it. What was she *thinking?* He wanted to *kill* her. Then kiss her. Then probably marry her, which might give him enough time to figure out who the hell she was.

In the meantime, Samantha was explaining that she didn't want trouble. She wasn't trying to interfere with the laws of supply and demand. She just wanted Artie to leave her and her friends out of it. "My dad," she said thoughtfully, "he really hates trouble. Says it's not good for business. Don't you agree? Of course, girls like me, we don't really get in trouble. And with dads like mine, even when we do ... we don't. But trouble, it's kind of Jason's middle name."

Artie shrugged. "Can't really argue. And you know I kinda love that kid. But he does piss me off."

"I think we all feel that way." Samantha Ward held out her hand. "Thanks for letting me win. I know you left that last shot open for me. All in all, I think it was a good plan." They shook hands.

Samantha motioned Pris and Dylan back from the doors and that was that. Done deal.

On their way out, Artie Fisher raised his brows at Jason and gave him his winning fractional grimace of a smile. Cool as hell. As if he hadn't set his sister's rapists to beat him like clockwork. As if he hadn't come to his school, hell, house, to get him to deal coke to kids. "See you back at the house, kid?"

Jason felt his fists form.

"No." Samantha and Pris spoke in unison, taking his fists in their hands.

42. WE ALL NEED SOMEONE
WE CAN BLEED ON

"Hey there, Lesbo Barbie." Jason's hair was growing out, but the t-shirt and even the army jacket over it looked strangely new. "How's it hanging? Oh, wait. You don't have one."

"Screw you, Devlin," Pris answered lightly. She and Samantha were sprawled out on the bleachers in the sunshine, waiting for football and cheer to get out. Samantha folded up the letter she'd been reading aloud. Apparently Jessica was getting into punk rock in prep school. The letter was light on other details, but maybe the school read her mail.

"Oh, excuse me, hey there, *Prissy*."

"Screw you seven times. With a poker."

"Ooh, so tough. Watch your friend's virgin ears, *Priscilla*."

"Screw you with my best friend, then, *Devil Man*."

Samantha kicked at Pris's boot. "Hey, best friend, sitting right here, and not up for that!"

Jason shot Pris a death glare and took Samantha's hand. "Babe? Me either. Promise." And he kissed her fingers. "Pris here is just trying to make sure I never sleep again."

Pris smiled. "Bingo." She turned to Samantha. "Sorry, Sam. What can I say? I saw an opening, and I had to—"

"Go for it, I know. Instinct takes over. But you forget, Jason here would have zero interest in watching two girls go at it in front of him, because he doesn't like *homosexuality*. He's still all freaked out that Freddie Mercury is gay, which, you know, came as such a shock cause he's the lead singer of a band called Queen."

Jason was still holding Samantha's hand but now made her slap herself with it. "Yeah, yeah. I'm working on it." He looked down and let the hand go.

"Okay. Look. After everything that's happened I realize—I need to be more flexible. I mean, we're young, right? We're not fully-who we're gonna be yet. We've all been through some shit and—now that I'm roomies with African Ken, and Diangelo is on medical leave—"

"I seriously cannot believe he got away with that shit," Pris sighed.

"Yeah. Well. Addiction is a terrible disease that needs our compassion. Anyway, he's gone, and Stagnita runs at the sight of me. It's like the mirror episode of Star Trek except it's a weird world *without* torture. So, who knows? Maybe now I am the kind of guy who'd dig going to bed with two girls and watching them go at it. I say—let's find out. Let's go to bed. We wouldn't have to even do anything." Jason looked up, the picture of innocence. "We could just talk."

"We're talking now," said Samantha evenly.

"Yeah, but think how much more interesting this conversation would be with no clothes on."

In unison, Pris and Samantha rolled their eyes and said, "Dream on."

"Now, see, Aerosmith. Steven Tyler? He's not gay."

"Your point?"

"Just, you know, not everyone is."

Samantha considered a moment. "Yeah, you're right. I mean, take Pris and me. We haven't really kissed with tongue since, what, you were in seventh grade, Pris? Remember," she said dreamily, "how on sleepovers we used to sometimes practice, for when we'd have boyfriends?"

Jason stopped breathing entirely for a moment and then just stared at them. "You're making this up."

"Of course, back then," said Pris, smiling, "I was pretending you were Jason."

Jason groaned.

Samantha went on, "Right. I remember you used to like it if I wore this little football jersey. Probably with his number on it. So it was almost like he was there." She sighed. "Of course, now if I were to kiss you with tongue, Pris, I'd probably be pretending *you* were Jason. "

Pris nodded, "Ironic, isn't it?"

"But that's all over now. Because—I wasn't gay. Not much, anyway. And you've got this steady girlfriend back in London. So it'll probably never happen again." Samantha shrugged. "It was fun while it lasted."

"Definitely," agreed Pris. "You know, Devlin, you really should've been there."

Jason leaned back and knocked his head against the bleachers. Twice. "You know, I don't see why you went to all that trouble to save my ass from scary coke dealers if you were just gonna fuckin' try to kill me when we got back."

Samantha exchanged a glance with Pris and smiled. "I guess we just didn't see why they should have all the fun."

"Yeah," said Pris, punctuating her speech with a little kick to Jason's shin, "I mean, they have all that cocaine, right? But me and Samantha, we have to make our own fun."

Jason buried his head in his hands again. "God help me."

"Don't worry, Jason," Pris flashed an enormous smile, "Suly's coming for Christmas. Soon I'll be having way too much amazing gay sex to worry about tormenting you."

Jason lifted his head. "I'm sure watching you have it would really help me evolve as a person. It would be so healing."

Samantha pushed his head firmly back into his hands and held it there. "You are such a cliché."

"I don't know what that means," Jason said, voice muffled against his hands, "I probably skipped that day of English."

"You're so full of B.S."

Samantha was still holding Jason's head down, but he managed to move his hands to the sides of his head. "My virgin goddamn ears, Samantha. Do you mind?"

Samantha picked her hand up to swat at him again, which let him raise his head. He stuck his tongue out at her.

Pris wrinkled her nose. "I can't believe you let him put that thing in your mouth."

"Tell me about it," said Samantha.

"I'll tell you about it!" Jason volunteered. "In detail. First, she—"

"NO!" Samantha and Pris gasped in unison and rushed to cover Jason's mouth.

He ducked and laughed. "You'd think you girls would learn not to pick a fight with me using my own weapons! Anyway, that's cool she's coming, how'd you swing a conjugal visit? I thought your parents were all Suly-skeptical, Pris."

Pris tilted her head in Samantha's direction. Samantha held up her hands, saying "Don't look at me!"

"Please. Everyone's always looking at you." Pris narrowed her eyes around her words in full pronouncement mode. "It is your blessing. It is your curse."

"It is your delusion," mimicked Samantha, screwing her eyes into tiny squinty slits until she burst out laughing, her whole body shaking. Her sweater slipped off her shoulder as her hair fell down her back.

Pris and Jason stared.

Jason breathed in sharply. "Jesus," he said.

"I know, right?" muttered Pris. "I'm telling you, for years no one even noticed I was in the room."

Samantha blushed. "You guys. *Stop.* Anyway, I had nothing to do with Suly coming." Samantha gestured towards the football team and the cheerleaders. "Kwame did it." Samantha pulled her sweater up again. "What could I do? I'm beyond grounded. I can only have Pris over because her mother literally begged my mother to let us be friends, and they play bridge together."

Jason frowned. "Is bridge, like, code for the CIA or covert ops or something?"

"No," Samantha said evenly. "Pool is. That's why we have a soundproofed billiard room in the basement."

Jason stared. Hard. "You're fucking kidding me."

"Mm. Hard to know. I can't really tell with my dad, sometimes, either. Anyway, Kwame, the quiet, easy-going one? who should probably be in the CIA himself, apparently? told his parents he needed a connection to his roots. He told them he had a "pen pal" from Africa and she was going to come to the US, and could she stay with them for a while. They were apparently all over it. They're dying for him to have authentic African experiences."

Pris snorted. "Maybe they're expecting her to bring lions. Maybe they'll buy the mohawk as tribal?"

"It was tribal. Just, you know, from New York State. Right?" Jason shrugged.

"Which is about as close to Eritrea as South Africa is, so that's perfect."

"Do you think that stuff bothers Kwame?" Samantha asked. "Do you think it's, like, weird to be him?" She frowned at her friends' startled look. "What? It's this thing I'm trying, where I imagine what it's like to be other people. It could help me rule the world." She paused. "You know, rule it better."

Jason stared at the figures on the field. "Weird to be everyone, I guess. But if I ask him about it, he'll just shrug and say his parents mean well. Dude is all kinds of surprising. He says these very quiet things and then suddenly shit is, like, arranged. Like I'm going out for varsity football next year as a condition of my living at his house, which I would've sworn I would never do, but instead I'm swearing on a stack of Lou Reed albums that I will. And like I would've said he gave a rat's ass about Africa or anything but football, but then he's going with us to the shantytowns and stuff."

"*You* go to the shantytowns."

"Yeah, but that's because apparently my life was recently bought with the ransom blood of toiling millions there, and I didn't know shit about it—"

"News flash, Devlin." Pris's eyes narrowed again. "All our fucking lives here were bought with the blood of toiling millions. Suck it up and do your best with what was stolen for you. Until the revolution, anyway."

"Fine, whatever, Anarcho-communist Barbie."

"Ooh. Big words. I love it when you use big words like that, Jason. It's like I can pretend you pay attention when I talk." Pris's eyes were still narrow and her hair stuck out from her head like prickles.

Fitting.

Jason reached out a hand and mussed the hair all over her head so it looked softer and she looked outraged, but somehow softer, too.

"I pay attention, vocab girl. What else do I have to pay with?" Jason stared at his boots. He found being helped hard to get used to. Even though, he had to admit, it was better than the alternative.

"So," Samantha said, staring straight ahead, body suddenly entirely rigid, "any sign of any, um, bald guys?"

The calls of the football players and cheerleaders grew louder as a thicker quiet took over on the bleachers.

Jason reached a hand out and rubbed it tentatively along Samantha's back. She didn't move. "No, babe. No sign. I'd tell you. First thing. No more secrets."

"There's still stuff you're not telling me," Samantha said quietly.

"Said the girl who is totally eager to introduce me to her friend from Chicago. What was his name? Snow? Oh, no, that was his product."

"I can't tell you other people's secrets," began Samantha.

"Back at you," Jason said.

"Everyone has secrets," Pris said, kicking at the bleachers. "Even someone like Dylan, like how no one thinks he's conscious."

"Dylan Dougherty's two surviving brain cells are for sure the biggest secret in town." Jason started trying to braid a strand of Samantha's hair and succeeded in tying it into tiny knots as her back stayed rod stiff.

"That's right. And with his covert brain activity, Dylan's keeping an eye out," Pris said quietly, "for, you know, bald guys. So secrets can be okay."

"Well, that should take care of everything," Samantha sighed, "I don't know why I'd ever worry again." She ran her fingers through her hair, carefully undoing the knots. "Except about my hair, obviously."

"Exactly. Nothing left to do but make our own fun," said Pris, sprawling back into the sunshine.

"Naked is fun." Jason stretched his arms up and his legs out wide.

"So are clothes." Samantha said, but she watched his shirt ride up as he stretched all the same. Then she turned away, looked down.

"I let you buy me a new jacket, remember?" asked Jason.

"Jason. Your jacket was held together with your own dried blood. It was disgusting."

"It looked tough!"

"It looked like a horror movie. And It's not like you let me buy you a fun jacket. It's still all Army surplus."

Jason folded his hands and raised his eyes skyward. "Any healthy relationship is based on compromise, Samantha."

Pris looked up. "Excellent and surprising use of the word 'relationship' in a sentence."

"The word relationship is a goddamn sentence on its own—the old Jason might have said," Jason added quickly. Pris rolled her eyes at him and mouthed the word "idiot."

"I did warn you," said Samantha slowly as she started peeling strips of green paint from the bleacher by her side, "that I might want to wait 'til I get married to, you know ..."

"And I respect that." Jason paused. "But did you know, we can get married right now, in some states? C'mon. Road trip. Who's up for another road trip!" Jason sat straight up and started playing air guitar to the first licks of "Sweet Home Alabama."

Samantha smiled but turned her eyes back to the field. "I don't know, I think I need to be sixteen most places, and even for that you need parental consent. Which, having met my mother, I think is unlikely. And I don't turn sixteen for months."

Jason shifted closer to Samantha, but not close enough that they were touching. "I don't know, see, I've been doing research, it's part of the new bookish me, and I read in New Hampshire we coulda gotten married in middle school."

"Not if you were really me and I was Pris, here."

"Good point. Except for making no sense at all."

"Anyway," sniffed Samantha, "I think you should take me out on at least one date first."

"Oh, come on, I took you all over Chicago, in a white Mercedes. We had those cute matching blood outfits."

"You guys did look adorable." Now Pris adjusted a few strands of Samantha's hair, watching as Samantha stiffened at the first touch, then relaxed. "Red is so your color, both of you."

Samantha shook her head free and swatted first Pris, then Jason. "You two think you're so funny."

Pris and Jason nodded. "We really do," said Pris.

"It's a big part of our charm," agreed Jason.

Samantha took a deep breath and fluffed her hair out down her back. "Well, just because I now hang out with burnouts and freakazoids does not mean that I don't know what a real date is. I want a dance club or at least a dinner without guns, or coke dealers, or creepy teachers or psycho moms. Clear? And I want you in a tux or at least another button-down shirt, and a clean car."

"No blood?" Jason rubbed his hair and looked skeptical.

"I may not have mentioned this? But I have standards."

Pris and Jason both laughed. "Um. You might have mentioned that. Once or twice."

"Good," and Samantha shook her head proudly, "as long as that's clear."

"Okay, so, I'll take you out. No problem. How long are you grounded for?"

"Last I heard, only until, like, 1992. It's come down for good behavior."

"Cool. It might take me some time to put the cash together."

"Cool." Samantha reached out stroked Jason's hair absently, happy to be back on the bleachers, and not eager to venture behind them any time soon. "It'll be worth the wait."

Jason took her hand and kissed it. "Babe, I'm not holding my breath." He paused. "Though I think we've established that I can—"

"Me, too—" Pris chimed in.

"Oh my God, guys. What. Ever.

If you enjoyed this novel, please consider leaving a review or telling a friend. For information about the author and updates about future books in this world, and visit www.annejamison.net.

CPSIA information can be obtained
at www.ICGtesting.com
Printed in the USA
LVHW010840270120
644555LV00006BA/184